TWO FOR JOY

Patricia Scanlan

BANTAM BOOKS

LONDON · NEW YORK · TORONTO · SYDNEY · AUCKLAND

TWO FOR JOY
A BANTAM BOOK : 0 553 81391 9

Originally published in Great Britain by Bantam Press,
a division of Transworld Publishers

PRINTING HISTORY
Bantam Press edition published 2003
Bantam edition published 2004

5 7 9 10 8 6 4

Set in 11½/12½pt Garamond by
Kestrel Data, Exeter, Devon.

Bantam Books are published by Transworld Publishers,
61–63 Uxbridge Road, London W5 5SA,
a division of The Random House Group Ltd,
in Australia by Random House Australia (Pty) Ltd,
20 Alfred Street, Milsons Point, Sydney, NSW 2061, Australia,
in New Zealand by Random House New Zealand Ltd,
18 Poland Road, Glenfield, Auckland 10, New Zealand
and in South Africa by Random House (Pty) Ltd,
Endulini, 5a Jubilee Road, Parktown 2193, South Africa.

Printed and bound in Great Britain by
Cox & Wyman Ltd, Reading, Berkshire.

Papers used by Transworld Publishers are natural, recyclable
products made from wood grown in sustainable forests.
The manufacturing processes conform to the environmental
regulations of the country of origin.

Dear God, this one's for you.
Thanks for all your help.

ACKNOWLEDGEMENTS

I love you, O Lord, my strength. The Lord is my rock, my fortress, my deliverer. Psalm 18.

When I sit down to write I light a candle and ask for inspiration to write the words that I am meant to write. To Jesus, Our Lady, St Joseph, Mother Meera, St Anthony, St Michael, and all my Angels, Saints and Guides I thank you so much for never failing me.

To my family, Mam and Dad, the best in the world, Donald, Hugh, Paul, Dermot, and Mary, Yvonne, Lucy, Rose, Catherine and Henry and to my nieces and nephews, the joys of my life. Fiona, Caitriona, Patrick, Laura, Rebecca, Tara and Rachel, and to our two new blessings, Matthew and Maria. Thank you all, I am so lucky and blessed to have such a lovely family.

To my godmother Maureen. My aunts Ita and Flo and all the Rosslare gang.

To the friends old and new, who enrich my life in so many ways.

To Breda, Kieran, Alison and Gillian, as dear as family.

To Deirdre Purcell (wise, witty and encouraging), Sheila O'Flanagan (computer whiz, thanks a million for printing out my MS when I was stuck!), Cathy Kelly (for the hilarious lunches and lovely emails), Anita Notaro (who's going to give us all a run for our money and who never forgets!), Anne Schulman (who says the nicest things) and to all my other writer friends, too numerous to mention, thanks for everything.

To Annette Tallon, Anne Jensen, Debbie Sheehy, Margaret Neylon, Ann Wiley, Margaret Daly, my stalwarts. All the characters in *Two for Joy* are fictitious except for Anne Jensen, who appears as herself.

To the 'hhhonourable' Anne Barry. '*Here we go again, happy as can be, all good friends and jolly good company . . .*' I've never laughed as much in my life!

To Olive and Christy Lonergan, great neighbours.

To Ciara, Ruth, Heidi, Jenny and Ella, my colleagues in HHI, I'm having a ball, hope you are too!

To Ger McPartlin who bosses me around like nobody's business. You're the best in the world!

To Alil O Shaughnessy and Tony Kavanagh, for all the love and laughs.

To Frank Hession, who has such a good heart.

To Peter Orford for the photo and the kind phone call.

To Ray, Frank, Margaret and Gerry, AIB Finglas, who take the greatest care of me, and to Sinead Burke and Mary Burke for sound advice.

To Sarah, Felicity and Susannah, not only the best agents, but the best friends.

To Nikki, Jean, Laura, Michelle (and Pauline on the high seas!) of Nikki's Hair Salon. They know I love the 'thinning scissors' so they indulge me.

To Francesca, editor and dear friend, and to all in Transworld. This one's going to be such fun! And to

Carmel Fitzgerald, my publicist (the best there is). I'm in training! And to beautiful Bob who collects me at Heathrow and drives me around London when I'm on my trips. You're the icing on the cake!

To Gill Hess and his gang . . . Hang on to your hats . . . here we go!!!!!

To all in New Island, here's to OPEN DOOR 4.

To John Carty (and Olive) of The Endorphin Release Clinic and Mr John Byrne (and Maria) of the Bons, who'll have my back sorted one of these days and who show me nothing but kindness.

To Doctors Nuala O'Farrell, Fiona Dennehy and Frankie Fine, the best and nicest you could ever meet. Thank you.

Two very helpful members of staff of the HARI Unit in the Rotunda patiently answered my queries. Thank you both.

And to all my precious readers whose encouragement and appreciation give me such a lift. May your lives be full of joy like this book was for me. Thank you all, you're the ones who make it all worthwhile. Hope you enjoy *Two for Joy* as much as I enjoyed writing it.

One for Sorrow
Two for Joy
Three for a Girl, Four for a Boy
Five for Silver, Six for Gold
Seven for a Secret Never to be Told

'The fragrance always stays in the hand that gives the rose.'

Hada Bejar

1

'Don't you dare do it before I do, Heather Williams,' Lorna Morgan warned her cousin imperiously. 'Besides, you don't know him well enough, yet.'

'Relax, Lorna, do you think I'm mad? I don't want to get preggers.' Heather took a sip of her white wine spritzer.

'Yeah, well, is he *really* the one you want to lose it to? You could do much better, you know.' Lorna arched her eyebrows dismissively.
'Neil's very nice once you get to know him,' Heather said defensively. She scowled. She hated it when her cousin slagged off her new boyfriend.

'Heather,' Lorna shook her head sagely, 'you always settle for second best. What is he? A mechanic working in his daddy's shack of a garage, in this poky, one-street town in the sticks. He's going nowhere fast.'

'Don't talk like that, Lorna Morgan! Kilronan isn't the sticks and Neil's going to take over his father's garage. He's got plans. He's going to expand, start selling cars as well as fixing them,' Heather retorted hotly.

'Big wow!' Lorna was not impressed.

'Well, we can't all date doctors' sons,' Heather snapped back sarcastically. 'Derek Kennedy no doubt is going to be a consultant.'

'Actually I'm thinking of ending it. He bores me.' Lorna sighed, a frown creasing her smooth forehead.

'For God's sake, who are you looking for? Einstein? Would you give the bloke a chance.' Heather nibbled on a handful of peanuts. She shouldn't be eating them. She'd put on two pounds last week, but she had terrible PMT and she craved salt.

'Why won't you move into a flat with me in Dublin? Then we could have a ball. We could socialize in Temple Bar, go night-clubbing, eat in fancy restaurants,' Lorna urged eagerly. 'You know it's a great place, the pubs and clubs are mega. We'd meet *real* men, Heather, not the clodhoppers we have to put up with in this place.'

Her cousin pouted sulkily as she took her hand mirror out of her bag and studied her reflection in it.

'Come on, Kilronan isn't that bad. And there's plenty of men here,' Heather argued. 'Look at all the tourists we meet. You might meet a millionaire on one of the cruisers out on the lake one of these days.'

'Oh for God's sake, stop talking nonsense. It's the back of beyonds and I'm sick of it. I'm not going to stay mouldering here for the rest of my life,' Lorna exclaimed tetchily.

'Well I like Kilronan. I like working in Mangan's—'

'Don't you want something more out of life? You'll be nineteen soon. I mean how old is that? Don't you *want* to go to clubs and drink champagne and be wined and dined in swanky restaurants? You're such a stick-in-the-mud, Heather. Sometimes you drive me mad!' Lorna glared at her cousin. 'At least bossy old Ruth has some get up and go.'

'Don't be such a wagon, and don't talk about my twin like that to me.' Heather flushed. 'I'm going home. I've had enough of this crap for one night. See you at Oliver Flynn's wedding reception tomorrow night.' She drained her glass, picked up her bag and stalked out of Nolan's pub in high dudgeon. Just who did Lorna Morgan think she was? She was so superior. Let her go to Dublin and find Mister Wonderful and go clubbing and drink champagne if she wanted to, Heather was happy just where she was. She'd visited Ruth in Dublin often enough in the past year since her twin sister had moved to the city and she'd enjoyed herself, but she was always glad to get back to Kilronan. Heather frowned. Maybe she was dull and boring, she thought glumly. Lorna could always make her feel so inadequate. Lots of her friends had left home as soon as they were able to. Ruth certainly hadn't wasted any time, much to their parents' dismay.

She sighed as she pulled her scarf tighter around her neck and pulled up her hood. Grey damp swirls of mist rolled in off the lake. Heather shivered at the unseasonably cold weather. Two days ago they'd been enjoying an Indian summer. She was hungry. She and Lorna had planned to go for a pizza after their drink but that was knocked on the head now. She'd told her mother not to keep dinner for her, so she'd have to get a chippie. She hurried along North Road, past the hardware shop and the estate agent's and the small side road that led to the marina, and stepped into the welcoming warmth of Fred's Fast Food Emporium.

'Snack box and a portion of garlic mushrooms, please.' She gave her order to the girl behind the counter and went to sit at a table by the window. She wouldn't be seeing Neil tonight, he was in Dublin doing a business start-up course so it was OK to eat garlic mushrooms without worrying about having to kiss him, reeking of garlic. There were only a few people ahead of her. She'd missed the worst of the Friday evening rush.

The mist had turned into heavy rain that battered against the big plate-glass windows that faced on to the street. She saw Lorna's red Honda Civic scorch past and scowled. It hurt being called a stick-in-the-mud. OK, so she didn't have her cousin's glitz and glamour, but she was sociable and outgoing and she enjoyed life in her bustling, lakeside home town. She was a member of the drama society, the basketball team, the tennis club, as of course was Lorna, but Lorna considered it all far too parochial, instead of enjoying it all.

Lorna could always make her feel inferior and had done so since they'd been children. Ruth was always telling her to tell Lorna to go take a hike but somehow Heather could never bring herself to. Ruth and Lorna didn't get on. Ruth had no time for her prima-donna cousin and Lorna was jealous of the sisters' strong friendship. Thinking of some of the sizzling rows the pair had had over the years, Heather smiled in spite of herself.

'She's just a stuck-up, spoilt little cow with notions, she always has to be the main course. Well, one day she'll find that she's just the leftovers,' Ruth fumed after a spat at a disco one night when Lorna had flirted with a fella that Ruth had her eye on. Ruth had been furious at her cousin's flighty behaviour as she watched the pair snog during a slow set, but Lorna didn't give a hoot and had ignored her cousin's frosty glower. Ruth had called her a tarty slut the next day and they hadn't spoken for weeks. Ruth was great at holding a grudge and keeping a fight going, but Heather always caved in after a day or two. She had no staying power when it came to rows. She hated falling out with people. If only she could be a bit more like her sister and her cousin, she reflected despondently.

Ruth had started out as a typist in a small but busy architectural firm in Dublin. After two months she'd been promoted when the boss's secretary had been headhunted by a rival firm. She'd proved her worth and when the company had taken on an extra partner, she'd been given the grand title of office administrator, plus a rise in salary. Ruth was efficient and ambitious, far more so than Heather, who had always been the quieter of the two. She shared a house with three other girls, near Phibsboro. Lorna envied her enormously, although she'd never let on to Ruth.

Heather and Lorna had stayed over several times

at weekends when Ruth had a free house. And it was because of these precious weekends that Lorna made a half-hearted effort now and again to stay on good terms with her cousin. Lorna was always in her element, drinking and bopping to her heart's content, revelling in the capital's frantic, fast-paced lifestyle.

It had been after a meal in the Bad Ass Café and a night's dancing and drinking in Bad Bob's that Ruth and Lorna had finally had a parting of the ways. They had been sitting in the back of a taxi on the way home when Lorna had felt the urge to puke.

'Don't you dare barf or we'll be turfed out of the taxi and we'll never get another one at this hour of the night,' Ruth hissed furiously when Lorna slurred that she felt a bit queasy. Ruth was a bit pissed herself, but not *that* pissed. Typical of Lorna, couldn't hold her drink. Heather was always nurse-maiding her and holding her head over toilets when they went out. If it were Ruth Lorna was depending on, her cousin would end up drowned in a toilet bowl, Ruth often assured her twin.

Lorna valiantly held on until the taxi driver rounded a corner at a fast lick and she could contain her nausea no longer. Quietly and discreetly she puked into her cousin's handbag, which just happened to be lying on the seat between them. Ruth was giggling at a joke Heather had made about the driver's obvious desire to race in a grand prix and was distracted momentarily.

Because the house keys were in her coat pocket, she hadn't needed to rummage for them in her bag and hadn't made the putrid discovery until around noon the following day when she reached into her bag to find her lipstick before going out to buy provisions for a fry-up. 'You skanky, dirty wagon, I'll murder you. I'll break your scabby, scrawny little neck,' she shrieked as she raced into the room Heather and Lorna were sharing. She hauled her drowsy cousin out of the bed and shook her. 'Get dressed, you, and get the hell out of here. I've had enough of you, Lorna Morgan. If you can't look after yourself when we go out you're not coming with us any more and that's it. And you're not staying here again. Go and stay with someone else when you come down to Dublin. That was a *gross* stunt to pull. Why didn't you puke in your own bag, you silly bitch?'

'It's a Lulu Guinness. It cost me a fortune!' Lorna bleated, horrified at both the unexpected assault and the notion that she should ruin a designer label handbag. Even in her hungover state, she knew her priorities.

'I don't care if it's encrusted with diamonds, you shouldn't have puked into mine — but it's the last time you'll pull an act like that on me, I can promise you that,' Ruth raged as she thrust a handful of clothes at her cousin. 'There's a bus for Kilronan at one thirty, leaving from the quays. Be on it.'

'Oh, get over it, it will be a pleasure, you grumpy old hoor! Come on, Heather,' Lorna snapped dismissively.

'*Excuse me*, Heather is staying here. *You're* the one who's leaving,' Ruth retorted icily.

Heather groaned silently. Why was she always dragged into it? She hated being the pig-in-the-middle when the other pair were fighting.

'Let Heather decide for herself, she doesn't have to do everything *you* tell her,' Lorna challenged.

Both of them turned to look expectantly at her. Heather's heart sank. This was definitely a no-win situation. One or other of them was going to be miffed with her, whatever she decided. It wasn't fair. The row had nothing to do with her.

'Leave me alone, I want to die,' she mumbled under the bedclothes. If she pretended her hang-over was worse than it was, they might have mercy on her.

'There! She's staying,' Ruth declared triumphantly.

'She didn't say that,' Lorna shot back. 'Are you coming or staying?' she demanded of Heather, determined to make her cousin choose one way or the other.

'I couldn't face a bus journey right now, Lorna, gimme a break.' Heather groaned and buried her head under the duvet.

'Thanks *very* much. Some friend you are.' Lorna grabbed her clothes and stalked into the bathroom.

'Ignore her,' Ruth advised.

'There's a pair of you in it, sometimes—'

'For God's sake, she puked in my handbag. How low can you get? Go home with her if you want to, see if I care,' Ruth retorted huffily.

'I don't want to,' Heather appeased. It was bad enough having Lorna in a huff, Ruth in a huff was the pits.

'I'll cook us a fry-up when she's gone,' her twin said over her shoulder as she left the bedroom to deal with the messy business of her handbag.

Lorna ignored Heather when she came back into the room to collect her shoes and precious Lulu Guinness handbag. Heather snuggled further under the duvet trying to regain her previous pleasantly drowsy state. But it was ruined. Lorna was in a huff with her and she resented it bitterly.

'Lorna, I—'

'Don't bother,' Lorna snapped. 'I know where I'm not wanted. I'm just a convenience in your life. Your *twin*' – she spat the word – 'is the only one who counts where you're concerned. Just don't come running to me the next time you're stuck for someone to go out with.'

She slammed the door behind her, leaving Heather fuming. How dare Lorna imply she had no one else to go out with. She had plenty of friends in Kilronan.

Lorna hadn't spoken to Heather for a fortnight until she wanted her to go to a pub quiz with her and breezed into the accountant's office where Heather worked as though nothing had happened. Arctic conditions still existed between her and Ruth and they had not socialized together since the handbag episode. Ruth wasn't a bit put out. She had her own life to lead and Lorna, happily, wasn't part of it.

Heather came back to the present as the girl behind the counter called over to her to ask if she wanted salt and vinegar on her chips. One of these days, she too would put Lorna in her place and not be a wimp about it, she promised herself as the delightful sizzle of frying batter and the wafting smells of garlic and vinegar made her mouth water.

Monday she was going to start. New diet. New fitness regime. New assertive attitude to life. And Lorna Morgan could take a running jump!

2

Lorna Morgan was thoroughly pissed off as she drove along North Road. There was no sign of her wishy-washy cousin. She'd hoped to over-take her trudging home in the rain and drive past with her head in the air. She gave a sigh that came from her toes. Heather was so staid and boring sometimes. She had no sense of adventure. Lorna *had*! She just knew that there had to be more to life than working as a receptionist in the Lake View Hotel and living at home with her parents and two younger brothers, Eoin and Aidan, who were the bane of her life. She was a month short of her nineteenth birthday, Heather was practically the same age, life was there for the taking and they were wasting precious time stuck here in the back end of nowhere. If only her cousin would come with her to live in Dublin. Everything would change. She just knew it.

She could go on her own, she supposed, but it would be very lonely. She didn't know anyone in Dublin apart from her obnoxious cousin Ruth, and *she* most certainly didn't count. Lorna wrinkled her pert little nose. She hadn't spoken to Ruth since she'd thrown her out of the flat and not even for a temporary place to stay in the city would she lower herself to ever speak to that ignorant cow again, she vowed, as she overtook a tractor at speed.

If she went to Dublin on her own where would she live, though? Good accommodation was hard to come by. She didn't want to live in a poky little bedsit in Rathmines. Certainly not. Or not even in a boring semi, like the one Ruth rented with her friends. Lorna had visions of herself in a smart apartment in town, or in the new, refurbished docklands. She was an avid reader of the property pages in the papers and spent many happy hours imagining herself entertaining new trendy friends in her own upmarket pad.

But first she'd have to get a job. There was a shortage of hotel staff in all the large cities according to the tourist board, so finding a position shouldn't pose a problem. Better get the job first before worrying about accommodation. Lorna sighed again. She'd had this conversation with herself a hundred times. If she didn't go and do *something* about it soon, she'd be so over the hill no one would want to give her a job. It was time to be proactive, she decided.

She liked the word 'proactive'. It had impressed her when she'd heard the manager use it at a staff meeting. It was a sophisticated sort of a word. Lorna was all for sophistication.

Yes, she thought, she would get the names of all the prestigious hotels in Dublin and send them her CV and references. Surely one of them would want a receptionist of her experience? The Lake View had a hundred bedrooms and a leisure centre, after all, and that wasn't to be sneezed at. She'd been working in the hotel every summer since she was fourteen and had got the job as trainee receptionist when she'd finished her Leaving Cert. As far as she was concerned she was now a fully fledged receptionist and she certainly wasn't going to mention 'trainee' in her CV.

Lorna chewed her lip. If only Heather would come with her to Dublin it would be perfect. She'd have someone she knew to rely on. She wasn't as brave as Ruth, going off to live in the city on her own. To tell the truth, she was a little in awe of her strong-willed cousin. She was much tougher than Heather. Heather could always be got around and prevailed upon to do what Lorna wanted her to do. Ruth was immovable once her mind was made up. For twins, they were chalk and cheese.

It was a bad move being snooty with Heather when she was trying to persuade her to leave Kilronan, she reflected ruefully. She'd better be nice to her at Oliver Flynn's wedding tomorrow. She'd get her pissed and try once again to persuade her to come and live in Dublin. Once they got there, Heather would love it, Lorna was sure of it.

She might as well go and have a session in the gym, she decided. She needed to look her absolute best for job interviews and who knew, maybe one of the guests using the gym while she was there might be a rich businessman taking a few days out of the rat race of city life. He'd see her working out and start chatting her up. Then he'd invite her out for a drink, or even dinner, and who knew

27

what it would lead to. If he was absolutely gorgeous she might even consider doing the business with him, she fantasized.

Lorna was longing to sleep with a man. A real man, not a wimpy doormat who let her walk all over him the way Derek did. She'd read so many articles in glossy magazines about fabulous sex. It really was time for her to experience it and become a sexual, sensual woman. Lots of her friends had had sex – she and Heather were practically the only virgins out of all the girls in their class. Dolores Redmond had lost her virginity at fourteen and had slept with loads of blokes. So had Margy Collins. It made Lorna feel extremely inadequate to know that she was practically nineteen, and hadn't done the business yet.

Ruth had.

Heather had confided this nugget to her one night when she was a bit tipsy. Lorna had been pea green. Ruth was not half as attractive as she was. Her cousin was well built, hardly a slender sylph like herself. She had thick, wavy chestnut hair that flew all over the place, unlike Lorna's groomed silken blonde bob. Ruth had nondescript grey-green eyes while Lorna's were the bluest of cornflower blue. And yet her cousin seemed to have no trouble attracting men. It was galling to think that she'd done it before Lorna.

Although she'd never admit it to her cousins, the thought of having sex scared Lorna. Once, when she was a little girl, she'd seen a man, not her father, doing things to her mother, when her father was at work. Jane Morgan had been making funny breathy moaning noises and Lorna was afraid. She slipped out of the bedroom, her heart pounding. Should she call a neighbour and say her mother was being attacked, she wondered frantically? What if the man came after her? She should hide. She ran to the little cubbyhole under the stairs until eventually she heard the heavy tread of footsteps and the man's voice calling a good-humoured farewell. When the man was gone her mother had been smiling and happy, humming to herself as she strolled into the kitchen in her dressing-gown, to make herself a cup of coffee.

'Hello, Chicken,' she'd greeted her, uncharacteristically warmly, when Lorna had slipped warily into the kitchen. Lorna knew something was different – 'Chicken' was an endearment that was rarely used by her mother, who was not maternal by nature. 'What are you doing here? I thought you were over playing with Ruth and Heather?'

'We had a fight. Ruth always wants her own way,' Lorna whinged sulkily.

'Hmm.' Her mother was miles away, her eyes dreamy and unfocused. It was clear she hadn't heard a word Lorna'd said. Usually Jane would be annoyed to hear of the cousins fighting among themselves. It suited her much better if there was peace and harmony so that her children could play over with their cousins, out from under her feet.

When Lorna was older, she'd seen a couple having sex in a film on TV and the memory of that distant, warm, Indian summer's afternoon had come back like a tidal wave. She'd looked at her slim, pretty mother and realized that she'd been

29

having sex with another man. It had shocked her deeply. She never thought of her parents as sexual beings. Parents didn't do the things to each other that film stars did on TV, kissing and touching breasts and worse . . . And mothers in Kilronan definitely did *not* have affairs! She became hostile towards Jane. Angry with her for not being like other mothers. Especially like her Auntie Anne, Ruth and Heather's mother.

Anne Williams, Jane's older sister, was a good-humoured, motherly woman who seemed effortlessly to produce very satisfying dinners for her family and not worry if bedrooms were untidy, unlike Lorna's own mother who was a poor cook but who went spare if anything was out of place in her spotless and immaculate home. Anne never worried about Hoovering and dusting, she was far too busy with her parish activities and spent as much time out of the home as in it. The Williams household was lively and chaotic, unlike Lorna's own regimented palace.

As Lorna grew into her teens she saw that her parents were not happy, and vaguely understood that Jane had looked to someone else for a need that was not being met in her marriage.

'Marry a rich, ambitious man and don't end up in a dead-end cul-de-sac like me,' her mother had said to her one Christmas when she'd come home from a party and was the worse for wear for drink.

'Go to bed, Jane,' Gerard Morgan said wearily, but Lorna had seen the flash of hurt in her father's eyes and felt a mixture of pity and contempt for him. Why didn't he tell her mother to shut up?

Why didn't he stand up to her when she put him down? Which she did constantly, nagging and bickering until she got her own way.

Lorna could get around her father too, wheedling and pleading until he gave in to her demands. He was a soft man and she could see that her mother despised him, despite the fact that he had given her a far better lifestyle than many of her peers, working all hours in his legal practice.

Jane, too, had wanted to live in Dublin. When she'd married the young handsome solicitor she'd set her cap at, she'd been the envy of all her friends and had felt full sure that they would buy a big house in the city and entertain smart, successful couples like themselves. But Gerard wasn't at the cutting edge of law. He'd only followed the career to please his father. He'd much rather have become a vet. Disappointment and resentment had slowly poisoned their marriage and although they put up a well-practised façade for their relations and neighbours, behind closed doors their relationship had long gone past the point of rescue.

Lorna was sure of one thing. The man she married would have to have plenty of ambition and be prepared to keep her in an affluent lifestyle to which she certainly intended to become accustomed.

Her current boyfriend, Derek Kennedy, was certainly not that man, she thought crossly. Derek had been trying to bed her for the last six months but she didn't fancy him enough. He had wet lips, which she hated. The only reason she dated him was because his parents were loaded and he was always able to give her a good time. Besides, dating the doctor's son gave her a certain social cachet in the town. He'd been invited to Oliver Flynn's wedding with his parents and had asked her to accompany him. Heather and her culchie mechanic had to make do with just attending the afters.

Derek was studying medicine at Trinity and he detested it. All he wanted to do was mess about on his boat on the lake. He came home most weekends, but tonight he'd had to stay late for a college event, hence the boring Friday night ahead of her. He didn't have much get up and go either, Lorna mused as she swung into the car park of the hotel. It was practically full. There was a wedding on today too. The hotel was extremely busy with weddings and conferences and had been full throughout the summer season. She drove around to the leisure centre and found a space without too much difficulty.

She looked through the big plate-glass windows, expectantly, and saw Nuala Logan and Ted Grimes, two locals, running on the treadmills. Not a businessman in sight, she thought dispiritedly as she trekked into the changing-room with a face like thunder. This could be her lifestyle for years to come if she didn't do something drastic. Grim-faced, she slipped into her leotard, a black lycra affair with a very high leg to show off her toned thighs to perfection. She was going to work her ass off tonight. No more faffing around.

It was time to get a life.

3

Oliver Flynn loosened the knot of his tie as he sat waiting for his wedding meal to be served. The sooner he got out of this monkey suit the better. He felt like a right idiot in his tails. He'd drawn the line at wearing a hat, much to Noreen's annoyance. She wanted everything to be just so, but there were some things a man had to take a stand on and wearing silly hats was one of them. He'd be glad when this palaver was all over and they were back from their honeymoon.

They were going to Malta. Noreen didn't want to go to any of the 'common or garden resorts' as she called them. She wanted something different. Classy. Noreen liked to impress people.

He didn't care where they went. He'd left all those decisions to his wife. He glanced at the gold ring encircling the fourth finger of his left hand.

He had a wife.

He was married.

He couldn't quite believe it. Marriage wasn't something he'd actively planned. It was just something that seemed to happen out of nowhere. Noreen had proposed to him. If it had been left to him, it would probably never have happened, he thought ruefully.

Oliver still remembered the queer lurch his stomach had given when she'd turned to him one evening during a walk along the lake shore and said, 'Oliver, I think it's time we got married. Will you marry me?' Otherwise she was considering going back to London. What could he say? He'd been seeing her for two years. He liked her, he got on well with her. He was a little bit in awe of her confident ways, she was good for him, but he didn't long for her or dream about her the way he'd longed for and dreamed about Kate MacDonnell when he was sixteen years old and too shy to say more than a quick hello when he'd meet her on the street.

Kate was curvy and flame-haired with sparkling blue eyes and a wide ready smile and he'd worshipped her from afar. The conversations he'd had in his head with her where he was witty and entertaining *stayed* in his head. He was far too tongue-tied and reserved to say the things he wanted to say to her and all he could manage was a pathetic 'hello' and a blush when he said it. He'd acquired more polish as he'd got older, but Kate had gone to London and never come back.

The girls in Kilronan liked him for some reason, but even though he went to the odd disco and dated several of the local girls, the challenge of his bashful reserve would eventually wear off when he'd be late for dates due to work, or when he wouldn't be free on Saturday to go to Dublin to shop and do the other things women wanted to do.

Or when he'd want to jump out of bed after having sex instead of spending hours kissing and cuddling.

Oliver sighed. There was only so much kissing and cuddling that you could do. But houses had to be built, contracts had to be fulfilled and new ones secured, and none of the girls he'd dated could understand that. They always took it personally, saying that he wasn't interested in them. He was . . . to a point. But work was a demanding mistress and best of all . . . it didn't nag.

That a woman as sharp and focused as Noreen Lynch would want to be married to him still surprised him. He didn't know what she saw in him sometimes. He cast a sideways glance at his bride. She was speaking to one of the waiters, issuing crisp, concise instructions. She looked so different in her white veil and elegant beaded wedding gown, her straight black hair brought back from her face emphasizing her wide, dark-lashed amber eyes, her best feature.

Noreen was a brisk, no-nonsense type who knew what she wanted out of life. She was always on the go, full of energy, while he was content to plod along in his own quiet way, working all the hours God sent, building up his construction firm and enjoying a pint after a long back-breaking day on site. Not that he actually needed to do any of the physical work himself, these days. He could spend all day in the office if he wanted to. But he hated being stuck indoors, and besides, it was good for him to mix with his men and be on site. He could keep a sharp eye on things. A Flynn-built house was a well-built house. Oliver took pride in his work and expected high standards from his workmen.

He was doing well, he thought with quiet satisfaction. He had thirty men working for him now and the books were full for the next two years.

He'd built a new home for Noreen and himself and it had given him pleasure to do the best job he possibly could. Noreen had been involved in every aspect, of course, but although he took her input on board, he was the authority on the project. One thing Oliver Flynn was certain about in life was his work, and no one could undermine him there. Noreen was impressed in spite of herself when he spoke with quiet authority as she argued with him about where she wanted her kitchen and utility room. She had a bossy side to her and he often agreed with her just for the sake of peace and quiet, but when he knew he was right about something, or just didn't want to do what she suggested, he could dig his heels in with the best of them. Building the house was his responsibility – she could decorate it whatever way she wished, but he'd had his way regarding the structure.

It was a fine house, nestled on a hillside overlooking the lake. A four-bedroom dormer, with en suite bathrooms and a conservatory facing west. 'Posh' his mother had called it. He hoped it would be a very happy home. Now that he was married he'd put his heart and soul into his new life and not waste time regretting the romantic notions of his youth. True love was just something that happened in films. It was a crush that he'd had on Kate MacDonnell, nothing more, nothing less, he decided, but he felt a little pang at the memory of her, which he irritatedly banished. It was ridiculous to be thinking of another woman on the day of his marriage. He and Noreen had a strong bond and a lot in common. It would be a very good marriage, he promised himself.

Hopefully he'd have at least one son to take over his business. 'Flynn & Son, Building Contractors' had a certain ring to it that pleased him. Noreen was anxious to have children sooner rather than later: she was five years older than him. Thirty-four, old enough for a woman to be having her first child. No more precautions once the ring was on her finger, she'd told him. If that was what she wanted that was OK by him.

A waitress placed a prawn cocktail in front of him. Oliver was ravenous. He'd give anything for a plate of spuds, flavoured with a scattering of salt and a lump of real yellow butter. He hated all the so-called buttery spreads that Noreen bought. She was into healthy eating and she was always buying light butters with polyunsaturates and the likes. Not his cup of tea at all. Or his mother's for that matter, he thought ruefully. Cora Flynn did not like Noreen, and the feeling was mutual. Cora never lost an opportunity to make disparaging remarks to the younger woman. And Noreen was not one to take anything lying down. She gave as good as she got, so there was a constant sniping and one-upmanship going on that Oliver found wearisome. He kept his head down and kept out of it as much as he could, much to his mother's fury, for she expected him to take her side as a matter of course.

His mother hadn't come to the wedding.

She'd bought the outfit, a flowery lilac two-piece with a wide-brimmed lilac hat that looked very nice, Oliver had thought when she'd tried it on at home for him. His aunt had taken her shopping for the day and she'd seemed to enjoy it by all accounts. But as the wedding day drew closer, she'd taken to the bed, blaming a variety of ailments, especially her sciatica, which according to herself made it impossible to walk or sit for long occasions such as a wedding.

In his heart of hearts, Oliver understood. He knew he was her pet, her youngest child. She'd been forty-two when she'd had him and when his brothers, Jim and Sean, had emigrated to Australia, he'd been there to take care of her when his father had died suddenly of heart failure. Cora had mothered over him to her heart's content and had been perfectly happy until he'd started dating Noreen. Somehow she knew that Noreen was different from the other girls he'd been with. Noreen posed a threat. She wouldn't kow-tow or make allowances for Cora's age. She wouldn't do as she was bid. Cora couldn't intimidate her.

'What do you want with her anyway? She's too old for you. If she's been on the shelf this long and couldn't get a man for herself before now there's something amiss,' Cora declared bluntly when Oliver informed his mother of the engagement.

'Stop that now, Ma. That's enough. Noreen and I are getting married and that's the end of it. I'd like it if you'd treat her a lot better than the way you've been treating her,' Oliver said in a tone that brooked no nonsense.

Cora was raging; he could see the way the dull angry flush of red mottled her cheeks. He'd ignored her anger and asked for another slice of currant bread, his favourite. That had mollified her somewhat. She was very vain about her baking prowess. Still she'd been unable to let the matter rest and had to have the last word. 'It's all right now, but when you've got two old women on your hands you'll only have yourself to blame. Mark my words!' she sniffed. Oliver gave an inward sigh and refrained from comment.

When he'd moved into the house with Noreen six months ago, she'd been horrified.

'Couldn't you at least wait until you're married! You'll be the talk of the parish,' she berated him, bereft that he was leaving her alone, and incensed that he would give people in the town an opportunity to talk and point the finger.

'Ma, people don't think that way any more, and besides, I don't like to leave the house empty,' Oliver explained patiently.

'Well, I think that way and *I'm* not people!' she said wrathfully. 'Let that Noreen one go and stay in it.'

'She doesn't want to stay in it on her own, she'd be a bit nervous,' Oliver had replied unthinkingly, until he'd seen the expression on his mother's face and realized that he'd put his two big feet in it and given her a heaven-sent opportunity.

Cora rallied triumphantly. 'Oh, and I suppose you don't mind leaving *me* here on my own. I might be nervous too, you know. Does madam ever think of that?'

Oliver groaned silently at the memory. Women, they were masters at manipulation. He'd assured Cora that she was welcome to come and live with them. There was plenty of room in the house. She'd even have her own bathroom, but she wasn't having any of it and had been in martyr mode ever since.

Her non-appearance at the wedding was not a complete surprise. The sciatica had got worse; she demanded that he get the doctor for her, even though he was up to ninety trying to get himself sorted. The doctor had given her more painkillers and anti-inflammatories and told her to put a pillow under her knee. He'd wished Oliver good luck on his nuptials and told him not to worry, that she'd be fine. Oliver had considered cancelling the honeymoon, worrying that she'd be unable to look after herself, and when he'd said this to Cora he'd seen the look of triumph on her face.

'You're a good son to me, Oliver. Thank you. As soon as I'm better you can go off somewhere.'

Noreen had nearly had a fit. 'Get someone in to mind her. We're going to Malta and that's the end of it,' she pronounced grimly. 'She's only putting it on. I'm a nurse. I know these things.'

'I can't go and leave her with strangers,' Oliver muttered.

'Well, get one of your brothers to stay a bit longer. You shouldn't have to shoulder all the burden. It's not fair. I know, it happened to me,' she said bitterly before slamming the kitchen door and walking off in a huff. She'd slept in one of the spare rooms that night. Putting him on notice that she wasn't going to budge an inch on the issue. He'd felt like calling the whole blinking thing off at that stage and going to live in the Portakabin on the site, where there were no demanding, huffy women to harass him.

In the end his Aunt Ellie had stepped in and announced that she'd stay and look after Cora but that she was going to the wedding and would leave after the meal to get home to her. His mother was furious, but couldn't refuse the offer and Oliver had felt a wave of relief wash over him. His life wouldn't have been worth living if he'd chosen Noreen over Cora and vice versa. As it was he was treading a very tight rope between the two women, and he knew things weren't going to improve. The older Cora got the more demanding she became.

Oliver sighed deeply. He knew his mother was at home in her big brass bed feeling hard done by and sorry for herself, but there was nothing he could do about it. He'd done his best for her, he could do no more. He knew his mother of old. She was as stubborn as a mule, and sciatica or no sciatica if she'd wanted to be at his wedding she'd have been at it. But it would have stuck in her craw to watch Noreen become Mrs Oliver Flynn. That was too bitter a pill to swallow. She'd lost the battle and she'd never forgive either of them. In his mother's eyes Oliver had betrayed her by marrying Noreen, and putting Noreen first. There was no going back. He'd just have to make the best of it.

His Aunt Ellie had taken the seat where Cora

would have been sitting and she was chatting away to the priest, in her element to have pride of place at the top table. She was a jolly, good-humoured soul who didn't stand for any nonsense and she was well able to handle her sister. She had been a rock of strength these past few days for Oliver and he planned to bring her back something really nice from Malta. Perhaps a good piece of gold jewellery. His aunt loved jewellery, earrings in particular. The thought of buying her something special in repayment for her kindness made him feel better.

He didn't really like to be under an obligation to people. But Ellie was different. She never made him feel that way, and besides, he'd built a new kitchen for her and only charged her the cost of the materials, and she'd always been very grateful for that. Ellie never forgot a kindness but there were plenty of people around who'd been ready to take advantage of his good nature when he was younger, until he'd copped on to himself and stopped giving credit and waiting months for payments that he had to chase people for. Now he put his cards on the table with clients, got deposits and payments upfront, and if they called him a mean bastard behind his back, as he knew they did, he didn't give a toss. He had a business to look after and if they didn't like it, they could lump it.

Oliver tried to be polite and pronged a prawn. Two mouthfuls later and he'd cleared his portion. His stomach growled. It seemed a long time since he'd grabbed a bacon sandwich at noon and it was after six now. If he didn't get some proper food soon, he'd faint from hunger!

*   *   *

Cora Flynn lay in her bed and watched the late evening sun stream in through her lace curtains. It had been a beautiful afternoon, even if there was a sharp nip in the air. Oliver was probably at the hotel by now, tucking into his dinner. The wedding had been planned for two o'clock and it had gone six. She'd heard the chiming of the Angelus bell break the silence of the evening a while back. She tossed and turned restlessly and eventually threw back the blankets and quilt and eased herself out of the bed.

She was stiff from lying in the bed these past few days, but the painkillers must have worked on her hip because all the twinges were gone. It hadn't been that bad a pain compared to other times, she acknowledged guiltily, knowing that she'd have been well able to make the wedding if she'd wanted to.

Cora wrapped her dressing-gown around her and walked slowly down the hall to her kitchen. Two big tears plopped down her cheeks. Maybe she was a bitter old woman but she just couldn't bear to watch that sharp-faced rip become Oliver's wife and take the Flynn family name.

Noreen Lynch had chased Oliver and taken advantage of his good nature and in the process got a fine mansion up in the hills and Oliver ready at her beck and call. He, of course, couldn't see it and got very snippy if she said anything critical about madam, so she had to bite her tongue frequently. It was all extremely difficult. She wiped her eyes, annoyed with herself for showing such weakness.

43

She filled the kettle and stared out the kitchen window at the big bank of autumn heathers that she'd planted a couple of years ago. Beautiful shades of violets and purples gave her garden a mountainy hue that reminded her a little of Wicklow, where she'd been born and bred. It had taken her weeks to clear and prepare it. Oliver had told her that he'd do it for her, but he hadn't a clue about gardening. Green-fingered he certainly wasn't, whatever his other attributes, she thought fondly. He was a good son to her. Quiet, reserved, traits inherited from his father. But he'd always driven her where she wanted to go and kept the home spick and span both inside and out. Every spring the outhouses and walls of the house were white-washed, and the windows painted the lovely cerulean blue she loved. He'd painted them this year before he'd moved into his own house.

Tears welled up again. Oliver moving out had been the worst thing that had happened to her since her husband had died. At least when Liam had died, she'd had Oliver to lean on and help soften the loneliness. Now she had no one. That Noreen one had made sure of that. Cora felt a surge of anger and bitterness. Oliver had turned his back on her. He'd made his bed and he could lie on it with that bony bitch and she'd be changing her will on Monday morning to make sure that Noreen Lynch never got a penny out of Cora's estate. If Oliver didn't like it, he could lump it. With a determined set to her jaw, Cora went back to her bedroom and took out the big brown envelope from under the clean towels and sheets in the big sandalwood chest at the foot of her bed. She went back to the kitchen table and spread her papers out carefully, papers that included the deeds to the house. Things were going to change, and Noreen Lynch could take the blame for it.

4

Noreen Flynn felt a deep sense of satisfaction as she surveyed her guests from the top of the table. Her wedding was everything she had dreamed of. Well apart from Oliver digging his heels in over wearing a top hat, she thought ruefully, remembering the rows. It would have looked so distinguished on him too. Both her sisters' husbands had worn top hat and tails at their weddings. But she hadn't been able to persuade him, no matter how much she'd gone on at him. Once Oliver made his mind up about something she could forget about trying to change it. He was as stubborn as a mule. She turned to look at her new husband and saw him gazing off into space.

Oliver had an interior life that hard as she tried she couldn't share. He withheld part of himself from her and it drove her mad sometimes. She wanted to know what was in his head, she wanted to know what he truly felt for her but the more she pushed, the less she got. 'A penny for your thoughts,' she'd often said, early on in their relationship.

'Not worth a penny,' he'd say in his offhand way

and that would be that. If he was in one of his quiet moods she might not get more than two words out of him. It could be extremely frustrating sometimes. He was an enigma to her. So self-sufficient in his own quiet way. He certainly didn't need her as much as she needed him. But that would change once he'd settled into married life with her, she comforted herself. She'd change him, make him more open and relaxed. He'd stop working so hard as well and they'd be able to do more things together, even spend more time in bed together, she thought in happy anticipation of some wild passionate lovemaking on their honeymoon. Oliver was good in bed.

He was drop dead gorgeous too, Noreen thought with quiet pleasure. He was the sexiest man she'd ever met and he didn't even know it. Tall, six foot, and lean and rangy, he had the most beautiful body that she could wish for, fit, hard and healthy from all the physical labour. She could never get enough of him. But it was his eyes that had really got to her. As blue as sapphires, he had a direct way of looking at you that could set her heart galloping in an instant and she certainly wasn't one given to romantic notions. She'd nursed too many men in her time and emptied too many of their shitty bed pans to be overcome by the sight of a man's body.

She'd been in a relationship that had brought her to her lowest ebb, thanks to a man's pure selfishness and her own lack of judgement. Noreen certainly didn't see men as gods to be worshipped on pedestals. But Oliver had something, a complete lack of awareness of himself that had attracted her

47

from the beginning. That she had landed a handsome, successful man like Oliver Flynn had given her younger, married sisters the shock of their lives. Smug bitches, she thought sourly. She had no time for Rita and Maura.

Noreen glanced down at them sitting with their fat, florid little husbands at a table in the centre of the room, and felt an uncharacteristic surge of superiority. She'd certainly got a better man than Rita and Maura had got with Jimmy or Andy. The thought of either of them pawing you was enough to give you the shivers, she thought smugly, thinking of how delightful it was to stroke her hands up and down the lean planes of Oliver's strong body and weave her fingers in the dark tangle of hair on his chest. He had a good firm mouth too, she liked kissing him. Jimmy had loose, slobbery wet lips. Even if she was to stay on the shelf for ever, she'd never have married a blob like Jimmy. And yet Rita had been ecstatic when they'd got engaged and treated her husband like a god! Whatever she saw in him. It was always 'Jimmy said this' or 'Jimmy said that' or 'Jimmy says'. When she spoke of him in the third person Noreen always felt she spoke in capitals. 'HE' likes to have a couple of drinks and a game of golf on Sunday. HE hates playing with women. Shouldn't be allowed on the course, HE says. Rita would give one of her silly ah-you'd-have-to-laugh-at-him titters that drove Noreen around the bend. 'HE doesn't eat lamb, would you order a well-done steak for HIM,' Rita had requested when Noreen had told her the menu for the wedding breakfast.

She'd felt like giving HIM a good kick up the ass. It was fat enough too, she thought mentally picturing a pair of flabby, pasty white buttocks. Oliver had a great ass, taut and firm and not at all pale and pasty but a sallow, olive hue, the same as the rest of his body. She loved watching him walk around naked, although she had to eye him surreptitiously. If Oliver thought she was ogling his body he'd be mortified. He never believed her when she told him he was magnificent. 'And I know . . . I'm a nurse, I've seen *hundreds*,' she'd add for good measure.

'Stop talking nonsense, woman,' he'd say, but she felt he liked it when she said it. He wasn't good at taking compliments, but then with a mother like Cora Flynn was that anything to be surprised at? Cora couldn't say anything positive or nice in case it would choke her. It was no wonder Oliver had no self-esteem. If she ever had children she would praise them to the skies and make sure they were full of confidence about themselves, Noreen promised herself. She was looking forward to having a family of her own and she'd rear them a hell of a lot better than Rita's pair. Brats, that's what her two nephews were, and already their mother was speaking about *them* in capitals. THOMAS and JEFFREY needed a good clip in the ear, as far as Noreen was concerned. She was glad that she had put her foot down and told Rita they could not come to the wedding. Rita had got into a fine snit, but tough. Those pair weren't going to ruin HER wedding.

Noreen gave a little smile. Today she was perfectly

entitled to think of herself in capitals. Today was the best day of her life and tonight was going to be extra special. She and Oliver hadn't had proper sex for a month since she'd come off the pill. She was so looking forward to tonight. And maybe if she was truly blessed she'd conceive a honeymoon baby as well. Oliver was so virile she might even have twins, she thought happily, giving him a little smile and a wink.

Sex with Oliver was good, better than she'd ever had with her ex, in all the on and off years she'd been with him, that was for sure, and she'd swear better than Rita or Maura ever had with those two little fat frogs who were stuffing their faces with bread rolls as they waited for the next course to be served.

Noreen knew that until she'd made the surprise announcement of her engagement, the shoe had been on the other foot and her younger sisters had looked down their noses at her and thought she was a dried-up old spinster with no life of her own. That was all changed now, she thought grimly. And how. When their mother had suffered a stroke, they'd more or less told her that she was Noreen's responsibility, her being a nurse and unmarried with, as they saw it, no responsibilities.

Noreen sighed. It was really the fact that she was a nurse that had been her undoing in terms of standing up for herself in that particular situation. Normally she was pretty good at standing her ground, she acknowledged wryly. She'd felt duty bound to come home from London, where she'd lived for the past ten years, and nurse her mother.

She'd liked London. No one knew her. There were no prying, nosy neighbours or superior younger sisters to ask when was she going to give everyone a day out? No one knew about her life in London or knew what a disaster her personal life had been. She bit her lip at the memory of Pete McMullen and a sadness darkened her eyes.

Stop it! Such nonsense at your own wedding. Oliver's a thousand times the man that shit ever was, she chastised herself. *Don't even go there!* Noreen sat up straight and surveyed her guests once again. There was a lively hum of chatter and laughter and the clink of cutlery against china. People seemed to be enjoying themselves. The Lake View had a deservedly good name for wedding receptions.

She heard Oliver's Aunt Ellie laughing at something the priest had just said. Ellie was a good old stick, stepping into the breach to look after that old rip of a termagant that was now her mother-in-law. Noreen's mouth tightened. Cora Flynn had done nothing but put obstacles in her way ever since she'd begun dating Oliver, but Noreen hadn't thought for one second that she would pull a stunt so low as to pretend to be ailing, to try and stop Oliver and herself from going on honeymoon. And as for not coming to the wedding, personally, Noreen was delighted but she felt it for Oliver. It was a real slap in the face for him. He'd been so good to her, the old bat. You'd think that she'd be delighted he was getting married and not going to end up a lonely old bachelor with no one to take care of him.

Cora was a different kettle of fish from her own

mother. Nuala Lynch had been a kind, quiet woman, who'd let her husband Tom bully and boss her. Tom had tried to bully and boss them all, but he hadn't got far with her, Noreen thought with satisfaction. She'd always given as good as she got and consequently her father had no time for her.

Tom had died drunk behind the wheel of his car, when it had gone out of control and hit a tree at high speed. Noreen certainly hadn't mourned him and she'd actually been glad for her mother, who after an initial period of adjustment had come out of her shell and begun to enjoy a whole new lease of life freed from the bullying and bad treatment that had been the bondage of her 'for better or worse' marriage.

Nuala had joined the local women's guild and the bowling club and, with no one to cook and care for apart from herself, for the first time in her life had time to lead the type of life she had never thought possible. She looked years younger and had a serene contented air about her that Noreen had never seen when her father was alive. Married to Tom, she'd been quiet and miserable. As a widow she'd blossomed and Noreen rejoiced for her.

It was a cruel irony that she had been struck down with a massive stroke from which she'd never recovered, and although her eventual death gave Noreen a freedom of sorts, she'd grieved for her mother and railed at the cruelty of fate.

It was through her mother's illness that she'd really got to know Oliver. She'd known him and his family to say hello to, although Mrs Flynn had always been a bit stuck-up and stand-offish, but

52

apart from the usual social interactions outside a shop or the church, she'd never had a conversation with him and knew just that he had a good reputation as a builder, a rare enough distinction.

When the hospital had told the family that they could no longer let Nuala occupy a bed as there was nothing more they could do for her, Noreen had tried to get nursing-home accommodation. But after a few weeks Rita and Maura had balked at the cost and said they couldn't bear to see their mother 'incarcerated in a home for the rest of her life'. However, they weren't willing to take it upon themselves to bring her to either of *their* homes. They hadn't nursing abilities like she had. 'And besides,' as Maura had sniffily told her, 'we've looked after her for the past ten years when you've been in London.' The way her sisters saw it, it was time she took some responsibility.

'What do you mean, you looked after her? She was never sick a day in her life and once Da died she had a great life,' Noreen retorted.

'Ah, you weren't here when he was drunk and making her life a misery. You got out pretty quick so you didn't have to be around for that,' Maura accused.

She had a point, Noreen supposed. She'd left home to train as a nurse in the Mater, and lived in Dublin before moving to London. She hadn't been at home to endure her father's increasingly bad behaviour.

Noreen had given up her job as a ward sister at St Mary's Hospital in Paddington and come home, simmering with resentment. If *she* had been married with children, would Maura and Rita have been so quick to land their mother on her, and would she have felt in a stronger position to refuse to shoulder the whole burden? It was as if she were being punished for being single, she thought gloomily, feeling uncharacteristically sorry for herself as she flew home from London to begin a new and uncertain life in her home town.

The small, poky family home wasn't suitable for Nuala's needs and Noreen had told her sisters in no uncertain terms that she needed an extension to the back parlour and that they could pay their share towards it. *That* money had been forthcoming without argument, increasing her resentment towards her siblings. They couldn't wash their hands of their mother quick enough, now that Noreen was home. Money for an extension was a small price to pay. Noreen had engaged Oliver Flynn's firm to build the extension for her.

He'd looked over the architect's plans, made a few suggestions of his own and told her that he'd be able to have it built for her in six months' time as they were currently working flat out. Noreen had been horrified. Six months was far too long to wait. She was thinking in terms of six weeks, she told him agitatedly.

'We're pushed to the pin of our collars, Noreen. I can't let my other clients down,' he'd said regretfully when she told him of her mother's circumstances and that she needed the extension built as soon as possible.

'It's not the Taj Mahal I'm looking for, Oliver, and it's not even a very big extension as you can see. Are you sure you couldn't squeeze me in?' she urged.

'I don't like to make promises that I can't keep, Noreen. Phil Hanahan in Redwood might be able to do it for you,' he suggested, helpfully.

'Phil Hanahan! Are you mad! He's an awful chancer. Did you not hear about the Nolans' new house? He and the idiot of a plumber got their hot and cold pipes mixed up and all the hot water was being flushed down the loo. Ma Nolan got the arse burned off her. I wouldn't touch him with a ten-foot bargepole!' Noreen exclaimed.

Oliver laughed. A good hearty chuckle. 'I hadn't heard about that. I'd better not go recommending him so,' he said, his blue eyes twinkling as they crinkled in amusement.

He's nice when he smiles, Noreen thought in surprise.

'Look, leave it with me, and I'll see what I can arrange,' Oliver said firmly and then he was gone, his hand raised in salute, and somehow she knew that he'd see to it that the extension was built for her.

Two days later he drove up in his battered old navy Volvo and she saw him loping up to the front door. 'I'll have a JCB here tomorrow to start on the foundations, if you want to start clearing out the room. I'll be doing a lot of it myself after work so I hope you won't mind putting up with a bit of noise and inconvenience in the evening. It's the only way I can get it done anyway quickly if that will suit you?' He leaned against the door jamb, his dark eyebrows raised quizzically.

'God, thanks a million, Oliver. I really appreciate this. I was at my wits' end,' Noreen confided. 'You've saved my bacon.'

'I know what it's like to have an elderly mother. At least mine is still relatively hale and hearty,' he said gruffly. 'The lads will be here before eight. See you, Noreen.'

She watched him stride down the path and thought, *he's a pretty decent bloke even if he's not very chatty*, before forgetting about him as she began to clear out the small back parlour that had been her mother's pride and joy the first time she'd walked into her new home. Now it was shabby and old-fashioned and Noreen felt no regrets as she rolled up the carpet and ordered a skip to take the old sofa and sideboard.

Her mother was going to have a nice bright room with a bed and en suite and a big French door to give her a view of the rolling hills. Paralysed all down the left side and hardly able to speak, she wouldn't have much of a life, but Noreen was determined that she'd have the best quality of life that she could give her.

True to his word, Oliver's men arrived with the JCB the following morning and that evening Oliver himself arrived to survey the work in progress and do his own bit. Noreen offered him tea and sandwiches but he told her, politely, that he hadn't time; she got the feeling that he'd prefer not to have to make idle chit-chat but just to get on with things, so she left him to it.

Every evening around six thirty he'd arrive and carry on where his men had left off, sometimes working until ten and after, as long as the light held good. It was an unusually dry couple of weeks and they were blessed by the weather. She often watched him, bare-chested, in the heat of the dying rays of the sun, and marvelled at the strength and fitness of him and made vague promises to herself that she would join the gym up in the hotel to tone up and give her an outlet to work off the tensions and frustrations of being a 24-hour carer. She knew she needed some focus and outside interests to keep her sane in the months and even years ahead.

One evening several weeks later, when the extension had its new tiled roof on, Oliver knocked on the door. His tanned face was streaked with grime and he looked tired.

'Howya, Noreen, just to let you know that the lads will be breaking through tomorrow, maybe you might like to go shopping for a few hours. It will be a bit noisy, to say the least.'

'OK,' she said. 'You look a bit knackered, are you sure you wouldn't like a beer, even, if I can't persuade you to have tea or coffee?'

He stretched tiredly. 'A beer sounds mighty good to me. It's a very humid night, isn't it?'

'Very,' Noreen agreed as she went into the kitchen and took a bottle of Miller out of the fridge. 'Glass?'

'Naw, thanks, I'll drink it out of the bottle. Are you going to have one yourself?'

'Oh!' she was surprised. 'Why not? It's been a long day.'

Oliver grinned and took a long draught of the

cool golden liquid. 'Larry likes to get started early,' he said, referring to the builder who came every morning at seven thirty on the dot. 'He's been with me a long time. He's one of my best. In fact he taught me a hell of a lot when I started out in the building trade, so I've no worries about the work being up to scratch. Larry's a perfectionist,' he said as he took another swig of beer.

'A bit like yourself, then,' Noreen remarked. To her surprise a dull flush suffused his neck and cheeks and she realized that Oliver Flynn was quite shy, despite his outwardly calm, businesslike reserve.

'If that's a compliment I'll take it,' he said, awkwardly.

'It's a rare commodity now to find people who have high standards at work. It's no wonder you're booked solid,' she said lightly, 'I'm just glad that you and your high standards and Larry the perfectionist are looking after my extension.'

'That's good. Thanks for the beer, Noreen. See you tomorrow,' he said briskly as he laid the bottle on the table and left.

Noreen closed the door after him, half sorry that he'd rushed off so soon. Oliver Flynn could be an interesting man if you could get behind the shyness long enough to get to know him. She'd been gone from Kilronan so long, she had no real friends left here now. She certainly didn't count Rita and Maura as friends.

She was lonely, she realized as she watched the lights of his car disappear over the hill. She'd been so busy sorting out things for her mother and getting the house and extension organized, she'd had little time to socialize. It had been nice having the bottle of beer with Oliver. She must get in a supply, and keep them cold in the fridge for the duration of the building works. Having a nightly beer with Oliver would be a pleasant way of ending the day; she might even get beyond his shyness and see what made him tick. Now that would be a challenge and a half, Noreen thought in amusement as she drew the curtains, locked the door, rinsed a few cups in the sink and switched out the lights.

As she lay in bed later, looking out at a full moon that slanted slivers of white gold light through her window, she replayed the events of the day and fell asleep thinking about Oliver, hoping that he would stay and have a beer with her after work in the days to come.

To her gratification when she offered him a beer the following evening he accepted and they chatted about inconsequential things. She deliberately kept the conversation light and made no personal observations. Oliver was a good listener and, over time, she found herself telling him about her resentment at having to leave her job in London to come home. 'It's not that I don't love my mother, I do,' she explained, anxious that he wouldn't think her a selfish wagon. 'It's just that Rita and Maura think that just because they're married and I'm not, I'm the one who has to give up everything to come home. They're offloading it all on to my shoulders.'

It was a huge relief to be able to verbalize her

anger and even though Oliver was practically a stranger, she'd felt he understood. 'Do you think I'm being totally selfish?' she asked curiously.

He'd studied her with his direct blue-eyed gaze. 'Not in the slightest,' he'd said reassuringly. 'But, even though it might not be much of a comfort at the moment, at least when your mother does pass away you'll have nothing to reproach yourself with. Your sisters might not be so lucky.'

'I suppose so,' she agreed, not having thought of that particular aspect.

By the time the extension was completed – to the highest standards of course – Oliver had become quite relaxed with her and she enjoyed their chats and nightly bottles of beer so much that she said forlornly as she wrote out the cheque for the outstanding balance she owed him, 'I'm going to miss our chats and beer, Oliver. I've kinda got used to them now.'

'We could always have the odd pint in the Haven,' he said diffidently and she saw the faint hint of a blush curling around his shirt collar.

Noreen was touched. He was a nice, decent bloke, even if he was a few years younger than her. She liked him. 'That would be nice, Oliver. I can try to get one of my sisters to come and spend a few hours with my mother when she comes home,' she responded easily.

'It's important that you get out and about, Noreen. Make sure those sisters of yours pull their weight a bit,' he said gruffly. 'I'll be in touch. See you.' He smiled at her and again she was struck at how much a smile changed his countenance, making him appear younger and more relaxed than his usual serious, watchful demeanour.

Noreen watched him get into his car and wondered why he wasn't married. Was it his shyness that kept him from being in a serious relationship? He was currently single, he'd told her, when she'd asked outright. He'd been surprised at her directness. She was nothing if not direct, she thought wryly. And bossy with it. Hadn't Pete called her a bossy bitch during one of their many rows? Maybe she was bossy, she conceded. It had stood her in good stead when she was promoted to Sister. She liked to call a spade a spade.

'And what about you? Is there a man waiting for you in London?' he'd queried back.

'Not any more. I lived with someone for five years, but it was over before my mother got sick.'

'I'm sorry to hear that, I hope it wasn't too rough on you.'

'I was a bit shattered to say the least,' she said quietly.

'These things happen,' he murmured, but she saw sympathy in his eyes and felt strangely touched by it.

He phoned a week after he'd finished the extension. 'We'll sort out that drink in the Haven if it still suits you, Noreen,' he said crisply and she exhaled a long breath. She'd been half afraid he wouldn't ring.

Noreen smiled at the memory. She'd had to organize all their dates from then on. She'd even had to take the bull by the horns after two years of courtship and ask him to marry her, or she'd still be going for walks around the lake and drinks in the Haven.

She would have preferred it if Oliver had proposed to her. She could still remember the startled look in his eyes when she'd bluntly said, 'Look, Oliver, I think it's time we got married, don't you? Will you marry me? We've been seeing each other for two years now and we're not teenagers any more. My mother's dead. I need to make plans for my future. If you and I don't move on, I feel I should go back to London.'

For one heartstopping moment she'd thought that he was going to refuse her but he'd sort of gulped and composed himself and muttered, 'I suppose you're right. When do you want to set the date?'

It certainly wasn't the proposal she'd ever dreamed of, but that was the way of it and she knew a tiny part of her would always wonder if he *truly* loved her and would ever have got around to asking her himself. Certainly there was no way she'd ever admit to her sisters or anyone else for that matter that she had done the proposing. It didn't seem right somehow, no matter how liberated women were. He should have asked her, then she'd know he'd really wanted to get married. It was the only thing that bothered her coming up to the wedding.

'Are you sure you want to get married?' she'd asked Oliver once when they'd been edgy with each other about the arrangements and he'd flatly refused to wear a top hat.

'Sure enough,' he'd scowled and she hadn't pressed him on it.

He seemed happy enough, she reflected as she saw him tucking into his lamb. Well, they were married now, she thought pragmatically as she cut into the tender moist meat and took a bite. It was a fresh start for both of them and it was going to be a success. Of that, Noreen Flynn was determined.

5

Neil Brennan ironed the collar of his best white shirt and frowned when he noticed the beginnings of fraying. He was very heavy on shirts – he'd better go and buy himself another few. After all, he'd need to look his best if he was going into the car sales business. People would expect a certain standard of dress when they were doing business with him.

He had great plans for his father's garage. He was going to ask Oliver Flynn to demolish the existing shabby, gloomy shack that stood on North Road and get him to build a gleaming glass and chrome showroom with garage and service facilities at the rear. It was going to cost an arm and a leg, but he had costed it all, drawn up an impressive business plan, and the local bank manager was willing to give him a substantial loan. His father too was willing to invest and be a sleeping partner. It was time to take the bit between his teeth and go with it. That business start-up course he was doing was practical and extremely informative. It was paying off already, Neil reflected as he ran the iron over the cuffs.

He stuffed a pile of newly printed business cards into the inside pocket of his freshly dry-cleaned grey suit. He was getting ready to go to the afters of Oliver Flynn's wedding. He'd serviced Oliver's car a couple of weeks ago and the builder had issued a casual invite to the afters of his wedding. Neil was delighted with the invitation. He'd looked after Oliver's cars for the past few years. It was nice to be appreciated. Weddings were a great place for doing business. He intended to go after potential customers in a discreet but determined manner. Neil knew enough about the business to know that most people hate In-Your-Face-Car-Salesmen. He wasn't going to be pushy but if the opportunity came up he'd use it.

He slipped on the white shirt and tucked the tail into his trousers. He was putting on weight, he noted glumly, holding his breath as he fastened his belt. He'd have to stop eating the big fry-ups his father cooked for breakfast.

He glanced at his watch – seven forty-five already. He'd want to get a move on – he was supposed to have collected Heather fifteen minutes ago. She wouldn't mind, he reassured himself. Heather understood when he was late for a date sometimes. She knew he had to finish working on the cars. And she knew Friday nights and Tuesdays were out because of his business course, but she didn't moan and whinge like Angie Hudson had before she'd given him the brush-off. She'd been a usey bitch anyway, he was far better off without her.

Heather saw the sense in what he was doing and

was extremely encouraging. Neil enjoyed talking to her about his plans. He was looking forward to going to the wedding bash with her tonight; the only drawback was that her stuck-up cousin, Lorna, would be there.

Neil grimaced as he knotted his tie. He really couldn't stick that girl. She thought she was *so* superior. She always had some snooty remark to make about bog-trotters and culchies, which was rich coming from her – she was as much a culchie as he was, he thought indignantly. He didn't know what it was about Lorna Morgan, but she could really get up his nose . . . and frequently did. One day, he'd be driving around in a brand new Beemer and living the high life and she wouldn't be sneering and looking down her pointy little nose at him then, Neil vowed as he slapped on some aftershave, ran a comb through his unruly black hair and grabbed his wallet off the dressing-table.

He pulled open one of the drawers and rooted until he found a packet of condoms. Might as well bring them, just in case he got lucky with Heather. They'd been dating almost two months now and zilch. Some girls he'd dated he'd shagged after *two* dates. Well, maybe that was a bit of an exaggeration. But Angie Hudson had let him shag her on the fifth date and that was after two weeks. She'd only been looking for a good deal on a Nissan Micra that he'd got for a song, he thought in hindsight. Being used like that had left a bitter taste. It had shocked him, actually, that a girl would be so duplicitous. He'd thought Angie was really into him. What an idiot he'd been. As soon as she'd got her fat little mitts on the car, she had dumped him like the biggest hot potato ever. Even now, his stomach knotted at the memory. He'd been made a fool of, but it would never happen to him again. And he'd never let a woman lead him by the nose again, either. He'd make the rules in any relationship of his from now on. Women were not to be trusted.

Heather Williams was a far nicer girl than that Hudson slag though. Maybe she was different, he conceded. She didn't have a car, yet. Neil smiled to himself. He'd keep an eye out for a nice Fiesta or Starlet for her and help her to arrange the financing too. She could be one of his first customers, but naturally because they were dating he'd give her a good cut on the price.

Whistling, Neil let himself out of the house and got into his pride and joy, a black Saab that gleamed and shone in the evening sun. It might be three years old, but it looked brand new. Once the business got going he'd change it for a new model. After all, if he was expecting people to buy new cars from him, he'd have to drive to impress. Maintaining the right image was crucial in business, any fool knew that. *Angie Hudson and Lorna Morgan just watch this space*, Neil thought jauntily as he sat into his car, gunned the engine and scorched down Larkin's Lane on to North Road.

Carmen tinkled tinnily on Heather Williams's mobile, causing momentary panic as she rooted in her taupe leather bucket bag trying to locate it. The ringing got louder and her rooting became more frantic as she delved into little inside pockets and compartments, cursing as she pricked her fingers on the sharp ends of a comb before finally locating the offending article. 'Hello,' she said breathlessly, expecting it to be Neil to tell her he was on his way. She was totally surprised to hear Lorna's *extremely* friendly tone ask gaily, 'Hi, Heather, are you coming? I'm pissed already, I thought you'd be here by now.' There was no trace of yesterday's ill grace. Lorna was her bright, breezy self.

'Oh! Oh! I'm just waiting on Neil to collect me, we shouldn't be too long.' Heather was flustered.

'It will be midnight before you get here, knowing him. He's never on time,' Lorna said tartly.

'Look, I'll be there when I'm there, OK,' Heather snapped.

'Well, just hurry, I'm bored out of my tree. It's *so* not happening here. I was sitting with Derek's parents and I had to behave myself and they're awfully dim. Doctor Kennedy is as dull as dishwater, he kept making really stupid jokes and Mrs Kennedy just kept glaring at him, saying, "Be quiet, Douglas." And Derek wouldn't even talk to them. As soon as the meal was over we sneaked off and had a couple of doubles to cheer ourselves up and I'm pissed and ready for action. I'm going to bop my brains out when the music starts. Get your ass down here pronto.' She giggled.

I'm not holding her head over a toilet tonight, Heather promised herself as she listened to her cousin rabbiting on. Lorna was well on the way to being smashed. Tonight she could look after herself.

Heather was going to enjoy herself with Neil and that was that.

'Are you there?' Lorna demanded.

'Yeah, look, I'll see you soon—'

'Oh God, here's Derek with two more drinks. Have to go, byeee,' Lorna trilled and then there was a thud and a clatter and Heather could hear her cousin cursing her mobile phone which had obviously fallen out of her grasp.

Heather shook her head. Lorna had no sense sometimes. Oliver Flynn's wedding was not the place to make a show of herself. There'd be talk and her mother would hear about it and Lorna's life wouldn't be worth living and she'd whinge and whine for months. She hoped she wouldn't start sniping at Neil when he arrived. They didn't get on at all, and it was uncomfortable sometimes listening to them having a go at one another. All of a sudden the evening she had been looking forward to for the past few weeks was beginning to lose its lustre. She glanced at her watch and bit her lip. It was almost seven fifty-five and there was no sign of Neil coming to pick her up. Perhaps he wasn't coming. He could be standing her up.

She heard a diesel car coming along the road and raced to the window hoping it would be the familiar black Saab, but no. It was a red car and her heart sank to her boots. Should she ring him? she agonized. But then he might think she was being pushy. Two months wasn't that long to be going with someone. He might take exception if she started demanding explanations or started giving out to him for being late.

But maybe there was a good reason that he was late, she dithered as her hand hovered over the phone digits. Maybe he'd had a puncture or something. The least he could do was ring though, she thought crossly. He was *never* on time and it was rude to keep another person waiting. It suggested that his time was more precious than theirs. She was going to have it out with him once and for all. He had to learn to have a bit of respect.

What was it with her? Men fell over themselves to please Lorna, but the blokes that she went out with never seemed to put her first. Heather scowled, remembering Colin Breen. She'd dated him for six months and there had been times when he'd be two hours and more late for a date. Whenever they went to the pictures it was always the picture that he wanted to see that they went to. Usually mind-boggling mental chewing-gum with Arnold Schwarzenegger or Sylvester Stallone.

Once he'd stood her up and when – furious – she'd phoned him up and eaten the face off him, he'd hung up and hadn't called her for ten days. She'd been so miserable. She'd cried herself to sleep every night. Every time the phone had rung at home or at work, her stomach had clenched into knots and she'd prayed that it would be him. The disappointment when it wasn't had been shattering each time. She'd almost called him a dozen times. In fact once she had, and when his flatmate answered, she'd lost her nerve and hung up. She'd been petrified that she'd never see him again and that she'd be left on the shelf. A shit boyfriend was better than no boyfriend, she'd reasoned. When he'd finally called her she'd eagerly agreed to meet him and had fallen into his arms when she'd seen him.

Heather blushed scarlet at the memory of her wimpiness. She had behaved like such a doormat — even now she cringed, thinking of it. It hadn't made any difference anyway, it turned out that the two-faced little ferret had been two-timing her all along and he'd ditched her unceremoniously one wet Friday night when she'd refused yet again to have sex with him, and called her a frigid cow.

Now, it was a huge relief to her that she hadn't slept with Colin. At least she hadn't let him walk all over her in that regard. She might be a wimp and a doormat but she wasn't a notch on Colin Breen's bedpost and that was a small crumb of comfort in what had been a total and absolutely disastrous relationship which had wiped out every scrap of confidence she had.

Heather studied her reflection in the big bevelled mirror over the hallstand. Chestnut hair with glints of auburn fell around her face in a smooth silky curtain. Heather wore her hair short, whereas Ruth wore hers wild and wavy, tumbling down her back. Heather wasn't really the wild and wavy sort, she thought ruefully. The reflection of solemn hazel eyes fringed with thick dark lashes stared back at her. Her eyes were OK, she supposed. Her nose was too wide, lips normal enough, and now, because she hadn't been dieting, her cheekbones were gone and her face wasn't the slightest bit thin and interesting. At least she had a tan, she comforted herself. Tans always made you look better. She decided to dab a bit more blusher on her cheeks to try to give the *impression* of cheekbones. She was wearing a plum bustier over black trousers, and a silky black jacket. The bustier gave her a good cinched-in waist and a flattering hint of cleavage but she wouldn't dare take the jacket off no matter how warm it got, her ass was far too big to be put on public display. Heather sighed deeply. Lorna no doubt was dressed to the nines, and not the slightest bit worried about her ass. Her cousin had a perfect figure.

She heard another car coming down the street and peered out of the window anxiously, her palms curling. A green car whizzed past. That was it! She'd had enough. If Neil wasn't here in five minutes' time she was going to go to the wedding on her own and to hell with him. She was just sick, sick, sick of being treated like a doormat. Tears glittered in her eyes. Was it her, or were all men selfish shits? Angry, hurt, disappointed, she blinked rapidly to dispel the tears. A thought struck her: it was Neil that had been invited to the wedding, she was going as his guest. She couldn't go on her own whether she wanted to or not.

Well, she just would go, Heather decided resentfully. Who'd notice? She was damned if she was going to take off all her make-up and finery after going to such trouble. She picked up her evening bag, a glittery purse affair, pulled out her lipstick and re-did her lips with 'Sensual Plum'. She'd have to stop biting her lips, they were in shreds, she noted forlornly. She tried to fit her phone in the bag, but it wouldn't fasten and bulged in an unsightly manner. Heather hated small bags with a vengeance. She liked bags that she could carry her bits and pieces in, they made her feel secure. She wished she had her twin's confidence, or even Lorna's. She wished she was more like them in every way. They could carry off small, smart evening bags, they could reveal their asses to the world without a care. They had men falling at their feet, men who were on time, even early for dates *and* they didn't take crap. She, at this precise moment, felt an utter and absolute failure.

She heard a familiar diesel engine thrumming outside and once again she flew to the window, feeling a huge wave of relief wash over her when she saw a familiar black car. Thank God he'd arrived; she sent the fervent acknowledgement heavenwards in grateful thanks. He hadn't stood her up after all. Maybe she wouldn't have it out with Neil about his punctuality tonight, but the next time he was late for a date she was going to give it to him hot and heavy, Heather assured herself earnestly, as she gave her bustier one last tweak before opening the door with a smile on her face.

6

Lorna gasped with dismay as she felt a sharp stab of pain. 'Oooh,' she groaned against Derek Kennedy's neck. Unfortunately Derek mistook her groan for a moan of passion and thrust into her even more frantically before collapsing on top of her, panting like a dog. Lorna's jaw dropped. That was it! That's what all the fuss was about. That's what all the begging and pleading in the back seat of Derek's car had been for, as date after date he'd urged her to let him have sex with her. She'd felt nothing, not even a tingle. She just felt sore, messy, uncomfortable and cheated.

This wasn't the way it was supposed to be. She'd read *She* and *Marie Claire* and all the other glossy mags (even *Cosmo* although that was seriously dated) avidly. She'd studied numerous hints to satisfy HIM 'n' HER and had looked forward to using them in a night of blissful pleasure and passion, but nothing that she'd read about had happened with herself and Derek. There'd been no touching and tasting and sucking and licking, no slow, sexy stripping, no massaging with oil, just Derek jumping on her, pulling off her panties.

Then, two minutes later, it was all over. They hadn't even snogged!

'Get off me,' Lorna slurred as Derek nuzzled her ear. He raised his head and looked at her, hurt.

'Didn't you enjoy it?' he asked, his brown eyes gazing blearily into hers.

'No, I didn't, you idiot.' She glowered at him.

'Well, I did,' Derek muttered and passed out.

Lorna wriggled out from under him and felt like thumping him as he snored noisily. She staggered into the bathroom and slipped out of her dress. She needed a shower, badly. She reeked of alcohol and other unmentionables. It had been a fatal mistake to confide that she could use one of the hotel rooms if she wanted to. Staff did it all the time when the hotel wasn't fully occupied. Derek had jumped at the idea, and half excited, half fearful, she'd led him up a back staircase, slipped into room 302, and then he'd pulled his He-man stunt and lunged for her. She'd been too smashed to protest, and besides, she'd thought it was only a prelude to lovemaking. She hadn't for one second thought that the whole thing would be over in two minutes flat, or less . . .

Lorna felt like crying as she stood under the shower, trying to keep her hair from getting wet. She felt a little more sober now. Funny how you could sober up so quickly, she thought just a trifle woozily. At least she could now claim she'd 'Done It', she thought dejectedly as she averted her eyes from the blood between her legs and hosed herself down with the shower, frantic to get rid of all traces of her unsavoury episode with Derek. Her disappointment was so strong, she could almost taste it.

The next time she had sex, *if* she ever had sex again and that was a very big *if*, she thought resentfully, she would make sure that she was stone cold sober and she would dictate the pace. She'd have her touching and tasting and sucking and licking and her sensual massage, by God she would. And she would have an orgasm come hell or high water. All those magazines couldn't be wrong! She would moan and groan with pleasure the way she'd heard her mother moaning and groaning all those years ago, Lorna vowed, and fell to her knees sobbing under the hot, steaming jets of water as that old, old memory that she had kept buried for so long invaded her head until she thought she was going to be sick.

'I don't want to think about it. I don't want to think about it,' she muttered wildly. 'No! No! Mam, why did you do it? Why did you let me hear you and see you? It's dirty, dirty, dirty.' Lorna wept uncontrollably, great wrenching sobs heaving from the depths of her.

Out in the rumpled double bed, Derek snored on. Oblivious.

Heather sipped her glass of tepid white wine and tried not to yawn. People were slow dancing to kd lang, but Neil was deep in conversation with some bloke about cars, and had been for the last half hour. Of Lorna and Derek there was no sign.

'Hi, Heather, would you like to dance?' Tony Mallin, one of Oliver's builders, sat down at the table beside her and eyed her hopefully. Neil never even noticed.

'Why not?' Heather said recklessly. She hoped Neil would get good and jealous when he saw her dancing a slow set. The evening had started off extremely promisingly: he'd been very attentive for about an hour but then he'd gone to the bar for more drinks and stayed chatting to some bloke for half an hour, leaving her like a lemon on her own, and now he was talking to another guy and she might as well be on the moon.

She followed Tony on to the floor and they started to dance. 'Are you enjoying yourself?' he asked as his hands slid down to her hips.

'It's OK,' she responded, disconcerted. He was being far too touchy-feely for her taste.

'If I had a lovely girl like you as my date, I wouldn't sit gabbing with a bloke,' he murmured, nuzzling her ear. 'That top you're wearing is dead sexy.' He drew away for a moment and gazed admiringly at her cleavage, before pressing himself close against her. She could feel his erection. Heather had just about had enough.

'Do you *mind*, Tony Mallin. What do you think I am?' she demanded furiously, twisting out of his grasp. 'Go grope someone else,' she snapped, marching off the dance floor leaving Tony with his mouth open in surprise.

Neil had never even noticed that she was gone. He was still engrossed in his conversation. Heather felt volcanic-size resentment engulf her, as she nibbled on a cold cocktail sausage, part of the finger food served to the evening guests. Her

77

boyfriend guffawed at something the other man said. Heather grabbed her bag. 'I'm going to the Ladies,' she hissed.

'Fine, fine.' Neil didn't even bother to look in her direction. Heather stalked out of the room to the strains of 'I Can't Get No Satisfaction'. 'Tell me about it,' she muttered. The Ladies, mercifully, was empty as she went into a stall, pulled down the loo seat and sat on it, biting her lip furiously. Neil was behaving really badly. He was being so disrespectful, ignoring her while he touted for business. Heather knew and understood that it was important for him to network. He had a client base to build up. But surely, she reasoned, good manners alone dictated that he look after his date for the evening – that was, she thought with sinking heart, if he felt anything for her at all. Maybe it was best to nip it in the bud now, she thought unhappily. There was no point in going through weeks of misery the way she had with Colin.

A tear trickled down her cheeks. She'd had such hopes of Neil. She'd thought that he was different. When they were alone, he told her all about his dream to open a big garage on North Road and then, when that was up and running, another one in nearby Navan. Eventually his dream was to open one in Dublin. She had helped him with his costings, had typed up his business plan for him and had been delighted to be part of it. It was exciting, exhilarating, and she felt that she'd contributed to and shared the dream. Until tonight. Tonight she felt totally excluded, unimportant, a nuisance even. And then being mauled by Tony Mallin on the dance floor. He could have raped her for all the notice her so-called boyfriend had taken.

Heather wiped the tears from her face and stood up. Neil could build up his client base, she was going home. Better to be manless than witless and wimpy. At least she could live with herself knowing that she hadn't behaved like a doormat this time. She heard someone come into the Ladies and silently cursed. One more minute and she could have slipped out and made her getaway. She ran her fingers through her hair, straightened her jacket and opened the door.

Lorna was standing with her back to her at the sinks. She was applying lipstick to her mouth but her hand was shaking. 'Where've you been all evening?' Heather asked dully, thinking that her cousin was probably pissed. She looked a bit rough. Her make-up was streaked and her flimsy slip-style dress was very creased.

'Don't ask,' Lorna snapped.

'OK, 'night,' Heather retorted.

'What do you mean 'night? Are you and loverboy leaving?' Lorna enquired truculently.

'No, if you must know. I don't have a loverboy any more. Neil Brennan can go to hell as far as I'm concerned. 'Bye.'

'No, hold on, Heather, what's wrong? What's happened? I saw Neil out there and he seems to be having a ball.' Lorna turned to face her. She looked ghastly. Pale, red-eyed.

'Are you OK, Lorna? You haven't been taking E's or anything?' Heather blurted.

'No I haven't, Heather. I . . . I . . . Oh Heather, it was horrible!' Lorna's face crumpled and she burst into tears.

'What is it? What's wrong?' Heather looked at her in dismay.

'Let's get out of here. I don't want anyone to come barging in. We'll go down the back stairs, there's a laundry room that will be empty. I need to talk to you, Heather,' Lorna said urgently, grabbing her cousin by the arm and propelling her out the door. They hurried down the corridor and pushed open the big heavy fire-doors to the back stairs. Two minutes later, Lorna led the way into a large tiled room full of big industrial washers and driers and steam presses and ironing boards. It smelt faintly of damp and washing powder.

'What's the matter? Where were you all evening? Where's Derek?'

'Don't talk to me about that bollox! Oh, Heather. I was going to pretend it was wonderful and boast to you that it was the best experience of my life, but it was disgusting and . . .' She started to howl.

'For God's sake will you tell me what's wrong with you, Lorna!' Heather shook her cousin.

'I did it, Heather. I had sex with Derek and it was revolting and I think I'm frigid,' Lorna bawled.

'Don't be ridiculous, you're not frigid. Let's face it, Derek's not exactly Colin Firth now, is he?' Heather said stoutly. She was a bit shocked that Lorna had had sex with Derek after all the giving out she'd done about him.

'I suppose not,' hiccuped Lorna. 'I mean,

Heather, he just jumped on me and it was over in a minute. I was so disappointed!' Her lip wobbled. 'I didn't feel anything, not horny, not tingly, or quivery, nothing.'

'Forget about it,' Heather advised, giving her cousin a comforting hug. 'At least you can say that you've done it. As far as I can see I'm going to end up an old maid.'

'What's the matter with you and the mechanic?' Lorna sat on a stool and lit a badly needed cigarette.

'I don't think he's really interested, to be honest. He spent most of the evening trying to interest new clients for when he's set up in business.'

'Huh!' snorted Lorna. 'That will be the day. He's all talk and no action.'

Now that she'd got it off her chest and confided in Heather she was feeling a bit better. 'Look, I just need to go back to a room, I left my pashmina there. Why don't we go home? I can stay the night and we can have a good moan. Better than sitting in this place.'

'OK,' agreed Heather. Even Lorna's company was preferable to being on her own tonight. 'What room were you in?'

'After I fixed myself up after Derek I went into 601, it was empty and I'd borrowed one of the maid's pass keys earlier. I didn't feel like rejoining the party I can tell you, so I just lay on the bed and I must have fallen asleep. Probably shock,' she said self-pityingly. 'Derek's in 302. I've a good mind to log him in on the computer as a guest and then he'll have to pay the room rate,' she added viciously. Her eyes brightened. 'Come on, we could raid the mini-bar, take everything and he'd have to pay for all that too, the dumb bastard.'

For a moment Heather was tempted. She felt like getting skulled, but visions of Lorna puking all night – she not being able to hold her drink – put a halt to her gallop. She didn't fancy cleaning up after her cousin tonight, she had a broken heart to nurse.

'No, come on, he's not worth the hassle. Let's get a chippie on the way home instead,' she suggested hastily.

'Oh! OK then,' Lorna said sulkily. She wanted to cause Derek as much grief as she possibly could. She stubbed out her cigarette, put the light out and followed Heather into the corridor. This time they took the lift to the top floor to retrieve Lorna's pale lemon pashmina. Minutes later they were in the foyer, passing the large reception room where the wedding reception was still going strong. Out of curiosity, Heather peered in to see if she could see Neil. He was at another table, chatting to a couple, not missing her in the slightest.

'Fuck you,' muttered Heather and followed Lorna through the big swing doors. The breeze was sharp as they walked down the gravel driveway, the pebbles biting into the thin soles of their evening shoes.

'I'm sick of this place. I'm really and truly sick of it,' Lorna said vehemently. 'There's not one decent man in the place. Well, apart from Oliver Flynn. He's a fine thing even if he is a culchie,' she said grudgingly.

'Yeah, Oliver's nice. We're his accountants. He's doing well too . . . for a culchie,' Heather said tartly.

'I wonder what he sees in her. That Noreen one. She's a bit of a battleaxe. You should have heard her giving out last night because she wasn't happy with the table linen. She told them that she wanted peach table napkins to match the trimmings on the cake. We only have cream of course, but she gave out stinko about it and said she'd requested peach napkins the day she booked the wedding. There was a right royal rumpus.'

'I bet Oliver Flynn wouldn't ignore his date all night,' Heather said bitterly.

'I wonder what he's like in bed?' mused Lorna.

'Noreen will find out tonight,' grinned Heather as they passed through the pillared entrance to the hotel and headed towards Fred's Fast Food Emporium.

'Come on, I bet she's done it before now, she's in her thirties. She's ancient,' scoffed Lorna.

'If I get to do it before my thirties I'll be lucky,' said Heather mournfully, feeling extremely sorry for herself.

Lorna stopped dead. 'Look here, Heather. This kip of a town is a dead loss for men. I'm always telling you that. Let's cut our losses and head for Dublin. Let's get a life for once and for all.' She stared at her cousin, willing her to say yes, her blue eyes bright and determined under the orange ray of the street light.

Heather hesitated. That would mean giving up Neil. She'd been hoping too, that perhaps she might 'Do It' with him. She'd felt he was the right one for her.

'Come on. Did he even come looking for you?

Did he? He's no better than that Breen low life!' Lorna pushed.

Heather took a deep breath. Her cousin was right. They needed a fresh start. All men couldn't be totally self-centred. Could they? At least in Dublin there'd be a lot more choice. Neil Brennan could build his poxy garage without any help from her. There was no point in her staying in Kilronan. She'd be too depressed for words. She turned to face Lorna. 'OK then. Let's do it. Let's go to Dublin.'

'Yes! Yes! Yes!!!' Lorna punched the air. 'You won't be sorry, honest you won't. We'll show them what we're made of, Heather. Let's get out of this kippy town as fast as our legs can carry us. Believe me, this is the best move you'll ever make.'

'I hope so,' Heather said with false cheer. If it was going to be the best move she ever made how come she felt so dispirited?

'Come on, let's make plans. We've to decide where we want to live. I think we should go for a glitzy apartment—'

'We've to get jobs first,' Heather pointed out.

'We'll have no problem. Certainly not in the hotel trade and I bet you'll have no trouble getting into an accounts firm. Think positive, Heather. We are two gorgeous women, single and free. We can do whatever we want.' Lorna was on a high, memories of her disaster pushed firmly to the back of her mind. Going to live in Dublin had been her goal for so long, she wasn't going to let her cousin spoil it with negative vibes.

Heather laughed. When Lorna was in this mood

she was unquenchable and her gaiety infectious.

'OK then, we try for jobs tomorrow and then we look at all the properties for rent. Let's go for it, girl.'

'You bet your ass.' Lorna waved her pashmina over her head like a flag and danced exuberantly along the street. Nothing and no one was going to hold her back now.

Noreen slipped the deep ruby negligée over her head and settled the pencil straps on her shoulders. Normally she didn't go in for such fancy nighties. But this was her wedding night and she wanted it to be special. The ruby brought out the colour in her eyes and suited her sallow skin. She lifted her breasts so that the seam of the cups settled more comfortably. If only she had another inch or so on her boobs, she thought wistfully, looking at the small neat pair that nature had endowed her with. That top that Heather Williams had on at the dance had been gorgeous, she thought ruefully. She'd never be able to wear a bustier. She'd nothing to fill it with.

She yawned, dabbing some Chloé on her wrists and at the nape of her neck. She was tired. It had been a long, long day, but it had gone exceptionally well, as well as she could have hoped for, she thought contentedly. The drive up to Dublin after they'd run through the archway of friends and family, showered with confetti and good wishes, had been peaceful and quiet. There was no traffic to speak of, and she'd sat beside her new husband making the odd comment here and there, but mostly content to sit in silence and listen to the soothing music of Lyric FM, and relax.

They had booked a room in the Airport Great Southern and Oliver had ordered two brandies from room service for them, which they had sipped companionably, chatting over the events of the day. This time tomorrow they'd be in Malta, Noreen thought happily. She'd chosen Malta because she'd nursed a patient who'd come from Valetta and told her how beautiful the port was, and what a lovely wild, rugged, historically fascinating place his native country was.

Rita and Maura had gone to Greece and the Canaries on their honeymoons, on package holidays. Staying in Malta in a five-star hotel was certainly not a cheapie package honeymoon, she thought smugly, giving her teeth a quick clean. She actually felt as horny as hell. Must be after all the excitement. And besides, she hadn't had proper sex for a month. She didn't trust condoms and she certainly didn't want people in Kilronan counting on their fingers, should she have conceived after coming off the pill. Well, they could count all they liked now. Everything was in order. She was Mrs Oliver Flynn and if she had a honeymoon baby, that would be the icing on the cake. Noreen opened the bathroom door and padded into the bedroom in happy anticipation, only to stand stock-still in disappointment as she saw Oliver, limbs spread-eagled, chest rising up and down rhythmically in a deep sleep.

That was good money wasted on a negligée, she thought grumpily as she slid into bed beside her husband and switched out the light. She lay beside him wide awake, staring into the darkness. The dull roar of a jet taking off broke the silence. Noreen sighed and turned over, putting an arm around her husband. She slid her hand under the sheet. He was naked. 'Oliver. Oliver,' she whispered. She slipped her hand between his legs and began to stroke him. He sighed and turned over on his side with his back to her, still sleeping soundly.

'Some start to a honeymoon,' Noreen said crossly, then felt mean. Oliver had worked his butt off before the wedding so that everything would be sorted before he took his two weeks off. They had their whole lives ahead of them. It was a pity though, she was ovulating right now and it could have been a night to conceive. She smiled in the dark. She'd waited this long – one more night wouldn't make any difference.

7

A Year Later

Noreen snuggled deeper under the bedclothes. Vaguely, a long way away she could hear a voice calling her. She roused herself to consciousness. Oliver was standing, fully dressed, in front of her holding a breakfast tray. She blinked rapidly, rubbed her eyes and sat up. 'Happy Anniversary, Noreen,' her husband said as he laid the tray on her lap.

'Mornin', Oliver. This is a treat,' she said, smiling up at him, delighted that he had remembered without any hints from her. 'Happy anniversary to you too. That year flew. Didn't it?' She leaned over and took a small box and card off her bedside table and handed it to him.

'There's something for you on the tray,' he said gruffly. Oliver always got embarrassed giving her a gift, even after three years of togetherness and one year of marriage. He was a strange fella, she thought affectionately as she unwrapped the slim, awkwardly gift-wrapped package. She opened the black case to reveal a beautiful string of white pearls nestled against red velvet.

'Oh Oliver, they're *beautiful*.' Noreen's eyes sparkled with delight. She'd almost doubted that he would remember and the fact that he had made the gift even more precious. 'They're absolutely gorgeous, Oliver. Thank you so much.' Wait until Maura and Rita saw these, she thought, delightedly. They'd been asking her for weeks now did she think Oliver would remember their wedding anniversary. She'd been more than anxious, to tell the truth, but she deliberately hadn't given any hints. She wanted proof that he loved her. Remembering their anniversary would be a sign that he did, she'd assured herself. Oliver wasn't one given to sentiment. She'd had to make him go and buy her a Christmas card on Christmas Eve when one hadn't been forthcoming.

'We're married now. What do we need to be giving each other Christmas cards for?' he'd demanded grumpily. 'It's pure nonsense.'

'No it's not, and I want Christmas cards, birthday cards and anniversary cards and presents to go with them,' Noreen had insisted. 'It's the little things like that that are important in marriage. Don't go taking me for granted. I want you to be the way you were and as attentive to me as when you were wooing me.'

Oliver threw his eyes up to heaven. 'That was then, this is now, Noreen. I was getting to know you then. You women have the strangest ideas.'

'We have and don't you forget them,' warned Noreen.

To give him his due, he hadn't forgotten, she thought happily, fingering the pearls gently. And what was more, his presents to her were always ones that he clearly put thought into. His choice of jewellery and perfume always impressed her, for a man who liked to give the impression that he was no good at romance.

'Do you like what I got you?' she asked anxiously. He was pulling the wrapping paper apart, eager to get at his gift, just like a little boy, she thought in amusement. She'd bought him a Bulova watch that gave the date and was water-resistant. It was a good solid watch.

'That's a beauty, Noreen. Thank you,' he said as he studied it from all angles. 'But I'll keep it for good wear, this old thing will do me at work.'

'It's a sturdy watch, Oliver, I bought it so that you could wear it to work,' Noreen assured him. 'Come on, take off that old thing and put it on,' she instructed.

'OK, then.' He smiled, undoing the battered leather strap of his old watch, and slid the silver-links on to his wrist. He had good strong wrists. The watch emphasized his tan. She wished he'd get into bed and kiss and cuddle her and be romantic, but knowing her husband, that would take a miracle. She knew she came a poor second to his work.

'That looks much better. Now you'll be home early, won't you?' Noreen took a sip of her tea.

'Why?' Her husband looked at her in surprise.

'Well, surely you're going to take me out to dinner somewhere. It's our first wedding anniversary,

Oliver.' Noreen couldn't keep the exasperation out of her voice.

'For God's sake, Noreen. I've to meet a fellow about a load of building blocks he's selling because his business has gone bust. I have to meet him. Aren't the presents and cards enough?'

'Jeepers, Oliver, have you any romance in you at all?' Noreen demanded irritably.

'None, Noreen. You married the wrong man if you're looking for romance. I'll see you when I see you and thanks for the watch. Don't wait for me to eat dinner, I'll stick mine in the microwave.' He strode out of the bedroom and she heard him running downstairs, anxious to be up and at the day. It was only seven thirty.

Noreen sighed, pushing the tray away from her. The toast had gone cold and besides, she felt queasy. Her period had come in the night and she was crucified with cramps. She reached over to her bedside table and shook two Ponston out of a container into her palm. She swallowed them with the lukewarm tea. Anything to get rid of those excruciating cramps. She lay back against her pillows and gazed out of the big French window that led to a tiled balcony.

The sun was beginning to rise over the low, rolling hills that surrounded the lake. A light opaque mist hovered over the lake's grey, glassy surface, faintly pink from the dawn's pale glow. The view from their bedroom was breathtaking, Noreen acknowledged. Every season had its own template, each uniquely beautiful. She was an extremely lucky woman. Living in the lap of luxury, she was the envy of most of the women in Kilronan for her walk-in-wardrobes alone. Noreen smiled. It was a stylish, peaceful bedroom with a king-sized double bed and gleaming brass bedstead. Although pastels were her own favourite colour schemes, Noreen had decorated the room in creams and terracottas to suit her husband's more masculine tastes. A luxurious cream Egyptian cotton duvet was highlighted with a terracotta throw and matching terracotta cushions. The shining maple floor was partly covered with a wide fitting beige and terracotta rug that Noreen had seen by chance in a carpet showrooms in Navan. It was the perfect match for her colour scheme and she'd been thrilled with it. Even Oliver had commented on what a good buy it had been. Cream muslin curtains draped the windows, allowing shafts of natural light to brighten the room. It was a serene, restful room. Her pride and joy, not cluttered with wardrobes and dressers and drawers. She had a walk-in wardrobe to house all their clothes and bed linens.

Maura and Rita had been pea-green with envy when she'd shown them around the house. Now *they* were in the poor relation category, and Noreen revelled in it unashamedly. Neither of them had houses half so grand, which was why she'd pretended to be welcoming and friendly. She knew they were dying with curiosity, and she'd kept them waiting a long time to see it. She'd wanted the house to be perfect. They'd been satisfyingly gobsmacked, not only at the size and grandeur of the house but at her taste. No knick-knacks and ornaments, no garish colour schemes. Just simple understated elegance and arrangements of fresh flowers in every room. She'd read her home interiors magazines and known just the look she wanted. Now she had it and it made her sisters' homes fade into the halfpenny place.

Noreen knew she was being bitchy, comparing, but she didn't care. They had made her feel the underdog for so long it was pure pleasure rubbing their noses in it. When they'd seen her fitted Shaker-style cream kitchen with its self-cleaning wall oven and ultra-modern hob, not to mention the working block in the centre of the kitchen, they'd been hard put to speak, apart from saying, a few weak 'very nices'. Giving her sisters the guided tour had been the most satisfying experience of her life. Which was pathetic, really, she thought dolefully as she placed the tray on the floor and snuggled back under the duvet. She was a grown woman. The eldest of her family and sometimes she behaved like a two-year-old. She should let go of all that old bitterness and concentrate on her new life. Her new, affluent, wonderful life.

When would this ache, this need and want leave her? Maybe she should go back to work, even do part-time nursing. Oliver had told her it was entirely up to herself whether she worked or not. He didn't mind what she did as long as she was happy. After eventually winding down after the wedding and learning to relax it had been wonderful. Especially during the summer. On hot sunny days she had lain out in the garden in a hammock, with her lake view and a few glossy magazines or whatever novel she was reading, and bronzed herself golden, feeling totally relaxed after the stresses and strains of the past few years. But lately, as the days had shortened and the nights had drawn in and autumn's nip had made its presence felt, she'd begun to feel bored and restless. She wasn't cut out to be a lady of leisure. She needed to work. She was on her own far too much.

Oliver often went back out to work after his dinner and the happy anticipation of nights curled up together in front of the fire had so far not materialized. Neither had sitting together in the swing seat she had bought for the garden. Nor had there been much entertaining, Oliver being too tired after work to do much more than sit nursing a pint, she thought resentfully.

Deep down Noreen knew the reason for her discontent. She'd hoped that by now she would have been a mother, or at least an expectant mother. As the months passed by, each time her period arrived she would feel a crushing sense of disappointment. Why was she not pregnant yet? They'd been having unprotected sex for a year now; surely the effects of the pill had long disappeared from her body. She always knew when she was ovulating and made sure to have sex with Oliver as often as she could during that optimum time.

Noreen sighed deeply. She wasn't getting any younger. Mid-thirties was late for a woman to be starting a family. Why wasn't it happening? Maybe she'd go to the doctor and have a check-up just to make sure all was in order, she decided, as her eyelids started to droop and the painkillers began to kick in.

It was almost noon when she woke, with a dull throbbing headache from having slept too much. She stretched and lay in drowsy stillness for a while, willing herself to get out of bed. Maybe it was a blessing in disguise that Oliver was meeting that chap tonight. She felt too lousy to go out to dinner anyway.

She didn't particularly feel like cooking dinner for herself either if she had to eat it on her own. She might order in a Chinese when Oliver got home. Such a difference from this day last year, Noreen thought wryly as she got out of bed. Wrapping her dressing-gown around her, she slipped her feet into a pair of mules and went downstairs to the lounge. She took her wedding album from its shelf on the specially built unit that fitted into the alcove beside the fire and curled up on the plump, luxurious sofa with it on her knees.

She began to flick through the pages, smiling at the photos in front of her as memories came flooding back. She had just put it aside and was trying to talk herself into having a shower when she heard a car pull up in the drive. Noreen hurried quickly to the window. A quick glance made her heart sink as she recognized Maura's Opel Corsa. She didn't pull back quick enough and Maura saw her and waved.

'Oh rats!' groaned Noreen, as she pulled her fingers through her hair and tightened the belt of her dressing-gown. Imagine being caught by her younger sister still not dressed at this hour of the day. It was even worse having to entertain her, the way she felt. She managed a feeble effort of a smile as she opened the hall door.

'Not up yet, you lazy wagon? Well, did Oliver remember your anniversary? What did he buy you?' Maura breezed in. Noreen felt like strangling her. *Nosy bitch*, she thought resentfully. *How dare you come into my house and ask me what sort of a present my husband has bought me.* And then she thought: *Thank God, Oliver remembered.*

'Hello, Maura,' she said drily. 'To what do I owe the pleasure?'

'Just popped in to wish you a happy anniversary. I've some news for you too. You look a sight. What's the matter with you?' Maura plonked into one of the big armchairs.

'Periods,' muttered Noreen grumpily, raging at being told that she looked a sight. Maura was actually looking extremely well. Her skin and eyes were glowing and she was wearing a lovely two-piece.

'Poor you,' Maura sympathized. 'I won't have them for another six months at least,' she added smugly.

'Why not?' Noreen asked listlessly, not copping on.

'Because I'm pregnant, silly. I've just been for my first scan. Look! Look at the photo.' She waved a black and white Polaroid under Noreen's nose.

It was as if time stopped. Noreen was aware of her fingers curling into her palms, and feeling the pressure of her nails as they pressed against the flesh of her hand. Maura was pregnant. Her stomach gave a crazy lurch. She felt physically sick. And the wave of bitterness and resentment that swamped her horrified her. What kind of a mean-spirited cow was she that she resented her own sister's first, obviously joyous pregnancy?

'That's great, Maura, congratulations,' she said faintly studying the picture with blurred eyes. *Don't let me cry, God. Don't let me be a bitch. Don't let jealousy eat me up.* She prayed silently to the Almighty, desperately trying to compose herself.

'Wouldn't it be great if you got pregnant too, they'd be company for each other?' Maura burbled happily, completely unaware of her sister's agitation. 'Are you and Oliver going to have kids?'

Noreen swallowed hard. Her mouth had gone very dry. 'We hope so,' she murmured. 'When are you due?'

'Eighth of March according to the gynae. I didn't really want to tell anyone until the three months were up. But it's been awfully hard. I've been bursting to tell people. Pity Mam's not here, especially if it's a girl. She always wanted a grand-daughter. That other pair were always so boisterous. Rita lets them get away with murder.'

Noreen made no comment. If she said anything critical about her nephews it might get back to Rita one day if Maura was in a bad mood, and she wasn't having that. 'At least the winter will be over. March is a good time to have a baby, it will be nice and hardy for the summer.' She made a supreme effort. 'Can I get you a cup of tea, Maura?'

'Lovely, and I'll have a couple of biscuits if you have them, now that I'm eating for two, I'm *starving*!

Now what did Oliver get you? I bet he forgot, Andy forgot ours.' Maura stretched her legs out in front of her and stretched happily. 'Could you pass me over another cushion, my back needs a bit of support.'

Oh, for God's sake, she's only three months gone! Noreen bit the inside of her cheek in irritation as she passed another cushion over to her sister.

'Well! Did he remember? I don't see any cards up?' Maura said smugly.

'He did remember.' Noreen managed to restrain herself from boxing her sister on the jaw. 'He bought me a beautiful set of pearls.'

Maura's eyes widened. 'Hmmm, nice. Let's see them – and stick the kettle on, I'm gasping.'

Noreen walked out of the room, fuming. That one was as cheeky. With bad grace she stuck the kettle under the tap and filled it. She flung a few china cups on to saucers and shook out a couple of digestive biscuits on to a plate. She had a packet of Tunnock's Teacakes in the biscuit tin but Maura could whistle for those, she thought childishly as she hurried out of the kitchen.

She climbed the stairs to get her pearls, heavy-hearted. If she'd been pregnant herself, she'd be glad enough for her sister but she couldn't help the envy seeping through her as she thought of Maura and the next six months of anticipation. If anyone knew what she was feeling they would be horrified at her begrudgery. She was horrified herself. What kind of a woman was she at all, she thought as her lip trembled and tears spilled down her cheeks. Frantically Noreen struggled to compose herself.

She could spend the afternoon crying as soon as Maura was gone, she told herself fiercely. Under no circumstances was she to let her sister see how upset she was. The last thing she wanted or needed was her two siblings yapping about her and what might or might not be wrong with her. She wiped her eyes, straightened her shoulders, and went into her bedroom to get her pearls. She was damned if she was going to show Maura her card. All it said anyway was:

> To Noreen,
> Love Oliver

and the card itself was fairly mediocre. Cards were not Oliver's forte.

'Aren't they beautiful?' she said with false cheeriness a few minutes later as she handed the box to Maura.

'Very nice,' Maura said flatly. She always said 'very nice' in a non-committal sort of way when she was mega impressed but didn't want to let on. 'Where's the card?'

'I'm not showing you my card, Maura, it's personal from Oliver to me,' Noreen snapped.

'No need to get hoity-toity,' sniffed her sister.

'I suppose you'll ask me what I had for breakfast next.'

'You don't look to me like someone who had any,' retaliated Maura.

'I'll make the tea, the kettle should be boiled,' Noreen said tightly. It couldn't be PMT. It had to be During MT. But her sister was in danger of getting clobbered. Noreen breathed deeply as she made and poured the tea. *Be civil for heaven's sake and don't be such a cow*, she chastised herself, disgusted with her behaviour.

'Here you go, Maura.' She handed her sister her tea and gave a weak smile. 'You're not having morning sickness or anything?'

'Not a thing so far, thank God. I keep expecting to feel a bit grotty but it hasn't happened.' Her sister beamed and Noreen felt even more ashamed of begrudging her sister her joy.

'That's good.' She sipped her tea, trying to quell her mean-spirited envy.

'So where's he taking you tonight?' Maura chirruped gaily.

'Oh! Oh, we're going to have a quiet romantic dinner at home,' Noreen fibbed. 'We'll probably go out at the weekend.'

'Of course the first anniversary is always the best, it starts to wear off a little bit after that.' Maura spoke with authority. 'Because I kicked up such a rumpus when he forgot ours, Andy took me to dinner in the Clarence and he had a room booked. It was great.' Maura sighed at the memory.

Little fat poser, Noreen thought sourly as she took a savage bite out of a digestive. 'Is he pleased?' she managed.

'Over the moon.' Maura was bursting with pride, and in spite of herself Noreen felt an odd little glimmer of affection for her sister that took her by surprise. 'He's even started a share portfolio for him or her . . . isn't that sweet?'

'Very far-sighted,' agreed Noreen, wishing Maura

would go so that she could go back up to bed and burrow under her duvet and be miserable in peace.

Maura took another biscuit and settled herself more comfortably in the chair. Her mobile phone rang. 'Sorry about this,' she twittered, 'the phone hasn't stopped all morning. Hello? Joan. Hi,' she said gaily and launched into a conversation with the person at the other end.

Noreen sat staring morosely out the window as her sister chatted nineteen to the dozen with her friend. She had a mobile phone but rarely got calls on it. Oliver never phoned unless he had something specific to impart and she had no friends in Kilronan to chat with. Maybe she should have gone back to London after her mother died, she thought morosely. She'd a good social life there, which was a lot more than she could say about her dull existence in her big house overlooking the lake.

'Noreen, I have to go.' Maura jumped up. 'I'm just going to have lunch with Joan and a few of the girls. I can tell them my news at last. I wanted the three months to be up before I said anything.'

'That's understandable,' Noreen murmured, her relief that her sister was going tinged with envy at the idea of a girls' lunch. Her own uneventful day stretched out unappealingly ahead of her. She followed Maura to the front door and waved unenthusiastically as her sister drove off happily.

Noreen closed the door slowly. It had started to spit rain. The clouds were dark and threatening over the lake. Bed was the best place to be on a day like today, she decided. She gathered up the cups and plates and shoved them into the dishwasher.

The digestive biscuit she'd eaten earlier had given her indigestion and her cramps were excruciating. Wasn't she lucky that she could go to bed, she told herself. She could be dragging herself around a hospital ward feeling grotty, or stuck on a tube in London. At least she could go to bed and feel grotty in peace and look out at the rain battering against the big windows, and read her book and snooze for the afternoon. The thought made her feel marginally better. She filled a hot water bottle and made herself a cup of hot chocolate. Ten minutes later she was snuggled up in bed, her hot water bottle on her bloated, painful tummy, sipping her drinking chocolate. The wind whistled around the house and rivulets of rain ran down the windows, the soughing of the trees making a soothing lullaby.

She'd go and have a check-up next week, she decided, drowsily, the double dose of Ponston she'd taken beginning to take effect. Maybe, if she was lucky, this was the last period she'd have for nine months. Maybe this time next month she'd be pregnant and Oliver would spend more time at home with her. Feeling a little more cheerful, Noreen slipped into a drowsy stupor.

She woke around four, muzzy-headed and hungry. The house was lovely and warm so she slipped into her dressing-gown, went down to the kitchen and made herself a cup of coffee. She buttered a chunk of Vienna roll and smeared it with blackberry jam. It tasted scrumptious. She hadn't realized just how hungry she was. She polished off the rest of the loaf and felt quite stuffed. She didn't fancy having dinner, but Oliver would be hungry when he came home and she always liked to have a substantial meal for him in the evenings after a hard day's work.

She had a pork steak in the fridge; she'd stuff it, and make some apple sauce to accompany it. While it was cooking she'd have a nice bath and freshen herself up. She'd open a bottle of wine and have a glass with Oliver when he was having his dinner. It would be nice to mark their first anniversary in some little way, just to try to bring back some memories of the happy wedding day they had celebrated a year ago.

Oliver was such a paradox: buying her beautiful pearls and obviously putting thought into the gift and then arranging to meet a fellow builder the evening of their anniversary. Romantic, yet not romantic. He was himself, she thought fondly as she crumbled some breadcrumbs to make the stuffing.

Noreen had had her bath and was just checking the pork steak when the phone rang. The smell wafting around the kitchen was delicious, and she thought she might have a small plateful of dinner with Oliver to keep him company. The table was set with her best china and crystal, long tapering lilac candles lending a romantic air. She hoped he wouldn't be too late. Maybe this was Oliver to tell her he was on his way.

It wasn't her husband. Her lips tightened when she heard the unwelcome voice down the line. Exactly who she didn't need to speak to, today of all days. When Noreen heard the clipped tones at the other end of the phone her cheeks reddened with fury. She said a curt thank-you, hung up, switched off the cooker and the downstairs lights and marched straight upstairs to bed. Oliver could go and get lost as far as she was concerned.

8

Oliver took a swig of hot tea and finished the remainder of his bacon butty. It was badly needed. He'd been on site for the last five hours, but he had to go and see his accountant and he needed to shower and change. His muscles ached but it was a satisfying ache. He'd put in a good morning's work and he knew the other men were always on their toes when he was around. No slacking. Although to be fair he had a good team of workers, with only the odd one inclined to swing the lead. He headed to the showers in the Portakabin. He could have gone home, he supposed. He shook his head, remembering how she'd taken the nose off him earlier. What was the big deal about anniversaries? Women set such store by these things. He'd bought her the pearls and the card. What did she need to go out to dinner for? He hated eating out in posh restaurants. He much preferred pub grub or a meal at home. Posh restaurants made him feel uncomfortable. Suave and sophisticated he would never be, no matter how much Noreen wanted him to be.

He gave a deep sigh as he flung his hard hat on

to a chair and shrugged out of his waterproofs. He knew he was a disappointment to his wife. She'd wanted to have dinner parties to entertain the 'high society' of Kilronan. To please her he'd agreed the first Christmas of their marriage to have a dinner for his accountant, Eddie Mangan and his wife. Noreen had also invited Doctor Kennedy and his wife and Gerard Morgan, Oliver's solicitor, and his wife, Jane.

Noreen had thoroughly enjoyed herself and had spent a week preparing for the party. She'd cooked a very tasty meal, Oliver couldn't fault it, but there'd been enough glasses on the table to fill a pub and the amount of cutlery had been daunting. He knew the basics of starting from the outside in, but it all made him feel uncomfortable, especially when the talk had turned to wine, which went way over his head as he didn't know a Chardonnay from a Chablis, or a Sauvignon from a Merlot. He'd kept quiet and concentrated on filling up his guests' wineglasses, hoping they'd get pissed and bugger off.

Noreen had been on a high for ages after, especially when their hospitality had been reciprocated and they had been invited to a plethora of parties in return. It had been his worst nightmare. He didn't mind talking to any of them in a professional capacity when he had to but making polite conversation was not him. Besides, Noreen did enough talking for the both of them, but she'd been annoyed with him, especially after Doctor Kennedy's party where she'd told him crossly that he was a party pooper and could make a lot more of an effort instead of sitting like a sphinx in the corner nursing his pint.

'I'm not a blinking social butterfly, Noreen, and you knew that when you married me,' he retorted, stung by her remarks.

'Look, I know it's not your scene, but if you made more of an effort you might enjoy it more,' she urged. 'You need to get out and about a bit more. There's more to life than work.'

'Ah, quit nagging, woman,' he'd snapped. She hadn't talked to him for a week. It had been their first big row.

Oliver stepped under the powerful shower spray and soaped himself briskly. What had Noreen expected? That once they were married he'd suddenly turn into a completely different person? There was an awful restlessness in her lately. She was hell-bent on getting pregnant and he was beginning to dread the middle of her cycle when it didn't matter whether he was in the mood, or whether he was totally knackered. She wanted sex no matter what. He liked sex as much as the next man, but having to perform on demand was beginning to get to him.

Then the disappointment when her period came. The tears, the depression. Noreen was so intense about things. He was sure that if she just relaxed about it all, it would happen. Of course when he said that to her he got the nose bitten off him again. It was all right for him. He was a man. He didn't have to worry, he could father a child into his seventies. He didn't have to worry about his fertility clock. He wasn't in his mid-thirties, which was old to be starting a family. The tirade had gone on and on. From then on he kept his mouth shut and just waited for the episodes to pass. The sooner his wife got pregnant, the better. A child would keep her occupied and she wouldn't have time to be nagging him.

He stepped out of the shower and towelled himself dry. From what he had known of Noreen before their marriage, he would never have guessed that she would get so agitated about something. She had always seemed so calm and in control, traits he admired. He found it difficult to deal with all this emotional stuff, especially when he felt that he was failing her in some way. It made him feel guilty. He wasn't great at giving succour and comfort, he thought glumly. Maybe he should try harder to be more sympathetic. Women set such store by sympathy. He'd been a bit abrupt about taking her out to dinner to celebrate their anniversary. He'd book a table at the Lake View for tomorrow night. That might cheer her up, Oliver decided as he dressed swiftly in clean jeans and a good shirt to go and see his accountant.

The meeting went well. The company was performing extremely satisfactorily – of course the countrywide building boom helped – and profits were up. Oliver felt good. He might not be a professional, like Mangan, Kennedy and Morgan were, but he'd bet his bank account was the equal of theirs if not better.

He strode out to his car light-heartedly. Surely his good news would cheer Noreen up. He glanced at his watch; he still had an hour to go before meeting Jimmy Kavanagh about buying his blocks. He'd visit his mother. She wanted him to fix a bulb in her halogen light. She'd been on to him every day for the last week; at least he could get that out of the way.

He was hardly in the door before Cora got going. 'Oliver, I've been thinking. I'd like a conservatory. I could sit out in it and do my bit of sewing and crochet when the evenings get brighter after Christmas. Bridie Sheehan got one, it's an awful Mickey Mouse of an effort. You'd do mine much better,' his mother assured him.

'Hold on now, Ma. When did you decide this?' Oliver demanded. This was all news to him. He'd recently refurbished the kitchen and bathroom for her and she'd mentioned nothing about getting a conservatory.

'I just decided I'd like one. It would be good for my sciatica to sit in the heat. Now when can you start it?' Cora demanded.

'Ma, I'm up to my eyes at the minute—'

'Ach, it wouldn't take *you* more than a day to build one of those yokes for me. There's not much in them, Oliver,' she interrupted.

'Ma, I'll do it but it will be after Christmas.' Oliver tried to hide his exasperation as he unscrewed a fuse in the fusebox.

'Huh! If that wife of yours wanted a conservatory, there'd be no problem,' Cora sniffed. 'But then I'm only your poor old mother.'

'We have a conservatory, Ma, if you remember,' Oliver said tightly as he opened the back door to get the ladder out of the shed.

His good humour was evaporating rapidly. It had started to rain again and his hands were slippy as he began to unscrew the nuts to the halogen light. He pulled a packet out of his jacket pocket and slid the narrow tube bulb on to his palm. He took out the faulty one, replaced it with the new one and climbed down the ladder to screw in the fuse. No light came on and he cursed under his breath. Those blinking bulbs were a temperamental nuisance. It took him three trips up and down the ladder before the light was finally working.

'That's sorted,' he told his mother as he wiped his hands.

'You'll have a bite of dinner with me, won't you? I've put a nice striploin of steak on the pan for you and I'll do a feed of fried onions with it.' Cora bustled around the kitchen, delighted to have her beloved son to look after.

'Mam, I can't. I've to meet a fella about a load of blocks.'

'He can wait. It won't take long; sit down there now and tell me all your news.'

Oliver stifled a groan. If he left, his mother would be in a mega snit, and besides, he'd been so busy lately it always seemed as though he was rushing in and out and brushing off her entreaties for him to stay. She was elderly, she lived on her own. Half an hour wouldn't kill him. He took his mobile out of his pocket and rooted in the pocket of his jeans until he found the slip of paper with Jimmy Kavanagh's number.

'Hey, Jimmy, Oliver Flynn here. I'm running a bit late, can you give me an extra half hour's leeway?'

110

'No problem, Oliver. See you later,' Jimmy agreed affably.

'Thanks.' Oliver put the phone on the dresser and stretched. He was tired.

'Sit down in the armchair by the fire, son. I'll have a bit of dinner for you in a jiffy,' his mother said happily.

The homely crackle of the flames, the smell of frying steak and the heat of the room relaxed Oliver and his eyelids drooped. Soon steady rhythmic snores rumbled from his chest. Cora hummed happily in the kitchen as she sautéed onions and mushrooms. Half an hour later, stuffed to the gills, Oliver bade his mother goodbye. He hoped Noreen hadn't cooked a big feed for him. He couldn't eat another bite. You'd think Cora had been cooking for an army.

Jimmy Kavanagh already had a pint in front of him when Oliver got to Nolan's Pub. He nodded at the barman and motioned Oliver to sit down. 'How's it goin', Oliver? I hear you're doing well, lucky bastard. The tax man is after me, may they all rot in hell. Don't get caught like I did, boyo, and watch yer back – there's always some bollox out there ready to snitch on you.'

'You're right there, Jimmy,' Oliver agreed. As far as he was concerned he paid his taxes and kept on the level, that way he didn't have to look over his shoulder and he could sleep easy in his bed. It was clear that the other man was digging in for a good whingeing session, but Oliver wasn't in the humour for a load of self-pitying moaning, especially when it was obvious that Jimmy was the architect of his

111

own downfall. Besides, he wanted to get home to Noreen, he didn't want her to feel he was ignoring their first anniversary. He hoped that she hadn't cooked anything too exotic. He was stuffed after the feed at his mother's.

The barman brought the pint to the table.

'Cheers, Jimmy.' Oliver took a swig, put his glass on the table and said briskly, 'Right then, let's see how we can be of some assistance to each other.'

Cora cleared the dinner dishes off the table and looked at Oliver's empty plate with pleasure. He'd eaten every scrap she'd put in front of him. That was extremely satisfying. She knew what kind of food her boy liked. None of those fancy *la sag neys* and the like that Madam Noreen was fond of cooking. It had been like old times, him having a snooze in front of the fire while she cooked the dinner, and then the chat between them while he relished every mouthful of her good no-nonsense cooking that he'd been reared on.

She sighed. It always cut her to the quick when he stood up to leave. It was terrible lonely living on her own, and she still hadn't got used to it. It was hard to believe that it was a year to the day since he'd got married. She hadn't wished him a happy anniversary. The wedding and marriage was something they didn't discuss.

She should have gone to his wedding, she supposed. She felt a bit guilty about it now, not because of Noreen, she still couldn't stand the girl. But she'd hurt Oliver, she knew that. Her sister had let her know that in no uncertain terms when she'd come home from the reception. Not that Oliver had ever remarked on it. Behind his gruff, reserved manner, he had a kind, soft heart.

Cora dried the plates, went to put them on the dresser and frowned when she saw Oliver's mobile phone. He was always putting his phone down and forgetting about it. Of course he was meeting that man about the blocks, so there was no point in ringing him at home.

A glint came into her eye. She put on her glasses and dialled. Noreen didn't sound radiantly happy, she noted with satisfaction.

'Hello, Noreen, Mrs Flynn here,' she said in the posh voice she assumed when talking to the younger woman. (She wouldn't dream of allowing Noreen to call her by her first name.) 'I'm afraid Oliver's gone off to his meeting and left his phone here, if you'd be so kind as to tell him. And he'll hardly be wanting any dinner, so don't go to trouble, he had a fine feed of steak, onions, mushrooms and spuds, here with me, so don't go to any bother.'

'Is that right?' Noreen said tightly. Cora smiled. She'd annoyed her daughter-in-law.

She gave a gay little laugh. 'Ah well, you know what they say about a mammy's home cooking. Sure it will save you popping something into the microwave . . . Give him the message, won't you. 'Bye-'bye, dear.' She hung up with immense satisfaction. She had let Oliver's wife know that she still knew all about his business, that was why she'd mentioned the meeting, and she'd also got in the little dig about fast-food meals out of the microwave. Yes, very satisfactory all round, and she'd see Oliver again when he came to collect his phone. She'd make a nice brown loaf for him. He was very partial to her brown bread.

Invigorated, Cora took out her baking bowl. Today had turned out to be an unexpectedly good day.

Oliver yawned as he put the key in his front door. It had been a long day, but he'd negotiated a good deal with Jimmy Kavanagh and it wasn't too late. If Noreen wanted to go out for a drink he'd take her out for one.

The house was very quiet. There was no light on in the kitchen or the lounge. 'Noreen?' There was no answer. The light was on upstairs. 'Noreen, I'm home.'

Was she asleep? he wondered as he took the stairs two at a time. The bedroom door was ajar, and lamplight spilled out on to the landing. Oliver poked his head around the door. His wife was curled up in bed, reading.

'You're in bed early. Did you not hear me calling you?' he asked.

'I heard you,' she answered shortly.

Oliver's jaw dropped at the curtness of her tone.

'What's wrong with you?'

'I'll tell you what's wrong with me, Oliver Flynn!' Noreen sat bolt upright and glared at him. 'I went to the trouble of cooking you a nice dinner for our wedding anniversary and you didn't even have the decency to let me know that you were eating at your mother's. That's what's wrong with me if you want to know.'

'I didn't know I was eating at my mother's. I went to fix her halogen light and she went and cooked a dinner for me and I didn't like to say no,' Oliver explained, trying to hide his exasperation. How the hell did Noreen know he'd eaten at his Ma's? He'd been all prepared to eat whatever his wife put in front of him when he came home even if he got rampant indigestion after it.

'Oh, but you don't mind saying no to what I've cooked for you,' Noreen exploded.

'I was going to eat it, Noreen,' Oliver said hotly. 'I appreciate that you went to trouble.'

'Huh! Don't bother. Throw it in the bin,' Noreen snapped, lying down again and turning her back on him.

'How did you know I was at my mother's anyway?' Oliver demanded. 'I never said I was going. It was a spur of the moment decision.'

'You left your mobile phone there, and she was delighted to be able to ring me up and tell me what a great feed you'd had and that I needn't bother sticking something in the *microwave* for you,' Noreen raged, keeping her back to him, obviously highly put out.

Oliver raised his eyes to heaven. 'Would you not be taking any notice of her,' he said brusquely. They were like children, the pair of them, always scoring off each other.

His wife studiously ignored him.

Oh, let her sulk! he thought irritably as he marched out the door scowling.

He went downstairs, took a can of beer from the fridge and went into the lounge and switched on the TV. The fire had died down so he threw a log on the embers and watched as a flame slowly took hold and began to crackle up the chimney. He could murder his mother sometimes. She went out of her way to antagonize and annoy Noreen. To be fair to his wife, she put up with a lot from Cora, without retaliating. But today, she'd got to her. Probably because Noreen was annoyed that he hadn't taken her out to dinner.

Oliver shook his head sorrowfully. Women! You couldn't live with them and you couldn't live without them. He switched over to the sports channel and watched a match. Noreen hadn't stirred. Around ten he called upstairs and asked would she like a cup of tea.

'No thanks,' came the terse reply.

No sign of a thaw, he thought ruefully as he surfed the channels.

By eleven he was yawning his head off. There was no point in putting it off any longer. He switched off the lights, locked the front door and sloped upstairs. Noreen's lamp was still on but she kept her back to him. He sat on his side of the bed and began to undress.

'Goodnight, Noreen,' he said as he slid into bed beside his wife.

''Night,' she muttered.

They lay stiffly, side by side.

'Don't be mad with me,' he said softly. 'It's our anniversary. I booked a table for us at the Lake View tomorrow night.'

Noreen gave a deep sigh. 'I got my period today.'

'Oh!' said Oliver. That explained her bad humour.

'And Maura called by. She's three months pregnant,' Noreen said forlornly.

Oh heck! thought Oliver in consternation. No wonder Noreen was in a foul humour. He rolled over on his side and put his arms around her. She relaxed against him. 'It will happen, Noreen, just relax about it,' he murmured against her hair.

To his dismay she started to cry.

'I'm worried, Oliver. We've been trying for a year. I'm going to go and have a check-up. And I just felt such a bitch. I was so jealous of Maura. I was disgusted with myself.'

'Don't say things like that. You're not a bitch,' he soothed her awkwardly. Weeping women unnerved him. 'Go to the doctor and see what he says. It could be something simple. Stop crying now and go to sleep.'

He felt her wipe her eyes and felt sorry for her. He tightened his arms around her.

'Everything will be fine, Noreen,' he said with as much conviction as he could. Nevertheless he couldn't suppress the niggle of unease in his belly. Just say there was a problem and Noreen couldn't have a baby. She'd be gutted.

Lord above, don't let that happen to her, he prayed as she drifted off to sleep in his arms, leaving him awake and troubled.

9

Heather yawned, took a sip of her Bud and felt utterly bored. Lorna was deep in conversation with an Armani-clad Brad Pitt lookalike, the air was thick with smoke and the din in the pub was giving her a headache. They'd trekked all the way out to Finnegan's in Dalkey because Lorna was convinced she was going to meet a pop star or a film star or a racing driver, or some sort of celebrity. 'Look, Bono, Eddie Irving, Lisa Stansfield, Pat Kenny, they all drink there. It's their local. All the rich guys hang out there, I'm telling you, Heather. One of the girls at work lives out here and she told me this is definitely one of the hot spots to nab a guy who's loaded, so we're going to make the effort and go out there on Saturday nights, OK?' Lorna had decreed.

The first time they'd gone Heather had enjoyed herself. It had been a novelty. Dalkey was chic and cosmopolitan. They'd eaten at a posh little Italian restaurant before heading for the pub, and there was a buzz in the pub that set the adrenalin flowing and the night had flown past. Lorna was on an absolute high the next day, and told Heather that from then on Finnegan's was going to be their local and they should even consider moving to Dalkey to live, it was so 'in'.

'Don't be ridiculous, we couldn't afford to live in Dalkey, and besides we'd have to spend hours commuting,' Heather retorted.

'Well, I think we should think about it. I'm fed up living in Drumcondra. Who lives in Drumcondra, for God's sake?' Lorna grumbled.

Heather took another sip of her beer and waved away a cloud of smoke wafting over the shoulder of a stunning blonde in a micro mini that hadn't much more material than a hanky. Lorna loved all this. She was in her element. Heather could take so much of it, and then she got bored. She would far prefer to come out to Dalkey in the daytime and stroll around the shops and art galleries, then have lunch and go for a long tramp up to Killiney Hill inhaling great lungfuls of fresh air. Lorna hated walking and fresh air!

They were so unalike really. Sometimes it amazed Heather that they'd survived living together in that poky little flat in Drumcondra for eight months. A thought struck her: it was around this time last year at Oliver Flynn's wedding that they'd made the decision to come to live in Dublin. That year had flown, she thought, a little shocked.

Once they'd made the decision to move, Lorna had got a receptionist's job in a new hotel out near the airport two weeks after sending out her CV. Heather had got a job as a wages clerk in a small printing firm. Unfortunately, four months after she'd joined they'd gone to the wall and she'd been jobless for two weeks, much to her dismay and Lorna's consternation.

'You'll have to pay your rent, I can't afford to pay for the two of us,' she'd said bluntly.

'Don't worry, Lorna, I wouldn't dream of asking you to pay my rent. I can always go and bunk in with Ruth if I have to, or go back to Kilronan. I won't be a drain on you.' Heather'd bristled but she was hurt by her cousin's lack of sympathy and support.

Mention of going to Ruth's or, worse, going home had shut Lorna up and she'd backtracked fast. 'Well, maybe for a week or so I could lend you the money,' she'd suggested a tad reluctantly.

Fortunately Heather had got a job in the letting agency section of a large auctioneer's.

Brooke, Byrne & O'Connell were a shower of chancers, Heather reflected as she popped a handful of peanuts into her mouth. She didn't like working for them. They didn't care what kind of tenants they got for their clients, once they got their money, and because of their lax, unprofessional attitude she was constantly having to deal with irate landlords and tenants. She was going to look for another job, she assured herself. One of these days.

The Brad Pitt lookalike excused himself to go to the loo and Lorna beamed at Heather. 'He's gorgeous, isn't he? He's an architect and he has a place in Killiney. He wants me to go back for a drink, you don't mind, do you, sweetie?'

'Oh Lorna, why didn't you tell me earlier? I'll probably miss the last Dart and it'll cost me an arm

120

and a leg to get a taxi.' Heather was furious. Typical Lorna.

'He only asked me a minute ago,' Lorna said indignantly. 'Honestly, why don't you make an effort and shift someone yourself instead of sitting there with a face on you?'

Heather grabbed her jacket and bag. 'Goodnight, Lorna,' she said tartly. 'Enjoy your drink.' She made her way through the throngs and cursed when she got outside. It was lashing rain and she wasn't dressed for rainy weather. She glanced at her watch – if she hurried she might make the last Dart. It was hard to run in her high heels and the rain whipped into her face as she raced along the high street towards the Dart Station. Five minutes later, she sat panting on the swaying train, relieved beyond measure that she hadn't had to get a taxi home. She'd be able to get a Nite link bus to Drumcondra from the city centre. Heather yawned again and stared at her reflection in the train window as it flashed past the expensive houses that dotted the coast. In daylight it was a picturesque journey, and it would be lovely to be able to live in such a glamorous setting, but it certainly wouldn't be practical. Left to her own devices, Lorna would make the move without thinking of the con-sequences. If she had her way they'd be living in an upmarket apartment in town, but they'd have no money once the rent was paid.

It was expensive living in Dublin. She had to spend far more than when she was living at home in Kilronan, she thought ruefully. Bus and train fares alone took a sizeable chunk out of her salary.

She'd been able to walk to her job in Mangan's at home. Suddenly she felt terribly homesick. She'd liked working in the small accountancy firm. She'd got to know so many people from the locality that she couldn't walk down the street without being greeted by someone or other. She missed the dramatic society and the socializing it involved. She missed the tennis club, even though she kept up her membership and played there on the weekends she went home. She missed Kilronan itself: just going for a walk along the lakeshore had always lifted her spirits no matter how down she was.

Leaving Kilronan had brought home to her how much she actually liked and appreciated her home town, whereas Lorna on the other hand was thrilled to shake the dust of Kilronan off her shoes and rarely went back to visit.

She was really a country girl at heart, Heather reflected, probably a totally un-hip thing to admit to. She smiled, thinking of how horrified Lorna would be to hear her expressing such sentiments. She was going to go home next weekend, she decided. Lorna could come out to Dalkey on her own.

She was glad to get off the bus and hurry down Botanic Avenue, then turn right to her little street with its row of redbrick houses. She was looking forward to getting into bed and not having to get up in the morning. Her heart sank as she neared the flat and heard the loud throb of music pounding through the front window. The girls downstairs must be having a party. She was just about to put her key in the door when it was pulled open and a young man staggered out looking extremely green around the gills. Two seconds later he was puking in the front garden.

Heather hurried up the stairs feeling queasy herself. She hoped he'd clean up the mess, not that there was much chance of that. The racket was deafening; it was a wonder the neighbours hadn't called the police. She opened the door at the top of the landing and let herself into her abode. It really was not at the cutting edge of interior design, she had to admit as she walked onto the landing with its shabby beige carpet and cream chip wallpaper. The sitting-room, which in another life had been a back bedroom, had an old-fashioned grate and black fireplace. At least they could light a fire, which was cosy enough in the winter. The cream chip wallpaper matched that on the landing and a worn gold and green pattern carpet covered the floor. A stained two-seater sofa, an armchair and a unit for the TV, all the cheapest of the cheap, comprised the furnishings. Heather never ceased to be amazed at the standard of furnishings that some landlords felt was sufficient to charge hefty rents for.

The poky little kitchen was basic and uninspiring. The bedroom that she and Lorna shared was fairly big and bright, the best room in the flat. At the moment it was in need of a good tidy. Neither herself or her cousin were the tidiest of people. The dressing-table overflowed with make-up, deodorant and a miscellany of dress jewellery and accessories. The two small linen baskets were full to the brim, clothes were draped on a wooden chair and hung higgledy piggledy from the door of the bulging wardrobe. Shoes lined the wall under the window, bags were shoved under the beds. 'All in all a bit of a nightmare,' Heather conceded as she snapped on the light. At least she'd made her bed. Lorna never made her bed; how she slept in it was a mystery to her cousin. For someone who was always so immaculately turned out, Lorna could be surprisingly slovenly in her domestic habits. She only cleaned the bath after much nagging from Heather, and her housekeeping, particularly in the kitchen, left a lot to be desired. Mostly they ate out, or lived on take-aways.

When Ruth had seen the state of the kitchen and bedroom she had nearly freaked. She was extremely tidy, and couldn't understand how someone could sleep at night in such an untidy room. When she and Heather had shared a bedroom growing up, the only rows they'd ever had had been as a result of Heather's untidiness.

One of the best things about being in Dublin, though, was seeing her twin regularly. They often had lunch in the cheap and cheerful restaurants dotted around Temple Bar, as both of them worked in the city centre. They didn't live too far from each other either, but her sister only came to visit when Lorna wasn't around. There had been no thaw between the pair and they kept well away from each other, which suited Heather. She'd found walking the tightrope between them when they had been talking a totally stressful experience.

A loud hammering on the front door stopped Heather in her tracks. The neighbours, she hoped –

maybe the racket would stop. Minutes later the deafening din eased and she breathed a sigh of relief as she kicked her shoes off and began to undress, looking forward to a peaceful night's sleep. She'd just snuggled under the duvet with a hot water bottle when the sound of 'There's Murder on the Dancefloor' nearly lifted the floorboards from under her bed.

'There'll be murder on the ground floor in a minute if you don't shut up that bloody racket,' she growled as she pulled the duvet over her ears in a futile effort to drown out the noise as the revellers downstairs partied long and loudly into the early hours. She had just fallen into an exhausted sleep when the phone rang, its shrill tone penetrating and insistent. In a complete heap, she staggered out to the landing. If someone was ringing at this hour of the night, it had to be bad news. A bleary-eyed glance at her watch showed her that it was just gone four thirty.

'Hello?' she managed.

'Hello Margy, sorry about earlier, I luv ya, yer a great ride,' a drunken voice slurred.

'I'm not Margy, you stupid git,' Heather snarled, slamming down the phone. It rang again and she glared at it.

'Margy! Margy, don't be—'

'I'm not Margy,' she raged. She flung down the receiver on the small table. He could stay there all night if he wanted to, she couldn't care less. She was leaving the phone off the hook too. She crawled into bed again. Her hot water bottle had gone cold and she threw it down on the floor and shivered. Lorna wasn't home yet either. She must have stayed the night with the guy she'd met in Finnegan's.

Heather thought she was mad. Lorna didn't know him from Adam, and he could be married or anything. She tried to mould her body into the warm spot in the bed and regain her lovely slumberous feeling. Lorna was her own worst enemy in terms of men. Wouldn't she ever learn? Even if she was to stay on the shelf for the rest of her life, and that was looking increasingly as if it was going to be the case, Heather thought sleepily, she hoped that she'd never be as desperate as her cousin was to find Mr Right.

She hadn't had a boyfriend since she'd told Neil Brennan where to get off after his treatment of her the night of Oliver Flynn's wedding. Heather's cheeks burned with resentment as she remembered how her former boyfriend had left her twiddling her thumbs while he worked the room for business. Neil had been astonished at his reception the following day when he'd called by to say he hadn't appreciated her leaving the hotel without even having the manners to say goodnight.

'How dare you talk to me about *manners*, Neil Brennan! You were nearly an hour late picking me up and then you left me to entertain myself while you sat up at the bar trying to sell cars, you ignoramus. I don't want to see you again. I'm not that desperate for a boyfriend,' she'd exploded in an uncharacteristic display of temper that had left him gobsmacked.

'But you know I'm trying to get business for the

garage, I thought you understood,' Neil tried to explain.

'I understand one thing, if you're so ambitious that you don't even have the manners to pay a scintilla of attention to your so-called girlfriend when you go to a function with her, there's not much point in you having a girlfriend. And if you find someone who's prepared to put up with being treated like dirt, fine, good luck to you and my heartfelt sympathies to her. Now get lost, Neil, I've better things to do with my life than be your doormat!' She'd closed the door in his face. It was her proudest moment. Lorna had congratulated her effusively when she'd heard the news. 'Good enough for the ignorant culchie,' she'd applauded.

He'd built his brand spanking new garage all the same, Heather thought drowsily. In Lorna's view he might be an ignorant culchie, but he was hardworking and ambitious and he'd put some of the lazy lumps Lorna had gone out with to shame. Maybe this architect guy might be different. Heather hoped her cousin wasn't heading down another road to disappointment. Having a man in your life wasn't the be-all and end-all of life and the sooner Lorna recognized that the better.

Still, it would be nice to have a man's arms around her, if only to keep her warm in bed, Heather thought longingly as she gingerly stretched out her leg and felt the coldness of the sheet. A depressing thought struck her. She'd be twenty in a couple of weeks, the oldest virgin in town.

'Oh, for God's sake!' she muttered. 'Go to sleep and stop talking nonsense!' It was bad enough being an old maid, without being haggard and baggy-eyed as well.

It took a mug of hot chocolate, two chocolate-covered Kimberleys and a fresh hot water bottle before Heather finally fell asleep.

10

Lorna tucked her arm into Carl's as they walked along the narrow, winding and, to her dismay, extremely hilly streets towards Killiney, where the architect lived. She was wearing strappy high-heeled sandals and her feet were killing her. At least her black skin-tight leather trousers protected her legs from the nippy breeze and drizzly rain, but her hair was getting wet and her red boxy jacket and white T-shirt were not really suitable clothing for a dank, cold autumn night. It wouldn't have killed him to get a taxi, she thought sourly as she stumbled on a broken cobblestone.

'Nearly there,' Carl encouraged. 'See down there,' he pointed. 'That's Enya's castle.'

Lorna was impressed. Enya was a neighbour! Wow! He must be loaded. He probably drove a Porsche, or was he more the Beemer type? She wasn't quite sure yet. She wondered did he have a sea view over Dublin Bay, or even his own stretch of private beach. He was exactly the type of eligible bachelor that she had come to Dublin to meet, she thought triumphantly. It was worth travelling all the way over to Dalkey and this should finally prove her point to Heather, once and for all. Honestly, her cousin would want to get with the programme or she'd end up going nowhere fast, stuck in that kippy flat. Lorna couldn't understand her. Heather was well placed to meet potential boyfriends when she was showing upmarket apartments for letting. But then, Heather was always saying to her that being a receptionist in a hotel was a great way to meet eligibles. It didn't really work like that. Usually the only men who were interested were married or deadly dull. She'd hit gold dust tonight though, she thought excitedly, trying to ignore her throbbing feet. She could feel a blister bubbling up under her big toe. Still, it would be worth it to hook a dishy-looking architect with a luxury pad in Killiney. Killiney was even more exclusive than Dalkey.

'Just up this little street here.' Carl took her arm and guided her up a steep hill lined with small cottages. Lorna was a tad disappointed to say the least. The sea was in the other direction. No sea view unless his place was at the top of the hill and had panoramic views. She felt a bit daunted, not to say out of breath, at the thought of walking much further, but to her surprise, Carl took a key out of his pocket and fitted it into the door of one of the cottages.

Was this it? Lorna was shocked. It looked so . . . so *ordinary* from the outside. No doubt it had all been changed and renovated on the inside. It probably had a mezzanine and lots of wood and glass out the back. There was a small, dirty Fiesta parked outside. Was it Carl's? There certainly wasn't a Beemer in sight, or a Porsche for that matter, she noted disgruntledly. She sincerely hoped it wasn't Carl's. It would be so uncool for his image. Even her own Honda Civic at least looked a little bit sporty and with it.

'Home sweet home.' Carl gave a wide toothy grin as he switched on the hall light and stepped over a clutter of tennis rackets, trainers and football boots. Lorna wrinkled up her nose. They didn't smell too sweet either, in fact, they were distinctly pongy. The tiny hall led directly into a small sitting-room, even smaller than the one she shared with Heather, and there wasn't a mezzanine or any other architect-designed features in sight.

'Is this your own place?' she asked, gazing around in dismay.

'God no! I'm just renting it with two other blokes.' Carl flung his jacket on the sofa.

'Oh!' Lorna murmured. 'And do you work in town? Where's your practice?'

'My practice?' he looked puzzled. 'Oh, my architectural practice,' he said hastily. 'It's in town, yeah. Now let's get ourselves a drink. Red wine? Beer? Don't have any spirits I'm afraid. We're mostly beer drinkers here.'

'You're not really an architect, sure you're not?' Lorna said bluntly.

'Yes I am!' Carl said hotly, but he couldn't meet her gaze.

'Well, if you're an architect, I'm a rocket scientist. Would you phone for a taxi for me please.'

'Oh, come on, don't be like that. Maybe I told a little fib. I'm an architectural technician, nearly as good as.' He gave a practised Aren't-I-Awful smirk and ran his hands through his tawny highlighted locks.

'I'd still like a taxi.' Lorna was ripping. She certainly wasn't going to waste time with a chancer who claimed to be an architect, and, even worse, didn't even own his own place, but was merely a tenant like herself.

'Phone yourself – it's in the hall,' Carl said sulkily.

'I don't know the address, and I don't know the southside numbers,' Lorna retorted frostily.

He brushed past her, went out to the hall and punched in a phone number with bad grace. She heard him give his address.

'You'll be waiting at least an hour, they said,' Carl reported triumphantly. 'It's Saturday night, don't forget. Come on – let's have a snog. You wanted to shift me, didn't you?' He grabbed her and tried to kiss her, his hands roaming all over her ass.

'How dare you. Get off me!' Lorna gave him a shove that sent him sprawling.

'Hey ya bitch!' Carl hauled himself up and advanced towards her, eyes blazing.

'Get lost,' Lorna snarled. She turned on her heel and raced out of the front door.

'Prick teaser! You were all over me in the pub!' he shouted after her.

Lorna turned and gave him the finger, furious. Now she had to go trekking all the way back to Dalkey unless she was exceptionally lucky and able to hail a taxi on the street. At least it was downhill, she tried to comfort herself, near to tears.

Her feet were murdering her. Her poor sandals were not meant for this harsh treatment and were grubby and mud-spattered. At least they weren't the fabulous Manolo Blahniks she'd been so tempted to spend an arm and a leg on. She click-clacked her tottering way down towards Dalkey, the rain beating into her face. She was frozen. A taxi passed her and she raised her hand and waved frantically, but even though he had no passengers he sped past and she cursed long and loudly.

It was an hour before she got a taxi. She was drenched to the skin and chilled to the bone and her teeth rattled as she gave the address. The taxi driver was none too pleased. 'Bleedin' northside. I could have three fares while I'd be driving across there,' he grumbled as he stepped on the juice none too gently. Lorna refrained from comment. All she wanted was to get warm and fall into bed and stay there. What a lying git that Carl had been. And to think she'd fallen for his crap in Finnegan's. She certainly wouldn't be telling Heather about this.

She should have known when he'd made her walk all that way in the rain that he wasn't what he seemed. He certainly wasn't a gentleman. Next time she was bringing the car, Lorna decided, as the taxi swerved around a corner at speed and came to a halt at a set of pedestrian lights. She was never going to be in a position like this again. If it meant giving up drinking when she was out socially, so be it. When she met the right man he'd have his own car and she wouldn't have to drive.

She was beginning to feel a bit queasy. The taxi stank of stale smoke and she knew that if the taxi driver lit up she'd be sick. She'd better not puke or the taxi driver would kick her out. She slipped a Polo mint into her mouth and tried to ignore the cold beads of sweat that were breaking out on her forehead and upper lip.

Hold on! she urged. They were driving up Dorset Street. He'd got across town very quickly and he hadn't even taken the East Link. She should never have had that last drink, she thought unhappily. She wished Heather was here to help. Through a supreme effort of will she held on and was never so glad to see Drumcondra hove into view. 'You can let me out here, I'll walk the rest of the way,' she said, not caring that her feet were covered in blisters. She couldn't risk another second in that taxi. She paid him the fare but didn't add a tip. He didn't deserve one, the cranky old bugger. The taxi driver gave her a filthy look, but she didn't care, she was too busy breathing deeply as she turned left at Fagan's and began to walk up Botanic Avenue. She passed a block of luxury apartments, with their neatly landscaped grounds, and wished mightily that she lived there. They overlooked the river. They were large and elegantly designed, not at all like some of the eggboxes she'd been at parties in. She was so busy gawking that she wasn't looking where she was going and she stumbled over a dip in the pavement. An excruciating pain shot through her ankle; she fell flat on her face, felt weak, sick and dizzy and then passed out.

'Ohmigod, ohmigod,' she moaned as she came to. Two men were kneeling beside her and one was talking into a mobile phone. Lorna tried to get up but squealed in pain and went white and almost passed out again.

'It's all right, girlie, we've called an ambulance, take it easy,' one of the men said. He was middle-aged and reeked of alcohol. The one with the phone tapped her on the shoulder.

'A word of advice, love, those things you're wearin' on your feet aren't the best for walking in,' he said paternally.

Talk about stating the obvious. Lorna closed her eyes and said nothing. This was a total disaster. To think she'd walked from Dalkey to Killiney and back in those blasted shoes and just on her own doorstep, practically, she'd come a cropper.

'I think she's fainted again,' the older man said. Lorna didn't disabuse him of the notion. The pain was so agonizing she couldn't speak even if she'd wanted to. She heard the ambulance siren in the distance with some relief. Soon she'd be looked after, snuggled up in a nice warm bed, after being tended to by a George Clooney type, who might even ask her to go on a date with him. Maybe this was meant to happen to her so that she could meet the man of her dreams, she thought woozily as the flashing blue lights of the ambulance made her blink.

'Are you all right, love? What's your name?' a red-bearded ambulance man asked her kindly.

'Lorna Morgan,' she whispered tearfully. 'I think my ankle's broken.'

'Anywhere else hurting?' he asked, his hands gently probing her ankle.

'Aaaahhh!!!!! That hurts,' she shrieked.

'OK love, OK, we'll have you sorted in a jiffy.' While he was talking, he had eased her up into a sitting position and almost before she knew it she was lifted into a red wheelchair-type thing, wrapped in a blue woollen blanket and whooshed up into the ambulance by the two ambulance men.

'We'll be there before you know it,' Redbeard said kindly. 'It's the Mater that's on call tonight.' True to his word, she was being wheeled into Casualty six minutes later. It was nothing like *ER*, she thought with horror as she was wheeled past a crowded waiting room and transferred to a hospital wheelchair while Redbeard had a few words with a staff nurse.

'Take care, and get a sensible pair of shoes, you're lucky you didn't break your neck!' He gave her a smile before rushing off to his next assignment.

It was four hours before she was even X-rayed. There wasn't a George Clooney lookalike in sight, just some extremely pale-faced, tired, harassed, busy young doctors and nurses. Casualty was a nightmare. Ambulances arrived every few minutes disgorging patients, some merely suffering the effects of too much alcohol on a Saturday night, others the victims of street fights and car accidents, as well as elderly people with heart attacks and other serious complaints. Patients lay on trolleys without even the privacy of a cubicle, some of them very ill and in distress.

She was way down the list of priorities and as she watched a drunk stagger and fall on top of a patient lying on a trolley, she felt scared and lonely as well as exhausted and in pain. She took out her mobile phone and rang the flat. She needed Heather badly. All she got was an engaged tone. How weird! Lorna glanced at her watch. It was five thirty a.m. What on earth was Heather doing on the phone at this hour of the morning? She burst into tears. No one took the slightest bit of notice of her and she sniffled and sobbed for a good ten minutes, feeling extremely sorry for herself. It turned out that her ankle wasn't broken but badly sprained, and after X-ray she was strapped up tightly, given a pair of crutches and a taxi was ordered to take her home.

It was almost bright as the taxi driver drove out through the hospital gates on to the deserted North Circular Road. The morning had a pale pink hue to it and the sun was struggling to shine. A Sunday morning calm enveloped the city and apart from a man walking his dog along the canal and a couple buying early morning papers the streets were deserted. The taxi driver took less than five minutes to get to her front door and he kindly helped her out of the back of the car as she struggled not to put her weight on her foot. In her left hand she carried her handbag and tattered sandal. She paid him and gave him a tip for his kindness and hobbled as best she could up to the front door. It was extremely difficult trying to get the hang of the crutches. She was going to have to crawl up the stairs, she thought sorrowfully as she managed to insert her key in the lock. She had tried the phone again, hoping that Heather could come and collect her to bring her home, but had got the same engaged tone.

Somehow Lorna managed to get up the stairs on her hands and knees, clutching her crutches, and hammered on the door to the landing. Silence.

Frustrated beyond measure, she managed to get the door open but lost one of her crutches in the process as it slid down the stairs.

'Heather!' she called loudly. 'Heather! For crying out loud, wake up!'

Her cousin staggered out of the bedroom, tousleheaded and bleary-eyed, in a pair of faded flannel pyjamas. Even in her distressed state, Lorna winced at the sight of them. How on earth could her cousin wear such passion-killers? Even if they were snug and warm.

'What on earth happened to you?' Heather demanded.

'Oh, Heather, I've had the worst night of my life,' Lorna blubbed, 'and I tried to ring you but the phone's not working.'

'Not working,' Heather echoed and glanced down at the small table between the bedroom and kitchen to see the phone off the hook. 'Oh, yeah, I got a funny phone call last night, well this morning actually, so I left it off the hook, and they were having a party downstairs and the racket was beyond belief. Just as well you weren't here.'

'Well, I wish I had been here,' Lorna sobbed. 'It was a real nightmare. Can you help me get into bed? I need to sleep. I was *sitting* in Casualty all night, I might as well have been invisible, and then I rang you to come and help me and the phone's off the hook. Some help you were.'

'Now hold on a minute, Lorna, don't get your

knickers in a twist. How was I to know you were going to end up in hospital?' Heather demanded. 'I didn't have such a good night myself either if you want to know.'

'Well, I've had enough! Anywhere has to be better than this crappy joint. If we don't move into a better place than this you can stay here on your own,' Lorna wept on a rising note of hysteria. She'd had a terrible trauma and her cousin wasn't being particularly sympathetic. It was time to call a spade a spade. Heather was holding her back, she thought resentfully. She hadn't been there for her in her hour of need. Maybe it was time to go solo.

11

'I suggest you relax about it, Noreen. Don't forget you've had a rough couple of years looking after your mother. Stress can do things to the body, so don't get hung up on it and let it take over your life. Enjoy this time with Oliver in your new house. Make the most of it.' Douglas Kennedy smiled over his bifocals at Noreen.

'I know you're right, Douglas. I think maybe I've too much time on my hands. To tell you the truth I'm a bit bored. I'm not used to being a lady of leisure,' Noreen said ruefully. 'Perhaps I'll go and get myself a job.'

The doctor looked at her thoughtfully. 'Back to nursing?' he queried.

'Well maybe. I might try a couple of the local nursing homes. Or do private home care.'

'I don't suppose you'd be interested in doing job-sharing with Kitty, here?' he said hesitantly. 'I have three surgeries a day, except Thursdays. Kitty does all the dressings, cholesterol checks, cryotherapy, ear-syringing and the like. But she wants to cut down to spend more time with her children, especially in the afternoons, now that they're going to school.'

'Oh!' Noreen was taken aback.

'Think about it?' Douglas Kennedy suggested. 'Have a chat with Oliver. I don't want to put you on the spot.'

'I will, Douglas,' Noreen said briskly, as she stood up to go.

'Great stuff. And don't worry about getting pregnant. If nothing's happening in another six months or so, we'll organize a few tests and take it from there,' Douglas said reassuringly as he held the door open for her.

Noreen walked out of the surgery feeling almost happy. Douglas was right, she had been under stress in the years leading up to her marriage and now she was putting herself under even more stress being hung up on getting pregnant. From now on she *would* enjoy her life with Oliver. Hopefully in six months she'd be pregnant anyway and life would be peachy. And she was going to get a job, she thought, feeling decidedly up. She'd had enough lolling about the house. A part-time job would suit her fine, and the idea of being a surgery nurse was quite appealing. It would be different to anything she had done before. She'd get to know a lot more people around the locality. *And* she was going to join the health club too, she decided.

It was so easy to sink into depression. She'd had enough of it. The last two months had been miserable. Time to nip it in the bud. Noreen got into the car and headed in the direction of the Lake View.

The annual membership was steep enough and as she wrote out the cheque she reflected gratefully that Oliver was very generous with money. He never questioned her spending and always seemed glad when she bought something new for herself. He was so different from her mean, spiteful, controlling father. Noreen frowned as she remembered how her mother would have to ask his permission to light the fire. Her father had nearly put her off men for life, Noreen thought grimly.

Oliver might not be very demonstrative in his affections but he was a good, kind husband and she'd been very moody with him lately. She'd make it up to him.

It was a cracker of a day. The lake shimmered in the pale magnolia sun. The air was crisp, bracing. It would be nice to go for a walk. She walked briskly through the landscaped grounds of the hotel. Russet, cinnamon and gold leaves crunched underfoot, and a squirrel scampered up the bark of a tree, his red bushy tail disappearing into the sun-dappled foliage. She pushed the creaking, groaning, red swing gates that had been there since her childhood, and came on to the tree-lined path that circled the lake. The water lapped gently against the shore. It was so peaceful here, the silence broken only by birdsong. She and Oliver had often walked here when they had been dating. She hadn't been for a walk with Oliver for ages. They should start doing things together. Noreen sighed. He worked so damn hard. He was driven. It wasn't for the money. It was as if his work affirmed him, who he was, what he was. It hurt sometimes that his work seemed to fulfil him far more than their relationship did. What had made him turn to his work rather than his relationship for sustenance?

Was it a result of his rearing? It wouldn't surprise Noreen. Cora Flynn was a tough cookie, domineering and bossy. In the time she had known her, Noreen had never heard Oliver's mother ever thank him, or give him a word of praise for all that he did for her. Her ingratitude and unreasonable demands infuriated Noreen, but she'd learned early on in their relationship to hold her tongue. She had been giving out to her husband about Cora expecting so much from him and he had turned and said quietly to her, 'Noreen, you looked after your mother when she needed looking after. I have to look after mine. I thought you of all people would understand that.'

There was no answer to that. How could she argue that her mother had been a gentle, undemanding soul, while Cora was a manipulative, demanding bitch? Oliver had a sense of duty that had been ingrained in him since childhood, and Noreen realized with dismay that she could never change that. Resentment niggled at her, though, and her relationship with Cora was prickly and uncomfortable.

Cora was confined to bed at the moment with a bad cold. She could call in and see if she needed any shopping done, it would mean Oliver wouldn't have to do it. And he'd be pleased that she had made an effort. Pity she didn't have a key. She'd have to get Cora out of bed and that wouldn't go down too well. Oliver had a key, but Noreen was still a 'visitor' in Cora's eyes, not part of the family. *Never* part of the family.

She walked along for another half a mile, trying to psych herself up to calling on her detested mother-in-law.

'Come on, do it for Oliver,' she murmured, skimming a stone across the lake. 'Be a good wife!'

She gave a wry smile and began to walk back to the hotel.

Cora was surprised to see her. 'And to what do I owe this honour?' she asked tartly.

'Oliver told me you weren't feeling the best. Would you like me to do any shopping for you?' Noreen responded cheerfully, determined not to be riled.

'Oh no! I'll get Oliver to do my shopping,' Cora replied in a tone that suggested Noreen wouldn't be capable.

'It's just he's up to his eyes, I've hardly seen him this week, so I thought I could do it to help him out.' Noreen tried a different tack.

'Oh! Well, if he's that busy, it's quite all right,' Cora sniffed. 'I don't want to put anyone out. I'll manage myself.'

Oh fuck! Noreen cursed silently. Now she thinks Oliver put me up to it. 'I just thought I'd pop in and suggest I'd do the shopping and maybe cook a bit of dinner for yourself and himself. He doesn't know I'm here – it would be a surprise for him,' she said casually. If Cora knew she was rattled she'd capitalize on it.

Her mother-in-law's beady eyes sparkled at the notion of her precious son having his dinner in her house. 'Get me a pen and a piece of paper out of my bureau there and I'll do a list. I don't want any fast-food nonsense now. You can get a nice piece of fresh cod, seeing as it's Friday.' Cora still didn't eat meat on Friday, despite the fact that the Church had rescinded that particular church law years ago. 'Yes, I think cod would be the best. You can steam it. That shouldn't be *too* difficult for you.' She was busy writing her list, so she didn't see Noreen's lips tighten in anger at her insulting barb.

'Could you make real parsley sauce? I don't want packet stuff,' she demanded truculently.

'I could, yes, Mrs Flynn.' Noreen kept her temper under admirable control.

'Get a couple of carrots and parsnips, you can mash them together and put a good bit of butter and pepper in them, that's the way Oliver likes them,' Cora ordered.

Yes your bloody majesty. 'Fine, can I get you anything from the chemist? Are you all right for paracetamol? Would you like any hot drinks?'

'I don't believe in any of those things. Hot milk and pepper and Vick's on my chest is good enough for the likes of me,' Cora retorted.

'I won't be long,' Noreen said grimly. The woman was a briar, there was no denying that. She scowled as she let herself out of the cottage and drove back to the town to get the groceries.

When she got back, Cora was dressed.

'You should have stayed in bed, Mrs Flynn,' she said lightly as she started to unpack the bags.

'That doesn't go there. Let me put it away.' Cora grabbed a jar of marmalade out of her hand.

145

'Now start peeling the potatoes. This is the knife I use. And call me when you have the vegetables peeled so I can show you which saucepan I use. And I'll put the salt in, I don't like too much or too little. I'll go and sit in the parlour for a while.'

Thank God for that. Noreen glowered at her mother-in-law's retreating back. She swiftly peeled the potatoes, and turned her attention to the carrots and parsnips.

'Make sure to cut the vegetables the same size so that they cook evenly.' Cora was back. Noreen almost jumped – she hadn't heard her coming into the kitchen.

'Tsk! You've left half the potato on the skins. Such waste. You young women don't know the meaning of frugality. I should have done it myself,' Cora remarked crossly, picking up a potato peeling and holding it contemptuously between finger and thumb.

Noreen remained resolutely silent. *She's old. She lives alone. Say nothing.* She chopped the parsley vigorously, waiting for the next criticism. She didn't have to wait long.

'You've chopped that far too early, you haven't even made the roux for the white sauce,' Cora scolded as she cut a chunk of creamy butter to melt in a saucepan. There were saucepans everywhere; she wouldn't entertain the idea of a microwave or a dishwasher.

'Go and phone Oliver and tell him his dinner will be ready in the next hour and to make sure he's home,' Cora instructed.

'Yes, Mrs Flynn,' Noreen said drily. *How high exactly do you want me to jump?*

'Why are we having dinner at Ma's?' Oliver sounded puzzled.

'It seemed like a good idea at the time.' Noreen kept her voice down. She had gone into the parlour to ring Oliver, not wanting Cora to earwig.

'Who's cooking?' She could sense the smile in his voice.

'Just get your ass here soon, I've already been lectured about my potato peelings and chopping the parsley too early,' Noreen whispered.

'How did it go at the doctor?'

'I'll tell you when we get home. Don't be long, sure you won't? At least you won't have to go and do the shopping. I did it earlier.'

'That was kind of you.'

'That's me. All heart!' Noreen laughed. 'See you soon.'

'You didn't have to scurry off to the parlour.' Cora was highly unimpressed.

'Better signal there.' Noreen fibbed. That shut her mother-in-law up for a second or two.

'You can set the table, dear,' she commanded. She only called Noreen 'dear' when she was annoyed.

Ha! thought Noreen triumphantly as she opened the drawer in the dresser and took out an embroidered tablecloth. She'd got one over on Cora. She knew she was being *extremely* childish but sometimes Cora drove her to it.

It was with a huge sense of relief that she heard Oliver's car crunch up the drive. She was ready to strangle her mother-in-law, who had found fault with her table setting, her washing-up habits (too much water and detergent used – 'I don't have shares in the ESB you know!') and the fact that she'd bought wholegrain brown bread and not a soda scone.

'Hello, women!' Oliver said cheerfully as he walked into the kitchen. 'That smells nice.'

'Oh, I hope it will be all right, Oliver,' Cora said tartly. 'Your wife and I have very different ways of coo—'

'It will be fine, Ma.' Oliver gave his mother a stern look. She turned back to the cooker, annoyed. He winked at Noreen, who threw her eyes up to heaven.

Dinner was a terse affair. Cora was petulant and abrasive; nevertheless she polished off a huge plateful of dinner, Noreen noted. She was obviously beginning to feel better. 'Oliver and I will have our tea in the parlour, and don't use too much water washing up,' Cora decreed imperiously with a wave of her hand as she stood up from the table.

'I'll do the washing up.' Oliver uncoiled his long legs from the chair and started to clear the dishes from the table.

'I'm sure Noreen won't mind doing it, after all you've been working hard all day and she is more or less a lady of leisure, aren't you, dear?' She challenged Noreen with a piercing stare.

'Oliver, go sit with your mother, she's poorly, and I've had the pleasure of her company for the last couple of hours.' Noreen smiled at Cora. 'Haven't I, dear?' she said sweetly. She'd prefer to wash up ten times over in peace on her own than to have to endure Cora for much longer. 'Go on, Oliver,' she gave her husband a little push.

'It won't take us a minute,' he protested.

'Go on, Oliver, I'll have it done in a jiffy,' Noreen assured him. She filled the basin to the brim with hot water and added in a good squeeze of washing-up liquid for good measure. It was amazing how used she'd got to a dishwasher, she thought in amusement as she scoured the saucepans. 'It was far from dishwashers you were reared,' she murmured as she rubbed at a particularly stubborn stain. Gimlet-eyed Cora would spot it in a second and remark on it if she didn't do it properly.

Maybe Oliver might like to go for a drink later. That would be nice, she thought. It would be good to spend more time together. Lately he seemed to be working all the hours God sent. She poured boiling water on to loose tea-leaves and took three china cups and saucers from the dresser. Cora did not approve of teabags or mugs – 'proper tea' should always be served in fine china according to her mother-in-law and perhaps she was right, Noreen acknowledged. Cora always served a very satisfying cup of tea. She placed milk and sugar on a tray and shook out some biscuits on to a plate. Another half hour max, and they should be able to leave, she comforted herself.

The fire was blazing up the chimney in the parlour, casting dancing golden shadows on the walls. It was an old-fashioned but cosy room, with chintz sofa and chairs dressed with pristine white antimacassars. A mahogany sideboard held an array of silver-framed sepia photographs of long-dead parents and grandparents, and in pride of place was a picture of Cora and her husband, Liam, on their wedding day. Cora sat ramrod straight on a hard wooden chair with Liam standing behind her, hand on her shoulder. Liam was a handsome, straight-backed man with a kind face and Noreen saw a lot of him in Oliver.

'Thank you,' Cora clipped as Noreen handed her her tea. 'I always put a doily under the biscuits when I'm serving them in the parlour,' she added sharply as she helped herself to milk and sugar.

'Did you not put the doily under the biscuits? Tsk,' teased Oliver, his blue eyes twinkling as she handed him his tea.

'Sorry!' she said with mock humility as she sat down beside him and took a sip of tea. Maybe instead of going out for a drink, they could open a bottle of wine at home and go to bed early. It was getting close to her ovulation time, and tonight might be the lucky night, she found herself thinking. *Stop it*, she chastised herself. *No more thinking like that from now on*.

'I met Lily Cleary at Mass last week, she was telling me that Mrs Nolan is going into a nursing home. Very sad. No one to look after her. Son in Australia and he wouldn't even bother to come home and see her,' Cora remarked as she helped herself to an undoilied biscuit.

'Aren't you lucky to have me?' Oliver said, straight-faced.

'I should think you *would* look after me in my old age. It's a child's duty to look after their parents.'

Cora sniffed. 'And speaking of children,' she turned to Noreen, 'I believe your sister is looking forward to a happy event, according to Lily. 'Don't you think it's time you started thinking in that direction yourself? You're not getting any younger you know,' she said forthrightly. 'You modern women and your family planning. In our day we took what the Lord sent when he felt disposed to.'

Noreen felt like slapping her mother-in-law's sharp, unfriendly face. 'As you say, Mrs Flynn, a child is God's gift and I look forward to receiving His gift as and when He sees fit,' she responded coldly. She turned to Oliver. 'I'm going to head off now, Oliver, I'll see you when you get home.' She stood up and walked out of the room without a glance at Cora. She was tempted to slam the front door but she didn't want to give her mother-in-law the satisfaction of knowing how much she'd got to her.

How dare she! she seethed as she got into the car and started the ignition. Cora was an interfering, judgemental old bitch who didn't deserve a son like Oliver. 'Snooty, pretentious fucking old cow with her fucking paper doilies,' Noreen cursed as she drove on to the winding road that led to the town. Tears came to her eyes. That snide remark about family planning hurt. Didn't any of them realize just how *badly* she wanted a child? She knew she was getting on. She was well aware of a lessening in fertility and all the rest of the medical stuff. She *was* a nurse for God's sake! She didn't need a fucking lecture from an ignoramus like Cora Flynn. Sobbing her heart out, Noreen drove home. She

151

didn't care who saw her. She didn't even bother switching on the lights when she got home, she just went straight to bed.

Oliver gathered the cups and saucers together with more force than was necessary and turned to face his mother. His blue eyes were flints of ice. 'Mam, I won't say this again. Don't you *ever* bring up the subject of children in front of Noreen again. It's none of your business for one and your crack about family planning is way out of line. We've been trying for a baby for over a year if you must know, and you and your smart comments don't help!' He was so angry he felt like flinging the cups into the fire. He marched out to the kitchen leaving his mother speechless. He rarely lost his temper but when he did, Cora knew better than to argue with him. Oliver rinsed the cups under the tap. He was like a bull. Of all the damn fool stupid things to say to Noreen of all people. Now she'd be way down in the dumps and she'd be wanting sex morning noon and night and then she'd be in floods of tears when her period arrived.

He groaned. If only she could get pregnant, life would be a whole lot better. The pressure would be off. She'd have a child to look after, that would make her happy, and he'd be glad for her. It was frustrating knowing that she wasn't content in their marriage. This wasn't the way it was supposed to be, he thought dispiritedly as he dried the cups. He knew now that when she turned to him at night it wasn't because she wanted intimacy and sex, her main objective was to become pregnant.

Sometimes when he was knackered and didn't feel like doing it, it would be nice to say, can we wait until tomorrow, or whatever, but he didn't feel he could refuse her in case it was her optimum time for conception. Sex was no fun any more, it was a bloody chore, he thought tiredly as he shrugged into his jacket.

'Goodnight, Ma!' He poked his head around the door. Cora ignored him, her lips a thin line of anger, her beady little eyes like two black olives.

'Great!' he muttered as he closed the front door behind him. His mother in a huff, his wife in the pits. Life right now was one big pain in the butt. He'd a good mind to go to the pub and get mouldy drunk. For a moment he was tempted, but the memory of Noreen's big brown eyes, hurt and pained, got to him and he knew he couldn't do it. He was her husband, she needed his support. He gunned the engine and headed for home.

He wasn't good at this emotional stuff. When he had problems he kept them to himself. He wasn't used to women's angst, it made him extremely uncomfortable. Marriage certainly wasn't a bed of blinkin' roses, he scowled, as he overtook a blue van.

Noreen was in bed when he got home.

'What are you doing in bed?' he asked off-handedly, making no reference to Cora or what had happened.

'I felt like it,' Noreen said sullenly.

'Come on, Noreen, get up and come downstairs. You can't live your life in bed, you know.' He tried to encourage her.

'Ah, I'm pissed off.' She gave a sigh that came from her toes.

'Look, you know what Ma's like. You know better than to let her get to you.'

'Well, she's just so bloody mean-spirited and judgemental. She hasn't a clue. And I'm sick of her,' Noreen exploded.

'I know, Noreen, just forget it. It's not worth getting into a state over,' Oliver said wearily, trying to hide a yawn.

'If I'm boring you, why don't you just leave me alone?' Noreen snarled, burrowing down into the bed and turning her back on him.

'Oh, for fuck's sake!' Oliver exploded, his patience worn thin. 'Women, you're all the same, drama, drama, drama. I've had enough. I'm going to the pub.'

'You do that,' Noreen snapped.

Without bothering to change out of his working gear, Oliver set off for the pub in a foul humour. When he got there, he ordered his pint, took his paper out of his jacket pocket and pretended to read it. He didn't want to talk to anyone. He just wanted a bit of peace and quiet. He nursed two pints for the evening, not wanting to drink too much; he had too much work on to be slowed down by a hangover. When he got home he had a quick shower in the big bathroom rather than the en suite, in case Noreen might be asleep. He fervently hoped she was. He'd had enough agro and stress for one evening.

Her bedside light was out and she was right over at her own side of the bed. He slid in beside her as

154

quietly as he could and felt her tense up. Pity she wasn't asleep, he thought, unwilling to engage in conversation. He turned on his side and lay there, willing sleep to come. Sometimes it would be nice to sleep in a bed on his own again. He thought longingly of his bachelor bed. Seconds later he was sound asleep, snoring rhythmically, much to his wife's annoyance as she twisted and turned beside him, lonely and unhappy.

Cora sat propped up against her pillows rubbing Vick's into her chest and sipping hot milk and pepper. It was very distressing that Oliver was angry with her. It was rare for him to speak to her with such disrespect. At least he hadn't spoken to her in such a tone in front of that wife of his. He should never have married her. A disaster from the start, but would he listen to her? Oh no!

Cora's nostrils flared as she picked up her rosary and prepared to say her prayers. If Noreen wasn't using family planning she was probably barren, Cora decided. Oliver should never have married a woman six years older than him. He should have left her an old maid on the shelf and got a nice young girl for himself. Well, he's made his bed, he'll have to lie on it, she thought crossly as she blessed herself and began to pray to the Almighty to give her strength for the crosses she had to bear. And that Noreen was the biggest cross of all. Life had been grand until she'd come on the scene to annoy her.

12

'You'd love it out there. It's *so* happening. The boutiques, the restaurants, the marina. It's a great place to live. Come on, Lorna, we need someone else to share. It would be perfect for you. What are you doing mouldering away in Drumcondra for heaven's sake? It's so un-cool.' Carina Carmody turned from her computer and stared at Lorna, who was printing out a guest's bill. She was still trying to persuade Lorna to move into the apartment she rented in Malahide. Her flatmate had moved to New York and Carina needed someone in to pay the rent, ASAP.

'I know, Carina. I'd love to and it would be just as handy to get to work. But what about my cousin?' Lorna gave a little helpless shrug.

'Let her go and live with her sister. You can't be her minder for ever.' Carina was not impressed with that as an argument and waved her hand dismissively. 'Stop making excuses. Just tell her that you're moving in with Lisa and myself and that it's handier for work. At least you won't have to drive through that awful traffic because of the Port Tunnel development. It's a gorgeous apartment, really,' Carina wheedled. 'You're lucky to be getting this opportunity. Look, tell you what, why don't you come home with me tomorrow and stay over and see for yourself? But I'll need an answer by Sunday, we really need someone else to pay the rent and if you aren't interested I suppose we'll have to advertise. It's just much nicer to get someone you know.'

Lorna studied her perfectly manicured French-polished nails. Carina was right. She *was* mouldering in Drumcondra. She didn't want to stay living there, and she didn't particularly want to keep living with Heather, who was getting on her nerves. Her cousin had been a good stop-gap until Lorna had found her feet in Dublin, but she was too much of a stick-in-the-mud. Lorna wanted to move up the social ladder and an apartment in the very chic Malahide Marina area was a most inviting prospect. Carina was extremely sophisticated and knowledgeable and had a host of well-connected friends. She was just the type of person it would be good to hang out with.

'Well?' Carina drawled quizzically.

Lorna took a deep breath. 'Sounds good. I'd love to stay. I'll bring in an overnight bag tomorrow.'

'And I need to know by Sunday if you're moving in.'

'Fine.' Lorna busied herself at her desk. 'No problem at all.'

But there *was* a problem, she acknowledged silently. Heather! How was she going to face her cousin and tell her that she was moving out to Malahide. Dumping her!

I'll think about it later. Lorna pushed the unwholesome thought to the back of her mind and was almost glad to see a coachload of Japanese tourists arriving for an overnight stay before flying home. For the next half hour it was all go and she was whacked by the end of her shift. She hurried across the staff car park to her red Honda Civic. There was a howling gale and the rain whipped into her face. What a stinker of a night; she was looking forward to getting out of her uniform and watching *Sex and the City*. She hoped Heather had taped it for her.

She could do with updating her car, she reflected as she slid in behind the wheel. If she was going to go and live in Malahide she'd need a good set of wheels to keep up the image. A five-year-old crock was not ideal. Maybe Neil Brennan, Heather's former boyfriend, might give her a good deal if she turned the charm on for him. He'd done well in the last year. A brand new chrome and glass showroom, built by Oliver Flynn, was almost completed. And his selection of cars had vastly improved. He seemed to be going for quality rather than quantity, which surprised her. She'd always thought of Neil as a hick second-hand car salesman.

Heather was watching *Frasier*, and already in her nightdress and dressing-gown. Talk about being middle-aged before your time, Lorna thought in disgust. Stuck in watching *Frasier*, drinking hot chocolate like an old woman!

'Did you tape *Sex and the City* for me?' she demanded.

'Yep,' murmured Heather, before laughing at one of Niles's one-liners.

'I'm going to have a quick bath.' Lorna kicked her shoes off with relief. Sometimes when she'd been on her feet all day her ankle still tended to ache where she'd sprained it. At least she was off those damn crutches. They'd been the pits.

'You might need to wait for a while for the water to heat up, I had a bath a little while ago,' Heather informed her as she dunked a ginger snap into her hot chocolate.

'Aw, *Heather*!' Lorna couldn't contain her irritation. She didn't often take baths in the decrepit cast-iron bath that graced their bathroom, but she'd felt like a quick lavender-scented soak tonight. Trust Heather.

'It won't take long,' Heather said mildly.

'I'll have a shower.' Lorna flounced out of the sitting-room in high dudgeon. Why on earth would she want to stay in this kippy hole with Heather when she could be living in the height of luxury in Malahide? And maybe when Heather had to live with a new flatmate she might learn to be a bit less selfish and not go using all the hot water, she fumed.

The following evening Lorna followed Carina's sleek, silver Peugeot off the dual carriageway, along the winding back roads to Malahide. They were going to go on a pub crawl later so she'd packed her new red matador pants and black bustier. Matador pants and the flamenco look were *so* key this season and they looked gorgeous on her. She'd been working out really hard at her local gym and

159

she was in excellent shape, she thought happily. Just as well, though. Carina, with her long willowy body and sleek black bob, was stunning and you'd need to look pretty damn hot yourself to get a look in if you were socializing with her, she thought ruefully. It wouldn't be like going out with Heather. Lorna knew she outshone her cousin easily. That was never a cause for concern when they went out.

She followed Carina with a mounting sense of excitement as they drove through the picturesque village of Malahide towards the exclusive apartment complex overlooking the Marina. This was what she wanted. Much more her! Carina indicated left into the complex and Lorna followed. Her colleague had told her to park in the bay beside her. The man who owned it was elderly and didn't have a car any more and Carina's ex-flatmate, Audrey, had appropriated it. 'You can use it if you move in,' Carina assured her airily.

The lobby was elegant, convent silent and smelling of polish. Lorna couldn't help but be impressed as the lift sped silently upwards to the third floor. 'This is us,' Carina declared as she stepped out on to a small landing and fitted her key into a door facing the lift.

Lorna followed her eagerly, dying to see the interior.

'Our kitchen,' Carina said with a flourish as she switched on the lights and led her along the wooden-floored hall with its elegant pine-framed mirror. Lorna gazed at the compact fitted white and grey kitchen with its breakfast counter, gleaming wall oven and sparkling hob and thought of the poky, chipped-tiled, ill-equipped hovel their landlord had the nerve to call a kitchen. She couldn't live there another second, Lorna decided there and then. She was moving in here as fast as she could.

'This is the lounge. We have our own balcony overlooking the estuary, it's really nice in the summer to have supper or drinks outside.' Carina led the way into a large rectangular room, switching on lamps here and there. Decorated in shades of lemon and blue, it oozed class. Two stylish pale blue sofas dotted with lemon and blue cushions that matched the curtains on the French doors and windows looked inviting. Various-sized smoked blue glass coffee tables held cream candles and some glossy monthlies. A vase of pampas grass and a large blue-framed mirror completed the decoration. A small circular cream table and six chairs fitted neatly into a lamplit corner at the other end of the room. Ideal for select dinner parties, Lorna thought in ecstasy.

'I have the en suite,' Carina said gaily as she moved back into the hall.

Quelle surprise! Lorna thought enviously. Carina Carmody would always be the one to get the en suite. She had a bossy way about her and an *I Come First* attitude that could be a bit grating. Still, Lorna could put up with it if it meant living in a palace like this.

'That's Lisa's bedroom, beside yours, which is here.' Carina opened the door and Lorna peered in. It was small. A boxroom with a single divan and a

161

drawer and wardrobe unit. Mint green patterned curtains with a hint of lilac that matched the duvet cover hung on a small window. It was very pretty, even if it was tiny, far nicer than the big untidy bedroom with its mismatched furniture and threadbare carpet that she shared with her cousin. Having a bedroom to herself, even if it was small, would be bliss. Some day *she'd* be the one with the en suite.

'Well, what do you think?' Carina beamed.

'I love it,' Lorna enthused. 'I don't have to wait until Sunday to tell you. I can move in tomorrow.'

'Tomorrow! Brilliant. But what about your cousin? Will she go and live with her sister?' Carina looked surprised at her impetuosity.

'Oh, I'm sure she will. She'll be fine,' Lorna said breezily, trying to ignore the lurch in her stomach. It so happened that Heather was going home for the weekend. In fact she was probably on the bus to Kilronan right this minute. Lorna could go back to Drumcondra tomorrow and pack at her leisure without having to give any awkward explanations. She'd leave her a note and say the vacancy had come up suddenly and it was too good an opportunity to miss. It being easier to get to work and all.

'Let's shower and change and have a quick bite to eat. I have some chicken wraps and salad. And then let's hit the town,' Carina suggested. 'Lisa's in London for the weekend, but you'll get on fine. You've met her. She's a pet.'

'Ya, she's very nice,' Lorna agreed. (She'd taken to saying Ya, like the southsiders with their posh

'Dort' accents. She must remember to keep it up now that she was ascending the social ladder.) Carina's flatmate was a human resources manager in a big multinational insurance company. She often had to travel. A quiet girl, with curly chestnut hair and a pretty face, she was no threat to Carina in the glamour or personality stakes.

Actually, Carina and Lisa reminded Lorna of herself and Heather. Thinking about her cousin caused another pang of guilt. It wasn't very nice, sneaking off in the dead of night so to speak, but Lorna couldn't quite bring herself to say it to Heather face to face. There'd be a row. Heather would be hurt, she might even start to cry, and it would be all too emotional! Better this way. She'd get over it, Lorna assured herself. And they could always meet for a drink or a meal every so often. It wasn't as if they'd never see each other again. But this type of lifestyle was much more her and at the end of the day, life was all about moving up the next rung of the ladder. If she stayed with Heather, she'd end up collecting her pension before she knew it, with nothing done with her life. It was unthinkable. She had to take the opportunities life presented her with, and this was a peach of an opportunity.

Lorna pushed all thoughts of Heather out of her mind as she stepped under the powerful shower spray in the tastefully appointed terracotta and cream tiled bathroom, which was a hell of a lot more inviting than the grotty, dirty hole with its old-fashioned, stinky, rubber-hosed shower that fitted on to the taps of that chipped and stained bath. She wrinkled her nose at the memory. How she loathed that bathroom. Well, no more distasteful baths there! she thought happily as she lathered foamy bath gel on to her smooth skin. This was it. There was no going back.

13

'Gone! what do you mean gone!' Ruth exclaimed. 'How could she be gone? Where's she gone to?'

'Her note says she's moved to an apartment in Malahide Marina. Everything's gone, Ruth. Her clothes, her make-up. The portable TV and vid—'

'The little yellow-bellied coward,' Ruth ranted. 'She couldn't tell you to your face. I warned you not to move in with that wagon—'

'Look, I have to go, I'll be late for work. I'll talk to you later. OK, I just have to collect a set of keys from a tenant and I'll be back in the office by eleven,' Heather interrupted hastily. Right this minute she wasn't interested in her sister's blistering I-Told-You-So's.

'OK, talk to you later.' Ruth was clearly furious and Heather knew there would be a day of reckoning with Lorna some day and her twin would take no prisoners. The thought made her feel marginally better.

She gazed around the bedroom, now denuded of Lorna's possessions. It was hard to take in. She still felt a little bit sick at the shock of it. She'd come back from Kilronan on the early bus, and because she didn't have to go directly to the office had taken the opportunity to drop off her weekend bag. She wasn't expecting to see Lorna as she was on the early shift at work, so she'd simply gone into the kitchen to make herself a cup of tea. The kitchen was strangely tidy, she'd noted. Normally when Heather came back to Dublin after a weekend at home she'd be greeted by a pile of half-washed crockery on the draining-board. Lorna's attitude to housework was 'Why bother?' It was only when she'd gone into the bedroom to unpack her bag that the uneasy sensation of something being amiss hit her. All Lorna's side of the room was bare, the open wardrobe door displaying empty hangers. The only reminder that Lorna had ever lived in the flat, her rumpled, unmade bed.

Then she'd seen the note stuck to the dressing-table mirror with Sellotape. Shock was her first emotion as she read her cousin's breezy missive, followed by hurt and then a red-hot anger. How low could Lorna stoop? How gutless of her not even to tell Heather to her face that she was moving out. It was unbelievable. Where was the friendship, the loyalty? Even kinship hadn't meant anything, Heather thought in dismay. She'd been dropped like a hot potato and Lorna had moved on to pastures new. Even if Lorna had spoken to her and given her some warning that she was moving out, it wouldn't have come as such a shock.

Tears stung her eyes. Now what was she going to do? If she wanted to stay living here she'd have to get another flatmate quickly. Her heart sank. Where would she get a flatmate? She didn't know anyone looking for a flat. She'd have to advertise. It would be horrible having to share with a stranger. Sharing a bedroom with Lorna had been bad enough. It didn't matter if Heather was asleep or not when she came in late at night, Lorna always switched on her light. And she'd hogged most of the wardrobe and the dressing-table. She wouldn't bloody miss her, Heather scowled as she shoved her weekend bag into the wardrobe.

What a way to start the week. It was bad enough coming back up to Dublin at the crack of dawn on a Monday morning. If she hadn't listened to Lorna she'd still be in Kilronan in a job she enjoyed, not stuck up in the capital working for a company she disliked and now facing a whole load of hassle.

That's what you get for being a doormat, she thought angrily. Lorna had once more walked all over her, because she'd let her. She had no one to blame but herself. She was going to have to cop on to herself and live her own life.

Heather yawned. She was sorely tempted to ring in on a sickie and just get into bed and sleep her brains out. Then she remembered she'd promised a tenant she'd call at his apartment to get his keys. Her trouble was that she was too conscientious. Some of the other girls in the letting department didn't bother to check the apartments when the tenants were leaving, asking them to post in the keys. Heather was afraid of keys going missing in the post. And she didn't want to have to explain that particular scenario to a landlord who was paying good money for a so-called professional service, so she always made sure to collect them, or asked the tenant to drop them into the office.

She must check on the Internet when she got into work to see if there was any place suitable for a single tenant that would suit *her* pocket, she thought glumly, staring out through the off-white lace curtains on to the windswept street below. Renting accommodation in Dublin was prohibitively expensive. She knew that from working in an estate agent's and letting agency.

She'd had more money in her pocket when she'd lived at home. *And* she'd had a better social life, she had to admit. She wasn't comfortable in Dublin, she felt out of step somehow. She couldn't quite explain it. Maybe it was the pace of life, but mostly what Heather didn't like was the anonymity. She felt no connection. At home there was always someone to stop and chat with, people saluted you on the street. She felt she belonged. Here she was just Miss Anonymous. Ruth and Lorna thrived on city life but she felt diminished by it. It was always balm to go home to Kilronan. Could she go back to live, she wondered? Would it seem like she was running away? Running back to Mammy and Daddy. Not able to hack the big smoke. How Lorna would despise her. 'Let her,' Heather muttered. It was nothing to the contempt she felt for her cousin right now.

She ran a comb through her hair, dusted her cheeks with some bronzing powder and outlined her lips with Mulberry Wine lipstick, the note lying on the dressing-table a stark reminder that Heather was on her own. She picked it up and read it again slowly.

Dear Heather,

I know this will come as a bit of a shock, but I've moved into an apartment in Malahide with a girl from work. It was an opportunity that came out of the blue and I had to make a fast decision unfortunately. It will be much easier for me to get to work, and I'm sure you'll understand. We'll sort out about the deposit, if you leave the flat. I'll phone you soon. I hope you don't mind but Malahide is much more convenient for work with that Tunnel thing being built,

Lots of love,
Lorna XXX

Heather shook her head. She didn't for a minute believe Lorna couldn't have waited to tell her personally of her decision to leave. It was such a flimsy excuse it was insulting. She really had no compunction about using people. Ruth had been right all along. Heather just hadn't wanted to see it. Well, it was staring her in the face now and she had to deal with it. As far as she was concerned, her cousin had done the hot potato act on her once too often. She was finished with her. From now on, Lorna was *persona non grata*, and she could go and whistle for her deposit. She'd broken the lease, Heather decided with uncharacteristic steeliness. If the shoe was on the other foot she was damn sure Lorna wouldn't refund her a penny. The nerve of her to even mention it! And how typical of her meanness. If Lorna came looking for a refund Heather would let her have it good and proper, she thought viciously as she

169

slipped out of her tracksuit and put on her navy suit.

The traffic was heavy and she arrived at the apartment in Clontarf five minutes late. 'I'm terribly sorry for keeping you,' she apologized to the young man who opened the door to her.

'No problem, you're not that late,' he said cheerfully. 'I'm still in good time for the airport.' He handed her the keys. 'Here you go. I organized for a cleaner to come in yesterday and she did the place from top to bottom. The company pays for that kind of thing, they're good like that, so if you just sign the list of contents when you've checked I think you'll find I can have my deposit back.'

'Sure, no problem.' Heather flashed him a smile. He'd been a dream tenant, no problems, no hassle. Corporate tenants were much easier to deal with generally. They knew the score, but with the downturn in the economy in the past few months they were getting scarcer and scarcer. Heather did a swift inspection of the apartment and ticked off the inventory. Everything was in order and the apartment was spotless. Some tenants left the apartments in terrible condition and kicked up ructions when they weren't returned their deposits. The grief they gave her was unbelievable, and then she had to deal with the aggrieved landlords as well. Well, at least this was one letting that had gone well. The manager of the lettings department would be on her back now until Heather had the apartment let again and Brooke, Byrne & O'Connell had secured a fine fat fee.

'I'll head off now, I have the car packed, I have

to give it back to the rental agency. Thanks very much, I hope I'll be as lucky in my next posting.' The man smiled at her.

'Where are you going?' Heather asked politely.

'Zurich.'

'Very nice,' she enthused.

'We'll see. Thanks again. I enjoyed my stay in Ireland.'

'That's good. Best of luck in Zurich,' Heather said warmly as she slipped the keys into her bag.

When he was gone, she got a final reading for the ESB and gas meters, straightened up the cushions on the sofas and made sure all the windows were closed and the cooker and immersion heater turned off. It was fine for viewing, and she'd had several enquiries already – the apartment was in a good location so hopefully it shouldn't take long to let it.

By the time she got to the office she was hungry, so she got a cup of coffee from a vending machine, and, because it was a day of trauma, she indulged in a Mars bar and didn't even feel a twinge of guilt.

'Was Seavale up to scratch?' Edith Palmer, the lettings manager, asked brusquely as Heather walked past her desk.

'It was fine. I have the keys. I'm just going to organize some viewings,' Heather replied, surprised at her boss's tone.

'Make sure I get to see the references of whoever is going in there next,' Edith ordered.

'Sure,' Heather said easily and carried on to her own desk. Something was definitely up. Usually the office was abuzz with chat and banter. She caught Tina Kelly's eye. Tina worked at the desk next to

171

hers. Her colleague gave an almost imperceptible shake of the head and put her finger to her lips. Heather took the hint and sat behind her desk and after a few sips of coffee and a welcome bite of her Mars bar, busied herself with arranging viewings with prospective clients.

Half an hour later Edith stood up. 'I've got to go to a meeting upstairs. Take my calls, Tina. Deal with what you can deal with, otherwise tell people I'll return their calls. If James Wentworth rings fob him off for God's sake!'

'Yes, Edith,' Tina said drily.

Edith gave her a sharp look but said nothing, before stalking out the door clutching her Versace briefcase.

'What the hell is going on?' Heather demanded when the door closed behind their boss.

'Talk about drama! You missed all the excitement. There's *ructions*!' Tina exclaimed gleefully, perching herself on the corner of Heather's desk. 'That dozy bimbo Dianne let a tenant into an apartment without checking his reference—'

'Sure loads of them do that,' scoffed Heather, who still found the totally slapdash and couldn't-care-less attitude of some of the staff, including Edith, it had to be said, mind-boggling. She wouldn't have the nerve to take the short cuts they took.

'No, this is really, really MEGA serious,' Tina explained earnestly. 'The guy she let in was supposed to be a lawyer. French, allegedly. The reference was a complete disaster. No headed note-paper. No telephone number. No letters after his name or after the guy, another lawyer, "allegedly",' she grinned, 'who wrote the references. Anyway the landlord wasn't happy when he heard that he'd moved in before he saw the references or signed the lease. When he finally saw the references he wouldn't sign the lease and the "lawyer" wouldn't provide him with another one and accused him of being racist and the landlord wants him out. He won't go and the landlord is threatening to sue *us*! Dianne's got the boot. She was told to have her desk cleared and be gone in ten minutes. Mr Brooke was roaring at her. And Edith's been hauled over the coals as well. I swear it was pandemonium this morning. It was a pity you missed it all.' Tina was thoroughly enjoying the drama, once she wasn't a participant.

'I'm glad I wasn't here. I hate things like that. You'd think old baldy-boots would have sacked her in his office instead of bawling her out down here.' Heather clipped her two meter readings together.

'He probably wanted to make sure we all saw it, so that it won't happen again,' Tina remarked sagely. 'If that landlord sues, we're up shit creek. Can you imagine the publicity in the papers? Landlords won't want to touch us with a ten-foot bargepole.'

'I wouldn't blame them,' snorted Heather. 'If I ever had a property to let I wouldn't go to a Mickey Mouse outfit like this lot, I can tell you. Would you?'

'You must be joking!' Tina snorted. 'This grabby, greedy shower are the most unprofessional cow-boys I've ever worked for and I've worked for a few of them in my time.'

'Is that right, Methuselah?' teased Heather.

Tina was saved the chance of replying by Edith's return. She was grim-faced and red-cheeked, totally unlike her usual cool, poised persona.

'I'll swing for that tart,' she muttered.

Tina stifled a giggle. Heather kept her head down.

'You two, get me the files on every letting we've done for the last two weeks,' she barked.

Heather's phone rang. 'Brooke, Byrne & O'Connell. How can I help you?' It was Ruth all ready to continue her Lorna rant. 'Look I can't talk to you now, things are mad here.'

'Right then, meet me for lunch if you can take a late one, I'll book us a table in Da Pino on Parliament Street. It won't break the bank and we can have a chat,' Ruth offered.

'OK, see you there around one forty-five,' Heather agreed hastily, as Edith's phone rang and she made Tina answer it, for fear it was the dreaded Mr Wentworth who was causing hassle about incorrect information regarding his property that Brooke, Byrne & O'Connell had placed on the Internet.

It *was* the dreaded Landlord Wentworth. Tina made a ferocious face. 'I'm afraid she's in a meeting, Mr Wentworth,' she lied smoothly.

There was an explosion down the phone that even Heather could hear and Tina held the phone away from her ear. 'I will tell her, Mr Wentworth,' she said wearily after the irate landlord had vented his anger at their incompetence, yet again. 'Edith,

I'm not taking that man's calls for you again. It's not fair. Will you just deal with it.' Tina was totally pissed off.

'I've told those idiots that look after the Internet to sort it. They're imbeciles! Morons! And incompetents!' Edith raged.

'Well, at least ring Wentworth back. He accused me of not passing on the messages and it's not fair on me,' Tina stormed.

'All right, all right, keep your hair on,' muttered Edith through clenched teeth.

Just to make sure that her boss was correct in her judgement of the people who looked after their website, Heather clicked on just out of curiosity to see if the apartment in Clontarf was correctly presented. She should have known, she thought irritably when she saw that her two-bed furnished with parking space was listed as a one-bed unfurnished with no parking. She sent a snooty memo to the imbeciles, morons and incompetents, knowing that it probably wouldn't make the slightest bit of difference anyway but it made her feel better.

'It's a crappy company and I'm sick of it. I'm going to look for another job,' she moaned when she finally sat down to lunch with her twin.

'Ah, you're always saying that,' Ruth scoffed as she perused the menu. The restaurant was choc-a-block but the girls liked it. It did an excellent cheap 'n' cheerful lunch special that suited their penury. The food was tasty, and it was handy to both their offices.

'I'm having the minute steak, please. And a glass of Diet Coke,' Ruth told the waiter.

'I'll have the lasagne and side salad, and a Coke as well, please,' Heather decided.

'So the bitch is gone.' Ruth sat back in her seat and fixed Heather with an 'I told you so' look. She looked a million dollars. Her glorious chestnut hair, swept back off her face, cascaded over her shoulders. She wore a taupe business suit with navy shoes and accessories and her eyes were bright and clear in her vivacious face. Heather felt like a frumpy drudge in her serviceable navy suit in comparison. And she certainly didn't exude the *joie de vivre* of her twin, she thought enviously. She really could do with a makeover.

'Yeah, she's gone.' Heather folded and unfolded her serviette.

'Am I surprised? In a word: no!' Ruth tapped her fingers on the table. 'Don't you dare give her back her deposit.'

'I've no intentions of,' Heather retorted coolly.

'Good for you!' approved her sister. 'And if it doesn't work out for her in Malahide under no circumstances are you to let her come running back to you,' dictated Ruth bossily.

'And exactly *how* high will I jump?' Heather enquired tartly.

Ruth had the grace to look ashamed. 'Sorry, Heather,' she apologized ruefully. 'I'm just so mad with the sly little cow. I really would love to give her a piece of my mind. What are you going to do? If you want to give up your place you can share my room until you get a smaller place of your own,' she offered.

'Thanks, Ruth, I might take you up on that, if

you don't mind. I can't afford to stay there on my own, and I don't really feel like sharing with a stranger.'

'Pity we're full up, but I know the girls won't mind you staying for a while until you're sorted.' Ruth smiled at the waiter as he placed her steak in front of her.

'You look great, Ruth, better than I've ever seen you look.' Heather arched an eyebrow at her. 'Is there something I should know?'

'Oh Heather, I'm in love,' Ruth bubbled.

'I knew it. Who is it this time?' Heather tucked into her succulent, creamy lasagne.

'No, this is *really* it. He's so different to any-one else I've ever met. His name is Peter, he's a carpenter.'

'A carpenter? Where did you meet him?' Heather was surprised. Ruth usually went for the 'suits'.

'I was at a party a while back and I was admiring a beautiful coffee table made out of redwood. The owner introduced me to Peter and told me he was the man who made it. He has his own small company and his handcrafts are gorgeous. So's he.' Ruth was definitely smitten.

'What age is he? What does he look like?' Heather forked some crispy salad into her mouth. After the morning's traumas, she was surprisingly hungry.

'He's twenty-eight. A six-footer with brown hair and the most gorgeous hazel eyes. He's got broad shoulders and a hairy chest—'

'Very important,' laughed Heather. She and Ruth had devoured romantic novels in their teens, and had always had a penchant for their broad-shoul-dered, hairy-chested heroes. 'Have you done the biz yet?'

Ruth shook her head. 'No, that's the thing I really like. It's as if we both know this is something very special and we don't want to rush it and muck it up. We get on so well, Heather, I'm dying to do it with him, he's gorgeous. But being friends first is so nice. I love being with him and I'm dying for you to meet him.'

'He sounds lovely.' Heather smiled enviously at her sister. 'You lucky thing. I wish I could meet a gorgeous bloke.'

'You'll meet someone special too,' Ruth com-forted.

'Yeah, when I'm ninety and past it,' Heather quipped.

'Don't be silly,' Ruth said briskly. 'Peter has loads of friends – I'll introduce you to them. I'm glad you're not living with Lorna any more. You were always too much in her shadow. Now it's time for you. That bitch has done you a favour,' Ruth declared, raising her glass to Heather.

It didn't feel that way, Heather reflected that night as she sat on her own by the fire and listened to the wind whistle down the chimney. The flat was morgue silent. It was amazing how noisy Lorna had been, but Heather had got used to her. She didn't like 'aloneness', she thought unhappily. It made her reflect on how empty her life was.

It hadn't always been like this. When she'd lived at home, she'd had a full, happy enough life. Was it because she hadn't put in enough of an effort here?

She did socialize with the girls at work occasionally, but it always ended up as a drinkfest where they spent the evening giving out about Brooke, Byrne & O'Connell. The same old thing.

Heather flicked the TV channels restlessly. Why was she feeling so totally inadequate? One of the girls at work, Margaret, was very into spiritual healing and meditation, and always seemed extremely sure of who and what she was and where she was going. Heather liked her. According to Margaret, when unsettling events happened in one's life it was time for what she called a growth opportunity and change. Did Lorna's leaving her in the lurch count as a sufficiently unsettling event? she wondered idly. Possibly the fact that she was forced to face up to how unrewarding her life was in Dublin was significant enough in the growth opportunity stakes. She didn't have to feel inadequate or any less of a person because she didn't like city life, Heather decided spiritedly. So she should stop beating herself with that particular stick. And so what if she hadn't met the man of her dreams in Dublin. She'd prefer to be with a man that she liked being with, no matter what he worked at. At least she wasn't an almighty snob and social climber like Lorna. And she got on well with her family. That was a big plus. Lorna had only gone home twice since they'd moved to Dublin and one of those visits had been for Christmas. That didn't count. Most people went home for Christmas.

She wasn't the failure, Heather decided, Lorna was, and she was never going to compare herself to

179

her cousin again. Heather felt surprisingly better about herself. Maybe this growth opportunity stuff wasn't a bad idea. She'd give notice to the landlord and move in with Ruth until she decided what to do. One thing she was certain of, though, was that she'd had enough of Brooke, Byrne & O'Connell. Maybe as well as a change of abode it was time for a change of career. In fact, Heather acknowledged, as she dunked a flake into her hot chocolate, it was time to take a good long look at her life and take stock. Time to make some changes!

14

Lorna's fingers hovered over the telephone keys. She just couldn't quite bring herself to dial Heather's mobile number. It was ridiculous. What was the harm in ringing and saying 'Hi'? Heather would have got over any annoyance she felt over Lorna's departure by now, surely. Her cousin didn't hold grudges and she never held a row. She'd be fine, Lorna assured herself. She'd ring and ask her out for a drink. It was worrying, though, that she hadn't heard from her at all. Not even an angry outburst. The first week that she'd moved to Malahide, she'd been expecting to hear from Heather and every time her mobile rang her stomach had tightened with tension. But Heather hadn't called. And that made Lorna uneasy.

She took a deep breath and dialled the number. She heard her cousin answer, in a surprisingly cheerful voice.

'Hi, Heather, it's me. Sorry it's been so long, I was mad busy. Would you fancy coming out for a drink?' she invited chummily.

'Get lost, Lorna, and don't bother ringing me again. You're the lowest of the low and I don't

want to have anything more to do with you.'
Heather's voice dripped contempt and Lorna's jaw
dropped at her tone.

'There's no need—' she stuttered, but she
was talking to herself. Heather had hung up. Well,
fuck her, Lorna fumed. She was raging now that
she had phoned her cousin. She'd given Heather
the chance to hang up on her. Bad move. Her
cousin obviously hadn't got over her departure.
She'd sounded so . . . so disdainful. Heather had
never spoken to her like that before. In anger, yes,
but never with such contempt. It stung. Lorna
didn't like how Heather's tone made her feel. Like
she was a slug who'd crawled out of a head of
cabbage or something.

How dare she? As if she were someone of
importance. Well, Heather Williams could get lost
herself. She certainly wouldn't be getting in contact
again. If Heather wanted to be friends she'd have
to come *crawling* back. And even then, Lorna would
freeze her. Then she'd be sorry.

Lorna poured herself a cup of coffee. She was in
the apartment on her own. Carina was working and
Lisa was away. It was quiet, very quiet, and because
she was a tad bored she'd decided to ring her
cousin. Lorna tapped her fingers impatiently
against the counter top. The phone call to Heather
had unsettled her. Forget it, she told herself crossly.
Just think she could still be living in that shabby
hovel instead of living it up here in Malahide. Life
was *brilliant* here. And now that she knew that
Heather didn't want to talk to her, she'd put her
out of her head and get on with it. It was closure,

she decided. She didn't need Heather Williams any more, and she'd certainly proved that by taking a leap into the unknown and moving to Malahide. It was a brave move, she congratulated herself. A move Stick-in-the-Mud-Williams wouldn't take in a million years. Now that she was feeling superior again, she felt much better.

Lorna strolled into the lounge, sipping her coffee, and went over to the French doors. The morning sun sparkled on the estuary, birds wheeled overhead in the sapphire sky, the Belfast train clickity-clacked northwards, sleek and elegant in the golden sunlight. Looking out, it was like a hot, sunny summer's day. Only the faint tracery of frost still on car windows gave a hint that the temperatures were below freezing. If she were still living in Drumcondra, she'd be shivering in whistling draughts and wrapped up in jim-jams and toasties. The central heating in the apartment was a dream.

She ran her fingers over her new silky black negligée. It was extremely sexy and she was hoping to get an opportunity to wear it tonight. Lorna's eyes sparkled with anticipation. On her first night out with Carina, the weekend that she'd moved in, she had met a dishy businessman in Gibney's. *The* pub in Malahide. His name was Bryan Taylor and he was a manager in a big mobile phone company. He drove a company Saab, and he *owned* a seafront apartment in the Marina! She'd played it cool in the pub, sensing his interest. When he'd asked her to come back to his 'pad' for a nightcap, she'd smiled sweetly and said another time perhaps. Neither would she give him her phone number, guessing correctly that she would see him again in Gibney's.

The following Thursday night herself, Carina and Lisa swanned into Gibney's, dolled up to the nines. A surreptitious glance around and she saw him at the bar. He didn't see her. So she played it cool, laughing and chatting with the girls until he came over eventually, tipped her on the shoulder and asked her did she like breakfast in bed.

'It depends who's serving it,' she replied coolly, half impressed by his very direct approach.

'I make a mean Buck's Fizz,' he boasted.

'Is that right? How nice for you,' Lorna replied non-committally, sipping her white wine spritzer.

'Maybe you're not a champagne girl.' He seemed a bit put out at her lack of enthusiasm.

'Oh, Barry, indeed I am,' she smiled sweetly, congratulating herself on a smart move, pretending not to remember his name.

'Bryan,' he corrected suavely.

'Of course you are,' she purred, slanting her eyes up at him, like Samantha, her heroine in *Sex and the City*.

'So you like champagne, then,' he persisted.

'Oh yes! I *adore* champagne' . . . she paused, *à la* Samantha . . . 'with the right man.'

'And is there currently a "right" man?' Bryan queried.

Lorna gave a Gallic shrug. 'Mister Right turned out to be Mister Very Wrong. But I live in hope,' she drawled. She knew he was waiting for her to ask about his status. He'd be waiting, she thought in amusement. She was extremely impressed with herself the way she was playing him. A far cry from that disastrous night in Dalkey when she'd trudged up hill and down dale in her high-heeled sandals after that lying little toad who'd called himself an architect.

'I think you haven't been drinking champagne with the right men, Lorna,' Bryan smiled, showing strong white teeth. He was quite handsome in a weather-beaten rugged way. And he had the most amazing black-lashed, green eyes. He had told her the first time they met that he went sailing. It sounded divine.

'Well, possibly not, Bryan. But what's a girl to do? How does a girl find Mister Right?' she teased playfully.

'Trial and error, beautiful Lorna. Trial and error.'

They'd played cat and mouse with each other for about two weeks before she finally relented and gave him her number. The following day he phoned her and asked her out to dinner. She told him she was busy for the next five nights but she was free on the Saturday. 'Fine,' Bryan said firmly. 'I'll book us a table at Tiger Becs, it's the new Thai restaurant part of La Stampa. You've been to La Stampa I'm sure,' he said casually.

'Oh indeed,' fibbed Lorna. Tiger Becs! She was impressed. It was *so* happening.

'Pick you up around seven thirty. Just tell me the number.'

Lorna stopped playing hard to get and gave him the information required. He was clearly interested in impressing her and she was all ready to be impressed.

Lorna went back out to the kitchen and refilled her coffee cup. She was feeling a tad nervous. She'd spent the entire evening the night before trying on this outfit and that. Discarding, selecting, changing her mind and starting the whole process again. She had half decided to wear her new black trousers and lilac Dolce & Gabbana halter-neck top that showed her cleavage to perfection. She'd been to the beauty salon and had fake tan applied. Her body was extremely toned, the nice shapely 'cut' on her arm muscles not too defined that she looked like a body builder but just delicately suggested to give her arms that high maintenance look. She'd splashed out and treated herself to a French polish. Classy but refined. That was the image she wanted to portray. The classy sophisticate. She'd never have been able to bring Bryan back to the flat in Drumcondra. It would have been too mortifying for words. Imagine him comparing his 'pad' to that crummy joint.

Here was fine, she looked around approvingly. Perfect for the Busy-Girl-About-Town. Her bedroom might be small but it was tastefully decorated and she could send him home after they did the woo, if they did the woo. Hopefully Bryan would be the one who would awaken the woman within. Maybe with him she'd finally have that elusive orgasm. None of her sexual experiences since her disastrous deflowering at the hands of Derek Kennedy had been anything to remember. Lorna was still mystified at the idea that sex was enjoyable.

Carina raved about it. She loved being shagged

senseless, as she described it herself. And indeed she didn't hide her enjoyment on the nights she took a man home. The bedsprings creaked and rattled, the apartment echoed to her moans and groans and Lorna, her head buried under her pillow, was reminded of that day a long time ago when her mother and that man had had sex and frightened the living daylights out of her.

Imagine, her mother had had mad passionate sex and seemingly enjoyed it all those years ago when it was something that was frowned upon outside marriage. Her mother had been adventurous to have an affair. It still confused Lorna to think about it and on the rare occasion that she went home, she studied her mother covertly and saw how deeply dissatisfied and unhappy she was with her life. Still, at least she'd known passion and pleasure once.

Lorna, in this modern day and age when no one lifted an eyebrow at sex outside marriage and everyone knew about the G spot, *still* hadn't a clue what all the fuss was about. She'd stopped reading articles in magazines about sex. It was just too dispiriting. At least Heather was still a virgin. She hadn't had an orgasm with a man yet either, as far as she knew, Lorna comforted herself. They were probably the only two women in the country who could make that claim, she thought wryly. And that was nothing to boast about.

By seven fifteen she was as ready as she'd ever be. She was extremely pleased with the finished result. Her blonde hair shone, the highlights glinting in the lamplight. Her blue eyes sparkled, her eyelids dusted with hints of mauve and pink eyeshadow, complemented by the colour of her silky top. Her lips glistened with frosted plum-coloured lipstick, and a hint of blusher high-lighted her cheekbones. She knew she was looking her best and it gave her confidence. She could carry herself anywhere. Pity she didn't have any decent gold, she thought regretfully. She had a fine gold chain that Derek had given her and a pair of gold earrings, a Christmas present from her parents. They'd have to do. She slipped the earrings into her ears and stood back to admire herself.

'Excellent,' she murmured, wishing she didn't have so many butterflies in her stomach. This was what she wanted. This was what she had come to Dublin for. She hoped Bryan didn't ask her too much about what restaurants she'd been to. Tiger Becs would definitely be her most upmarket. One of the girls at work had been there and raved about it. She'd just play it all very cool, and at least this time she'd know better than to make a *faux pas* as humiliating as the one she'd made in Mao's in Dun Laoghaire soon after she'd come to Dublin.

Even now her cheeks burned at the memory.

One of the girls at work had been telling the rest of them about the fabulous range of Christmas presents in Meadows & Byrne and a few of them had decided to go out to Dun Laoghaire on the Dart to have a browse around. Lorna had adored the elegant, stylish shop and had bought some beautiful wooden serving dishes for her mother and a gift basket of delightful goodies for her grandmother. They'd spent a happy two hours shopping and were just going to sit down in the little coffee shop to have coffee and something to eat when Shelly, the head housekeeper, said briskly, 'I know, let's go into Mao's and eat there. We can have cocktails.' That suggestion had gone down a treat and they'd all trooped out of Meadows & Byrne with their shopping and made their way against the buffeting winds to the cheerful red and blue wooden-floored restaurant further down the shopping pavilion.

Giggling and chatting they perused the cocktail menu and Lorna ordered a Margarita and felt completely happy. This was the life, she assured herself. Sitting sipping cocktails, in a hip, cool restaurant, buzzing and vibrant. It was just like *Sex and the City*. Kilronan was so hicksville in comparison. Eventually they'd decided to eat and Lorna had thought she'd go for the Malaysian chicken and jasmine rice dish. Shelly was going for the tempura of sole.

'I don't know about the Malaysian chicken,' Viv, one of the other girls, murmured. 'It might be too hot . . . the chillies!'

Lorna read the dish's description again: there was no mention of chillies, that was why she'd gone for it. She didn't like 'hot' food. 'It doesn't say anything about chillies,' Lorna declared.

'It does,' argued Viv.

'It's number eleven I'm talking about.' Lorna was perplexed at the other girl's insistence.

'There's no numbers on th— you *idiot*!' Viv shrieked with laughter. 'That's not number eleven, that's two chillies. That lets you know how hot it

189

is.' She guffawed with laughter and some of the others joined in.

'Oh, silly me, the Margarita's gone to my brain.' Lorna had tried to pass it off but she was mortified at her ignorance and the episode had quite ruined the meal for her, even though the others had forgotten all about it and spent the next hour discussing men, as they enjoyed their meal.

That certainly wouldn't happen tonight, she assured herself. She'd stick to something innocuous.

The doorbell rang and her tummy gave a little flip-flop. Taking a deep breath she sprayed some Issey Miyake on her neck and wrists and went to open the door.

'Well *hellooo*, Gorgeous!' Bryan bowed as he handed her a white rose.

'Oh, that's lovely!' Lorna exclaimed in delight, extremely pleased at this romantic gesture and completely forgetting that she was playing it cool.

'A lovely rose for a lovely lady.' Bryan smiled wolfishly. He was looking rather dishy in a black jacket, black open-neck shirt and black trousers. Very dark and brooding. He looked casually but expensively dressed. A man of taste and style, she thought happily.

'I think this might look nice here,' Bryan said suavely, taking the rose from her. He broke the stem, expertly, Lorna thought, sensing that he'd certainly done this before. Then he slipped the rose down into her cleavage, the merest touch of his forefinger against the creamy skin of her breast, and all the while he stared into her eyes with a deep intense look that made her nervous. She willed herself not to blush. Sex icon Samantha Jones would *never* be so uncool as to blush.

Thinking of Samantha was a great help and she knew exactly how to play it. 'Well, aren't you the romantic one?' she drawled, arching an eyebrow at him. 'A regular Sir Galahad!'

Bryan drew back and laughed. 'Let's go and eat. I was out in the boat today and I don't know about you, but I'm starving!' He eyeballed her when he said 'starving' and she knew exactly what he meant. 'Nice place, by the way,' he said as they descended into the lobby. 'I hope I'll get to see a bit more of it later on.'

'We'll see.' Lorna slanted a smile at him.

He was extremely well groomed, she noted approvingly as he drove out of the marina, the cuticles of his neatly manicured nails white against his tanned fingers. The Beautiful South played on the stereo, and she started to relax as they drove out through the *porte-cochère* and headed for the city.

By the time they'd parked and begun to walk towards Dawson Street she was feeling a little apprehensive again. Keeping up an ultra-cool façade wasn't as difficult as she thought. Sometimes it even seemed that she was standing outside herself, looking at herself zipping out smart one-liners as though she were a character in a film. But now she was going to have to sit opposite Bryan for at least two hours and keep it going while eating, with that sure knowledge that he wanted to have sex with her tonight. It was unmistakable, the way he looked at her, the way he touched her lightly on the knee in the car when he leaned over her to get another CD. Being desired boosted her confidence and she banished her momentary flash of apprehension.

She could almost taste the vibrant buzz of chat and laughter as they descended the steps under Samsara Café Bar to Tiger Becs. It was a long, narrow design, with an exotic African ambience. Tables edged a central platform which led to a small bar set against an unusual stained-glass panel. Lorna was mega impressed. It really was hip 'n' happening! Lots of gorgeous-looking girls and cool guys. A greeter, model thin, looking extremely chic, led them to their table. The oriental wooden carvings on the wall and myriad of mirrors lent sophistication to the restaurant. If she'd been here with Heather she would have thoroughly enjoyed the experience, gawking around at all the glitz and glamour and taking it all in. As it was she had to pretend to be totally blasé.

'What will you have to drink?' Bryan asked as they were seated at a small table for two with tasteful linen, cutlery and glassware.

'I'll have a white wine spritzer, please,' Lorna replied, although she was longing for a couple of VRBs. Tonight wasn't the night to go heavy on the booze. She needed to keep her wits about her.

'And a Tiger Beer for me,' Bryan ordered as he unfolded his artistically arranged napkin. They chatted about this and that as they waited for their drinks to arrive. He told her a little about his job, which all went over her head and sounded terribly technical and boring, and she told him about being a hotel receptionist and threw in a few amusing anecdotes about some of the guests she'd had to deal with. They perused the menu and decided to have the combination starter, which Lorna privately felt wasn't too scary as she'd often had the Thai combination in Chinese takeaways. Chicken and pork satays, spring rolls, fishcakes and prawn toasts were not 'danger zone' food. For her main course she played it relatively safe and ordered the stir-fried king prawns. Bryan went for the steamed seabass with lemongrass and chilli dressing. Animatedly he informed her that there was nothing like the thrill of catching a bass, reeling it in and cooking it fresh that night. The reeling in bit sounded a bit gruesome to her, but she pretended interest.

He was something of a contradiction, she decided, the poseur side of him slipping every so often when he got talking about his love of sailing and fishing.

She nibbled at the starter platter when it came, anxious not to appear too ravenous, even though she was peckish by now. She'd been hardly able to eat all day, she'd been so nervous. Her nervousness annoyed her. This was what she wanted in life, to be wined and dined by handsome men. She remembered so well telling Heather that in no uncertain terms the night they'd had the row before Oliver Flynn's wedding. What she wanted had come true. Unfortunately she felt unable to completely relax and enjoy it. Bryan wolfed down the starter and made short shrift of his not very large portion of seabass. 'It's nice, but this sort of stuff,' he forked some pretty cut floral carrots and a piece of salad, 'doesn't fill a man whose been on the briny all day.' He tucked into a helping of Phed Makeur Wao, while she nibbled at some Phad Thai vegetarian rice noodles. Her eight king prawns had been nice enough, the dressing sauce tasty and not too hot, but she'd kept well away from the dipping sauce garnished with a slice of green chilli, guessing that it was breathtakingly hot. Bryan was impressively dextrous with his chopsticks, she noted enviously, resolving to buy a pair and practise using them at home, but for now she kept strictly to the knife and fork.

For dessert she threw coolness to the wind and indulged in a mouth-wateringly scrumptious Thai banana roll. The crunchy honey-glazed sesame seed coating was just what she needed after the spiciness of her prawn dressing. After coffee, while Bryan was taking care of the bill, she tried to hide her self-consciousness as she walked the long walk between the tables to the loos at the end of the restaurant.

There was a queue, and she could feel perspiration between her breasts as she tried to stare nonchalantly around her. Eventually and with relief she got into the very small cubicle, and when she was finished she flushed the loo, pulled down the seat, sat down and did some swift running repairs to her make-up. There wasn't room to swing a cat outside – she was as well off where she was. She applied some deodorant and perfume, and touched up her face make-up with bronzing powder. A quick flick with her lipstick and she was ready. Taking a deep breath, Lorna opened the door and made her way back out to the restaurant, where she swanned down to her seat, head held high, aware that everyone at the tables on either side could see her and that Bryan was waiting with an appreciative glint in his eye.

'Would you like to go clubbing?' he asked. 'We could go to Renard's, it's not too far.'

'Fine,' she agreed. 'Why not? It's early yet.' It was only eleven thirty.

'If you don't mind we won't stay too late. I've a race tomorrow and I had a hard day today.' He barely managed to hide a yawn.

'Oh, don't go on my account,' Lorna interjected, a tad miffed. Feck his race. He should be making sure that *she* was having a good night. She didn't want to seem too eager though, and although she would have loved to see Renard's she knew she couldn't afford to drink too much, as she could end up disgracing herself by puking on the way home. The rich sauce that had dressed her prawns was already giving her a touch of indigestion.

'Are you sure, Lorna?' He sounded relieved. 'Maybe next weekend, I don't have to race next Sunday.' Bryan couldn't hide his relief as he yawned again.

So there's going to be next weekend, she thought happily. *Great!*

'You look as if you could do with some beauty sleep,' she said airily, glad that they didn't have to walk too far to the car. Her ankle was beginning to ache.

'Is that an invitation?' Bryan said wickedly and she laughed.

'Subtle you're not, Bryan,' Lorna remarked and was rather stunned when he pulled her into his arms and kissed her soundly.

'You're gorgeous,' he murmured huskily against her ear.

'I try to please, but not here,' she murmured pushing him away.

Further down the street a youth was puking, his friends laughing at him. It was gross. Anyway she just didn't like the unromantic way Bryan had launched himself upon her. Sixteen-year-olds did that. They didn't talk much on the way home and as they got nearer to Malahide she couldn't decide whether to put him off or ask him in and get it over with. She liked him well enough. He had been a courteous and generous escort and he was good-looking and attractive, all she wanted in a man. He'd surely be an experienced lover. Tonight could be the night.

His kiss had been hungry. He wanted her. That gave her power already, she thought, as Bryan parked outside her apartment and got out of the car and opened the door for her.

'Well, lovely Lorna?' he asked meaningfully.

'I had a very nice time, Bryan.' She eased herself gracefully out of the car. 'Would you like to come up for coffee?'

'I wasn't sure if you were going to ask.' He grinned at her and she laughed. He was honest about it anyway and she decided there and then to go for it. He followed her into the lounge, his arm around her waist, and she liked the feeling it gave her.

'So. Coffee?' she arched an eyebrow at him. 'Aren't you afraid it will keep you awake? And you with a race to run tomorrow.'

'Is coffee all I'm going to be offered?' he asked huskily.

'It's only our first date,' Lorna reminded, slipping into his arms.

'I know, will you respect me in the morning?' His green eyes twinkled.

Lorna laughed. Bryan was nice, she thought happily, as she raised her lips to him and he kissed her soundly. He slipped his fingers up under her top and she was thrilled to feel her nipples harden and quivers begin to tingle deep in her pelvis. He was very experienced, she realized that immediately the way he caressed her and she gave herself up to the pleasure of his touch, relieved beyond measure that her body was responding.

She led him into the bedroom and they undressed each other, slowly, sensuously.

'Sorry the bed's so small,' she murmured. 'I was last into the apartment.'

'All the better, lots of body contact.' Bryan gazed at her naked body in admiration. 'You're a sexy woman, Lorna, I wanted you the minute I set eyes on you,' he whispered against her hair as he eased her down on the bed and entered her. He was considerate, she couldn't fault him, whispering her name, asking if he was giving her pleasure, but her quivers and tingles had faded away and all she could think of was how heavy he was and that his breath was flavoured with beer and chilli, which was almost as bad as garlic. She pretended to come, breathing his name and groaning and moaning into his shoulder as his arms tightened around her and he gave a long, satisfied sigh before rolling off her.

'That was great,' he said drowsily, his rumpled hair making him look younger. 'Pity you don't have a double bed, I could stay the night. Next time we'll go to my place. And I promise I'll make you the best Buck's Fizz you ever had.'

'Mmm, sounds good,' she murmured. She couldn't wait for him to go, so that she could sob her disappointment into her pillow and curse her mother for that aching, horrible memory that wouldn't go away.

15

Heather yawned. She was knackered. Sleeping on a fold-away bed in Ruth's room was not conducive to getting a good night's sleep. She'd been at Ruth's for the past ten days and she knew that she'd want to get her ass in gear and get a place of her own sooner rather than later. It wasn't fair to be cluttering up her sister's room. Heather was finding it extremely unsettling. She was sleeping badly and dragging herself into work every day and she was finding it hard to concentrate.

She had a viewing arranged for tonight, from six to six thirty, so it wouldn't be too late when she got home, she comforted herself. Right now she felt like putting her head down on her arms and sleeping her brains out, but somehow she didn't think it would go down too well with her boss who was sitting scowling into space. The atmosphere in the office had not improved since the 'non-reference' debacle. Two days later an apartment owner had walked in on one of her colleagues, Tommy Walsh, shagging his girlfriend enthusiastically in the apartment he was meant to be showing with a view to letting. The owner had been mightily unimpressed and had taken her business to another letting agency. Both Tommy and Edith had been on the carpet, Edith for not having more control over her staff, Tommy for his complete lack of professionalism. He hadn't been sacked because they were short of staff, but he told Heather he was going to leave anyway, and they could stick their crappy job.

Heather cursed as she typed in the wrong figure, and wearily pressed the delete key. She was sending out an invoice to a landlord. It had to be correct. It had been a relief to let that particular apartment. It had been on the market for over a month and the slowdown in property and rentals was becoming more noticeable. She hoped the one she was showing tonight would move quickly; she didn't want Edith breathing down her neck.

The day dragged, and by the time she'd made her way to the apartment in Smithfield she was completely browned off, the only saving grace the fact that she wasn't too far from home. Ruth wanted her to go to a booze-up in the Turk's Head in Temple Bar and she knew they'd end up in the nightclub downstairs. All she could think of was bed. Even if it *was* lumpy and springy. *How pathetic she was!* You'd think she was ninety the way she was going on.

She should go out with Ruth. She was turning into a right couch potato and that should be nipped in the bud immediately. Sometimes she felt totally inadequate when she saw the girls at work heading out enthusiastically night after night. She just wasn't particularly interested in sitting in pubs or nightclubs. Lorna had always made her feel a social failure in that respect. But maybe that was because she wanted Heather to go out with her. She'd just been using her.

It was different going out with Ruth. At least she knew she'd have a bit of a laugh with her sister. She *would* go out tonight, she decided. A couple of drinks would ensure that she'd sleep no matter what. And she might even meet a nice guy. She'd met Ruth's new boyfriend, Peter, and had to admit that her sister had landed on her feet. He was funny, kind, handsome, and it was clear that he and Ruth had really clicked. Heather got on like a house on fire with him and he'd been great about inviting her out with them. She was conscious of being the proverbial gooseberry and had only gone out on the razz with them twice but it was high time she got a life of her own, and even a man of her own, she thought wryly as she pressed the print key and watched her document slide smoothly out of the printer.

At four thirty she'd had enough of work. She was going to go home, have a shower and get changed. She could go directly to Temple Bar after she'd finished showing the apartment. She tidied her desk, shut down her computer and stood up. 'I'm off,' she announced. Edith looked at her in surprise and threw a look at the board.

'You're not showing until six thirty,' she remarked coldly.

Heather was raging. What a cow! This was the first time that she'd left the office early in all the time she'd worked there. And why had she picked on Heather? Edith never said anything to the others when they left early if they had an evening viewing. She eyeballed her boss frostily. 'Correct, Edith, but if I took all the time I was owed, I wouldn't be here for a week. And if I skived off a bit more like you and some of the others, I still wouldn't make it up.'

Edith's jaw dropped. Heather had never spoken to her like that before. In fact Heather was one of the best she'd ever worked with. 'Well, if you're due time, that's fine, I'm sure. There's no need to be so rude!' She wore a deeply wounded expression.

Heather, uncharacteristically, didn't apologize. She was fed up with being treated like a doormat and had come to the conclusion that people took advantage of her because she was too nice and too soft. So no more Miss Nice Girl. She marched out of the office with her head in the air, leaving Edith open-mouthed.

'That told her,' Heather muttered as she took the lift to the ground floor. She was rather shocked at her outburst, but it had shut Edith up and she might think twice about picking on her again.

That was twice in the last couple of weeks that she'd stood up for herself, she thought as she walked briskly along the rainswept street. She was definitely getting more assertive and it felt good. She remembered Lorna's phone call and scowled. It had infuriated her that Lorna would think that all she had to do was ask her out for a drink and everything would be fine between them.

Her cousin was incredibly self-centred, but maybe her doing the hot potato act on Heather might have been the best thing that had ever happened to her – the 'growth opportunity' her friend Margaret had talked about. Now that she'd asserted herself a couple of times she was damned if she was going to take bad treatment from anyone any more.

At seven forty-five she got a phone call from Ruth enquiring about her whereabouts. 'I'm on the quays, won't be long,' she puffed. She really wasn't fit. She'd have to get in trim.

'Oh, I'm just at the Halfpenny Bridge, I'll wait for you at the Clarence,' Ruth said cheerfully.

'OK, won't be a minute.' Heather put on a spurt, weaving in and out of late-night shoppers, and before long could see her sister looking casually chic in jeans, suede boots and figure-hugging black polo under her black fur-trimmed coat.

Heather, wearing a pair of black trousers and a jade chenille jumper that covered her ass, wished heartily that she had her sister's slender figure. She'd been comfort eating for the past month over the stress of moving flats and the waistband of the trousers was uncomfortably tight. She longed to wear a jumper tucked into jeans but her rear at the moment was not for viewing. Her short jumpers were packed in a black plastic sack and long and relatively loose was currently the wardrobe of the day.

'Hi.' Ruth gave her an affectionate hug and they strolled along chatting about the events of their day. They were walking past Eden when the doors opened and a gaggle of laughing girls spilled out on to the footpath. Heather and Ruth were about to circle around them when they bumped right into Lorna.

'Oh! Oh, hi,' their cousin said brightly as the other girls moved off.

Ruth glared at her, 'Well, hey! If it isn't Cowardy-Custard-Morgan. You know . . . the one who does a runner at the weekend and doesn't even have the guts to say she's moving out. Don't you *dare* say hi to us.'

'Oh, shut up, you,' Lorna flared, clearly taken aback. 'I'm sorry, Heather, if you're still upset, but I did explain in my letter that I had to make a decision on the spo—'

'Why don't you just run along to your new friends, just think, you can puke in *their* hand-bags now. I'm sure they're much more up-market than mine was,' Ruth said cuttingly. 'Come on, Heather.'

'Yeah, go on, Heather, let little twinnie tell you what to do like she always does,' Lorna jeered. 'Well, I'm glad I moved to Malahide. I've made great new friends that aren't mouldy old stick-in-the-muds. I live in a fabulous apartment and I've got a dishy, rich boyfriend who thinks I'm the bee's knees,' she boasted.

'The poor deluded git,' Heather retorted coldly. 'He'll find out what a user you are too, just like poor old Derek Kennedy.'

'Bitches!' Lorna swore as she stalked off. Heather and Ruth looked at each other and started to laugh.

'She's so childish,' Ruth shook her head in disbelief. '*I've got a dishy, rich boyfriend and he thinks I'm the bee's knees*,' she mimicked her cousin. 'She's a sad wagon.'

'She looked fantastic,' Heather noted enviously. Lorna had been dressed to the nines in tan leather trousers and matching jacket. That was definitely it, she decided. She was starting another diet on Monday. There was a great three-day one that was guaranteed to lose ten pounds and you could even have ice-cream on it. Come Monday morning she'd be having two teaspoons of peanut butter on dry toast for breakfast. It was that kind of diet. And she wouldn't go overboard on the sauce tonight either. She could do without the calories and the hang-over. Meeting Lorna had given her a jolt and she'd seen the way her cousin's eyes had flicked up and down over her, checking out what she was wearing. Well, one day Lorna was going to see her and her eyes were going to pop out of her head, she'd look so stunning, Heather vowed.

The booze-up was great fun. Heather thoroughly enjoyed herself and was first to agree to heading downstairs to the nightclub at closing time. The encounter with Lorna had been unexpected but in some strange way it was like the tie had finally been cut and Lorna was out of her life. And the great thing was, it didn't matter any more. That was the liberating thing. She'd seen her cousin with her new swanky friends and it didn't bother her. Since their childhood, she'd been Lorna's little handmaiden, and now it was over and she didn't care.

She was in flying form, thanks to one Bud too many. Heather grinned at Ruth as they bopped effervescently to Kylie. 'I'm really glad I came out tonight.'

'Say that to me in the morning,' laughed her twin knowingly.

The following morning, Heather packed her weekend bag, trying to ignore her throbbing head. 'I'm never going out with you again,' she groaned as her sister breezed into the bedroom looking as fresh as a daisy.

'Here's a cup of coffee and a bacon sandwich, that will fix you,' Ruth declared kindly.

'Oh, thanks!' Heather brightened up. Hangover or not, she was hungry.

'I'd better fly. Tell the parents I was asking for them and tell them I'll be down with Peter on Sunday.' She sprayed some Allure in the direction of her neck, grabbed her bag and ran. Heather sat on Ruth's bed, took a bite out of the hot bacon sandwich, relishing the oozing melting butter, then sipped her coffee. She was so looking forward to going home. Tonight she'd be sleeping in her own snug, comfortable bed and tomorrow she was going to walk the round of the lake and breathe in that rich, clear, fresh, frosty country air. Not even Edith Palmer could put a dent in her good humour today, she smiled, as she applied her make-up.

Edith couldn't have been nicer to her as it happened. *It pays to stand up for yourself*, Heather thought in amusement as her boss gave her a saccharine smile and thanked her profusely when she handed her some references to inspect.

At six p.m. she was standing on the quays in gale-force winds and pouring rain, waiting for the

Kilronan bus. The weather was atrocious and she was longing to get her seat on the bus and immerse herself in *Harry Potter and the Prisoner of Azkaban*, the third part of the Harry Potter series. She'd been babysitting for a friend of hers in Kilronan one night and out of boredom, and interested in seeing what all the fuss was about, she'd picked up *Harry Potter and the Philosopher's Stone* and started to read it. After the first chapter she was hooked. As soon as that damn bus arrived she was going to stick her nose in her book and enjoy the journey home. A sharp beep of a car horn made her jump and she saw a dark blue BMW pull in to the bus stop. Somebody must be getting a lift, she thought, as she peered along the lines of traffic to see if there was any sign of the Kilronan bus. It was dark and rain blurred her eyes, and she couldn't really see.

'Heather! Heather, do you want a lift?' Someone was calling her name, a vaguely familiar voice. Startled, she looked in at the driver and saw Neil Brennan smiling out at her. Her heart gave a little lurch. She hadn't seen much of her old boyfriend since she had given him his marching orders. He was the last person she'd expected to offer her a lift. 'Come on, get in. It's a horrible night and the traffic's crap and I'd better get out of here.'

Oh God! she dithered, but he had the door open and automatically she passed him her bag and he threw it on to the back seat. Before she knew it, she was sitting in the plush passenger seat and Neil was moving out into the traffic.

'So! How are you, Heather?' Neil flashed her a sheepish grin. 'Can we let bygones be bygones?'

She laughed. 'Of course we can,' she said easily, not being one to hold a grudge. 'You're doing well. I like the wheels.'

'Not bad, sure they're not. Oh, Heather, it's been a hell of a year,' he said eagerly. 'Wait until I tell you . . .' He launched off into a description of how he'd finally got a financial package together and how Oliver Flynn had agreed to build his showrooms for him. 'I wouldn't go to anyone else locally, Oliver's a great builder. There's no messing at all. He does what he says he'll do,' he observed as the rain battered against the windows and the wipers swished rhythmically, creating a lullaby of their own.

'I like Oliver, there's something nice about him,' Heather agreed as she settled back into her seat more comfortably. She was pleasantly relaxed, her initial moment of awkwardness long vanished. It was just like old times in a way, she reflected. Neil and herself had always been able to talk and she enjoyed listening to him talking about his plans for the business.

'So now I'm mostly involved in the selling end and I have two mechanics working for me in the garage, but I need a receptionist, someone who can do the paperwork and send in those damn VAT returns. They're the bane of my life,' he confided as they inched along in bumper-to-bumper rush-hour Friday-night traffic.

Heather laughed. 'Are you getting nasty letters telling you that court proceedings will be initiated and the sheriff will be at your door in ten days? The clients in Mangan's used to go spare when they got those.'

'Yeah, but the infuriating thing is that I'd sent in the return and the cheque and because of some delay in *their* office, it wasn't processed in time. They send out those stinkers of letters and never have the manners to apologize,' Neil exclaimed indignantly. He turned to look at her. 'Of course you worked in Mangan's, didn't you? So you'd know all about VAT and stuff. You're not looking for a job, are you?' he joked.

Heather felt the hair rise up on the back of her neck. Her friend Margaret, who believed in 'growth opportunity', had told her that there was no such thing as 'coincidence'. That when something that seemed coincidental occurred it was really the Universe, or God, whichever you preferred, presenting you with an opportunity to change or grow or take a new step in life. Was this apparent coincidence, this lift from Neil and his job offer, one of those gifts from the Universe that Margaret was always going on about?

Neil studied her hard. They were stopped at red lights and only the sound of the engine purring and the wipers swishing broke the silence. 'You're not looking for a job, are you?' he asked uncertainly.

'I don't know,' Heather hesitated. 'I don't like the job I'm in, I was thinking of looking for another one. But I don't know if I was really planning on going back home.'

'I suppose not.' Neil backtracked. 'Why would you leave the bright city lights for boring old Kilronan?'

'I don't think Kilronan is boring. I miss it,' Heather remarked.

'Do you?' he looked at her in genuine surprise. 'I thought you'd love city life.'

'No, I don't really like Dublin to be honest. I think I'm a country girl at heart.'

'Well, why don't you come back?' he challenged. 'I meant it when I said I needed someone to look after the office and answer the phone. The business is getting too big for me to run on my own. I want to be professional. I'm not a small back-street garage merchant any more. I'm in with the big boys now and I need back-up. Come on, Heather,' he urged. 'Think about it. I'd pay you good money, you'd be back in Kilronan. It could be great. We get on well, don't we? Well, apart from our little hiccup the night of Oliver's wedding,' he amended.

Heather gave a wry smile. 'Hmm,' she said drily.

'Aw, Heather, I *am* sorry about that. Honest. It was bad manners. I miss you, you know. We got on very well.'

'We got on very well because I let you walk all over me,' she retorted.

'Ah, don't be like that. Look, will you think about the job? I think we could make a great team. I'll pay you a good wage. More than what you're on.'

'Aren't you afraid I'd give you an inflated salary figure?' she teased.

Neil laughed. 'Naw, you're too straight, Heather. That toffee-nosed cousin of yours might all right.'

'Don't talk to me about her.' Heather's mouth tightened.

'Why? What did she do on you? I thought you were sharing a flat with her.'

210

'Not any more as it happens.' She gave him an edited version of the saga.

'Sounds like you're better off without her,' he observed as he overtook a lorry.

'I know, but I've got to go and find a place to live. I can't hog Ruth's bedroom for much longer.'

'You don't have to. Come back to Kilronan and sort me out. You won't have to go looking for a new flatmate or a new place to live.' He paused. 'Of course you probably wouldn't want to live at home, is that it?'

'I haven't really thought about it,' Heather admitted.

'Look, I've a couple of rooms built over the office. I was thinking of letting them as offices, but I could always get Oliver to do them up as a flat and get rent that way for it. So what would you say to that? A place of your own, no commuting, and me for a boss?' Neil grinned at her.

'I don't know.' Heather was a tad stunned. This was almost surreal. Less than an hour ago she'd been standing at the bus stop minding her own business waiting for the bus to Kilronan, knowing she needed to find accommodation and a new job, and now she was sitting in Neil Brennan's BMW with the prospect of a job and a flat presented to her on a plate. There had to be some trick, some flaw. Could this be a dream? She gave herself a little pinch, noting that there was plenty of flab to pinch from. Nope, this was for real.

'Look, think about it over the weekend,' Neil advised. A thought struck him. 'Are you seeing someone in Dublin? I never thought of that. Is that what's keeping you there?'

'No, I'm manless as well as practically homeless,' Heather said wryly. 'How about you? Are women falling all over you? You're fairly eligible now with your big showrooms.'

'To be honest I've been so caught up in the business I haven't really been out and about much. Maybe we could go for a drink tomorrow night if you like, seeing as we're both footloose and fancy free?'

'Well, I usually meet the girls on Saturday night when I come home,' she demurred.

'Oh!' he looked crestfallen. 'I work on Saturdays so I can't meet you in the daytime. Pity.'

'Well look, I'll arrange to meet the girls for lunch and I could meet you tomorrow night if you want, then,' she suggested. She wasn't going to be a doormat this time and she wanted him to know that she wasn't sitting in waiting for him to provide her with a social life either.

'Great. I'll pick you up around seven thirty. It will be like old times,' Neil said cheerfully.

'It better not be like old times. You were always late. Seven thirty on the dot,' she warned.

'OK, Heather. Seven thirty on the dot,' he agreed.

Although the traffic was heavy the journey flew by. They chatted easily together and when he drove away from her house, having refused the offer of coffee, Heather was as happy as she'd been in a long time.

'Hi Ma, I'm home.' She practically danced into

the sitting-room where her mother was watching *Fair City*, one of Heather's favourite soaps.

'Hello, love.' Her mother stood up and gave her daughter a hug. 'You look great. Much better than the last time you were home. I'll get your dinner for you. You can have it in front of the TV.' She took her coat and motioned her to the sofa. 'Sit down, relax.'

'Wait until the ads are on, Ma. *Fair City*'s really good lately, that Nicola is a walking wagon.'

'She reminds me of Lorna,' her mother sniffed. Heather remained diplomatically silent. Lorna was certainly not flavour of the month with her mother at the moment. And if Anne got her hands on her there'd be wigs on the green. Anne was ripping with her for doing the dirty on Heather and had been all prepared to ring her niece at work and give her an earful, only Heather had warned her in no uncertain terms to do no such thing.

'I don't need Mammy fighting my battles for me. I'm a big girl now, Ma,' she'd informed her mother firmly.

'It's not right what she did and I want to tell her so,' argued her mother. 'She's got away with too much for far too long.'

'No Ma, it's for me to deal with. Don't get involved,' warned Heather, knowing that if her mother lost her cool, there'd be a right royal row and the whole family would be dragged into it.

'Look at that Nicola one, the way she looks down her nose at Farrah, that *exactly* the way that little consequence Lorna goes on. I'm glad you're not living with her any more. I always felt she was

213

using you. She has airs and graces way beyond her standing,' her mother declared as the ad break came on and she went out to the kitchen to heat up her daughter's dinner.

Heather snuggled up on the big comfortable sofa as the aromatic scent of chicken and mushroom pie wafted in from the kitchen. The fire was crackling up the chimney, the wind was keening around the house. The rain lashed against the windows. This room was so cosy, and homely, she thought gratefully, remembering lonely nights when she'd been on her own in that gloomy, draughty sitting-room in Dublin.

There really was no place like home. Her mother arrived in with a tray loaded with a plate of steaming pie, roasted vegetables, a dish of golden crème brulée and a glass of chilled Chardonnay.

'Eat up,' she ordered. 'I hope you're not going out tonight. I have the blanket on for you upstairs. You look as if you could do with a good night's sleep. Look at the bags under your eyes! There's plenty of hot water for a bath. Run up while the news is on and get into your nightie. And come down and watch the *Late Late* with me and we'll finish off the wine. Your father won't be in till late, he's gone to a golf thing.'

'Why didn't you go?' Heather forked a piece of feather-light pastry into her mouth.

'Oh no, it wasn't a do, it was a committee meeting,' her mother explained as she sat down in her armchair and took a sip of wine. 'Is the pie all right?'

'Oh Ma, it's gorgeous,' Heather said fervently,

214

relishing the creamy sauce filled with succulent chicken and mushrooms.

'I know you, you probably live on frozen rubbish and never eat a vegetable,' her mother chided. 'And Ruth seems to live in restaurants. She's always eating out.'

'Well, it is handy to eat in town at lunchtime,' Heather pointed out.

'And costs a fortune,' her mother said tartly.

'Not really.' Heather took a bite of roasted baby onion. 'The other day we went to a place in Temple Bar called Bendini & Shaw's and I had a spinach wrap with chicken and red onion and it was very tasty and not dripping in calories either and it wasn't too expensive. I had a lovely café mocha after it and that did me for my main meal of the day.'

'If I gave you spinach you'd turn your nose up at it but go to a restaurant with a fancy name and it's *tasty*!' snorted her mother. 'Right then, it's spinach for you from now on but you'll have to do with common or garden coffee, we don't do fancy stuff here.'

It had been a peach of an evening, Heather thought drowsily several hours later as she curled up in her warm bed and pulled the patchwork quilt under her ears. She was totally relaxed, having soaked in a hot, lavender-scented bath. After which she'd sat chatting to her mother as they finished off the wine between them, watching Pat Kenny conduct a spirited and entertaining debate on the *Late Late*. She hadn't said anything to Anne about Neil's proposal. She knew her mother would jump at the idea of having her back home. She might be a bit miffed about her going to live in a flat. The thoughts drifted in and out as her eyelids drooped.

Anyway, she wasn't quite sure yet if she was going to come back to Kilronan. She'd go for a long walk around the lake tomorrow and have a good think about it. It was great to have options, was her last conscious thought before she fell asleep listening to the wind sighing in the trees and knowing that she could sleep in as long as she liked in the morning.

Neil Brennan opened his bulging briefcase and spread his files on the kitchen table. He rubbed his eyes wearily. There was so much paperwork involved in selling cars. He was barely keeping on top of it and he knew come hell or high water he was going to have to get someone in to take care of it. If Heather would come on board all his troubles would be over. She'd be good at the job, he was sure of it, and besides, she was genuinely interested in what he was doing.

He poured himself a glass of Carlsberg and took a long draught. He wouldn't mind a couple of drinks tonight but he had to catch up. Anyway he'd be seeing Heather tomorrow night, he could indulge then, he comforted himself as he took out the dreaded VAT form. He scanned it resentfully. He hated the damn things. Office work was not his strong point, selling cars was. Heather had been impressed with the BMW, he thought proudly. He was damned impressed himself. He still couldn't believe it and he loved driving around in it, impressing the locals. Wait until that stuck-up cousin of Heather's saw it. It might knock the superior look off her mush. Seeing Heather at the bus stop had been a bit of a shock. It had been an impulsive decision to pull in and ask her did she want a lift. She'd always been very cool with him when she'd seen him around after she'd given him his walking papers.

It had been very enjoyable talking to her on the journey home. Heather was real easy to talk to. That was one of the things he'd liked about her. In fact he'd liked a lot of things about her. If he got a chance to go with her again he'd make sure to be more considerate and not take her for granted this time.

But even if she didn't go out with him, if she took the job he'd be on the pig's back. It would leave him free to get out there and really hustle for business. He was doing well. He'd achieved his goal of a big chrome and glass showroom that every motorist who drove through Kilronan on the way to Dublin couldn't miss. State-of-the-art show-rooms were a must now in the cut and thrust of the motor industry. He'd heard of a few dealerships being withdrawn because the garages and show-rooms weren't up to scratch. His premises were an investment in his future, as he'd told some of the old fellas in Kilronan who'd accused him of having notions about his station in life.

He wanted to have a team of salesmen in place in the next five years. He wanted it all and Heather could help him get it. He wanted to have the biggest car dealership within a hundred-mile radius.

He wanted to be a top-notch businessman that people in Kilronan looked up to. And he wanted to be rich. He never wanted to have to scrimp and save again. The BMW had cost an arm and a leg and he'd had to take out a whacking big loan for it, but image was everything and he knew that. He couldn't have a big car showroom and drive around in a crock. It was a business decision to buy that car.

Heather obviously hadn't bought a car yet, or she'd hardly have been waiting at the bus stop for the bus to Kilronan. He could offer to give her one of the second-hand cars out on the forecourt at cost price. That might be an added incentive for her to take the job. He'd really woo her tomorrow night. He'd take her to dinner in the Lake View and he'd ring Oliver Flynn first thing in the morning to talk about fitting out the rooms over the office as a flat. If she agreed to take it, he'd tell her she could decorate it in whatever colour schemes she wanted. Women liked that kind of thing. With Heather on board, Neil had the strongest feeling that things could only get better.

Hoping that it would be the last time he'd have to do it, he flattened out the dreaded VAT return and began to fill it in.

16

Noreen curled drowsily against Oliver and his arms tightened around her. They had just made love and she knew by his breathing that he'd be asleep in seconds. She would have liked it if he'd stayed awake a bit longer to talk to her. He was so busy these days she hardly ever saw him, and those few minutes in bed when he was relaxed and they talked were precious.

Tonight might be the night they'd conceive their much-longed-for baby. It was slap bang in the middle of her cycle, and they'd done it twice. Surely this time they'd be lucky. She felt a pang of guilt as Oliver started to snore rhythmically. The poor fella. She was wearing him out, she thought ruefully. He would have gone asleep after the first time but she wouldn't let him. Just as well he was fit and healthy. With Pete, she'd been lucky to have sex twice a week, let alone twice a night. That was the drink of course. Drink had ruined their relationship . . . ruined everything. A sharp, stabbing pain of sadness enveloped her. Wouldn't it ever go . . . wouldn't it ever leave her? Would she have to carry the grief of it for the rest of her life?

Don't think about it. Don't think about him! She snuggled in closer to her husband, feeling the warmth of his body against hers, wishing she could wake him up and tell him of the heart scald that tormented her.

She shouldn't keep harking back to the past. Her life was very good now. She was married to a decent, kind man . . . *That you had to propose to . . .* the thought came unbidden.

'For crying out loud, Noreen, will you stop this crap,' she muttered, irritated with her negativity. She made herself think about work. She was starting in Douglas Kennedy's surgery tomorrow and she felt uncharacteristically nervous. It was so long since she'd worn the uniform that was now washed and ironed and hanging in her wardrobe ready for wear again. She'd tried it on earlier in the week. It had been strange to see herself in the attire that for years had almost defined her in her sisters' eyes, and in which she had sometimes defined herself if she was honest about it. Sister Noreen Lynch she'd been. Calm, proficient, conscientious. They were traits in herself that she liked. They helped balance the unsure, self-doubting, needy, vulnerable part of her that threatened to overwhelm her sometimes. After her disastrous relationship with Pete McMullen she'd sworn that she'd never let a man see that side of her again, but despite her best intentions sometimes she'd slip into neediness, trying to get Oliver to admit that he loved her, or showing her despair when her period arrived.

Poor Oliver. She stroked his hand. Providing emotional sustenance was difficult for him. He hated it when she got upset and would be like a cat on a griddle until she composed herself, or he could escape to one of his beloved building sites. Sometimes she simply needed him to put his arms around her and hold her. Being held was always balm to her soul.

Noreen sighed. She wasn't being fair to her husband. He didn't know what lay behind her distress, nor would he ever. That was in the past and there was no going back. Tomorrow was the start of her new job and she was looking forward to it. It would be immensely satisfying to be doing what she was good at. She was sure it would do much to restore her emotional equilibrium and that could only help her to conceive. She drifted off to sleep and dreamed that her mother was beside her, telling her gently that everything would be all right.

'Good luck today, don't kill anybody,' Oliver teased as he towelled his hair dry the following morning.

'Smarty-pants. You'll be sorry if you ever have to come to me for a tetanus injection,' Noreen said drowsily as she lay back against the pillows and watched her husband get dressed. It was six forty-five, the crack of dawn. She'd long since stopped trying to persuade Oliver to get up at a *reasonable* hour.

'Do you want a cup of tea?' he asked, as he always did.

'No thanks, I'm going to have a little snooze, get up, and prepare the dinner so that I'll have it all ready when I come in from work.' She yawned.

'God, it sounds so weird to be saying when I come in from work.'

'You don't have to go to work, you know that now, don't you?' Oliver said firmly.

'I know that, Oliver. I just think it will be good for me. I'm turning into a right couch potato, I need to get out and about again. I won't neglect you though. I'll have your dinner on the table every evening.'

'That's not why I'm saying it, Noreen,' Oliver said indignantly.

'I just want you to know you're still my number one priority,' she assured him.

'That's nice to know,' he said gruffly as he tucked his shirt into his trousers.

'Come here.' She sat up in the bed and wrapped the sheet around her bare shoulders.

Oliver looked at her warily. 'What?'

'I only want to give you a kiss.'

'That's all now, Noreen,' he warned. 'I'm running late.'

'Oliver, don't be like that,' she protested, hurt. 'Wouldn't it be worse if I didn't want you?'

'Ah, Noreen!' Oliver grimaced as he sat on the bed and leaned over to her. 'Come on, give me a gooser and go back to sleep.'

She kissed him on the cheek. 'See you later,' she said quietly and turned away. She heard him give a deep sigh.

''Bye,' Oliver said in a resigned sort of tone and then he was gone and she could hear him running down the stairs.

As if he couldn't get away from me quick enough. She was hurt, angry, hating him for making her feel undesirable and demanding. It wouldn't have taken long to have a quickie. He knew it was her ovulation period. Why couldn't he be more considerate? Sometimes she felt he wasn't interested in having children. They might take him away from his fucking work, she thought bitterly, raging with him for ruining her day.

Oliver gulped down a cup of tea and smeared butter over a slice of brown bread. He felt utterly oppressed, guilty, angry and resentful. He knew that Noreen had wanted him to have sex with her this morning, but they'd done it twice last night and he was in rag order. Why couldn't she relax about it like the doctor had told her to? One of these days he wasn't going to be able to get it up, the way she was going on, he thought wearily. He'd suggested they look into adoption but she wouldn't hear of it. Took the nose off him and said she wanted a child of her own. He'd only been trying to help in his own ham-fisted way. He hadn't referred to it again. He didn't know if Noreen enjoyed sex any more. He didn't think that she did. She was too focused on getting pregnant, spending a fortune in the chemist on yokes that told her when she was ovulating, and when they were having sex making sure that she was lying in the optimum position for conception. There was no spontaneity any more. Pregnancy was the be-all and end-all as far as she was concerned and he was beginning to feel like nothing more than a sperm machine.

She was up in bed now, angry with him because he wouldn't have sex with her, and part of him felt like a heel, and that wasn't fair. He shouldn't feel like that. He was doing his goddammed best, he thought savagely as he rinsed his cup under the tap and threw it in the drainer.

Noreen stood in front of the mirror and straightened her shoulders. Her uniform was looser on her than when she'd worn it a couple of years ago. Her sessions in the gym and pool were certainly toning her up, but she was getting a bit thin. Angular even. Her bust was beginning to disappear. Pregnancy would sort that out, she told herself briskly as she slipped into her coat and wrapped a deep mauve scarf around her neck. She glanced at her watch. Just one thirty. Surgery began at two. She wanted to be there for quarter to. It was a fresh, bright, cold day and she inhaled the air appreciatively as she walked out to the car. It was a far cry from fume-smothered London, yet she'd been happy there when she went to work there first. Her work had been challenging, satisfying, and she'd made good friends among the nurses and doctors that she'd worked with. And then she'd met Pete. Brown-eyed, smooth-talking, hard-drinking, undependable Pete.

She'd fallen for him hard. He was a systems analyst in a big IT firm and they'd met at a mutual friend's engagement party. 'Do you believe in this engagement nonsense?' he'd whispered conspiratorially as they toasted the happy couple.

'Don't knock it till you've tried it,' she whispered back, liking his twinkling sloe eyes and infectious smile.

'That'll never be me. I'm not the marrying kind,' he declared, looking her straight in the eye.

What woman could resist a challenge like that? Not her, that was for sure, she thought wryly as she twisted the key in the ignition. He'd reeled her in hook line and sinker with his 'I'm not the marrying kind but try and catch me if you can' crap, and she'd played his games, and sat waiting for the phone to ring and watched him flirt with other women, and lent him money when he was skint, which was often, until she'd been wrung dry. She still despised herself for her weak, pathetic behaviour but he was the first man she had ever really loved and his treatment of her only reinforced what she had learned at the hands of her father. That all men were lousy, selfish, demanding bastards who used women with callous disregard for their welfare and emotional needs.

'Jesus, Mary and Joseph, Noreen, will you stop going back there,' she growled, her hands clenched in her lap. Why were all these memories coming back to haunt her? Was it because Oliver had made her feel unloved, unwanted and unwomanly this morning? Just the way Pete used to make her feel when he wanted to punish her. Her lip trembled and she bit it hard. *Stop it!*

She'd want to cop on to herself, she reflected as she spun the wheel and reversed to face down the drive. She was turning into a neurotic basket case. She breathed deeply and managed to compose herself. It frightened her when she lost control like that. The first person she saw when she walked into the surgery was her sister. Maura sat flicking through a magazine, her bump a nice soft curve under her jumper. Noreen's stomach lurched. Maura was the last person she wanted to see. She felt guilty for not keeping in touch to see how her sister's pregnancy was progressing.

'Well, hi, what's wrong with you?' her sister demanded when she looked up to see Noreen walking towards reception.

'Not a thing, Maura,' she said crisply. 'I'm doing a few hours here as surgery nurse.'

Maura's eyes nearly popped out of her head. 'Really? Why on earth do you want to go back to work? Isn't Oliver making enough to keep you in the style to which you've become accustomed?' she tittered.

'Oh, indeed he is and *more*, I just hate sitting at home doing nothing.' Noreen couldn't resist the barb. 'See you later.' She smiled at the rest of the patients in the waiting-room and walked into reception. Eileen Gannon, the receptionist on duty, welcomed her warmly.

'How are you, Noreen? Let me show you to your domain, I've a few awaiting your ministrations already.' She led her to the room marked 'Nurse' and Noreen looked around the clean, sterile, well-equipped room with the window overlooking a well-tended back garden and was glad she'd made the decision to return to work. This was where she would come into her own. This was where she'd come back to the confident, in-control woman she'd once been.

The afternoon passed quickly and she was kept going, attending to cholesterol counts, warts removals, dressings, and other assorted procedures. She enjoyed the sense of calm that enveloped her when she was working and she was exhilarated when Eileen came in at the end of surgery with a cup of tea for her. They were joined soon afterwards by Douglas and they chatted easily about the patients that had passed through the afternoon surgery and their various requirements. She felt as if she'd been there for ever and it was a very good feeling.

She was dying to tell Oliver all about it over dinner. She stopped at the off-licence and bought a six-pack of Bud, remembering how, when he'd been courting her, they'd chatted companionably over a beer in the evening when he was finished work. She wanted it to be like that again. She'd been very contented when she and Oliver had been courting.

She phoned him when she got home. 'Where are you? What time will you be home at?' she asked gaily. 'Will I put the dinner on?'

'OK. I'll be home in about half an hour, I just want to check out Neil Brennan's place. The lads are nearly finished there. How did it go?' He sounded relieved that she was in good form.

'It was great, Oliver,' she enthused. 'I'm really glad I took it on.'

'That's good, Noreen,' he said warmly. 'If it's what you want. I'm happy for you.'

'Thanks, Oliver, that means a lot to me.' There was silence for a moment and she heard her husband clear his throat.

'Listen, Noreen, I'm sorry I was a bit tetchy this morning,' he apologized awkwardly.

'That's OK, Oliver. Hurry home, I've got a few cans of Bud for us and I'll have the fire lighting. I'll tell you all about my afternoon,' Noreen said cheerfully. ''Bye, love.' She hung up and set about putting the finishing touches to their dinner, humming to herself as she did so. She hadn't felt so energized in a long time.

Oliver stopped at the local florist and selected some irises and lilies he thought his wife would like. He felt as if a load had been lifted off his shoulders. Noreen had been bubbling down the phone. She sounded like a different woman. Maybe this job was just what she needed to get her out of the rut she was in. She was right. Staying at home gave her too much time to dwell on herself and her desire for a baby. This job would give her another interest and help her to get to know people around the area.

She needed to make friends and go out and about a bit more. He was glad she'd joined the gym. She seemed to enjoy that. It was a pity that she wasn't close to her sisters. It would have been nice for her to socialize with them. Women needed friends and family to confide in. He knew he wasn't the best when she was teary and upset. It just made him feel very uncomfortable. He never knew what to say to comfort her. He'd never thought that Noreen would be the emotional sort. She hadn't given him that impression when he'd been dating her. It all seemed to come from this immense need for a baby. Pity she was that bit older than he was. She kept saying that the mid-thirties was old to be starting off, but he'd heard of women in their mid-forties getting pregnant. His own mother had been in her early forties when she'd had him. Of course when he'd said this, he was told she didn't want to wait until she was forty to get pregnant and besides, Oliver was Cora's third child. Hopefully now that Noreen was working her job would keep her occupied. He'd even suggest that she invite the Kennedys to dinner soon if it would keep her happy. Whistling, Oliver laid the flowers on the front seat beside him and drove home to have dinner, sip beer and chat with his wife.

Noreen pulled into a parking bay in Blanchardstown shopping centre. It was a frosty December morning and she'd come to Dublin to do some Christmas shopping. She wanted to buy Oliver some warm fleeces. But first of all she had a very important purchase to make. Her heart raced with anticipation. She was a week overdue and her excitement knew no bounds. She knew she could have a pregnancy test in the surgery but she was paranoid about anyone finding out. She was going to buy a pregnancy test kit, here where no one knew her, and in another few days she was going to use it. She hadn't even told Oliver that she was late. She was praying that it wasn't a false alarm.

Despite the early hour, the centre was abuzz with Christmas shoppers. The deep, rich tones of Bing Crosby singing 'White Christmas' gave an added touch of seasonal cheer and Noreen felt a glow of happiness. This might be her best Christmas ever, she thought happily as she walked briskly into

McCabe's Pharmacy and scanned the shelves looking for pregnancy test kits.

Two hours later she sat having a croissant and coffee feeling very pleased with herself. She'd remained totally focused and made great inroads into her Christmas shopping list. Even though she'd warned Oliver that he was taking a day off to come Christmas shopping with her, she'd bought some of their joint presents, including a beautiful pale green bedjacket for Cora. Today, not even her mother-in-law could put a dent in her joyful humour.

Surgery was even more busy than usual and she was tired when she got home that evening. She filled the kettle to make herself a cup of tea and then popped the steak and kidney pie she'd made earlier into the oven. Her handbag rested on the counter top. Inside it, two pregnancy test kits. She'd bought two, knowing that she'd feel much safer to have a back up if she did test positive. She took it out and read the instructions, feeling her heart begin to flutter. Part of her wanted to do the test there and then but she was scared. What if it proved negative? She put it back in her bag and tried to forget about it.

'What did you buy me for Christmas?' Oliver teased as they sat drinking coffee after their dinner.

'Mind your own business.' She grinned at him. He might be getting the best Christmas present of his entire life, if she was pregnant. She'd have a terrible time not telling him until Christmas Day, but wouldn't it be the most wonderful thing to wake him up on Christmas morning and tell him that he was going to be a father?

17

'Heather, I think it's a terrific idea, why don't you say yes, it would save you a fortune on bus fares, coming home every second weekend.' Anne Williams beamed at her daughter. Heather had just told her about Neil's job offer. 'Take it, take it, take it,' she urged.

'Now stop it, Ma, and if I do take it, I might move into the flat over his offices,' Heather warned.

'Now what do you want to do that for?' Anne chided. 'And a perfectly good home here for you.'

'I can come and visit every second weekend,' Heather joked as she tucked into a fry-up with gusto. 'One of the reasons I'm not going to live at home is because I'd end up like an elephant. I'm starting a diet on Monday, I want to lose at least half a stone before Christmas—'

'Stop your nonsense and eat up your breakfast, you can run around the lake later on,' her mother ordered, sliding a crispy slice of fried bread on to her plate.

'Oh Ma,' groaned Heather, 'this has got to stop.' She dipped a piece of bread into her fried egg, pressed some mushrooms on to the fork, flavoured it with tomato sauce and savoured every bit of it.

Two hours later she was walking around the lake, the wind whipping her hair around her face. The rain of the night before had cleared to bright frosty weather and the cold nipped at her nose and cheeks, all that was visible as she tramped swiftly along the path that circled the lake. Little whitecap waves lapped the shore, and the sound of the water was music to her spirit.

Heather breathed the air deeply. She loved this place. Birdsong filled the air. A little robin perched on a bare branch gazed at her with curiosity, quite unafraid. Winter heathers, holly bushes, and orange-berried pyracantha and evergreens lent splashes of colour amid the bare-branched foliage of the trees. White powder puffs of cloud scudded across a clear blue sky and a pale yellow sun cast prisms of light on to the rippling waves.

This was where she felt happy, Heather reflected. Not in pubs and nightclubs and grimy city streets. She'd been in Dublin a little over a year and it still felt alien to her. This was home, this was where her roots were. She didn't have to wait for Neil to persuade her over a drink tonight. This was where she wanted to be.

With a spring in her step and happiness in her heart, Heather looked at the little robin and exclaimed exuberantly, 'I'm coming home!'

Lorna shivered. She was freezing and soaking wet. Spray spumed up from the bow of the boat as it sliced through the waves and the harsh glint of sunlight on water was giving her a headache. There was nothing glamorous about sailing, she thought in dismay, as Bryan ducked under a sail, flashed her a grin and said, 'It's great, isn't it?'

'Fantastic,' she fibbed, hoping to God she wouldn't get seasick as they bounced along the water, the slap of the sea as the boat dipped and rose into the waves making her queasy. Bryan had had to lend her a waterproof when her expensive pink fleece had got soaked.

For this, she'd got up at the crack of dawn – well, eight o'clock, she amended – so that her new boyfriend could take her out in the boat he co-owned with some of his friends. He was like a child showing off his new toy, telling her about jibs and spinnakers and mainbraces, as if she gave a fiddler's. She should have put more tinted moisturizer on, she fretted. She'd be like a weather-beaten old prune when she got home.

'You OK? You're very quiet and you look a bit green around the gills,' Bryan asked kindly.

'It's a bit rough,' she ventured.

Bryan guffawed. 'Rough! My dear girl, it's practically a mill pond!' He ducked under his sail again and did something to loosen it out and the boat really took off.

'Oh God,' groaned Lorna. She really was going to up-chuck in a minute, and that would be absolutely mortifying. She scrabbled around in her precious Bill Amberg bag and found some chewing gum. It helped a little. She'd even taken the pre-caution of taking a Sea Legs but perhaps she should have taken more than one. It was the longest hour of her life and eventually Bryan took pity on her and headed for the Marina.

'We'll drop you off, and I'll see you tonight,' he said briskly and she felt like telling him to impale himself on his jib, whatever his jib was.

'Fine.' Her teeth chattered. Pneumonia was probably imminent, she thought sorrowfully, as the boat sailed gracefully into the Marina and her boyfriend tied it up expertly.

'Guess you're not a mermaid. Pity,' he said ruefully as he helped her off the boat.

Lorna couldn't even think of a Samantha-like retort. All she wanted was to soak in a hot bath to warm herself up. She'd never leave dry land to go sailing again, she vowed, as she trudged past Caruzzo's towards her block.

'Well, what was it like, you lucky tart? Trust you to land an eligible with his own boat! I'd *love* to go sailing,' Carina declared enviously when she came home from her shift later that afternoon.

Lorna, who'd soaked herself for hours, fortified by several hot ports, had recovered her equilibrium.

'It was fabulous,' she drawled. 'I felt like I was on the Mediterranean. I'd say it's divine in the summer.' Not for an instant would she let on that it had been a disaster. Carina's envy made sure of that.

At seven thirty, dressed up to the nines, Lorna sat waiting for Bryan. Carina and Lisa had gone to the launch of a photographic exhibition and were going clubbing later. She was the only one of the trio to currently have a boyfriend, she thought smugly.

At nine o'clock, she gave in to her rage and phoned him.

'Where are you?' she demanded furiously when he answered his mobile.

'Sorry about that,' he slurred. 'I'm drinking with the lads—'

'Well, fuck you,' Lorna spat and slammed down the phone. He could take a hike. No man stood her up and got away with it.

Some Christmas this was going to be, she'd been banking on a nice piece of jewellery at least. Not to talk about having a hunk on her arm to escort her to Christmas parties.

Now she was going to have to start from scratch.

Noreen's heart sank to her boots when the old familiar cramps assailed her as she lay on her mat using the Abs Toner at the gym. Maybe she'd just stretched too hard and pulled a muscle, but the nagging pain in her lower back brought fear to her heart. The pounding music on the stereo couldn't compete with the pounding of her heart as she picked up her towel and water and made her way through the crowded gym out to the toilets.

The smear of blood on her white panties was like a knife to her heart.

'Oh God, where is your mercy?' she sobbed into the towel, heartbroken. Eventually she managed to compose herself and made her way to the locker-room, hoping that people would think her red face was the result of her workout. She didn't even bother to change out of her gym gear, just pulled on her coat and hurried out to the car. All she wanted to do was to get home.

She started crying again as she was driving. She'd never been late before, she was always regular — that was why she'd been so hopeful that this was finally it. At least she hadn't said anything to Oliver. He wouldn't have his hopes so cruelly dashed the way she had, she thought bitterly as she pulled into the drive.

The house was mausoleum quiet. Would it ever ring with the happy laughter of small children playing? If they had children would Oliver spend more time at home? How could he work six days a week, week in week out, and enjoy it? Sometimes she felt it was because he didn't want to be at home alone with her.

He'd cleaned out and set the fire for her this morning before he went to work. Even though they had central heating, he knew she liked to curl up in front of the fire. He was good like that. Thoughtful in his own way. She'd better get her crying over and done with before he came home, she thought desolately as she set a match to the fire and watched it flame up the chimney.

She made herself a cup of tea, took a couple of Ponston and lay down on the settee. A terrible weariness enveloped her and she fell asleep curled up in a childlike huddle. Dusk was beginning to fall as she awoke, and she lay drowsily watching the flames cast dancing shadows on the walls, feeling a relief of sorts that at least the uncertainty was over. She should have used the damned pregnancy test yesterday when she'd bought it and put herself out of her misery instead of believing that God had granted her a miracle. What a naïve idiot she was, she thought in self-disgust. She switched on a small table lamp and picked up a glossy magazine she'd brought home from the surgery. Idly she flicked through it and then sat bolt upright as she began to read an article.

'God, I never thought of that,' she muttered, half excited, half dismayed.

She heard her husband's key in the door and turned to face him as he came in. 'Oliver, come here, sit down. I need to talk to you,' she patted the settee beside her. 'And promise me you won't get mad.'

'Why would I get mad?' he asked. 'Did you prang the car? Could happen to anyone,' he said as he sat down beside her and stretched and yawned.

In spite of her trauma she had to smile. 'No, Oliver, I didn't prang the car. Look. I've just been reading this article about infertility.' She turned and gazed into his blue eyes, noting the sudden wariness. 'Oliver, would you do something for me?' she asked hesitantly.

'If I can, Noreen.' He looked perplexed.

'Oliver, it might be that the problem conceiving doesn't lie with me. Would you go and have a few tests done?'

'Oh, for fuck's sake, Noreen.' Oliver rubbed his eyes wearily and her heart sank.

'Please, Oliver,' she pleaded.

'God Almighty, Noreen, would you give me a break.' He stood up angrily.

Resentment flared. 'No, *you* give me a break,

237

Oliver, and don't be so selfish,' she yelled as he stormed out of the sitting-room. 'You don't spend any time with me, you work morning noon and night and you won't even see if it's your fault that I can't have a baby. You're a selfish bastard,' she shouted, at the end of her tether, as she heard the front door open and then slam behind him.

Oliver gunned the engine and heard the gravel crunch under the tyres as he practically skidded down the drive. Now she was saying it was his fucking fault that they couldn't have a baby. Why couldn't she just leave well enough alone and let it happen when it was meant to happen?

It had been too good to be true; this peace and harmony they'd had for the past few weeks when she'd started working had been a respite for them. He'd actually enjoyed coming home from work to her and that was something that hadn't lasted beyond the early months of their marriage. Now the heat was on again and he could feel his stress levels rising.

He parked outside the Haven and went in and ordered a pint. It was quiet enough in the bar, too early for the Saturday night revellers, so he sat on a bar stool and waited for his pint to settle. What kind of tests did she want him to have? It would mean going to doctors and he hated the breed. Stay well away from that shower was his motto, you'd go to see them half healthy and come home dying.

Oliver gave a sigh that came from the depths of his being.

'Can't be that bad,' the barman said cheerfully. Oliver quelled him with a look. What did he know?

Was he selfish, he asked himself as he took a draught of the cool golden brew. He provided very well for Noreen, he did the heavy chores around the house, he wasn't mean, yet she was always giving out to him for not being at home, for not spending more time with her.

If she'd quit nagging he might be more inclined to go home, he thought grumpily, staring into space. Women! They were an enigma to him, he'd never understand them. There was no point in even trying. He stared at his pint. He had two options right now, get mouldy drunk and tell Noreen that under no circumstances was he having any damned tests or go home and try and sort this mess out once and for all.

18

'It looks terrific doesn't it?' Neil was like a little boy as he followed her from room to room. Heather broke into a melon-slice grin, and just stood staring around the small bright sitting-room that would be her new home from now on. Having the furniture in and the curtains up made such a difference. She had no complaints at all.

'I think you can take it that the woman is happy enough, Neil,' Oliver Flynn said in amusement from where he was leaning against the door jamb, his hands shoved into the back pockets of his jeans. He'd come to give it the final once-over and see if she had any complaints.

Heather remembered her manners. 'It's lovely, Neil. I'm mad about it. You did a great job, Oliver. Thanks a lot.'

'You're welcome, Heather. So you're coming back to us for good?' Oliver smiled down at her from his lofty height, his eyes crinkling into a smile.

'I sure am. I don't know why I stayed away so long. I saw the sun rise over the lake this morning and felt sorry for all those poor sods in Dublin where all you can see are rooftops and houses and

240

more houses. I can see the far end of the lake from my bedroom window here. It's great, isn't it?' She was bubbling with excitement and happiness.

'So you didn't want to be a city slicker then?' Oliver glanced at Neil, who was gazing with pride down at his forecourt filled with gleaming cars.

'It's not me, Oliver. I'm a country girl at heart,' Heather said merrily.

'And a hard taskmaster!' Neil interjected teasingly. 'I have to fill out my cheque stubs or it's like the Spanish Inquisition if I don't!'

'Those blinking things. I know what you mean. I get that from Marie in the office.' Oliver threw his eyes up to heaven. 'Well, if you're both happy enough, I'd better get a move on. A very Happy Christmas to you both and the best of luck here, Heather. If you have any problems let me know.'

'I will, Oliver, and thanks very, very much. I love it.' Impulsively she leaned up and gave him a hug, and laughed when he blushed. He gave a bashful grin and hurried down the stairs but turned and gave her a wave when he reached the front door.

'He's shy behind it all, isn't he?' Heather remarked in amusement as she went back into the sitting-room.

'I suppose he is if you say so, but he's a damn good builder,' Neil declared as he gazed around at his latest investment. 'This adds fifty thou or more on to the value of the place. I like those curtains,' he added. 'You've a good eye for colour.'

'Well, thank you.' Heather grinned, forgetting all about Oliver as she looked around at her new domain. The sitting-room, which overlooked the

241

forecourt and the treetops that opened out on to the lake across the road, was a rectangular room that she'd had painted in a shade of warm, creamy yellow. A maple floor gleamed in the wintry sun. She'd buy some nice rugs to cover it in the January sales. Her mother had made the lilac curtains and matching cushion-covers to go on the oatmeal three-piece that was a Christmas and moving-in present from her parents. The small, circular, smoked glass dining-table and chairs were a present from Ruth. There wasn't a fireplace in the room so she'd got an electric coal-effect fire that was quite realistic. It gave a nice focal point to the room. Neil had given her a small portable TV and video on its own unit, much to her delight. She had a pine nest of tables to serve coffee on, and some book-shelves on the wall opposite the window. Any-more furniture would have made the room look cluttered.

It was new and clean and smelt of fresh paint, light-years away from the shabby flat in Drum-condra. Heather thought she had died and gone to heaven. She was as happy as a lark!

Giving in her notice at Brooke, Byrne & O'Connell had been one of the best days of her life. It was a gloomy, chilly Monday morning following her delightful weekend at home, and her boss glared at her as she came into work five minutes late and fished in her bag for her letter of resig-nation, typed up on Neil's computer the night before. Edith Palmer nearly had a seizure when Heather placed the letter on the desk in front of her and said cheerfully, 'I'm resigning.'

'But you can't go,' her boss protested. 'We're dreadfully short-staffed and January can be quite busy for us.'

'Sorry, Edith, and don't forget that I have leave accrued so I'll be taking that.' Heather stuck the knife in deeper, enjoying her boss's discomfiture.

'But that means you'll be gone two weeks before Christmas. That's just not on, I'm afraid. Tommy Walsh has applied for leave, he's going to New York. You'll just have to wait until after Christmas and that's the end of it!' Edith said bossily.

'I think not, Edith!' The cheek of her boss, trying to bully her into staying and talking to her as if she were a child. Just who did she think she was? Neil's job offer couldn't have come at a better time. Heather was thoroughly sick of Miss Superiority with her patronizing attitude. 'I have a challenging job, with lots of responsibility and a big wage increase to boot, waiting for me. I don't care to wait any longer. That's my letter of resignation effective from this date,' Heather said coolly, enjoying her new sense of power *immensely!* She'd often daydreamed about resigning, as indeed did most of the rest of the staff in the office, but even in her wildest dreams it hadn't felt as good and as deeply satisfying as the real thing. And even better, Tommy Walsh had confided that he wasn't coming back from New York so Edith and Brooke, Byrne & O'Connell were going to be rightly up the Swanee in January.

'But what about your loyalty to the company?' Edith demanded, staring in disdain at the white envelope Heather had placed on her desk. Heather laughed heartily at the notion. Loyalty to the company indeed! Was Edith for real?

'It's no laughing matter,' Edith said icily.

'Oh Edith, get a life,' Heather retorted as she turned and made her way to the vending machine for a much needed cup of coffee.

Because of her leave she only had to work out a week of her notice and the following Friday found her sitting in the family station-wagon at four thirty, having left the office early, surrounded by black plastic sacks containing all her clothes and bits and pieces. Her mother had driven from home to collect her from Ruth's and as they drove past Phibsboro, northwards to freedom, Heather felt a weight lift from her shoulders. She'd done city life, had a bit of fun, seen a bit of life, but all in all, hadn't greatly enjoyed it. Now she was going home to get a life for herself, just as she'd urged Edith Palmer to.

Maybe she was running away. Lorna would definitely view her return to Kilronan in that light. She didn't care. City life wasn't for her, she admitted, as the car in front made an illegal right turn at Whitworth Road, causing her mother to swear loudly and jam on the brakes. She wouldn't miss city gridlock in the slightest, she thought happily, as they resumed their forward motion but stopped again a minute later, blocked by a car parked on double yellows.

Her first week working for Neil had been a bit daunting, to say the least. Excellent as he might be at selling cars, his paperwork and accountancy were a shambles. Folders, stacks of demands and receipts from the Revenue, paperwork for his car sales, were strewn higgledy piggledy on a large desk in the back office. He also had a small office reception area where he dealt with new customers. That at least was presentable, she noted. His computer desktop was a disaster!

'I want a computer of my own, with Microsoft Office First Run and Excel,' Heather announced as Neil stood sheepishly amid the detritus of his paperwork. 'And I want a four-drawer filing cabinet for the time being, until you expand even more.' She flashed him a grin. 'Actually there's an office supplier's in Drumcondra, Lawlors, they have a good catalogue. I'll get them to send us one and we can go through it for our office supplies. You could do with having some headed notepaper and "With compliments" slips. I'll get that organized too.'

Neil enveloped her in an unexpected bearhug. 'This is brilliant, Heather. You're just what I need.' He waved a hand expansively around the office. 'This is your domain. Do what you want. I won't be interfering. I'll be out selling cars. You can look after the wages, I'll explain the way it works—'

'I hope everything's above board,' she said sternly, snuggling in to him.

'Oh, it is,' he assured her. 'All PRSI and the rest is paid. It's too risky not to.'

'Right, get out of here and let me try to put some sort of manners on the place,' she ordered.

'OK,' he agreed, smiling at her. She smiled back and then before she realized what was happening he started to kiss her and it was as though they'd never been parted.

'Go on, get out of here,' she whispered, breathlessly, red-cheeked, as she heard one of the mechanics call Neil's name.

'Let's go out for a meal to celebrate.' Neil kissed her again.

'OK, OK, go on,' she giggled, pushing him away. And smiled to herself for at least twenty minutes before the full reality of his total disorganization took the smirk off her face as she settled down to some serious sorting.

By the time Christmas Eve arrived she had the office organized to her liking, and a system set in place that suited the needs of the business. She was working hard, but it was enjoyable, knowing that this side of the business was her responsibility and that Neil was happy for it to be so. She also acted as receptionist and telephonist so her day was varied, dealing with customers, suppliers and enquiries as well as her paperwork. She had never been so happy in her life, especially when the flat really began to take shape.

She'd bought more curtain material with her mother and Anne had spent hours at the sewing machine working away, delighted that one of her darlings was back home in Kilronan. Her mother had cleaned the place with her from top to bottom to remove the builder's dust and as the four-roomed apartment became more homely, and she saw the happiness in her daughter's eyes, she stopped fretting about the fact that Heather was not going to live at home. It was a huge relief to Heather that her mother wasn't kicking up a fuss, it made her return to Kilronan much easier all round.

When Oliver had called in on Christmas Eve to make sure that she and Neil were happy with the finished product, Heather was practically dancing on air. This truly was going to be the happiest Christmas of her life, she thought, as she stood at the bedroom door and looked into her new room. A double bed, dressed in a lightly quilted white and lilac coverlet that matched the curtain material, dominated the room. Two pine bedside lockers and a pine wardrobe and dressing-table unit completed the simple furnishings, but she was enthralled with it. The walls were painted white with a hint of pink. It was a warm, south-facing room from which she could see the lake in the distance. Across the landing a small galley kitchen looked on to the fields behind Neil's garage. A nice view to watch the changing seasons when she was cooking. Beside the kitchen a tiled bathroom with a walk-in shower unit completed her living arrangements.

She felt she was living in a palace.

'Like it?' Neil asked, slipping his arms around her.

'I love it,' she assured him. 'You know what I think we should do?' she added, staring him steadily in the eye.

'What?'

'After we've christened the bed, I think we should put up a Christmas tree.' A blush crept up her cheeks at her forwardness.

His jaw dropped. 'Do you mean it?'

'If you want to,' she said shyly. 'I've never done it before though, so I mightn't be very good at it.'

'Don't be silly,' he said tenderly, kissing her nose.

'I bet you'll be brilliant at it. Come on, let's give it a try.' He linked his arm into hers and they walked over to the bed.

'I'm not a twig,' she said doubtfully as he started to unzip her fleece.

'That makes two of us,' he laughed as he slipped his hands under her top and expertly unhooked her bra. His fingers started to caress her, sending delightful quivers careering all over her, and she forgot about not being a perfect size ten as she began to eagerly open the buttons of his shirt, suddenly as eager to make love as he was.

Later as she lay drowsily in the curve of his arm she smiled up at him. 'Did you enjoy it?' he asked lazily.

'Yessss,' she murmured. 'It was lovely. I just feel *soooo* relaxed. Poor Lorna, the first time she did it with Derek Kennedy was a real let down, she was in bits after it and said it was a disaster.'

'Now why does that not surprise me?' Neil remarked. She gave him a little puck in the ribs.

'Don't be like that,' she chided.

'Nothing would ever be right for the likes of her,' Neil observed perceptively. He turned to her and kissed her. 'What are we talking about *her* for when we can do this?' he murmured, cupping her breast in his hand.

It was late into the afternoon before they finally went off, hand in hand, in search of a last-minute Christmas tree. The two happiest people in Kilronan.

19

Noreen shivered and tucked her chin deeper into her scarf as she walked with Oliver towards St Joseph's church for midnight Mass. It was a cold, frosty, starlit night and a full flaxen moon seemed to sit on the point of the spire casting an ethereal glow over the church grounds. Neighbours and acquaintances called white-breathed seasonal greetings as the Mass-goers streamed towards the great teak doors, festooned with wreaths of red-berried holly. It was a beautiful night, and normally Noreen would have enjoyed the Christmas atmosphere and joined in the carol singing with gusto. Last year she'd been very happy going to midnight Mass. Her first as a married woman. She'd felt serene, contented, and very optimistic. Now she had to make a conscious effort to try to stem the tide of resentment, anger, disappointment and unhappiness that constantly threatened to engulf her.

She cast a sideways glance at her husband's profile. Jaw set, firm mouth drawn down, he looked as miserable as she felt. She sighed deeply as they crunched their way up frosty, pine-cone-filled steps. There had been a strain between them since the night she'd asked him to go for tests. After his explosive reaction to her suggestion, she hadn't expected him to arrive home within the hour or expected him to say grimly, 'I'll go for those tests if you want me to, just tell me what you want me to do.'

As matter-of-factly as she could, she'd explained that he'd have to go to a maternity hospital to give a semen sample to test his sperm count. She'd get a letter of referral from Doctor Kennedy.

'I don't want him knowing my business, I'll go to someone else,' he said brusquely and that was the end of the conversation.

So far he hadn't mentioned a word about it and it was getting to her. He knew how important this was to her, he could at least make an effort and get his skates on. Time was of the essence in case she needed fertility treatment. If he didn't do something about it soon she was going to go and have her own tests done. At least she'd know then, one way or the other, whose fault it was and if anything could be done.

'I want to sit up at the front, Oliver,' Cora declared as they went into the porch. They had given Oliver's mother a lift to Mass and her eyes were bright with anticipation. She loved midnight Mass and proudly informed Noreen that she hadn't missed one in the past thirty-five years. She'd chattered away in the front seat of the car and for once Noreen was glad of her presence, as it meant she didn't have to make an effort to talk to Oliver. And that was what it was lately, she thought sadly. An effort. He'd gone quiet and moody and shut

250

himself off from her. Maybe he might thaw over Christmas; if she was lucky he might even make love to her. He hadn't come near her in the last few weeks and she missed their intimacy and the comforting feel of his strong arms around her.

'Well, helloo,' Maura trilled gaily as she stood with Andy chatting to one of their neighbours. 'Happy Christmas, and to you too, Oliver, and Mrs Flynn.'

'Happy Christmas to you both,' Oliver said politely. Cora gave a regal nod, as if accepting homage, and proceeded into the church and up the aisle. Noreen smiled into her scarf. Maura might think she was someone, but in Mrs Flynn's eyes she was well below the salt.

Maura patted her substantial bump. 'It has to be a fella, he's hopping and lepping like a flea in there. The kicks!' She rolled her eyes up to heaven theatrically.

'A full forward for sure,' Andy exclaimed jovially and Noreen could smell the brandy fumes off him. He'd obviously started seasonal celebrations early.

'How are you keeping, Maura?' Noreen asked civilly, wishing she hadn't bumped into her sister and brother-in-law.

'Great, not a bother, thanks. Listen, we're having a few people in for champagne and smoked salmon after Mass, why don't the two of you call in? We'd love to have you,' Maura invited cordially.

'Yes, yes, come along and have a couple of snifters!' Andy whacked Oliver on the back.

'Ah . . . ah . . . we have to bring Mrs Flynn home after Mass,' Noreen pointed out hastily.

'Bring her along too,' Andy said ebulliently.

Maura flashed him a look of irritation. 'It might be a bit late for her. Why don't you come back with us, Noreen, and when Oliver has dropped his mother home he can join us,' she said smoothly. 'Come on, we haven't seen the pair of you in ages.'

Noreen glanced at Oliver in dismay. She knew a soirée at Maura and Andy's was the last thing he'd want. It was the last thing *she* wanted, for heaven's sake, but she felt churlish saying no and she felt more than a little guilty for not being more supportive to her sister in her pregnancy.

'Well, I suppose we could go for an hour or so,' she said doubtfully.

'Excellent,' Maura approved. 'We'll wait for you in the porch after Mass. We'd better go in or we won't get a decent seat.'

The strains of 'Silent Night' wafted through the decorated church, as Oliver and Noreen hurried up the aisle and slipped into the front row with Cora.

'What do you want to go back there for?' growled Oliver as they settled themselves in the seat.

'What else could I say?' hissed Noreen. 'I didn't see you coming up with any brilliant excuse and besides, she *is* my sister,' she added tartly. 'You don't have to come if you don't want to.'

He didn't answer her, just picked up the Mass leaflet and studied it intently.

Noreen sizzled silently. *Peace and Goodwill to all mankind indeed*, she fumed as Cora cast a censorious look in their direction. The choir began to sing

'Hark the Herald Angels Sing', incense wafted around the altar, and Father Walters's kindly tones welcomed them all to church before beginning the Mass. Noreen tried her best to immerse herself in the comforting, familiar ritual, hoping for some sort of spiritual sustenance.

Two and a half hours later she was enjoying sustenance of a rather more secular nature. The hum of chatter and laughter surrounded her as she nibbled on smoked salmon and brown bread and quaffed her third glass of champagne. Maura was in her element bustling around and Andy played the expansive host with great aplomb, his hail-fellow-well-met veneer even more exaggerated with the amount of drink he had consumed.

Noreen didn't like him, she acknowledged a little tipsily. He was a gropy, leery drunk and she'd seen him making the most of his snoggy kisses with various women under the mistletoe. She'd made sure to keep well out of his way. She didn't really know why she was here. It was almost to spite Oliver, she thought glumly, wishing paradoxically that he would come and rescue her.

'I must show you the nursery.' Maura came up to her and offered her another canapé. 'I went for neutral colours, lots of Winnie-the-Pooh bits and pieces, because I don't want to know whether it's a boy or a girl. Although I do think it's a boy. You know the way they say you can tell by the way you're carrying? What do you think?' her sister asked earnestly.

Noreen swallowed. 'It's hard to know, Maura, and obstetrics aren't my area of expertise, but you do seem to be carrying to the back, so it could be a boy. Have you any preferences?'

'I don't mind really as long as it's all right.' She cleared her throat and drew her sister to a quiet corner of the large, ornately decorated room. Maura went in for lots of swags and frills and glass cabinets full of china and ornaments. Noreen looked at her quizzically, wondering what was coming. It wasn't like Maura to want tête-à-têtes with her.

'Noreen, I was just wondering . . . ahh . . . well you see Andy doesn't like the prenatal classes, he fainted at the birth video and he doesn't want to be there . . . and besides, I read somewhere that men are put off sex after watching a birth, so I was just wondering if you'd come with me when I'm giving birth? I'm a bit petrified to be honest,' she blurted anxiously. Noreen had never seen her normally bumptious younger sister so flustered. Her heart softened in spite of herself.

'Of course I'll come,' she answered without hesitation, wanting to kick Andy in the goolies. She could see him mauling some new arrivals.

'Oh, thanks a million, Noreen! Look, here's Niamh and Sophie Lindsay. I'd better go and say hello. I'll be back in a sec.' Maura gave her an awkward pat on the arm and hurried over to greet her guests.

Noreen watched her go, astonished at her own reaction to her sister's request. *Blood must be thicker than water*, she thought wryly. Imagine her agreeing to be there for the birth. She the barren woman. Tears smarted her eyes and she turned her head and brushed them away, afraid someone would see.

Why didn't Oliver hurry up and come to bring her home? It was mean of him, mean, mean, mean, she seethed. And she'd damn well let him know what she thought of him before the night was over.

Cora bustled around happily making tea for Oliver. What a bonus to have him to herself after midnight Mass. And even better, himself and Noreen looked as if they were having some sort of tiff; they hardly had two words to say to each other. Maybe he'd realize now that he should have listened to her and stayed single. Stayed with her to look after him as only she could.

'Now Oliver, here's the first piece of Christmas cake, I cut it specially for you,' she said, proudly handing him a slice on one of her good china plates. She was delighted with the cake this year. It had turned out beautifully rich and golden, the fruit evenly distributed throughout. The previous year her cake had got slightly burned at the edges and the fruit had sunk a little and she'd been very vexed about it.

She poured herself a cup of tea and sat in her chair by the fire, the log she had thrown on the embers when she came in flaming nicely. She watched her son covertly. He was eating the cake, but his mind was miles away. He looked tired, stressed, and was it her imagination or were there grey flecks at his temples and were the lines around his mouth and eyes grooved deeper than she'd ever seen? Oliver normally had a healthy, energetic air about him but tonight he was certainly not himself. She felt a niggle of worry. She didn't like to see him like this. What if there was something wrong with him? He wasn't the sort to go confiding in her. It had never been his way. They weren't much for hugging or kissing either, she felt awkward with that kind of nonsense, but if there was something wrong with him she'd like to know. She cleared her throat. 'Er . . . aahh . . . you're very quiet tonight, Oliver, and you're not looking the best. What is the matter with you?' she ventured.

Oliver took a gulp of tea and shook his head. 'Not a thing, Ma, not a thing,' he said easily. Too easily, Cora thought crossly. Something was up and he wasn't telling her and the sooner she got to the bottom of the matter the better.

Oliver shivered and pulled the collar of his coat up to his ears as he slid the bolt into his mother's gate and got back into the car. It was freezing hard and he set the wipers to fast speed to get the ice off the windows, the hot water he'd already poured on them freezing up again. He yawned tiredly. It had been cosy and warm at his mother's and he would have loved to have gone for a snooze in front of the fire and then stumbled bleary-eyed to bed in his old bedroom, his limbs stretched to the four winds with no one to bother him. He glanced at the clock on the dash. It was gone two a.m. Noreen would be doing handstands wondering where he was. His heart sank at the thought of going to make polite conversation with his in-laws. They'd all be well lubricated and he'd be stone cold sober and Andy would be trying to force brandy on him even though he was driving.

He sat staring out at the starry night, the Plough and Orion's Belt etched into the inky black sky, Mars and the North Star twinkling steadfastly and the swirling curlicues of the Milky Way as mysterious as the first time he'd seen them. Normally the sight would delight him, he never wearied of gazing at the stars, but tonight the magnificence of the universe could not lift his spirits. As soon as Christmas was over he'd better get his ass in gear and get himself to some doctor to get the damned letter of referral for that damned test. He'd told Noreen he'd do it and he never went back on his word. But now that she'd put the idea in his head that the fault might lie with him he was worried. If he couldn't father a child and she wouldn't adopt, what lay ahead for them? The thought oppressed him.

Reluctantly he put the car into gear and drove off along the winding road, wondering how his life had gone so badly astray.

'God Almighty, Oliver, you might have come and rescued me a bit earlier,' Noreen grumbled as she got into the car. It was almost three a.m. and she was pissed, tired and extremely fed up. 'And then when you finally did come you sat in a corner and wouldn't say two words to anyone. You could try to make the effort,' she nagged.

'I leave that to you, you're so good at it,' he muttered irritably.

'Don't be a smart bastard, Oliver.'

'Look, I didn't want to go there in the first place,' he snapped. 'That fool Andy couldn't get it into his thick skull that I wasn't going to drink and drive and he pestered me the whole time I was there to have a bloody brandy, and Maura was as bad. If I get caught for drink driving I may throw my hat at it, you think they'd realize that without it having to be spelt out for them, bloody idiots.'

'Don't call my family bloody idiots,' Noreen exploded.

'Well, they are.' Oliver was in no humour to be trifled with.

'Yeah, well, what about that old witch of a mother of yours that I have to put up with?' she raged, her cheeks scarlet with drink and temper.

'You knew what you were getting into when you married me,' Oliver growled. 'You had a choice.'

'So did you,' she flared. 'Sometimes I wonder just why you married me?'

'Because you asked me to,' Oliver said coldly.

Noreen felt the blood drain from her cheeks as the impact of his words washed over her like an icy shower. Suddenly she felt stone cold sober.

'Oh Oliver!' she said faintly. 'That was a cruel thing to say.'

'Maybe it was, but you asked me and I told you the truth,' Oliver said angrily. He knew he'd hurt her. The words had burst out of him, there was no point in backtracking and making it worse, not in the humour both of them were in.

The remainder of the journey passed in silence and when they got home, Noreen went straight upstairs, got her nightdress and dressing-gown from their bedroom and went into the guest room down the landing.

Oliver, now that he was home and didn't have to worry about drinking and driving, poured himself a large tumbler of whiskey and drank it neat. Tonight he wanted to sleep and no troubling thoughts of Noreen's hurt feelings were going to keep him awake, he fumed, raging with himself for hurting her, even if a small part of him deep in his heart acknowledged the truth of what he'd said.

Noreen lay wide-eyed in the unfamiliar bed, her heart thumping rapidly. Her deepest fear in relation to their marriage had been manifested. Oliver had bluntly stated that he'd only married her because she'd asked him. She should never have done it. She'd have been far better off to live with him, waiting for *him* to ask rather than forcing the issue. At least then she could have walked away relatively easy with her head held fairly high when it had all collapsed in a heap around her.

Marriage made it much harder to walk away. She bit her lip to stop it from trembling. She'd never forgive Oliver for making her feel like this. She'd never thought he had it in him to hurt her so viciously. She knew he could be moody and un-communicative, but in his own way he could be very kind and thoughtful. She'd never expected such deliberate, wounding callousness from him. He didn't love her. That was the be-all and end-all of it, she thought forlornly, and it was that thought that finally made her cry.

None of them loved her. Not her father. Not Pete, and certainly not Oliver.

20

Lorna was bored out of her tree. She didn't bother to hide a yawn as the choir broke into a rousing rendition of 'Adeste Fideles'. She hadn't wanted to attend Mass on Christmas morning with her family. She hadn't really wanted to come home at all, if truth be told. Nothing was going right. The plan had not been for her to be standing on her own in church on Christmas morning. The plan had been for her to swan up the aisle on Bryan's arm, flashing a stunning new piece of jewellery for the whole parish to see and talk about and then, after Christmas lunch, to get back to Dublin as fast as they could.

Attending Mass with her family was so uncool. It embarrassed her even to think about it. She'd be the talk of the parish, she thought mournfully, as Mrs Campbell, the chief soprano, hit a woeful high note, wobbled dangerously but regained control at the 'Venite adoremus'.

Imagine living in Dublin over a year and still being manless. It was mortifying and she wasn't admitting it to a sinner. To all intents and purposes she had a boyfriend and no one would know otherwise. Her shameful secret was safe now that she was no longer living with her cousin.

She wondered idly if Heather were at Mass. Maybe the Williamses had gone to midnight Mass. She hoped she wasn't here. She didn't fancy meeting either of her cousins after the way they'd behaved when they'd bumped into her in Temple Bar. The hymn ended and she sat down gratefully. She had a fierce hangover. She'd helped herself to a few shots of vodka when she'd arrived home the previous evening, to find that her parents were gone to a dinner party at a friend's house.

Some welcome home, she thought crossly as she read the note propped up on the hall table. Her two younger brothers were out, and the house was like a morgue. There wasn't even a dinner waiting for her and she felt extremely hard done by as she raided the fridge, helping herself to the remains of a macaroni cheese and some trifle.

She'd wished she was talking to Heather. At least she'd have been able to go and have a drink with her cousin if they'd been on speaking terms. She'd been tempted to phone her and offer her a lift home, and possibly would have if Bryan had still been on the scene and she could boast about him, but she didn't want Heather spreading it all over the town that her big romance was off.

She scowled, thinking of Bryan. He really was a let-down. She'd been all prepared to let him eat humble pie for a week or two and then take him back. He'd breezed into Gibney's on the Tuesday after he'd stood her up, as if nothing had happened.

'Hi, doll.' He winked.

'It's you,' she said coldly.

'Don't be frosty.' He gave her a boyish grin and kissed her on the cheek. 'I've got an invite to a big corporate bash at work. Day at the races, meal, free drinks, the works. Do you want to come?'

Lorna struggled with her pride. She had several options. She should tell him to get lost . . . and never see him again. She could play it cool and keep him dangling for an answer, or she could play it safe and agree to go, and tighten her grip on him in preparation for Christmas.

'When is it?' she drawled.

'Next Saturday.' Bryan ran his hand down her thigh. 'Come on,' he urged. 'It will be a blast!'

'And if I say yes, how do I know I won't be left waiting like I was the other night. I *do* have a life, you know!' she added pointedly.

'I know, sorry about that. I got skulled with the lads. Won't happen again,' he assured her silkily.

'You can say that again,' she retorted, but she let him buy her a drink and that night she stayed at his place and pretended to enjoy his passionate lovemaking. Lorna sighed at the memory. As usual the sex had started out well and she'd been eager and anticipatory, but once again the quivers had fizzled out to nothing and she'd put on an Oscar-winning performance, writhing and moaning in a way that had Bryan secretly congratulating himself on being a world-class lover. She'd lain awake as he snored beside her and despaired of her abnormality.

She'd dolled herself up to the nines the following

Saturday in her black leather trousers and a black bustier and had been rewarded by the look of pure admiration in Bryan's eyes when he'd arrived to pick her up. The day was a blur of drink. She'd even been tempted to indulge in a spot of coke when Bryan had snorted some, but self-preservation held her back. She wasn't sure how she'd react to it in front of all these strangers. She might even puke, knowing her, and that would *totally* ruin her image. And to Lorna, image was sacrosanct.

She found the racing boring but pretended to enjoy it, placing bets on horses she hadn't a clue about, but as Bryan got steadily more high, his eyes glittering brightly, she felt uncomfortable, especially when he pressed her to have sex with him behind a horsebox.

'No, Bryan,' she hissed as he tried to unzip her trousers.

'Come on, you sexy bitch,' he muttered. 'Come on.'

'No!' She pulled away from him, and tottered back to the crowd with her ridiculously high heels sinking into the mucky ground. He didn't speak to her for the rest of the evening and when they got back to town he turned to her and said coldly, 'You can piss off, I don't want to see you again.'

One of his colleagues said, 'Steady on, buddy. You're not in the right mind to be making decisions like this.'

Lorna was horrified at being dumped so publicly. And she was as mad as hell that *he* had dumped her and not the other way around.

'Do you think I want to see *you*, cokehead?' she retaliated stoutly. 'You're a sad bastard! Believe me, Bryan, the feeling is mutual. And another thing.' She pointed a shaking finger at him. 'You think you're God's gift to women. You think Casanova has nothing on you. You don't even know when a woman's faking it! Pathetic git.' She stalked away, head held high, feeling she had reclaimed the high ground.

Tears brimmed in her eyes at the memory. She'd messed up once more. What was it with her? Why couldn't she get it right? Lorna swallowed hard as tears threatened to spill down her cheeks. *Stop it*, she ordered herself frantically. If people saw her crying in Mass it would be all over Kilronan. Her street cred would be *ruined!* She blew her nose and to take her mind off her heartache she scanned the congregation to see who she recognized. All the usual faces. To her right she saw her Aunt Anne and Uncle Marty and then with a funny little lurch she saw Heather smiling up at Neil Brennan.

So that was all on again, she thought, half dismayed and half annoyed. What on earth did her cousin see in that culchie? Although she had to admit that he had smartened himself up considerably, *and* the grey suit that he wore looked well on him, *and* he'd lost a bit of weight, *and* his hair suited him better cut tight. She saw Heather slip her hand into his for a second or two and saw him smile back down at her and realized immediately that they were lovers. She'd seen couples totally engrossed in each other too often not to know the signs. It looked like her cousin had finally done the deed and she looked exceedingly happy too. Heather had an unmistakable glow about her and Lorna could not suppress the surge of jealousy that ignited like rocket fuel.

Are you mad to be jealous of her, you idiot? Just because she's dating a country bumpkin. Lorna shook her head at her stupidity and once superiority was regained she felt a little better.

At least she's got a man on Christmas Day. The unwelcome thought popped into her head.

A man! Lorna gave a mental snort remembering the unedifying sight of Neil Brennan arse up to the sky when he was bending over the bonnet of a car, the tip of two pasty white cheeks escaping from the top of his jeans. *A man*, she echoed silently. *I think not.*

It was a relief when Mass was finally over and she made her escape quickly, not wishing to talk to her relatives. Once lunch was finished she was going to go back to Dublin. She'd far prefer to spend Christmas on her own in the apartment, watching films on TV and reading, than spend another day in this dead-end hole. She drove home angrily, annoyed at seeing Heather's happiness even if *she* wouldn't touch Neil Brennan with a ten-foot bargepole. She slowed down as she passed the gleaming glass and chrome showrooms, impressed in spite of herself. He had made something of his poky little garage, she grudgingly admitted. Brennan Motors was a classy addition to the main street. She noticed that curtains hung in the upstairs rooms over the office and wondered was that where he was living now. At least he'd have somewhere to entertain Heather. Envy seeped through her at the thought of her cousin enjoying a stress-free sex life.

'You scooted off very quickly,' Jane Morgan chastised later as she walked into the sitting-room where Lorna was curled up on the settee flicking through a magazine. 'You could at least have stayed to wish Anne and Marty a happy Christmas.'

'Oh, give over, Mum, I had a headache,' Lorna said sulkily.

'Two minutes is all it would have taken, for heaven's sake. Go and set the table for me in the dining-room, please. Your father's gone to visit Malachy Sinclair, he's never here when you want him, and that other pair,' she scowled, referring to her sons, Eoin and Aidan, 'have gone to have a drink with the Buckleys. They're far too young to be drinking beer but will they listen, and your father's hopeless with them.' Jane grumbled as she tied an apron around her slender waist and walked into the kitchen followed by Lorna. 'I hope this bloody turkey's OK. Your father can deal with it. I'll take care of the veg and potatoes. I wanted to go away to a hotel but he wouldn't have it.'

She threw a couple of carrots into the sink and began to scrape them. 'You never told me that Heather had moved back to Kilronan,' she remarked as she began slicing the peeled carrots.

'What!'

'She's moved back to Kilronan. She's working for Neil Brennan and living over the offices. Oliver Flynn turned the upstairs into an apartment,

266

according to Anne. You never said. She's been home over two weeks now.'

Lorna was stunned.

'Well . . . I . . .' she blustered.

Jane turned to look at her. 'Didn't you know? What's going on with you pair?'

'Nothing,' Lorna fibbed.

'Are you two having a row? That's why you didn't stay back after Mass? Well honestly! What happened?' her mother demanded crossly.

'I moved out of the flat and she got into a huff,' Lorna said irritably.

'But you told me she was going to live with Ruth!'

'That's why she went to live with Ruth. Honestly, Mum, we're not tied at the hip. I'm not her minder, she wouldn't go anywhere or do anything and I hated living in that flat, so get off my case.' Lorna felt a surge of irritation at having to explain herself.

'I see.' Jane frowned. 'Well, there's no flies on her, she's landed a very eligible bachelor if the way they were looking at each other during Mass was anything to go by. Why don't you go and get a nice ambitious, professional chap for yourself? I thought you would have found an eligible bachelor in Dublin,' Jane remarked.

'Is that right, Mum? Was he a nice ambitious professional who screwed *you* while Dad was at work?'

Where it came from she would never know, but it burst out of her with a pent-up force of anger and bitterness that was stronger than any other emotion she had ever experienced. Her eyes

267

glittered with fury and contempt as she stared at her shocked mother.

The blood had drained from Jane's face. 'I don't know what you're talking about,' she said weakly, her knuckles white as she gripped the handle of the small knife.

'Don't you? *Liar!* I'm talking about the man that was in our house, having sex with you, when I was a child, and you didn't even bother to make sure we were out of the way. I thought you were being attacked. I hid under the stairs because I was terrified. But you didn't care about that, did you? Did *YOU?*' she screamed hysterically and ran out of the kitchen sobbing uncontrollably.

'Sacred Heart!' Jane muttered, horrified. She stood, stunned, her heart racing wildly. How did she deal with this? she wondered helplessly.

Lorna flung herself on to her bed and howled like a baby, her grief and sorrow coming from some place deep inside of her. She couldn't stop crying. Nothing was working out in her life and now that she had confronted her mother with the secret that had held her in bondage for most of her life she didn't know whether she was glad or sorry.

'Lorna?' she heard her mother call her name hesitantly from the doorway.

'Go away!' she wept.

'Lorna, we have to . . . we should talk—'

'I don't want to talk. I just want you to go away.'

Jane started to cry, a harsh choked sobbing that startled Lorna. 'Please don't tell your father, Lorna, that's all I ask,' she pleaded.

'I'm not going to hurt Dad. Don't worry, your

sordid little secret is safe with me.' Lorna managed to compose herself.

'Lorna, please don't be like that. You don't understand.' Jane pressed her hand to her trembling lip.

'No I don't. All I know is that you're my mother and it wasn't right that I saw you and heard you. Do you know what that's done to me? Do you? Do you? It's mucked up my head. That's what. I can't enjoy sex. I think it's dirty and disgusting!' She started to cry again.

'You have sex?' Jane said weakly.

'Oh, get real, Mum,' Lorna sniffled.

'I hope you take . . . precautions,' Jane managed.

'Don't worry, Mother, I'm not going to disgrace the family name.' Her tone dripped sarcasm and Jane blushed.

'Why did you cheat on Dad?' Lorna's curiosity got the better of her. Looking at her mother, shaken out of her usual poise, unsure and apprehensive, Lorna felt a wave of remorse for being such a bitch.

'I'm sorry, Mum, I should never have said what I said. I hadn't planned to say it, it just sort of . . . sort of . . . burst out of me, I don't know why,' she said gruffly.

'Oh Lorna!' Jane came and sat on the edge of the bed. 'What have I done to you? I'm so, *so* sorry.' She hung her head and started to cry again, her thin, angular shoulders shaking.

Lorna swallowed hard. She didn't like seeing her mother in such distress. She was used to a poised, controlled, almost distant woman who flitted in and out of her life between social engagements and lunches with her well-heeled friends.

'Stop crying, Mum. Everyone will be home soon and we don't want them to . . . well . . . well, we don't want them to know anything,' she said awkwardly, giving her mother a tentative pat on the shoulder. Jane wiped her eyes with the back of her hand in a vulnerable gesture that Lorna found strangely endearing.

'Look, we won't mention it again,' she said firmly, feeling more like the parent than the child but rather liking the feeling of being in control.

'I'd like to . . . I think I should give you some sort of explanation.' Jane cleared her throat. Lorna bit her lip, embarrassed. This wasn't the sort of conversation she wanted to be having with her mother.

'You don't have to.'

Jane sighed. 'I think it's the least I owe you. It's not that I didn't have feelings for your father. I'm very fond of him. But I made a mistake when I married him.' Her eyes took on a faraway look. 'I thought it would be so different, I thought he would be ambitious. As ambitious as I was. I didn't think we'd end up staying here.' She managed a twisted little smile. 'I was like you in that regard, I couldn't wait to shake the dust of Kilronan off my feet but it never happened for me. Your dad didn't want to practise in Dublin. He never really wanted to practise law anyway, he wanted to be a vet, of all things.' She met Lorna's eye. 'Could you imagine me as a vet's wife?'

'Not really.' Lorna gave a shaky smile.

'It hasn't been easy, Lorna. Not on me and

certainly not on Gerard. He knows he's failed me, he knows I'm disappointed at the way our life worked out. And when I was younger . . . and more resentful, I did meet someone, exciting, successful, who was interested in me. I'm sorry you saw what you saw.' She ran her fingers through her fine, highlighted hair.

'What happened to him?' Lorna was curious in spite of herself.

Jane shrugged. 'He got bored after a while and moved on to his next conquest. I was just a bit of a diversion for him, looking back.' She couldn't hide the bitterness in her voice and Lorna felt uncharacteristically sympathetic towards her mother. What a sad, lonely, empty life she'd led. Unfulfilled and unhappy. Lorna made a silent vow not to end up like Jane.

'Em . . . Lorna, if what you saw affected you to such a degree, would you . . . I don't know . . . would you consider counselling?' Jane blurted.

'Maybe it will be better now that we've talked,' Lorna murmured. 'Forget it, Mum. I think that's the best thing for both of us.'

'I don't want you to be miserable because of me, listen to me now. I want you to have a *happy* life, Lorna. I want you to have the life that I didn't have, please don't let anything I did ruin it for you.'

'I do have a good life,' Lorna lied.

'Well, have an even better one, then. Don't ever let anything or anyone hold you back,' her mother urged.

'I won't, Mum. I'm sorry if I upset you. I really

didn't mean to. I don't know what came over me. It must have been PMT or something.'

Jane got up and stood in front of her daughter. In a rare display of tenderness she reached down and stroked Lorna's cheek. 'No, dear. I'm the sorry one. You'll never know how sorry I am that I put you through this. I hope you can forgive me.'

'I do, Mum. I do,' Lorna said fiercely as she pressed her mother's hand tighter to her cheek. Mother and daughter had never felt so close as they did at that moment and for Lorna, it was as though a huge burden had been lifted from her. Maybe Christmas wasn't going to be such a disaster after all.

21

Oliver's palms were damp with sweat as he locked hard and reversed into a parking space between two cars. The drive to Dublin had seemed to take an eternity. His heart was like a lead weight and his stomach was tight with anxiety. He had never been so nervous in his life. He switched off the engine and looked around. Three-storey redbrick houses lined the street. Bare branched trees dropped snow on to the bonnet of his car. Buses and lorries trundled past and in the distance he could see the gates leading into the Phoenix Park.

The gleaming gold plaque on the gate opposite him told him he was at the surgery of Doctor Miles Lawson, M.B., B.C.H., B.A.O., D.Obs., M.R.C.G.P. He had scoured the Golden Pages looking for a male doctor handy enough to the M50. The idea of going for a walk in the Phoenix Park after his ordeal appealed to him, so Miles Lawson it was.

His appointment was for ten fifteen. It was five minutes past ten. He'd told Noreen he was going to a business meeting. She knew it was something out of the ordinary because he'd dressed in a suit, but because the atmosphere between them was still extremely frosty, she hadn't pursued it. He sighed deeply. She was still sleeping in one of the spare bedrooms and every time he tried to apologize she said curtly, 'I don't want to talk about it.' So he'd given up. He could be as stubborn as she was.

Christmas had been a miserable affair. He was glad it was over. She'd hardly looked at the gold earrings he'd bought her and when he'd thanked her for the leather jacket she'd bought him she'd ignored him.

He'd never been so glad in his life to see the festive season end and get back to work. Maybe if he went and got this bloody sperm test thing done, she might soften towards him and life could get back to normal. And then he'd never open his big mouth again, he vowed as he got out of the car and reluctantly walked to the door. A tired-looking receptionist took his name. 'Oh yes, you're a new patient. I'll just take your details if you don't mind. Please sit down.' Oliver sat. He could see that there were two other people in the waiting-room. He could be here for another three-quarters of an hour at least, he thought glumly as he gave his date of birth and tried to remember whether he'd had mumps, measles and chickenpox. He could remember the mumps, they'd been bloody painful. He'd got them in his teens and been in agony for a week.

'And have you ever been hospitalized?' the receptionist asked in a bored tone.

'No.' Oliver was tempted to tell her not to bother asking him any more questions. Once he'd got the letter for his test and everything was OK he wouldn't be coming back here again, but he restrained himself, and kept answering the questions.

By the time he finally got in to see the doctor he felt he was going to have a heart attack. He was rigid with anxiety and was perspiring freely. Doctor Lawson was a plump, bespectacled man in a tweed jacket. He smelt of pipe smoke and Oliver felt himself relax a little.

'Mr Flynn.' He glanced at the file in front of him. 'Oliver, take a seat there.' He reached over his desk and shook hands. His hands were stubby, but his grip was firm.

'So, Oliver. What can I do for you?' He leaned back in his worn leather chair and peered over his bifocals at Oliver.

Oliver cleared his throat. 'Well, ahh . . . that is . . . er . . .' Oliver wanted the floor to open up and swallow him. 'Well, my wife wants me to have a test,' he gulped. 'We've been trying for a baby, and nothing's happening,' he added lamely.

'I see,' Doctor Lawson said calmly. 'And how long have you been trying?'

'Well over a year,' Oliver said miserably. 'I didn't want to go to the doctor at home, my wife's a nurse, she works for him. I didn't want him to . . . I just preferred to go to someone out of town.' He felt the need to explain.

'That's fine, Oliver,' Doctor Lawson said kindly. 'I quite understand. I just need to ask you a few questions. Let's see if we can get this matter sorted. It's a good idea for the man to get tested and evaluated first. Much less invasive than what a woman has to undergo. It's a very simple procedure: you can go and get it over and done with today if you want. I'll give you a letter for the Rotunda Hospital for a semen analysis. You just go to the laboratory reception desk. They will give you a container, you go into the loo and give a sample. If you lived nearby you could do it at home, but unfortunately they need the sample within two hours. It's quite straightforward though.'

Oliver felt his tension rise again. He hadn't expected this. He thought he'd be waiting a week or so to get an appointment, thought he'd have time to prepare himself for the next ordeal. Still, maybe it was better to get it all over and done with. He wouldn't be going for any walk in the Phoenix Park, he thought ruefully as he paid his bill.

An hour later he was standing in a tiled hospital toilet cubicle with a sterile container in his hand, his trousers and underpants down around his ankles. He'd never been so mortified in his life, going up to the girl in the lab reception area with his letter of referral. Even now his face was hot with embarrassment. He was sure everyone outside knew what he was doing, or trying to do. He scowled and looked down at himself. Dead as a dodo and not a sign of life. He felt himself break out in a cold sweat. Why in the name of God was he standing here? He felt a huge surge of resentment towards Noreen. No point in thinking of her, she wouldn't do it for him the way he was feeling at the moment. He better do something, he couldn't stand here all day. The sooner it was over and done with the better and that was it. He'd done his bit, Noreen would have to put up with the consequences. He closed his eyes and thought of flame-haired Kate, took a deep breath, and got down to the business of providing a sample that would tell whether he'd been shooting blanks or not.

Noreen removed the protective cover from around Mrs Delahunty's neck and handed her a sheaf of tissue to wipe around her ears.

'I thought I was going deaf, couldn't hear my mobile. Thank God it was only wax,' she twittered as she took out her compact and dusted down her heavily rouged cheeks. 'Thanks for syringing me, Nurse Flynn. Send me the bill please, I don't have any cash on me at the moment.'

Mean old bat, Noreen thought grumpily as she watched her patient totter out of the door on impossibly high heeled boots. Her boxy fur jacket, which had seen better days, and the skirt that showed far too much of her bony, skinny shanks were totally inappropriate for the wintry weather. Mrs D, as she was known in the town, was notoriously tight-fisted and renowned for not paying her bills promptly.

Noreen glanced out the window. The garden was covered in a fresh mantle of snow. Hedgerows and branches iced with a powdery coating. It was quiet out in the surgery, only the diehards like Mrs D and a few flu sufferers braving the weather. It was good to be back at work and in a routine again, she reflected as she tidied up and sterilized her instruments. Better than sitting wallowing in despair at home. She couldn't get Oliver's words out of her head. Why had he said them to her? Didn't he know how much they would hurt her? Had he *wanted* to hurt her? Over and over she tormented herself with questions to which she had no answer. Maybe it was his way of getting back at her for all the pressure she was putting on him about having a baby. But he didn't understand. He didn't know what need and want drove her. No one knew, it was her burden and she carried it alone.

He'd been all dressed up this morning in his good suit. He'd muttered something about going to a meeting but she wouldn't give him the satisfaction of asking who it was with, although she was curious. Oliver didn't often dress up in his good gear, which was a pity. He looked extremely well in his suit. His lean frame carried it well. The leather jacket she'd bought him looked great too, although she hadn't told him that. He'd worn it on Stephen's Day when they'd taken Cora to visit her sister and she'd felt he was trying to make amends. She knew she'd hurt him by hardly looking at the earrings he'd bought her. But she'd wanted to hurt him. Her eyes darkened. She wanted to hurt him as much as he had hurt her.

Those four caustic words, 'Because you asked me', were gouged into her heart and as long as she lived she didn't think that she was ever going to be able to put them out of her mind. She was as lonely as hell sleeping in the back bedroom, but it was better than lying stiff and tense beside him, the air frosted with the resentment that was always between them these days. If Cora knew their present situation she'd be delighted. She'd had the knives out for Noreen from the first time Oliver had brought her home. If their marriage broke up, there'd be no happier woman in the universe.

'Don't think like that,' she muttered. It was unthinkable. She and Oliver would weather the storm, eventually. She just wasn't ready to forgive, let alone forget, yet.

Oliver sat in a smoke-filled restaurant close to the hospital wolfing down a fry-up. He took a drink of hot, sweet tea and for the first time that day started to relax. He'd done it. Got the doctor's letter of referral, presented himself at the hospital and performed as required. He hoped he never had to go through a day like it again. It had been the most embarrassing day of his life. He took another gulp of tea, which tasted like nectar.

He was glad he hadn't gone to Douglas Kennedy. Not that he had anything against the man. He was a good enough doctor and had dealt with Oliver competently on the rare occasions he needed him but it would have just been too mortifying to have to answer the kind of intimate personal questions Miles Lawson had asked him. Imagine meeting him in a social situation afterwards! Noreen would probably have a fit when she found out that he'd gone to a stranger but let her, at least he'd gone and had the bloody test done for her.

Doctor Lawson had thoughtfully provided some

information for him to read. He'd drive home and park somewhere near the lake and have a glance at it maybe, although part of him wanted to ignore the whole thing. He finished his meal, paid his bill, tipped the waitress and trudged through the slushy snow over to the ILAC car park. The January sales were on, the ILAC Centre was jammers and he weaved his way through the throngs, impatiently. How anyone could voluntarily want to live in a city was beyond him. He couldn't wait to get out of the place. Noreen would talk about London longingly, sometimes. She seemed to have liked it when she was working there. Sometimes, Oliver felt she really missed her old life.

There was a queue at all of the lifts. Oliver didn't even give them a second glance. He loped up the five flights of stairs easily, located his car and heaved a sigh of relief as he finally reached the exit, drove past the hospital, which he dearly hoped he'd never have to set foot in again, and headed for home. It had started to snow again and by the time he got to Navan there was a full-scale blizzard.

It was a relief to drive into Kilronan as drifts of snow piled up on the wipers and he gave up on the idea of going to the lake. Noreen was still at the surgery and he felt relief that he didn't have to try to make strained conversation and be rebuffed. He raced upstairs and got out of his suit and shirt as fast as he could. Ten minutes later he had put a match to the fire and was sipping a cold, refreshing Bud, the stresses and strains of the day easing away from him as he lounged in his armchair, flicking through the information Doctor Lawson had given him.

It was a bit of an eye-opener, he had to admit, as he read that in 60 per cent of couples experiencing infertility a male factor was involved, primarily male in 40 per cent of those couples and in an additional 20 per cent a combination of male and female factors. They weren't great odds, he thought with a start. Oliver frowned, concentrating as he read on about something called varicoceles, which made him wince as he read the treatment. Manfully, he kept on reading about abnormalities in the seminal fluid, problems with the ductal system, obstructions of the epididymis, immunolegic infertility, testicular failure . . . it went on and on and the more he read the more worried he got. He drained his can of beer and went out to the kitchen for another. After reading that lot he didn't care if he never had sex again, he thought dolefully as he plonked back down in the chair and switched on the TV. The warmth of the fire, the stress of the trip to Dublin which had kept him awake half the night with worry, and the calming effect of the beer soon had him snoozing and before long his chest rose and fell rhythmically as Oliver slept and dreamed of horrible things happening to his bits and pieces.

Noreen drove home at a snail's pace as the snow swirled dizzily, making it almost impossible to see. She wondered where Oliver was. She was worried about him. The roads were treacherous, dusk was falling and she hadn't even asked him where he was going. He could be stuck anywhere. She inched along until she came to the turn off the main road that led towards the lake and their house. She could see the house in darkness through the gloom, but then, rounding the bend, saw that his car was in the drive. He could at least have put a light on, she thought crossly, annoyed that she had wasted time worrying about him. She parked and hurried into the house, the snow almost blinding her, and saw the flames of the fire flickering in the darkened sitting-room. She could see Oliver stretched out in his chair as she divested herself of her coat and scarf before going into the kitchen. When she saw that the table hadn't even been set for the dinner, she grew angry. The least he could do was set the bloody table, she fumed as she snapped on the light and began clattering knives and forks on the table. She turned the heat on under the hotpot she'd made earlier and buttered some chunky slices of Vienna roll to serve with it.

When it was ready, she marched into the sitting-room to call Oliver. He was snoring his head off now, which added insult to injury, and she was just about to give him a rough shake of the shoulder when she caught sight of something he'd been reading that had slipped down on to the floor. Curiosity got the better of her and she picked up the leaflet and slipped out into the kitchen to have a look.

'Oh, Oliver,' she whispered as she read the material her husband had been reading. Here she was thinking that he didn't care and he'd gone to the trouble of getting information on male infertility. And gloomy reading some of it made too, she thought forlornly as she scanned the contents. She sighed as she replaced the pages beside him and gave him a little shake.

'Oliver, Oliver, your dinner's ready.'

'Wha . . . what!' He jerked awake as she switched on a side lamp, his eyes heavy and slumberous.

'Dinner's ready.'

'I'm sorry, I meant to set the table.' He rubbed his hand wearily over his face and yawned.

'What's this?' she asked lightly, bending down to take the pages off the floor.

'Never you mind,' Oliver said hotly, snatching it from her, a deep red flush creeping up his face and neck.

'Don't be so bloody rude,' Noreen exclaimed, stung that he wouldn't share the fact that he'd been reading up about male infertility.

'Oh, don't start,' he snapped uncoiling himself from the chair. 'If you want to know I went and had that semen test today. So now are you happy?'

'Why didn't you tell me? Who gave you the letter of referral?' she demanded, going straight into hostile mode at his surly behaviour.

'What does it matter? It's done now. I did what you asked me to do, Noreen, so now can we forget it until the results come and let's go and eat our dinner.'

'I'm not hungry,' she muttered, walking out of the room and up to her bedroom, despairing of the gulf that seemed to deepen daily between them. He'd gone and had the test, had gone through that ordeal on his own and never told her so she could have been with him to support him. She knew how shy he was. It must have been torture for him to talk to strangers about such a private matter, let alone go to a hospital and give a sample. He would have been cringing. She knew in her heart and soul how difficult it would have been for him. And yet he preferred to go through it on his own without her. That said it all about the dismal state of their marriage. She slipped to her knees beside the bed and bowed her head. 'God, please,' she beseeched, 'let everything be all right with Oliver, please don't let it be his fault that we can't have a baby. I'm sorry, Lord, I should never have put him through that. Please, please don't let it be Oliver's fault.'

22

'Did you have a good christmas?' Carina enquired as she dumped her travel bag on the floor and flung herself into an armchair.

'It was OK. I came back to Dublin on Stephen's Day. I was going to come back after lunch on Christmas Day but I got a bit smashed and couldn't drive. It was *so boring* at home. It did my head in,' Lorna admitted.

'Really? I'd a great time. I wasn't in bed before five any morning. I really need to detox.' She arched an eyebrow in Lorna's direction. 'Any drink in the place?'

Lorna grinned and held up a glass. 'Cider, there's some left in the fridge, help yourself.'

'Ta, I will. I'll detox tomorrow,' Carina assured herself. 'What was work like today?'

'The pits. Half staff. Guests complaining because their rooms weren't ready on time. I hate this time of the year.' Lorna made a face. 'And there's a staff meeting tomorrow. Something's going on. Freddie Murphy looked really worried today.'

'He's the manager. It's his job to look worried,' Carina drawled.

'Something's up,' Lorna reiterated. 'You'll see.'

'You were right,' Carina whispered the following morning as the manager made the shock announcement that the hotel was being taken over and would close for at least three months for renovations, after which staff would be notified if they were to be re-employed by the new company. They were being given two weeks' notice as of today.

Lorna listened to the speech and felt totally irritated at being out of control. It bugged her that unknowns had the power to make decisions that affected her life. She couldn't say that she was desperately upset at leaving the hotel. She'd been feeling bored lately and since her disastrous relationship with Bryan she'd felt the urge to start afresh somewhere else. She wouldn't mind living somewhere nearer town, around the IFSC or the new docklands developments, she thought dreamily.

'Well, bugger this,' Carina scowled. 'I've had enough. I'm going to New York. A friend of mine is out there and she's making a fortune waitressing—'

'Waitressing!' Lorna turned up her nose.

'Don't be a snob, Lorna. Who cares when the money is great? Are you coming?'

'But don't you need visas and all of that stuff?' Lorna felt a flicker of excitement. New York! City of dreams. What could be more exotic than living in New York? Fifth Avenue, Tiffany's, Gucci, Armani, Saks! So her. She was sure of it. *And* she'd have someone to go with, she wouldn't own. She didn't think she'd ever have the nerve to go to New York solo.

'You can stay for three months on a tourist visa. I'd stay there longer if I could but Fiona, my friend, said that after 9/11 they've got really strict on illegals. A friend of hers came home and couldn't get back in. But just think, we might meet two millionaires and marry them.' Carina grinned. 'Park Avenue, here we come.'

'I'd love to live near Central Park—'

'Get real, Lorna, we won't be living in Manhattan, we'll be commuting,' interjected Carina drily. 'Unless you're in a rent-controlled apartment, and they're like gold dust, renting in Manhattan isn't for the likes of us.'

'Maybe we could live in Greenwich Village or TriBeCa or somewhere like that. It doesn't have to be the Upper West Side,' Lorna suggested.

'Lorna, you can go and pay a fortune on rent and come home penniless if you want to. I want to make a load of dosh and have a good time. Yonkers will do you fine. It's one of the suburbs. Are you coming or what?'

'I'm coming, I'm coming.' Lorna felt scared and excited at the same time. Maybe she might meet a Wall Street trader who'd fall madly in love with her; maybe this was where she was meant to be all along.

'Right, I'm going to email Fiona and then you go check out flights,' Carina ordered.

'I don't have a lot of ready cash,' Lorna said doubtfully.

'Sell your car. I'm going to sell mine,' Carina

retorted. 'Your mam and dad will give you some-thing, I'm sure. Say it's a loan. They never expect you to pay it back. My dad's always helping me out.'

'Good thinking,' Lorna agreed. She'd sell the car for sure. When she got back from New York she'd have enough for a nice jazzy, sporty soft-top at least. She'd probably have a deposit for a place of her own too, she thought happily as she surfed the net to get flight details.

Two weeks later she was jobless, and homeless. She and Carina had had to leave the apartment. Both of them were staying at their respective family homes for the next two weeks. They were flying to New York in the first week in February. Lorna was dizzy with excitement. 'See you in a fortnight,' she waved gaily as she loaded her belongings into the boot of her car. She looked up at the apartment. She'd miss it. She'd liked living in it. One day she'd own one a thousand times as posh, she assured herself. Every time she watched *Sex and the City*, or any programme with clips of New York, she felt she couldn't wait to get there. As she drove out of the Marina and headed for home she felt as if her life was truly beginning. Living in Dublin was chickenfeed compared to what it was going to be like in New York. Let Heather moulder away in Kilronan with her hick boyfriend. They'd never amount to anything. Not like her. This was her big chance. Dublin hadn't worked out for her. But New York would be a hell of a lot different. Lorna was going to make it big in the Big Apple.

23

Heather hummed to herself as she sorted a batch of new VRFs. Neil had had a delivery of six brand new cars and she was completing the paperwork on them. The sun was streaming into her office and she was as happy as Larry.

She could see Neil out on the forecourt inspecting his new babies. She smiled. He was ambitious for his garage. It was great to see, and he couldn't thank her enough for sorting out the business side of things. He'd badly needed sorting though, the place had been in chaos. He hadn't even got a proper filing system set up. It must have been hard going trying to do everything. She was constantly on the go, answering phones, dealing with customers, arranging services, paying bills and wages and doing the dreaded VAT, but she'd never been as happy in her life, she thought happily, remembering their lovemaking of the night before.

In the space of a month her life had turned around completely. She was back home in the place that she loved. She was in a job that she enjoyed and that challenged her. She was practically her own boss. Neil was more or less living with her, spending less and less time at his dad's place. It was like a miracle. Everything had fallen into her lap without any effort on her part . God had looked most kindly on her, she thought, gratefully offering up a little prayer of thanks.

'Aren't they beauties?' Neil barrelled through the door, eyes bright with satisfaction. 'This is what it's all about, Heather. I want you to send out the brochures to all our customers. I was thinking we could officially open Brennan Motors with a launch party. Invite local businessmen—'

'And women,' interjected Heather. 'Half your customers are women, you should target them.'

'Good thinking,' agreed Neil. 'What do you think? It would be a good excuse for a hooley, and I could do a special offer on the night for trade-ins.'

'I think it's a great idea. Who could we get to do the opening?' Heather enthused.

'I could ask Fintan Cullen—'

'No. Not a politician, Neil. I really don't think that's a good idea because it might put people off, thinking you were associated with a political party. How about Lorcan Kelly from the Chamber of Commerce? He might have some good contacts for you.'

'Good thinking again,' Neil agreed. 'Look, Oliver Flynn's just pulled into the pumps. It's time he changed his car, I'm going to work on him. I'll leave you to organize the launch,' he declared airily and then he was gone, leaving Heather a tad taken aback. He'd come up with the idea of the launch and she was the one left organizing it. Typical, but her adrenalin was flowing and she sat down at her desk and began to make out a list of calls she'd have to make. Lorcan Kelly being the first. She should ring around a few caterers to get quotes, and then she should organize invitations. And she had the brochures to send out. She'd get some invites printed up as fast as she could and include them with the brochures. Existing customers had to be looked after and made a fuss of.

The day flew by. January was Neil's busiest month with new car sales and by the time she closed her office and went upstairs to cook dinner for them she was tired. Neil always kept the showrooms open until eight, but came up to the flat long enough to have dinner.

She chopped some onions and garlic and sautéed them in the pan before adding thinly sliced pieces of chicken. She let them sizzle away before adding a carton of cream and turned the heat down low. Thirty minutes later, Neil was sitting down to creamed potatoes, carrots and sweetcorn and tender chicken in a creamy sauce. He shovelled it into him. 'This is scrumptious,' he said, between mouthfuls. 'Why don't we invite Lorcan Kelly and his wife to dinner some night? He'd be someone to be well in with. It was a good idea to get him to do the opening. It shows the town we mean business.'

Heather made a face. 'You want me to cook? Couldn't we go to a restaurant?'

'Lorcan's wife's a bit odd. She doesn't like eating out. So he has to entertain on his own a lot. But she might like a home-cooked meal. It would be worth making the effort to stay on side with Lorcan.

You're a great cook,' Neil assured her. 'This is very tasty.'

'That's only because you lived on chops and peas,' Heather laughed. 'I'm a very plain cook, Neil, I don't know any fancy dishes.'

'Do this. It's lovely,' he said. 'We'll wait until he's done the opening and invite them.'

'We'll see,' she demurred, hoping he'd forget the notion. Hosting dinner parties for strangers was not something she'd bargained on. Neil looked out the window when he heard a car draw up on to the forecourt. 'Better go, I'll have dessert later. Bring me a cup of coffee, would you?' He jumped up, gave her a kiss on the cheek and left her to finish her meal alone with a sink full of dirty saucepans and dishes awaiting her attention. She finished her meal, did the washing up and made a pot of coffee which she brought downstairs.

'That was a bloke looking for a second-hand Polo, I told him I'd look out for one for him. I'll make a few calls tomorrow and see what's on offer. The banger he's trading in isn't worth a damn, but it would be a new customer on file for us. The next time he's buying he'll be trading up, once I've finished with him.' Neil grinned at her. 'Give us a kiss, Heather,' he said, grabbing her.

Heather giggled. 'Stop, people will be able to see.'

'So what?' Neil kissed her soundly until she was breathless. 'The coffee will be cold,' she chided, pushing him away, aware that they could be seen from the road by all the passing traffic and anyone who was walking past. She poured their coffee and perched on the side of his desk, sipping the welcome brew. She always enjoyed drinking her coffee with him, talking about the day's events and making their plans. Then when the showrooms were closed they'd stroll up to the Haven and have a couple of drinks before racing home to fall on each other in bed. Sex was a joy to her. The novelty of being able to have it whenever she wanted, in the privacy of her own place without worrying about flatmates or parents, was exhilarating.

She'd invited her parents to dinner soon after she'd moved in. They weren't stupid and Heather was sure they'd realized that Neil was more than her boss, but they'd made no comment at any time other than to say how glad they were that she was back home in Kilronan, happy with her life. They'd never been the kind of parents that gave her hassle, she thought gratefully, knowing of the ordeals of some of her friends who still lived at home and could only have furtive, hurried sex when the occasion arose. Heather had landed on her feet, was the general consensus and she happily agreed with them.

She was engrossed at her computer a couple of weeks later when a familiar red car scorched on to the forecourt. She saw Lorna slide elegantly out of the front seat and sashay over to one of the mechanics, who pointed her in the direction of Heather's office.

'Shit,' she muttered, diving under her desk to look for her bag. She slipped into the back office, closed the door and redid her lipstick. She was wearing black trousers and a lilac chenille jumper which looked presentable enough, but nothing as glamorous as the suede skirt and jacket that her cousin was wearing. What the hell did she want anyway, she wondered as she heard Lorna call sweetly, 'Anybody in?' Heather took a deep breath, composed her features and opened the door.

'Can I help . . . oh, hello, Lorna,' she said coolly, pretending she hadn't seen her cousin arrive.

'What are you doing here?' Lorna chirruped as though nothing had happened between them.

'I work here,' Heather replied, sitting down behind the desk.

'Lucky old you,' Lorna drawled and Heather wanted to slap her.

'Can I help you?' Heather raised her eyebrows.

'Well, it was Neil I wanted to see, actually,' Lorna said slowly. 'Is he here or when will he be back?'

'He's at a meeting, but he'll be here after four I should imagine. Can I take a message?'

'Not at all, I'll call back later. See you.' She turned her back dismissively on Heather and swung out the door.

Heather glared at her cousin's retreating back. What on earth did she want with Neil? She was hardly going to buy a car from him. She had never had a good word to say about him when he and Heather had been dating before. Maybe she was just being nosy. Aunt Jane must have told her that Heather was working for Neil. It certainly wasn't like her cousin to come home to Kilronan for a weekend. She wondered if Lorna would call back.

'Take no notice of her,' Neil ordered when she

told him of her cousin's visit. 'I'll deal with her if she comes back.'

Heather was upstairs cooking the dinner at six thirty when her mobile rang. It was Lorna. 'Hi, Heather, I was just wondering was Neil back.'

'I'm not at work,' Heather said shortly.

'Oh don't be silly, Mum told me you're living over the garage, just tell me if he's there or not,' Lorna commanded.

Just who did she think she was? Heather thought furiously. 'Hold on a minute,' she snapped. She knew full well that Neil was downstairs waiting for her to call him for his dinner. She dawdled downstairs. Let it cost Lorna for the phone call, she thought nastily. 'Lorna's on the phone, she wants to know if you're here,' she told her boyfriend. He grimaced.

'Better get it over and done with, tell her I'll be here for the next fifteen minutes.'

'Yes sir,' Heather grinned. 'I'm dying to see what she wants.'

'A good kick in the ass,' scowled Neil. Heather laughed and ran upstairs light-heartedly. Lorna could get lost, she wasn't going to get into a bad humour over her.

'He'll be here for fifteen minutes,' she said airily into her mobile. ''Bye, 'bye.'

Twenty minutes later, Lorna drove up in her Honda Civic. Heather peeped through the curtains. She'd kept the light off in her sitting-room so she wouldn't be seen. Her cousin was still dressed in her suede outfit, but this time she was wearing a pair of high-heeled suede boots. Heather sighed enviously. Her cousin looked the height of fashion. She looked like a model. In the bright lights that illuminated the forecourt she could see that Lorna was made up to the nines. She saw Neil walk out to greet her. He didn't shake hands as he usually did, she noted with satisfaction. She saw them converse for a while and then Neil walked around the car and had a look at it. He opened the driver's door and peered inside. She must be selling, Heather surmised from her darkened vantage point. Why had she come to Neil? Probably thought that she'd do well out of him because she was Heather's cousin. Typical!

She saw Lorna throw back her head and laugh and then touch Neil on the arm. Heather's jaw dropped. What was that witch up to? Trying to flirt with him to get a good price? What a hypocritical cow. She felt like going down to the forecourt and kicking the shins off her.

She saw Neil shake his head and saw her cousin put her head to one side flirtatiously. Heather gritted her teeth. He'd better not start flirting back, she thought furiously. Surely he could see through her. They strolled into the showrooms out of view and Heather went back into the kitchen in a temper. She banged pots and pans around. He'd better not be late for his dinner. She could ring down and tell him it was nearly ready. She rooted in her bag for her mobile, and couldn't find it. That bloody phone drove her mad, she could never lay her hands on it when she needed it. She rummaged around the sofa and found it between the cushions. She keyed through the directory until she came to the garage number. She pressed call and heard it start to ring. Hastily she pressed cancel. It would look childish, she thought ruefully, and Neil might not appreciate her behaving like a possessive 'wife' in front of Lorna. She swallowed her resentment and went back to her cooking.

Today he was having fried plaice, mushrooms, peas and chips. The chips were sizzling away in the oil – if he didn't hurry up they'd be cremated. Ten minutes later Neil bounded up the stairs. 'That smells good.' He inhaled appreciatively.

'What did she want?' Heather couldn't contain her curiosity or her irritation. Did he not realize that she'd be dying to know? Men were hopeless.

Neil loosened his tie and sat down at the table. 'She's selling the car. She's going to New York.'

'New York! It'll suit her down to the ground. Did you do a deal?'

'She's a gas artist, even though I don't like her I have to admire her style. Do you know what she asked me?'

'What?'

'She wanted me to give her the cash for the car but to let her hold on to it for another two weeks until she goes. She didn't want to be stuck in Kilronan without a set of wheels, as she said herself.'

'The cheek of her!' Heather exploded. 'Did she think you came down in the last shower? I hope you told her where to get off.' She placed Neil's dinner in front of him.

Neil shrugged. 'I told her I'd give her a cheque at the end of next week—'

'And?' Heather stared at her boyfriend. 'Don't tell me you're letting her keep the car. What happens if she crashes it?'

'Didn't think of that,' Neil admitted sheepishly.

'But why?' Heather demanded. 'You don't even like her. She's often been very rude to you.' Privately she felt her boyfriend could have shown *her* a bit more loyalty. He knew all about Lorna doing the hot potato act on her.

'Look, she's a potential client, you don't let personal feelings interfere in business,' Neil explained patiently. 'She's talking about buying a soft-top when she comes back—'

'And you believe her? She saw you coming, Neil,' Heather scoffed.

'Don't be like that, Heather,' Neil reproached. 'Have you no faith in my business acumen?'

'I just know her, that's all,' Heather said sulkily.

'We'll see, Heather, we'll see,' Neil retorted.

Indeed we will, thought Heather but she remained resolutely silent.

24

'Are you sure that you're not going to New York because of . . . er . . . after our talk at Christmas?' Jane enquired delicately.

'No, Mum. Will you forget about that?' Lorna was embarrassed.

'It plays on my mind,' Jane said quietly.

'Well, don't let it. I'm going to New York because I have the chance to go and I'm really looking forward to it,' Lorna declared firmly.

'I envy you.' Her mother smiled at her. 'I would love to have gone to New York when I was young.'

'For God's sake, Mum, you talk as if you were Methuselah. Come over when I'm there, why don't you?'

'Will I?' Jane said eagerly.

'Yeah, give me a month or so to settle in and get to know the place. You'd love it, Mum, I know you would. You could buy a whole new wardrobe.' Lorna's eyes sparkled at the thought. 'The only thing, you'd probably have to stay in a hotel. Carina says we're going to live in Yonkers or some place. She has a friend looking for a place for us. Do you think Dad will come?'

Jane chewed her lip. 'I think if I'm going to go I might go on my own. He wouldn't be into shopping and the like. I think I'd like to do my own thing just once in my life.'

'I think you're right, Mum. There's nothing worse than going shopping with someone who doesn't want to be there. And what else would you go to New York for except to shop?'

'Well, I wouldn't mind going to see some of the museums. I was reading about an exhibition they had of Jackie Kennedy's clothes when she was in the White House, I'd *love* to have seen that,' Jane said wistfully.

'Oh, one of the girls at work saw it, she said Jackie was tiny. She saw the pillbox hats and everything. It was quite moving, she said. We could go and see her apartment on Fifth Avenue.' Lorna felt another wave of excitement hit her. She couldn't believe she was going to New York.

'I'd love to go on the Staten Island ferry too,' Jane said animatedly. 'Oh, Lorna, I'm starting to look forward to this.' They smiled at each other. 'Are you sure you want me to come and visit?'

'Of course I'm sure, Mum. Let's go and look up some hotels on the Internet.'

'Maddie Costello always stays at the Waldorf Astoria, she says it's the best hotel in New York,' Jane remarked as they went into the den and switched on the computer.

'She would say that,' Lorna said drily. 'Maddie Costello loves boasting. Just because her husband's a pilot and she gets free flights. Lisa, the girl I used to share with, was telling me about this hotel just minutes away from Tiffany's, Saks, Bergdorf Goodman and Central Park called Le Parker Meridian. It's got a rooftop pool – bet the Astoria doesn't have that – it's nearer to the posh end of Fifth Avenue, and it has a restaurant called Norma's which is one of *the* hot spots for brunch in New York. I think you should have a look at it.'

'I'll look at anything,' Jane said happily over her daughter's shoulder.

They spent two gloriously satisfying hours surfing New York's finest hotels and had to agree that Le Parker Meridian sounded and looked just peachy. They drooled over the brunch menu.

'I'll visit it, see if it's all it's made out to be, and if it is, you can book there and then, right?' Lorna said.

'Right,' Jane agreed. 'I hope Gerard won't mind.'

'I don't think Dad will, Mum. I think he'd like you to go on a holiday. I'll say it to him tonight if you want.'

'Well, you could just mention it.' Jane switched off the computer and gave her daughter an unexpected peck on the cheek before going out to check on dinner.

Lorna felt strangely happy. Her outburst at Christmas seemed to have been the best thing that could have happened between herself and her mother. They were drawing quite close . . . for them. That peck on the cheek was a sign of it. Jane was rarely affectionate. It was nice to see an animated sparkle in her mother's eye rather than that look of distant resignation that she often wore.

It would be a pleasure to go shopping with her mother. Jane had a great sense of style and loved buying clothes, the one interest they had always shared. Looking at the hotels on the Internet made it all so real. Soon Lorna was going to be there. And Le Parker Meridian and Norma's, Saks and Tiffany's were all going to be very real to her. Lorna did a little twirl of delight, only to stop short when her sixteen-year-old brother Eoin stuck his head in the door and jeered, 'Who do you think you are, Britney Spears?'

'Get lost,' she snapped. There was no love lost between her and her youngest brother – he was the bane of her life and always had been.

'Get lost yourself, Brit,' Eoin reciprocated cheerfully and went off to see if dinner was ready. Lorna scowled. She wouldn't miss him.

Later, after dinner, when her father had retired to his study to read up on a case he was working on, she slipped in and sat on the arm of his chair.

'Hi, Dad, how's it going?'

Gerard looked out over the top of his glasses at her and smiled.

'Not bad, love. It's nice to have you home. Are you sure about going to New York?'

'Oh yes, Dad,' Lorna said enthusiastically. 'I wish I had a bit more money of course. It happened so unexpectedly I didn't have time to save, but I'm so looking forward to it and it's only for a few months anyway.'

'Three, or you'll be an illegal,' her father pointed out.

'Oh Dad, I might stay a bit longer, we'll see.'

'Just be careful. And I'll give you a few bob when you're going.' He patted her knee.

Lorna gave him a little hug. He looked tired, she noted guiltily. She never made much fuss of her father, just took him for granted. She knew when she said about not having enough money that he'd subsidize her, he always did. He always took extremely good care of his family and got very little in return.

She cleared her throat. 'Er . . . Dad . . . I was just wondering if you'd mind if Mum came out for a few days when I'd settled in? I know she'd adore the shopping, but I don't think it would be you somehow or another.'

Gerard laughed. 'Dead right it wouldn't be me. I'd love for your mother to go. And you think she would?' He looked at her in surprise.

'I think so,' Lorna said noncommittally. 'I just don't think she'd feel good about you not coming. I don't think she'd feel it was fair.'

'I'll sort that out, don't worry.' Gerard smiled, visions of a week's fishing beginning to take shape.

'Great.' She kissed the top of his bald head. 'I won't disturb you from your work.'

'You're never a disturbance,' her father told her fondly. 'Maybe before you go you should sort things out with Heather. It would be a shame for you to go off if you're having a bit of a tiff,' he added, out of the blue. Lorna was surprised – she hadn't realized that Gerard knew anything about her estrangement from her cousin.

'Well, I was talking to her today and I tried

to be friends but she was very snooty,' she said defensively.

'Persevere.' Her father smiled.

'OK,' she agreed, thinking privately that if Heather wanted to stay snooty she could. It was no skin off Lorna's nose. She went out to the kitchen and made herself a cup of hot chocolate. Heather had been extremely cool today and she certainly wasn't going to get down on bended knees and beg her cousin to talk to her. She really thought she was someone now just because she had a fella, she thought crossly. She was dead cute though. Neil Brennan was going to be rolling in it eventually. That garage was no Mickey Mouse affair and Neil had told her he was going to expand. Lorna believed him. She recognized ambition when she saw it and he was ambitious.

He'd laughed at her when she'd told him she wanted to keep the car for two weeks, but he'd played it well, she thought, faintly admiring. He wouldn't give her the cheque for a week but he'd agreed that she could hold on to the car until she left. She'd half expected him to turn her down outright. She had given him a hard time in the past but he hadn't held it against her when they were doing business. He might be a country bumpkin, but he was an ambitious country bumpkin, she acknowledged, and Heather had made a smart move coming back to Kilronan.

She paced around the kitchen. She was bored. If she and Heather had been talking she could have gone and had a drink with her. Maybe she'd go up to the gym in the Lake View and do a work out early in the morning. She needed to be absolutely toned and fit for life in New York so that she could stride down Fifth Avenue in her designer gear with the best of them.

She was doing a swift jog on the treadmill at nine a.m. the following morning when Heather and Neil sauntered in. Damn, she cursed silently, holding her tummy in tighter. Heather was not a bit pleased to see her, she could tell by her expression, but Neil gave a friendly wave and called 'Hi.'

She waved back and kept on jogging. Fancy seeing them here. Heather could do with a few sessions in the gym, she thought cattily. Neil seemed to have toned up a lot since she'd first known him.

They stepped on their treadmills and began to walk briskly. Not able to jog, Lorna thought smugly as she increased her pace. Ten minutes later she lay on a bench and began to lift light weights. She could see through lowered lashes that Neil was looking at her and she stretched and lifted, making sure to stick her boobs out and tuck her tummy in. *Eat your heart out, babe, all you'll ever get is lumpy, dumpy Heather.*

They left before she did, and she felt a little flat. They seemed happy together, joking and laughing. What was she going to do for the rest of the day? Nothing. The great metropolis of Kilronan had nothing to offer her. On an impulse she decided to go for a swim and a sauna. She had her bikini in her sports bag. She did a quick change, took a shower before going into the pool and walked through the swing doors. She slid gracefully into the pool and

305

began to swim a length. It was nice to feel her limbs relax in the warm water after her workout and she turned on her back and lazily floated along.

'Hello again.' Neil Brennan surfaced beside her. She got such a shock she swallowed some water and came up spluttering.

'Whew.' She wiped the water from her eyes, wishing she wasn't wearing a totally silly bathing hat.

'Where's Heather?' she asked.

'Over there.' He pointed to the other side of the pool.

'She's not too friendly,' Lorna said in her 'poor little me' voice. 'Do you think if I swam over and asked her to go for a drink she would?'

'I have no idea.' Neil laughed. 'Good luck!' He swam away from her, much to her chagrin. How dare he turn away from her in the middle of a conversation. A proper country bumpkin. She eyed her cousin. Heather was scowling at her. For two figs she wouldn't bother, but if she didn't make it up with Heather she was stuck here for the best part of two weeks with no one to go out with. She took a deep breath and crawled lazily across the pool to where her cousin was doing some exercises.

'Hi, Heather.' She pretended everything was perfectly normal between them.

'What do you want?' Heather said bluntly.

'Please don't be like that,' Lorna wheedled. She was quite astonished that Heather was holding the row for so long. It really was so unlike her.

'Why not?' Heather said coldly, doing the bicycle underwater.

'Look, I'm sorry. I didn't behave very well. I admit it. Can't you let bygones be bygones? I'm not going to be here for very long. I'm going to New York in two weeks. I was made redundant,' she threw that in for the sympathy vote. 'Please, Heather, stop being so cold.'

'Well, it wasn't nice what you did, Lorna.'

'But look, you didn't stay in Dublin. You're back home with Neil, in your own place. You've really got it made. I've nothing,' Lorna protested.

'Well, no thanks to you,' Heather muttered.

'I know, but you're a lucky wagon all the same,' Lorna persisted. She felt she was getting somewhere. 'Look, why don't you and I go and have a drink tonight—'

'No, Neil and I are going out. He's going back to work now,' Heather retorted.

'Fine, let's go and have a coffee and a chat. Please, Heather?' she urged.

'OK then,' Heather sighed. 'After I've had a sauna.'

'Great. I was going to have one too. Whenever you get out I'll follow,' Lorna said gaily as she did a back flip and swam away. Passing Neil going in the opposite direction, she gave a triumphant thumbs-up. She sighed happily. She and Heather were talking again. She wasn't going to be stuck on her own for two weeks, and she'd have someone to impress with her tales of New York.

Life was getting better and better, she decided as she sliced through the pool with firm, powerful strokes.

25

Heather was frazzled. It was the day of the official opening and her phone was buzzing constantly. Caterers, invitees, as well as the normal run-of-the-mill phone calls she usually dealt with. The last two weeks had been hectic, getting the invites printed up and sent out and then organizing the event itself.

Lorcan Kelly, head of the local Chamber of Commerce, who was performing the ceremony, was taking it all very seriously and had been in constant contact. He was a serious, intense man in his mid-fifties who had a tendency to make mountains out of molehills. He'd insisted on approving the guest list and adding a few more names of his own and he was getting on Heather's nerves.

She couldn't grumble to Neil, he was as bad. He was hyper, rushing around getting into a tizzy over the slightest thing. He'd become even more driven than when she first knew him, Heather reflected as he asked her for the umpteenth time whether she'd organized the bouquet of flowers for Lorcan's wife. Personally, she felt he was going over the top and wasting money, but he told her Mrs Kelly too was a potential customer, the same as everyone else, and it was good to keep in with her.

A red car shot on to the forecourt. It was Lorna. Heather sighed deeply. She really wasn't in the humour to listen to her cousin rabbiting on about New York. She'd had it shoved down her neck for the past two weeks. It was all Lorna could talk about. Though she was trying, she couldn't quite feel the same about her cousin. Lorna had been all friendly and bubbly when they'd gone for coffee the Saturday they'd met in the gym. She'd been all over Heather, saying how wonderful it was for her to be back with Neil. Heather didn't believe a word of it. She'd never had a good word to say about him before. She was such a hypocrite. Still, the three of them had arranged to meet for a drink on the Sunday night and Lorna had been so sweet to Neil it was sickening.

'She's not that bad, I suppose. She's quite entertaining,' Neil had remarked as they walked home hand in hand. Heather had said nothing. One day, Lorna would revert to her true self, and Neil wouldn't be quite so smitten. *Entertaining* indeed!

Her cousin waved at her. Heather waved back. She could see that Lorna was dressed to kill in a pair of black leather trousers, black polo, and short black leather jacket. She wore a pair of black sunglasses and looked for all the world like a film star or model. Automatically Heather tightened her tummy muscles. She'd seen her cousin doing a punishing workout, and running fast on the treadmill. She worked hard for her stunning figure, Heather couldn't deny it. She always felt like a plump frump beside her. She was definitely going to walk at least a mile a day, she promised herself as Lorna swanned into the office.

'Hi, I just dropped by to say I'll be dropping the car in after I say goodbye to Gran this afternoon. What time's your do?'

'One thirty, why don't you come?' Neil had just come into the office.

Lorna lowered her sunglasses. 'What, for a glass of warm plonk, a wilted sandwich and boring speeches? I think not,' she drawled.

'Excuse me, we have caterers in to do the food and the wine is *not* plonk,' Heather said tartly.

'Wow, I'm impressed!' Lorna ran her fingers through her hair provocatively.

'Give me the keys and I'll drive the car around the side. It's filthy, I'm not having it on my forecourt.' Neil held out his hand. Heather could see he was annoyed.

'I'm not leaving it in *yet*, I was just telling Heather I wanted to say goodbye to my gran,' Lorna perched on the side of her cousin's desk.

'Is that right?' Neil retorted. 'Well, maybe it so happens that I'd like you to leave it in now so I could get my mechanics working on it.'

'Ooohhh, isn't he masterful.' She pouted. 'Come on, Neil, an hour or two isn't going to make any difference. Stop getting on your high horse just because I teased you about your wine.'

'You've a hard neck you know.'

'*Moi?* Surely not.' Lorna pretended innocence, eyes wide.

Neil laughed and turned to Heather. 'I'm just

going to collect the beer from the offie. Any important calls give them my mobile number. Ring the caterer and tell them to get a move on, they need to be here soon, and will you collect my suit from the cleaner's? Here's the docket. Good luck in New York, Lorna, in case I don't see you later.' He raised his hand in salute and hurried out of the office.

Heather was furious. How *dare* he talk to her and order her around like she was some little dogsbody. How *dare* he tell her to collect his suit from the cleaner's. And in front of Lorna too! He was in for it when she got him on her own.

'Big day for Neil,' Lorna said, unaware of her cousin's fury. 'I have to give it to him, I never thought he'd amount to much but he's done well for himself.'

'Lorna, if you don't mind, I'm kinda busy. Have to get a move on.' Heather was in no mood for Lorna's patronizing guff.

'Oh, I suppose you are. I better get a move on myself. I thought you might be having coffee,' she said hopefully.

'Not a chance,' Heather said briskly. 'If you want coffee go over and get a cup in the deli, you could collect that suit for me if you've nothing better to do.'

'I'm not Neil Brennan's maid,' Lorna said indignantly. 'Collect his suit indeed. And if I were you I wouldn't either.'

'Oh, I don't look at it like that,' Heather fibbed. 'When you're in a relationship you don't mind doing little things like that.'

311

'Well, I never intend to be a drudge in a relationship,' Lorna said insultingly but Heather didn't care, she knew by the flash of annoyance on her cousin's face that she'd got one over on her.

'I certainly don't consider myself to be a drudge, Lorna,' Heather said smoothly. 'Neil and I' (she really liked the sound of 'Neil and I') 'are a partnership. I do things for him, he does things for me.'

Lorna was fit to be tied. 'It sounds *so* boring, Heather.' She yawned. 'If you don't mind my saying so. I'm glad I ended it with Bryan before going to New York. I'm footloose and fancy free and I can do what I like.'

She's jealous, Heather thought with a little jolt. For the first time in her life, Heather felt superior to her cousin.

'Have a ball,' she encouraged. 'Now, Lorna, scram. I've got to get on with things here.'

'Poor you, having to work your butt off. I think I might go up to the hotel and have a swim,' Lorna said airily.

'Don't drown. See you.' Heather bent her head to her keyboard and pretended to type a document.

Lorna picked up her bag and sauntered out of the office. Heather kept her head down. She knew her cousin had been trying to impress her. She knew when Lorna was laying it on with a trowel. It was really getting to her that Heather had settled down so well back in Kilronan and that she was practically living with Neil. Her eyes had widened when she'd seen a shirt and tie of Neil's lying on top of the linen basket in Heather's bedroom, and his dressing-gown on the back of the door. For all

312

her sophistication, she'd never lived with a man, Heather thought smugly, enjoying the unusual feeling of superiority. Smiling, she lifted the phone and dialled the caterer's number.

By one thirty everything was going as planned. The caterers had arrived and set up the drinks and finger food. The guests were assembled. Neil was wearing his dry-cleaned suit that Heather had collected for him, and Lorcan Kelly was making a boring speech that lasted ten minutes. After his wife had cut the ribbon on the door into the showrooms, Neil invited everyone to help themselves to food and drink. He was as proud as punch and Heather forgot her previous anger and indignation and gave him a quick hug.

'It's going great,' she whispered.

'I've orders for two new cars and about four interested in the second-hand ones. This is brilliant for business,' he whispered back, on a high. 'Have to go and chat with Douglas Kennedy, he's interested in a top-of-the-range four-wheel-drive. Make sure they all have enough to drink.'

'One each will do them fine,' Heather retorted. Sometimes Neil thought he was Donald Trump, or the likes. She had taken him to task a couple of times about his expense account, telling him to cut back on his swanky restaurant bills.

'I have to entertain clients,' he protested.

'Get real, Neil, you don't have to go overboard,' she said drily. 'Your profits aren't exactly in the stratosphere.'

'Look, Heather, you have to realize, image is everything in this game. The more successful you behave, the more business you attract,' he explained patiently.

'Look at Oliver Flynn, you wouldn't think he had two pennies to rub together and he's very successful—'

'That's a different game, Heather. Let me worry about attracting the business and you worry about what happens when we get it.' Neil grinned.

Maybe he was right, Heather reflected. He certainly had enough drive and ambition to get the chain of garages he wanted. The buzz in the showroom was lively and good-humoured. Even if ten of the 150 guests bought a car they'd be doing well.

She was chatting to Martin Doyle, the manager of the Lake View, when she felt the elastic on the top of one of her pop socks give way, and felt it slowly begin to slide down her leg. *Oh no!* She gave a silent groan. How totally unsophisticated. She looked down when Martin paused to wave to someone and saw it wrinkly and loose around her shoe. She looked just like Nora Batty and she felt mortified. If she could ease her way into her own office, she could run upstairs and get a new pair. That's what she got for wearing pop socks, she thought dolefully. Lorna wouldn't be seen dead in them. No woman of sophistication would. She could feel herself breaking out in a cold sweat as the sock slid right down under her trousers.

'Excuse me, Martin,' she murmured. 'I just want to make sure there's enough wine.'

'Fire ahead, Heather,' Martin beamed. He'd had more than a couple of glasses and was in great form. Red-cheeked, Heather moved as casually as she could through the knots of people, aware that her sock was now hanging over the back of her shoe. She was sure all eyes were upon her and by the time she got into her office she was cringing with embarrassment.

She closed the door behind her and unlocked the interconnecting door to her flat. She hurried upstairs, cursing vehemently. She rampaged through her sock drawer, finding pairs that didn't match or were laddered. 'For crying out loud,' she muttered, mad with herself. She'd been meaning to sort out her socks and tights since she'd moved in and had never got around to it.

'Heather, what are you doing? The phone's going mad ringing, the least you could do is answer it. I've taken it off the hook,' Neil demanded irritably, as he erupted into the room.

'The blasted elastic in my sock broke and I need to get a new pair. Look at me. I'm like Nora Batty.' She lifted her leg to show him.

'For God's sake, Heather, would you try to dress a bit more appropriately for this kind of thing. Look at the way Lorna dresses. Get a few tips from her. It's important to have a good image,' Neil lectured, finding nothing amusing in her predicament.

She couldn't believe her ears. He was telling her to be more like *Lorna*! What an insensitive bastard.

'How *dare* you, Neil Brennan. It could happen to anyone. And if you prefer the way Lorna dresses get her to be your dogsbody and answer your fucking phone,' she yelled. 'I've worked my ass off

315

for you since I came here, I've worked twelve-hour days to get your bloody launch organized. How dare you,' she shrieked, incensed.

'Will you shut up!! They'll hear.' Neil nearly had a fit.

'I don't give a fiddler's who hears. Get out of my bedroom. I pay rent for it, I'm entitled to have whoever I want in it and I don't want you. And I'm taking the rest of the day off so go and answer your own bloody phone and brown nose that shower downstairs because I've had enough of it.'

'You'd better get back down there and don't leave me to do this on my own,' Neil warned, purple with indignation.

'Go sit on a pitchfork,' Heather snarled as she marched into the bathroom and slammed the door. She heard him curse viciously and then there was silence. She flipped the top of the loo down and sat on it. She was *raging*. How dare Neil speak to her like that. She always dressed smartly for work. OK, she wasn't in Lorna's league in terms of style, she was well aware of that, but few women were. Tears of humiliation smarted her eyes. This should have been one of the most exciting, satisfying days of her and Neil's life after all the work of the past couple of months and instead they were having a vicious row. He wasn't one bit grateful for anything she'd done. Well, she was damned if she was going downstairs any more. She could see through the small window that the guests were beginning to drift off anyway. People were anxious to leave once the drink and food were gone, there were other things to be done on a Saturday afternoon. He could bloody well clean up after it by himself. She'd had enough of being dogsbody for one day.

She went into the kitchen and switched on the kettle. There was a packet of unopened chocolate Kimberleys on the counter top, and she opened them and unwrapped one, staring out on to the far distant lake. By the time the kettle had boiled she'd eaten three. Disgusted with herself, she made a cup of coffee, locked her front door with the latch so that he wouldn't get in with his key, undressed and got into bed. It had started to rain outside, and she snuggled down under the duvet, tired after the stress of the past week. Neil Brennan would want to start treating her with a lot more respect, she thought angrily. She'd behaved like a doormat with him before. But those days were gone. He wasn't getting back into her bed until he'd eaten a large slice of humble pie.

She waited for him to knock on her door and apologize, but the hours passed and dusk deepened into night and she lay unhappily wondering if this was the end of them. After all her boasting to Lorna about being in a relationship, wouldn't it be ironic if she and Neil were finished? How Lorna would crow. That would be the worst thing of all, Heather fretted as hot tears slid down her cheeks.

Neil gazed around at what had five hours previously been an immaculate showroom. Paper plates, crumpled serviettes, lipstick-stained wineglasses, food trodden underfoot, and the stink of cigarette smoke. It had been a great success, he congratulated himself. He was someone in Kilronan now and it felt good. He'd bring his father out for a pint and regale him with all the details. His father, crippled with arthritis, had opted not to come. It wasn't really his scene. Neil would have liked him to have been part of the celebrations, but perhaps it was just as well he hadn't come. He wouldn't have been able to look after him, he would have had to leave that to Heather, and after the row they'd had, his dad would have had to fend for himself, seeing as Heather had left him to host the remainder of the launch alone. She'd really let him down. He couldn't believe it of her, just because he'd taken her to task for sloppy dressing.

Surely she realized how important it was to look her best at all times. She was often the first point of contact with the company, he thought self-righteously. Today was a special occasion. Wearing stockings that were falling around her ankles was just too much. And the way she'd cursed at him with such viciousness, he hadn't realized she had such a temper. He was damned if he was going near her for the rest of the night. He wasn't going to let her spoil the best day of his life. Pity she wasn't here to help him clean up though, he thought ruefully as he made a half-hearted attempt to clear away a few plates.

He saw Lorna Morgan drive on to the forecourt in the red Honda Civic. She'd left it late enough to come back. There was probably another thousand miles up on the clock since he'd bought it off her. He wasn't in the humour for her either. He scowled as she walked into the showrooms, keys jingling in her hand.

'You can let your precious mechanic go to work on it now.' She held out the keys.

'Fine.' He pocketed them. 'Have a good time in New York.'

'I intend to,' she purred, slanting her blue eyes up at him. 'It looks like everyone enjoyed the warm plonk.' She gazed around at the clutter. 'Where's Heather?'

'She's got a headache,' Neil lied. He wasn't going to let on to Lorna Morgan that he and Heather had had a row.

'Well, don't expect *me* to give you a hand clearing up.' Lorna wrinkled her pert little nose at him.

'Somehow I don't see you as the cleaning-up type,' Neil retorted.

She smiled at him. 'Ten out of ten for spot-on observation. I'm more the drinking champagne type as you've probably guessed, and if Heather is incapacitated and you've got no one to celebrate with, I'll allow you to buy me a glass of champagne, or two as the case may be.'

Neil stared at her. She was so sure of herself. She really thought she was it. But it wasn't every day a stunning looking woman with a gorgeous figure asked him out for a drink, even if she was a snob of the highest order. Heather might not be too happy if she knew he was off sculling champers with her cousin, but she'd let him down badly and she could go take a running jump.

'Let's go order the Dom P.' He flashed a smile at her, switching off the lights and locking the doors behind him. He'd organize a clean-up of the place tomorrow. Tonight was for celebrating the start of the Brennan Motors chain of garages. Tonight was the start of it. Champagne it had to be. At least Lorna Morgan realized it was a night for celebration, seeing as Heather certainly didn't. He held open the door of the BMW for Lorna and saw her sit elegantly in the soft leather seat.

'Nice set of wheels,' she approved, flicking back her blonde bob.

Neil closed the door on her. She looked far better in the front seat than Heather did, he thought guiltily as he drove on to Kilronan's main street.

26

'Do you think Heather will mind?' Lorna murmured as they drove into the car park of the Lake View Hotel.

'Why should she? What is there to mind?' Neil looked at her in surprise.

'Not a thing,' Lorna said nonchalantly, wondering privately what kind of an idiot he was. Any woman would mind her boyfriend quaffing champagne with another woman. Heather was so smug, going on about being in a 'relationship'. Two and a bit months wasn't that long, but the way Heather was going on you'd think they were practically married.

Mind, she had felt a few darts of envy when she'd seen Neil's dressing-gown beside Heather's on the back of her bedroom door. It looked so intimate and companionable. She'd never been in a relationship long enough to have her toothbrush in the bathroom, let alone her dressing-gown hanging up.

She had to admit she'd been impressed when she'd seen her cousin's flat. It smelt new and fresh and clean and it was so bright and airy. Heather had really landed on her feet without making the slightest bit of effort and she didn't mind rubbing Lorna's nose in it. '*When you're in a relationship you do things for each other.*' Who did she think she was talking to? She watched Neil up at the bar ordering the champagne. His suit was expensive. He looked the part of the young, successful man about town. He'd definitely smartened himself up a lot. He'd told her on the car journey to the hotel that he was considering buying a garage in Navan in the next few years but that his dream was to own a big showroom in Dublin. At least he had a bit of get up and go in him, he wasn't going to stagnate in Kilronan. He wasn't bad-looking in a rough sort of way, she thought grudgingly. His black hair, cropped tight, was much more attractive than the wild mop of longish hair he used to have. He had nice brown eyes too. She could possibly fancy him if she let herself, she decided. And she knew she could have him too, if she wanted. She'd seen the way he'd looked at her in the swimming-pool and gym. That might wipe the smug smirk off Heather's face. If she couldn't keep her boyfriend, that was her problem. It might shut her up boasting about being in a 'relationship'.

'Would you like to have dinner? I'm hungry,' Neil declared out of the blue as he came and sat in the chair opposite her.

'Why not?' Lorna agreed. It was better than sitting at home twiddling her thumbs. She was all packed and ready to go, her parents were out at a golf dinner, she was at a loose end.

322

'We didn't book, that's the only thing,' Neil remarked.

'I'll have a word with the maître d'. I know him,' Lorna offered.

'Friends in high places,' Neil teased and she laughed. Half an hour later they were sitting at a candlelit table and Lorna was quite giddy. She'd drunk three glasses of champagne on an empty stomach, and she'd even begun to feel that Neil was an interesting bloke. He was ambitious. Just like her. He didn't want to stay in Kilronan and vegetate.

'You should come and visit me in New York. I'd say you'd love it there,' she invited blithely.

'I suppose we could come out for a long week-end or something.' Neil topped up her glass.

'Oh, I forgot about Heather,' Lorna said wickedly. 'I meant *you*!'

'Don't think I'd manage to get away for a long weekend by myself, Lorna. Heather might object.'

'So is it serious with you two?' Lorna sat back in her chair and eyed him curiously.

Neil shrugged. 'Bit soon to say, I suppose.'

Interesting, thought Lorna. *He's not swearing undying love*. The arrival of the main course interrupted conversation momentarily. The monkfish and wild mushrooms smelt absolutely divine and it was melt-in-the-mouth when she tasted it.

'Food is good here,' Neil said as he forked a sliver of sole into his mouth. She'd half expected him to order steak and chips, but he'd surprised her with his selection of lemon sole and he seemed *au fait* with the wine list, she noted, as he ordered the wine confidently. Not such a country bumpkin after all. She felt a little *frisson* of admiration for him. When she'd first known him he'd been unsophisticated and extremely ordinary. But he was making something of himself, learning to pass himself off in society, just like she was. Acquiring a polish that was far from what he was reared to. She didn't doubt that he'd have his garage and showroom in Dublin. He was hungry just like she was. They were quite alike, she thought with a little shock.

Her mobile phone rang and swiftly, discreetly she located it and answered the call. It was Carina confirming that they would meet at nine thirty in the airport.

'Are you excited?' Neil enquired as she turned off her phone and put it back in her bag.

'I can't wait. I'm going to explore Manhattan from top to toe.'

'We'd better get another bottle of champagne to toast you,' Neil said expansively, raising a discreet finger to the wine waiter.

Three hours later they were giggling and laughing as if they were the best of friends. Lorna was quite pissed. 'I've had a terrific night,' Neil exclaimed after he'd paid the substantial bill, his eyes bright with drink and admiration.

'Me too,' Lorna assured him earnestly.

'Do you think they'd let us use the residents' lounge? We could have another drink?' he asked.

Lorna patted his arm drunkenly. 'I've a better idea, leave it to me.'

Ten minutes later they were in one of the

unoccupied mini suites with another bottle of champagne on ice.

'My treat.' Lorna giggled.

'What a woman!' Neil declared. 'You're way too much woman for the likes of Kilronan. You go pop your cork in New York.'

'Do you mean that?' Lorna murmured seductively.

'Of course I do. Take New York by the scruff of the neck and shake it.' Neil held up his glass in a toast.

'No, do you mean the bit about being way too much woman?'

'Are you crazy? I think you're magnificent! I didn't like you when I first knew you, I thought you were a stuck-up cow,' he admitted, his tongue loosened by all he'd had to drink. 'But after tonight, talking to you over dinner, and getting to know you, I think you're something else,' he said warmly, his eyes glittering with admiration as he gazed at her.

'I didn't like you either. I thought you were a country bumpkin.' She giggled again.

'I know you did. You were a snooty, superior wagon. And now?' he grinned wolfishly.

'I guess I made a mistake,' she murmured, swaying into his arms. They kissed passionately, lustfully.

'We shouldn't do this,' Neil muttered when he came up for air.

'I know,' Lorna agreed and kissed him again, tugging at his shirt buttons.

'Oh, Lorna,' he groaned. 'You're dead sexy. I want you.'

'I want you too.' Lorna could feel the desire curling inside her and an immensely satisfying feeling of triumph that she had conquered him. They undressed each other frantically and he lifted her up and carried her to the bed. 'Come on,' she moaned. 'Come on, do it to me.' He needed no second invitation. She wasn't sure if she came or not, she was so smashed, but she had a vague feeling that the quivers lasted the whole time, not dying away as they usually did, and she would have liked him to do it to her again but he'd fallen asleep very quickly afterwards.

Lorna lay beside him, her head swimming. It had been better than anything she'd had with a man before, she thought woozily. What an irony. A man she had most despised was the one who had given her most pleasure sexually. She knew if she pushed hard he'd leave Heather for her at the drop of a hat. That thought too gave her immense satisfaction. But she'd hold him in reserve. New York and its millionaires were waiting for her.

The phone woke her out of a deep, dreamless sleep. It was the night porter. 'Aren't you going to New York today?' he asked. 'You'd want to get moving.'

'Oh shit! What time is it?' She leapt up and ran her fingers through her hair. Beside her, Neil snored contentedly.

'It's ten to seven, do you want coffee or anything?'

'Thanks, Dan, don't have time. I better get going, 'bye.' Her parents would be going berserk. They were driving her to the airport and they'd want to leave by eight. She picked up her mobile and rang home. Her father answered, sleepily, she noted with relief. 'I'll be home in ten minutes. Get up, Dad,' she instructed.

'Where are you?' her father asked groggily.

'Heather's,' she fibbed. 'See you soon, 'bye.' She raced into the shower and stood under the steaming jets feeling like hell on earth. She should never have drunk so much last night. She was her own worst enemy. Neil was still sleeping by the time she'd dried her hair and dressed. She gazed at him in irritation. 'Big lazy lump,' she muttered crossly, not feeling quite as fond of him as she had the previous night.

'Wake up, Neil.' She poked him roughly.

'Wha . . . what's wrong, Heather?'

'It's not Heather, it's me,' Lorna said coldly.

'Oh crikey! Lorna. Sorry . . . sorry about that. I was half asleep,' he apologized profusely, rubbing his bloodshot eyes. 'Oohh, I feel rough,' he groaned. 'How much did we drink last night?'

'It doesn't matter. I have to go. I'll be late getting to the airport. You better get going too, I gave Dan Leeland thirty smackers for this room, he'll have to have it made up before room service get here.'

'Oh. Oh, right!' He looked at her admiringly. 'I suppose we don't have time for a quickie?'

'No we don't, Neil Brennan,' she snapped. 'Look, I'm going. I'll see you when I see you.'

'Hey, wait. Look, don't go like that. Here, take my card. Keep in touch with me on my mobile or email,' he said hastily.

'Give it to me, quick.' She practically snatched the card from him and stuffed it in her bag.

'I'd a great time last night, I'll never forget it,' Neil said quietly. Lorna looked at him, stubble-faced and tousled, and felt her heart soften.

'I did too, Neil. It will be one of my better memories of Kilronan.' She smiled at him and leaned down and gave him a quick peck on the cheek. 'Not a word to Heather.'

'Definitely not,' he grinned and waved at her as she slipped out of the room.

She hurried to the lift, sizzling with impatience, two jack-hammers beating a tattoo inside her head. She felt queasy as it glided silently to the lamplit, empty foyer. 'Dan, thanks a million for waking me, see you whenever.' She blew the night porter a kiss as she flew past reception, out into the dark, blustery morning. It was a nuisance having no car, and as usual her shoes weren't the best for walking. At least she didn't have too far to walk.

It was only half past seven by the time she got home and she congratulated herself on her speed. Adrenalin was flowing. She could go to sleep in the car, she promised herself as she let herself into the house. Her father was standing in the kitchen munching brown bread and marmalade.

'There's coffee in the pot,' he pointed to the coffee percolator. 'You could have let us know you were staying over at Heather's.'

'It was a spur of the moment thing, and besides you were out yourself,' she retorted, pouring a cup of hot strong coffee for herself.

'I'm glad you and Heather are friends again.' He patted her arm. 'Heather's always been a good friend to you.'

'Yeah, Dad,' Lorna said uncomfortably. If he'd seen what she was up to last night he'd be totally horrified, and she would be off her pedestal so quick it didn't bear thinking about. 'Look, I'm just going upstairs to change my clothes. Is Mum coming?'

Gerard nodded. 'She's having her shower. She's really looking forward to visiting you. I haven't seen her in such good form for years.'

'That's good, Dad.' Lorna planted a hasty kiss on his cheek and his eyes lit up with pleasure.

'I'll miss you,' he said. 'Even though we didn't see you that much when you were in Dublin, you were only an hour and a half's drive away, not a six-hour flight across the Atlantic.'

'It's only for a while, Dad, not for ever. Now I'd better go get sorted.'

Thank God I packed last night, she thought gratefully as she surveyed the two large cases on her bedroom floor. One of them was practically empty but was being brought to accommodate her shopping for the return flight home. She eased her legs out of her leather trousers and pulled her black polo over her head. For the trip to New York she'd chosen a taupe trouser suit and a black T-shirt. She'd carry her snug pure wool coat on her arm, in case it was freezing cold in the Big Apple. After all, it was still only the beginning of February.

Her head throbbed and she swallowed two Panadol, wishing she'd at least drunk water the previous night as she sometimes did when she'd been on the tear. She'd slept with Neil Brennan, Heather's boyfriend, she thought with a vague sense of astonishment as she gazed at herself in the mirror. Her cornflower blue eyes were puffy and red. Her hair, which hadn't been dried properly with the hotel hairdryer, was not its usual sleek bob. It was too late to do anything with it now, she thought grimly as she rubbed gel between her fingers and tried to calm her flyaway fringe.

It was her own fault for not going home. Imagine having dinner in the hotel and then going to a room with Neil. It would be all over the town. She must have been mad. Still, Heather wouldn't be stuffing that relationship nonsense down her neck again, if she ever found out. Lorna was still smarting at her cousin's smug jibe. Her mother knocked on the door and peered in. She looked as if she'd just stepped out of *Vogue* in her smart Louise Kennedy trouser suit.

'Ready?'

'As ready as I'll ever be.' Lorna wrinkled her nose.

'We'd want to go. Say goodbye to your brothers.'

'I'm not waking them up, they'd kill me,' Lorna said indignantly. 'Tell them I said goodbye when you get back.'

Gerard appeared at her door. 'Let me take those cases. Go and get in the car.'

If only she hadn't got the mother and father of a hangover, this would be the most exciting moment of her life. Leaving a dark, quiet backwater town for the bright lights of the most famous city in the world was a once in a lifetime experience and she'd ruined it by drinking too much. By the time Gerard's Volvo had cruised past Neil Brennan's showrooms, her hangover was really kicking in, and she closed her eyes and tried to sleep.

She did sleep, in fits and starts, and as there was little or no traffic on the road at that hour of a Sunday morning, her father made good time to the airport so that she was standing in departures at nine thirty peering around for Carina. 'Look, you go on, we'll probably have coffee after we check in and then we've got to go through immigration. There's no point in you hanging around,' she said to her parents.

'We'll wait until Carina arrives,' her father told her firmly. 'Imagine if she didn't show up and we had to turn back from wherever we were to collect you.'

'There she is. Now go,' Lorna ordered as she saw her friend struggling with her case at the entrance. 'Thanks very much for the money, Dad,' she added. Her father had given her five thousand dollars in traveller's cheques.

'It will probably only buy you a pair of trousers in Armani's or wherever, knowing your taste in designer labels,' he teased, 'but have a good time and don't become an illegal. Come back when your time's up.' He hugged her tightly and to her dismay she felt a lump rise in her throat. She swallowed hard and turned to her mother.

'Mum, see you soon. I'll check everything out as soon as I get there and phone you. Give me about six weeks to get settled.'

'Have a great time. I'll be dying to hear all about it,' Jane said animatedly. Her father was right, Lorna reflected. She'd never seen her mother so sparkly about anything.

'Go on now, I hate long drawn out goodbyes,' Lorna said gruffly, giving both of them a little shove. She turned her back on them and walked towards the monitors where Carina was looking for their check-in desk. When she turned to look back her parents were gone. That was the best way to have it, Lorna thought with relief. Sentimentality was not her style.

'Hi.' She marched up to Carina. 'Did you come here on your own?'

'My dad dropped me at the set-down, I didn't want fond farewells.'

'I know the feeling,' Lorna said ruefully. 'I hope to God it's not a bumpy flight or I'll puke. I've the mother and father of a hangover.'

'Me too,' groaned Carina. 'I'm never drinking VRBs again. *Ever*!' she added vehemently.

'Wait until we get to New York. I believe the cocktails are toxic! They serve them neat.'

'I'm staying on the dry,' Carina retorted. 'I wonder is the bar open yet?'

'Let's have a coffee,' Lorna suggested weakly. The thought of alcohol made her queasy.

They found their check-in and joined the long straggly queue. Everyone seemed to have huge amounts of luggage and it seemed to take for ever before they were hauling their cases up on to the conveyer belt and assuring the ground hostess that they had indeed packed their own cases.

'I think we should have our coffee in the departure lounge, we've to do the immigration stuff too.' Lorna glanced at her watch.

'OK,' Carina agreed wearily. 'Look at us! Like

two wet rags, we should be shot. I couldn't bear the thought of duty free. I've bought a whole load of vacuum-packed rashers and sausages in my case for the gang in Yonkers. That will have to do them, we can get drink on the plane for them. I think I just want to die,' she moaned.

'I know, me too,' Lorna agreed as they trudged to the security check before going airside.

'It's a bit shabby down here,' Lorna murmured in disappointment twenty minutes later as they filled in their immigration forms in the transatlantic departure area.

'And the fucking coffee bar's closed,' Carina swore.

'I thought it would be really jet setty and glamorous.' Lorna gazed around, unimpressed by the drabness of it all as she queued to give her card to a bored immigration officer. 'The departure lounges for Europe and the UK are far superior. Still, I suppose we're lucky we can go through immigration at this side instead of having to do it when we get there. I'll run upstairs and get us a coffee.'

'OK.' Carina collapsed on to a hard chair and closed her eyes.

Lorna made her way upstairs, after an argument with one of the immigration officials, who told her in no uncertain terms she should stay where she was.

'Look, buster, the coffee bar's not open. My friend and I have hangovers to die for and if you don't want us puking all over this kippy hole you'll let me go upstairs for coffee.' Lorna was in no mood to be trifled with.

'OK, lady, just this once.' He backed off hastily.

'Yeah, well, if your coffee bar was open I wouldn't have to go to the trouble of going upstairs,' Lorna snarled.

'Nothing to do with—' but Lorna was gone, leaving the man to protest to thin air.

The queue to the self-service upstairs was out the door and Lorna nearly cried in frustration, twenty minutes later, as a foreign tourist in front of her spent ten minutes sorting out loose coins to pay for her big fry-up. Lorna practically shoved her out of the way to pay an arm and a leg for two mugs of coffee and two Danish.

'What a rip off,' she panted as she finally plonked the tray in front of Carina, who looked a bit green around the gills. 'Here, drink this, it will sort you.'

They had to gulp the last of their coffee as the gate opened to board and as Lorna finally made her way on to the huge Airbus she couldn't help the way her heart pounded with excitement. She was going to New York and one day, she promised herself, she'd never turn right into economy on an aircraft again. It would be left and first class all the way.

They sorted themselves and their hand luggage and sank gratefully into their seats. 'Get a bottle of vodka and a bottle of gin, if you're allowed, and wake me when we get to New York,' Carina instructed as she tucked her little white pillow under her head and promptly fell asleep, before they'd even taxied off the apron.

As the huge jet rose into the air, Lorna felt tense with excitement. This was it. Life was giving her a chance to make it big and she was going to take it. All around her there was a buzz of excitement and anticipation that she'd never experienced on a charter flight to the Med. This was *so* different, it was thrilling, she thought giddily wondering how Carina could sleep through it all. She flicked through the in-flight magazine and the duty-free brochure. She wanted some Yves Saint Laurent Touche Éclat, she needed it badly, she thought ruefully.

What a night. What a morning. In her wildest dreams she'd never thought that she'd end up having sex with Neil Brennan and, what was more, half enjoying it. Maybe she wasn't as abnormal as she thought. Hopefully her hang-up about sex was disappearing. She could put that memory of her mother out of her head once and for all. If she could enjoy sex with Neil, she could enjoy it with anyone, surely. He could come to New York for a dirty weekend if he wanted, she'd enjoy that. But that was it, she decided. Heather could have him. She had new fish to fry. Big fish to fry. The adventure was just beginning.

27

Heather shivered and sleepily stretched her hand out to feel for Neil. He wasn't there. She lay, puzzled for a minute, before memories of their row flooded in. Her heart gave a painful little lurch. He hadn't come home at all. She glanced at the small luminous clock on the bedside table. Seven thirty. She'd slept well considering, she thought in surprise as she reached down and turned on the electric blanket. Lorna would probably be on her way to the airport, she remembered. She'd been a bit abrupt with her yesterday, she thought guiltily, nor had she wished her well for her trip to New York.

The heat of the blanket infused warmth into the bed and she snuggled under the duvet. In the distance she could hear the lowing of cattle, so different from the harsh roar of traffic she'd woken to in Dublin. A few months ago she'd been living in the city and hating it. And, until yesterday, she'd been the happiest girl in the universe, until Neil had made his horrible crack about getting tips from Lorna. He couldn't have picked a more hurtful remark if he'd spent hours trying to think of something to say to wound her.

Why had he said it to her? Had he stopped fancying her? She'd seen him eyeing Lorna appreciatively in the gym. All the time they'd been living and socializing together, Heather had got used to men only having eyes for Lorna. That was one of the reasons Neil was so special to her. He'd never made her feel she was inferior to her cousin. Until yesterday she'd always felt confident with Neil. Now he'd ruined it.

If the relationship was over, she could hardly stay working for him, she thought glumly. And she'd have to go home and live at her mother's, but she was damned if she was going back to Dublin. If she had to get work as a housemaid in the hotel she'd do it, to continue living in Kilronan.

Stop being dramatic, it's only a row, you'll get over it, she told herself. Trust her to think the worst. She fell asleep again, as the wind whistled outside and the eastern sky began to lighten.

Neil showered and dressed at a far slower speed than normal. His head was thumping. He had expected to wake up and find it was all a dream. He couldn't believe that he'd shagged Lorna Morgan. He'd certainly been a more than satisfactory lover, he thought proudly, remembering the way she'd writhed and moaned beneath him, telling him over and over to do it to her. He wouldn't have minded going again with her this morning, he thought longingly as he began to stiffen. Remembering her words about the night porter, he reluctantly put all thoughts of her out of his head and finished dressing.

'Morning, Dan,' he said brazenly as he walked through reception. There was no point in skulking around as if he had something to hide. He was beginning to realize that he'd been far from discreet. If Heather ever found out that he had spent the night with Lorna that would be the end of them. She'd flip bigtime. He hadn't behaved very well, he acknowledged, but how many men would not take an opportunity when it was presented to them on a plate? And what an opportunity Lorna was. Any red-blooded male would have done the same.

It had all been so unexpected, he thought ruefully as he got into the car and wondered where to go. He really wanted to go back to bed and sleep his hangover off. He could go to his dad's house if he wanted to, he supposed. Tell him he'd been on the batter and there'd be no questions asked. It was probably his best option.

As he drove past the garage he could see that Heather's curtains were still drawn and the place was in darkness. He remembered too that the showrooms were in a sorry state and would have to be cleaned up before opening hours the following morning. Neil groaned. Later, he'd worry about all that later. Right now he felt as though red hot pokers were being twisted up inside his skull.

His father chuckled when he said he was dying from drink and told him to get up to bed and he'd do him a big fry-up later on. Ten minutes later, Neil was snoring.

*　　　*　　　*

338

When Heather woke up the second time, weak sunlight filtered through the curtains. It was still windy, but the rain had stopped. She was hungry. She glanced at her clock. Ten thirty. Half the morning was gone. She'd bought roast beef for dinner but she was damned if she was going to cook Neil Brennan a roast dinner after his cavalier attitude. She wondered dully where he'd spent the night.

She wrapped her dressing-gown around her and went into the kitchen and made herself tea and toast. She sat forlornly at her breakfast counter, smearing butter and marmalade on to the hot toast, lonely for Neil. She'd got so used to having him around. It was nice not having to eat meals on her own. Sunday mornings were always particularly nice. He'd get up and go over to the deli and get croissants and Danish pastries and they'd have them in bed, reading the Sunday papers. When they'd showered and dressed they'd go for a walk around the lake, if she could persuade him. Neil hated walking and did it to humour her.

She'd go on her own, she decided. She could do with some fresh air anyway.

An hour later, dressed in a tracksuit and runners and with her big lilac scarf wrapped around her neck and ears, she set off briskly. Great gusts of wind buffeted her and she was half sorry she'd come, as she almost slipped on a mucky patch. She was even sorrier when a single magpie landed in front of her. What a bad omen, she fretted, anxiously scanning the skies for his mate. Not a sign. Trust her to find the only solitary magpie in

Kilronan. After fifteen minutes battling against the wind she turned and walked back the way she'd come. It wasn't as bad going home. The wind was at her back, which helped enormously. She saw a man trudging in her direction, shoulders down, hands thrust into pockets, head bent into the buffeting wind, and recognized Oliver Flynn. He looked as pissed off as she did.

'Morning, Oliver,' she said politely.

'Morning, Heather. It's windy,' he answered, not breaking his stride.

'You can say that again,' she agreed, but her words were carried off on the wind and she kept on walking. She glanced at her watch. It was just twelve. People were streaming towards the church gates for last Mass. It wouldn't kill her to go, she thought glumly. She could do with some spiritual sustenance. She wasn't really dressed for it though. Trainers and track suit were a tad casual for church in Kilronan. She could sit at the back, not that it really mattered. God wasn't one for dress codes, she reflected. She was just walking into the porch when she felt a tap on her shoulder. It was her Uncle Gerard.

'Hello, Heather, we've just come from bringing Lorna to the airport. I just wanted to say, I'm glad you're friends again. It was nice that she spent her last night with you. I hope you'll get a chance to get out to New York.'

'Yes dear, I'm sure you'll enjoy it.' Jane Morgan smiled. 'Gerard, we'd better go in, the priest has come out to the altar.'

'See you, Heather.' Her uncle smiled warmly at

her, leaving Heather completely at a loss. What did he mean that Lorna had spent last night with her? She must have been up to something and fibbed. Typical of Lorna, she could have landed her in it rightly.

She sat in the end seat, wondering where her cousin had spent her last night in Kilronan and with whom. The strains of 'Here I am Lord' rose up to the rafters as the choir sang lustily.

Yes Lord, here I am and it's all going wrong. Help, she prayed. Growth opportunity! She was so sure someone had spoken the words aloud she turned her head. Now why had her friend Margaret's oft-used phrase popped into her mind? *Oh no!* she groaned silently. Growth opportunity in her experience was never a very happy occurrence. '*Please Lord let me and Neil be all right*,' she prayed. But she had a funny feeling in the pit of her stomach that something wasn't quite right and she wished that today of all days she hadn't seen that bloody single magpie.

After Mass she called home to visit her parents and was persuaded without too much difficulty to stay for lunch. 'Where's Neil, why isn't he with you?' Anne asked as she spooned meat juices over the roast and put it back into the oven for browning.

'He's doing something with his Dad,' Heather lied, stirring the gravy. The aromas wafting around the kitchen were making her mouth water and after her walk in the fresh air she was starving. She certainly wasn't the type to lose her appetite during emotional stress, unfortunately, she thought ruefully as she nibbled at a mushy pea that had fallen on to the worktop.

If she came home to live she was going to be the size of an elephant, she thought half an hour later as she gazed at the steaming plate her mother had put in front of her. She cut into a crispy roast potato and dipped it in the rich gravy. Her mother made the most perfect roast potatoes. Crisply roasted on the outside, light and fluffy on the inside, and the beef was melt-in-the-mouth. Heather forgot her worries and tucked in. By the time she'd had a portion of home-made apple crumble she was bursting and annoyed with herself for her gluttony. She need not have had second helpings of *everything*. Just as well she wasn't playing a basketball match the following day, she'd be dragging herself around the court like a leaden lump.

After she'd washed up with her mother, she went into the sitting-room and snuggled up on the sofa. The fire was lighting, her father was dozing in his armchair, his paper half-way down his knees, *Calamity Jane* was on the TV, the wind was howling like a banshee outside. Where would she be going on a day like today? She settled back to watch Doris Day singing 'The Black Hills of Dakota' and wondered would Lorna feel the slightest twinge of homesickness or would she take to New York like a duck takes to water? Most likely the latter, Heather reflected. *She* would go berserk sitting at home on a Sunday afternoon watching TV with her parents. She'd never find comfort in old, familiar routines, that hadn't changed since childhood.

Thank God I'm not in that grotty flat in Dublin. Heather tried to look on the bright side. She was feeling terribly hurt that Neil hadn't contacted her on her mobile. It was mean of him to hold the row, especially when he'd started it. She didn't feel like going back to the flat and being on her own. She didn't know if he was going to come home tonight. Well, he could come home if he wanted. She wasn't going to be there. Tonight she'd sleep in her parents' house, get up early in the morning and go back to the flat to change for work. That might give him something to think about.

'Why didn't you come home last night?' her boyfriend demanded the following morning when she let herself in to the flat at eight fifteen.

'Why didn't *you* come home the night before?' she retorted tartly.

'Sorry, I went on the beer and got pissed. I stayed at Dad's,' he confessed sheepishly.

'Oh! Well, you could have phoned,' she accused.

'I didn't get up until four in the afternoon. Then I took Dad to the pub and when you weren't here when I got home I figured you might not want to talk to me anyway,' Neil said defensively. He looked a tad the worse for wear, she admitted.

'Yeah, well, you behaved like a shit, and you weren't a bit nice on Saturday, going on the way you did about image and everything. I'm not Lorna and I never will be, so if you want someone like Lorna, go and get them. I'm me and if you think I'm not good enough say it to my face,' Heather said coldly.

Neil blushed. 'Sorry. I was way out of line.'

'Yes, you were.' She pushed past him into the bedroom and rooted in the wardrobe for a pair of trousers and a jacket. 'Will these do for work?' she demanded sarcastically, her pent-up hurt in free-flow.

'Look, Heather, I really am sorry. I didn't mean it. I was just up to ninety,' Neil apologized.

'Yeah, well, we can't stand here talking about it now. I've to get changed. It will be time to open up soon.'

'And I haven't cleaned up after Saturday,' he groaned.

'Well, you better get down and do it now,' she suggested.

'Will you give me a hand?' he wheedled.

Heather weakened. She hated rowing, it was horrible. 'Go on, I'll be down in a minute.'

He put his arms around her. 'I'm sorry. You're the best,' he said before kissing her. Heather's heart lifted. They were almost back to normal. All she had to do was try and erase the 'Lorna insult' from her memory.

They were almost finished tidying up when she asked him who had he gone on the piss with. 'You don't really know them,' he hedged. 'I had a bit to eat with Lorna before I went drinking, so at least my stomach was lined,' he said casually, tying a black plastic sack full of rubbish.

'With *Lorna*?' Heather was astonished.

'Well, she dropped back the car and she was at a bit of a loose end. She asked me where you were and I said you had a headache. I wasn't going to tell her we had a row. She seemed a bit disappointed so

344

she asked me did I want to have something to eat because her parents were going out. Bit mean on her last night at home.'

'Where did you go?' Heather couldn't get her head around the idea of Neil and Lorna having a meal together.

'The hotel,' Neil said offhandedly.

'The bar?'

'Naw, the dining-room!'

'The dining-room!' Heather was gobsmacked. 'The full works?'

'I didn't want her to think I was a cheapskate, you know, she has such a poor opinion of me at the best of times,' Neil said light-heartedly, as he finished tying a second sack.

'I suppose,' Heather said sulkily. Lorna and Neil having dinner in the Lake View was just a bit too cosy for her liking. Lorna was such a bitch, she thought resentfully, muscling in on her man. And Heather knew she was just using Neil because she was bored. It was nice of her boyfriend to be so accommodating. She just wished it wasn't with Lorna.

Neil glanced at her and saw her scowling. 'You don't think I *enjoyed* it? Did you?' he teased. 'Lorna! Me! God, she really does spoof. She *loves* the sound of her own voice. No wonder I got pissed, I was trying to drown my sorrows, listening to her. She's a rare bird all right. Where they got her from I don't know. I think she was surprised that I could order a bottle of wine!'

Heather laughed, relieved. 'Yeah, she's good at being superior, New York won't know what's hit it.'

345

'Look, why don't you and I go and have a nice dinner in the Slieve Russell—'

'Hmmm, posh,' Heather said appreciatively.

'Well, you deserve it,' Neil declared as he carried the sacks out to the wheely-bins.

Heather took out the mop and filled a bucket with hot water. Dinner in the Slieve Russell sounded lovely. And Lorna was gone out of their hair, so she could forget about her and get on with her life with Neil.

Neil dumped the bags into the bins and heaved a sigh of relief. That hadn't been too bad. The row was over and he'd slipped in the news about having dinner with Lorna. Better to hear it from him than someone else. At least if anyone mentioned it to her she'd know about it. He felt he'd carried it off OK. She'd been a bit shocked to hear it was the dining-room of the Lake View and not the bar, but his excuse about not being a cheapskate had mollified her. As long as Dan Leland kept his mouth shut, Neil would be fine. It was a one-night stand. Men had them. It didn't mean a thing. He glanced up at the sky. Lorna was in America by now. A weekend with her in New York would be something to look forward to, if she agreed to it, but how would he get away with it?

He could always say he was going to a sales conference in the UK, or Europe even. Ford had had a huge sales conference for salesmen from all over Europe, in the Don Carlos in Marbella. It wasn't unheard of for car salesmen to travel to conferences. He'd think of some way to get around

346

it. He'd worked his butt off the past few years, he deserved some of the good things in life. He hoped she'd contact him. She'd taken his card with his mobile and email address. It was up to her. Would she? Wouldn't she? He didn't know. That was part of the attraction, he supposed. He hoped she did. Whistling, he went back into the showrooms, glad to see that Heather was mopping the floor.

Heather tucked a pair of clean white socks into her
sports bag, made sure she had all her toiletries and
hefted it on to her shoulder. She was looking
forward to practice; she'd missed it the previous
week on account of preparing for the launch and
she knew from experience that if she left going for
too long her fitness levels slipped rapidly.

'See you later,' she called to Neil, who was
ensconced in front of the TV drinking beer.

'Have a good game,' he called back and she
smiled. A game of basketball would do him all the
good in the world. She hurried downstairs. She was
late; just as well it was only a practice and not a real
match. She walked along the main street enjoying
the light breeze in her face. The weather had turned
mild. The scent of spring was in the air. Buds were
bursting out on trees and shrubs and the cherry
blossoms were out, swaying in the breeze. What
bliss to be at home in springtime. She was so
incredibly lucky, she told herself as she raised
her face to the sun. It was getting stronger too.
There was heat in it, definitely. And the nights were
much brighter. She felt alive, exhilarated and happy

as she breezed into the changing-room in the sports hall. Women in various stages of undress paused to look when she came in, and was it her imagination, but had conversation come to a halt?

'Hi,' she said awkwardly. 'What's up?'

'Not a thing,' Lena Burton said hurriedly. 'We were just saying how good St Mary's are lately. We're playing them next Saturday so we'd want to get in a good practice today.'

'Sure,' Heather agreed. 'That new player they got is great at long shots.'

'Yeah,' agreed Norah Sinclair. 'Let's get out on court, I intend for us to whop their asses.' Everyone laughed and Heather relaxed.

They started with lay-ups to warm up and before long were engaged in a keenly fought practice match where no quarter was given. Heather took possession of the ball, dribbled fast and dodged Norah, to aim at the basket. The shot went in and she felt extremely gratified. She still had a good aim. She might get Neil to put up a basket at the back of the flat so she could practise shooting. It was an extremely satisfying morning and they all agreed to put in some extra practice during the week before their big match.

The following Wednesday night, after practice, she was just going into the loo when she heard Norah and Lena engaged in an argument.

'I'm telling her. It's only fair, Norah,' Lena declared. 'I'd much prefer if someone told me. If I was in that position.'

'It's none of our business, Lena,' Norah retorted.

'We're her friends. It is. Everybody's talking about it.'

'Well, wait until after the match, then,' Norah said angrily. 'We don't want her off form.'

Heather turned away, mystified. She didn't want to barge in on their private conversation. She'd wait until she got home to go to the loo. Whatever was going on, Norah wasn't allowing it to interfere with the match. Good captain. Had her priorities right, Heather grinned as she left the sports hall and walked briskly towards the garage. She was in fit mode and had been watching what she was eating. She was determined to lose a stone by the summer. Then she'd be able to buy smarter clothes, and Neil would never tell her to take tips from Lorna again. She wondered how her cousin was getting on. Needless to say she hadn't contacted Heather. Her usual hot potato act. Jane had told Anne that she was living near friends of Carina's in the suburbs but that she intended getting an apartment in Manhattan. She was loving it, Jane said.

Neil was at his computer when she popped into the showroom, which to her surprise was still open. He was engrossed in an email, most unlike him, she thought in surprise as she bent to kiss the top of his head. Neil hated computers and could make a hames of the slightest little thing. He'd mastered email only after a couple of hours tutorial from her.

'Hi,' she greeted him.

He nearly jumped out of his seat. 'You gave me a fright,' he said hotly, his face red and flushed. Heather was taken aback by his response.

'Sorry,' she apologized. 'Who's the email from?'

'Aw, just a fellow in Dublin. I told you Douglas Kennedy wants a four-wheel-drive. He's looking after it for me.' He closed his emails and turned to look at her. 'How did the practice go?'

'Good,' she said cheerfully. 'It's nearly nine, why don't you close up and I'll make us some supper?'

'Sounds good to me. Any chance of cheese on toast?' he asked hopefully.

'Every chance,' Heather assured him. She was feeling peckish herself after her practice.

'Do you want to have our dinner in the Slieve Russell this Saturday?' he asked a while later as she made their supper.

She made a face. 'Can't this Saturday. We'll either be celebrating a win over Mary's or drowning our sorrows.'

'Oh, I forgot about the match. How about the following Saturday?'

'Sounds good to me.' She gave him a cuddle.

'I might have to go to a sales conference in the UK some time in April,' he said diffidently. 'No wives or partners unfortunately. Will you hold the fort here?'

'Sure,' Heather agreed.

'I might go over early and visit a few showrooms, get some ideas, talk to people. Might go from Thursday to Sunday.'

'Good idea,' she said enthusiastically. 'Might as well make the most of it while you're there and see if they have any updated office programmes. Find out what systems other garages use.'

'Yes, Mam.' Neil saluted and she laughed.

'Am I too bossy?'

'No, you're not bossy enough,' Neil said quietly and gave her a funny look.

'Oh well, I can change that. Make the hot chocolate while you're standing there,' she ordered briskly as she sprinkled Lea & Perrin's sauce on the bubbling golden cheese.

She shouldn't have eaten that, she thought guiltily afterwards. She was doing well, she'd lost a few pounds, she wanted to keep it like that. Even running around at basketball she noticed that she was fitter and she wanted to really contribute to the match on Saturday.

It was a hard-fought match, but she scored the point that brought them level just seconds before the final whistle went and she was surrounded by cheering team-mates. It had been a bit of a fluke shot – she hadn't even taken proper aim, she admitted, but no one cared. They hadn't lost to an exceptionally good team and there was something to celebrate tonight after all.

They went for a meal in a new Italian restaurant at the far end of the town and as they sat sipping wine waiting for their main course, she felt perfectly content. This was such a good time in her life, she reflected as the waiter placed the calamari in front of her. Unfortunately, her calamari was the only blip in her good life, she acknowledged ruefully as she chewed on what seemed like warm rubber bands.

Beside her Lena prodded at her runny, greasy lasagne with distaste. 'This is crap,' she murmured.

'So is this,' Heather whispered. 'Won't be coming here again.'

'Ditto, the bloody garlic bread's cold in the middle. This is outrageous. I'm going to complain.' A heated argument ensued with the waiter, as ten disgruntled women let their feelings be known about a less than satisfactory meal.

An hour later, eschewing coffee and desserts, they made their way to the pub, vowing never to set foot in Aldo's Trattoria again. By the time they were on their third round, Aldo and his crap food were a distant memory and they were feeling no pain.

Around eleven, Heather stood up to go.

'Where you going?' Lena demanded. 'The night's only starting, it's not as if you have two kids to face in the morning like I have. Don't be such a party pooper.'

'Ah well, I haven't seen much of Neil this week with all the practice,' Heather explained. Lena's face darkened. 'Fuck him,' she said viciously.

'*Lena!*' Heather exclaimed, shocked. Norah gave Lena a tug on the arm.

'You're pissed, Lena,' she said warningly.

'You should tell her, Norah. It's not fair,' Lena said indignantly.

'Tell me what?' Heather demanded, suddenly feeling sick as she remembered the argument she'd overheard between her friends the previous week. Silence descended on their table and nine faces turned to look at her with various expressions of concern and embarrassment mirrored on their faces.

'Tell me what,' Heather said quietly. 'Please. I want to know what's going on?'

Norah took a deep breath. 'Come outside with me if you really want to know.'

'OK,' Heather agreed, totally sober by now.

'I'm sorry,' muttered Lena. 'I just think—'

'That's enough, Lena,' Norah interrupted.

Heather followed her captain through the crowded pub until they came to the front door. 'Come on. Let's sit on the seat over there,' Norah suggested, making her way to a wrought-iron seat outside Carleton Auctioneers.

'Just tell me what you have to tell me,' Heather said quickly, sitting down on the cold, hard iron.

'You know my boyfriend Dan's a night porter in the Lake View?'

Heather nodded, wondering what on earth Dan Leland had to do with her.

'Well, he told me that Neil spent the night of his bash with Lorna Morgan in a mini suite and she didn't leave until after seven the next morning. She gave him thirty Euros for the room. I'm sorry, Heather. I didn't know what to do. Lena felt very strongly that it was only fair to tell you. She felt you'd want to know. I wasn't sure,' she admitted honestly.

Heather hardly heard her. Neil and Lorna. It couldn't be true. He couldn't do that to her. Lorna couldn't do that to her. Could they? She felt frightened. Her face crumpled. Tears spurted down her cheeks as she gave a low howl. 'Noooo, no, no, it can't be,' she cried as Norah patted her awkwardly on the back and kept apologizing.

'Let me walk you home to your parents,' she offered kindly.

'No, no, I want to be by myself. I need to be by myself,' Heather said wildly. 'I have to go.'

'But where? You won't do anything foolish?' Norah said anxiously. 'Let me go with you.'

With a superhuman effort, Heather composed herself. 'It's OK, Norah, go back to the girls. I'm not going to do anything silly, I just need to be by myself for a while.' She stood up. 'Thanks for telling me,' she said quietly. 'I know it was hard.'

'Lena wasn't being malicious. You know that,' Norah said miserably.

'Of course I do. Lena's got a big heart. I can see where she's coming from.' Heather wiped her eyes. 'Better to know now than to go on making a fool of myself.'

'I'm really sorry, Heather. That Lorna Morgan is a bitch,' Norah swore.

'And Neil Brennan's a bastard,' Heather added quietly as she walked purposefully towards the garage.

The light was on in the flat, so he was there, she thought with a sick feeling in the pit of her stomach. She took out the keys of the showrooms and let herself in quietly, switching off the alarm. She didn't switch on the lights. The small light on Neil's desk would do fine. She flicked on the computer and went to email, scrolling down through them with a racing heart. Nothing in the 'in' box. She went to deleted emails and scrolled down through them. Neil was so lazy and so computer illiterate that he rarely deleted completely and it was often left to her to delete forty or fifty emails at one sitting.

She came to the one she was looking for.

Lorna Morgan as brazen as anything on the screen. Subject. N.Y. She opened it, feeling more angry than she'd ever felt in her life.

Hi, Neil,

Just a quickie, although not as satisfying as our quickie ha ha. You've got to get over here, you'd love it. Tell Heather you're going away on business and I'll book us into a fantastic hotel for a weekend. Rates very reasonable, I'll allow you to treat me. Believe it or not, I miss you. Loved what you did to me that night in the Lake View. Email me back!

Lorna

Sick to her stomach, Heather opened his reply.

Hi gorgeous,

wish I was having a quickie with you now, I feel horny just at the thought of it, you wild sexy woman, who's too much woman for Kilronan. Will definitely try and arrange that weekend, and of course I'll treat you, if you're verrrry good to me, wish I was inside you right now. Make sure it's a good strong king-size bed!

Neil

'Oh my God,' she whispered. 'Oh God. Why? Why have you done this to me? Why have they done it? What am I going to do?' She sat there in shock, wounded to her core. She clicked on the print icon and watched as the laser printer slowly eased out the distasteful document.

Switching off the computer and the light, she set the alarm and locked up after her. He wouldn't be able to deny this, not when she handed him the printout. How could she have been so wrong about him? So completely and utterly wrong. Lorna's behaviour didn't come as a total shock, although Heather had huge difficulty accepting that she would betray her like she had. They were cousins. They'd been so-called friends all their lives. What a fool she'd been. Lorna had never been her friend. She was a total user. It was clear she felt no loyalty, nothing, for Heather. She was the pits. The lowest of the low.

Neil was asleep in the chair when she walked into the sitting-room, several empty cans at his feet. Silently, she stared at him and felt hatred erupt inside her.

'I hate you, you gutless bastard,' she swore viciously as she kicked him hard on the shins.

'What the fuck— Heather! What the hell did you do that for?' he demanded, puzzled and dazed.

'So you're going to a sales conference in the UK are you? Aren't I the fool?' she yelled. 'I know all about you and that slutty cousin of mine. I know all about your night in the mini suite in the Lake View. So you wish you were inside her and you're all horny, are you? You fucking wanker, Neil Brennan!' She shoved the printout under his nose.

'You get out of here right now. I'm going to pack my stuff and I'll collect it tomorrow and I never want to see you again. Get out, you bastard, you're welcome to her and she's welcome to you. You were made for each other.' She whacked him hard across the face, wanting to rake her nails down his cheeks.

Neil pushed her away from him.

'Don't do that!' he warned.

'Why, what will you do? Hit me?' she taunted. 'Get out, Neil, before I get really mad and do something I'll regret. Get out,' she yelled, shoving him out of the door. He went, saying nothing. He didn't try to defend himself because he couldn't and as she closed the door behind him she sank to her knees sobbing, knowing that she'd never trust another man as long as she lived.

29

'I'm sorry it's not better news, Oliver, but you and your wife can attend the fertility clinic in the Rotunda. Maybe you'd be suitable for IVF. It is possible for men suffering from azoospermia to have small amounts of sperm harvested—'

'No, Doctor,' Oliver interrupted, his face taut and grim. 'I don't want to go down that road. I don't think my wife could cope if it didn't work.'

'Well, look, Oliver, both of you can come back and see me if you change your mind, you know where I am.' Miles Lawson patted Oliver on the back and shook hands with him.

'Thanks for all your help, Doctor, I appreciate it,' Oliver replied, managing a small smile. Miles Lawson had been kind, helpful and sympathetic as Oliver had been called back for more tests, explaining as simply as he could about sperm count, morphology, motility and the like as Oliver struggled to come to terms with the fact that he was very unlikely to father a child.

As he sat into the car and drove towards the Phoenix Park, he felt a lump rise in his throat. He'd never thought much about having children. He felt awkward around them, but he'd assumed he and Noreen would have them eventually and that he'd do his best to be a good father.

To be told that this was unlikely was like being kicked in the stomach, hard. He felt a complete failure. Half a man. He might be able to do the business, but in terms of providing for Noreen's need for a baby, he'd failed her and he was dreading telling her. Life was bad enough now, how would they be when she found out that the infertility was his fault? She'd probably start putting him under pressure to have that harvesting thing done and go for IVF and he just couldn't face it. If it failed, she'd be devastated.

He turned left off the roundabout opposite the American ambassador's residence and drove down the narrow tree-lined road to where the Visitor's Centre nestled among the trees. He needed a cup of tea. He had the mother and father of a headache, something he rarely suffered from. He felt so tense that he almost jumped when his mobile phone rang.

He was surprised to see Noreen's number come up. They rarely rang each other these days unless for a specific reason. 'Hello?' he tried to keep his voice as normal as he could.

'Oliver, Maura's gone into labour early, so I'm driving up to Holles Street with her. I don't know how long I'll be. There's steak and chops in the fridge if you want to—'

'Don't worry about me, Noreen. I can have a pub lunch or something. Tell Maura good luck, keep in touch,' he said heavily.

The irony of it all. There were times he felt God had a most peculiar sense of humour. There was Maura about to give birth, the very day he found out he couldn't give his wife a baby. He'd better hold off a few days before telling Noreen. It was going to be even more difficult now for her. Holding a little baby in her arms always put the longing on her. What would seeing Maura's child born do to her?

The restaurant was not busy and he carried his tea and scone up the circular wooden stairs to a table by the window. Shafts of sunlight slanted on to the wooden floor, and outside were signs of spring's exuberance, unmistakable in the budding trees and new growth in the grass and flowerbeds. Hard to believe this green peaceful glade was in the middle of a large city.

Maura would probably be up to ninety, she was about a month early. He hoped the child would be all right. He'd been surprised when Noreen had told him she'd asked her to attend the birth. He thought she would have asked her other sister, they seemed much closer. It was probably because Noreen was a nurse and she'd feel safer, he surmised, buttering his scone. Maura was a bit of a user to say the least. He could understand why Andy didn't want to be at the birth. Oliver wouldn't have fancied it himself, nevertheless it wasn't very manly of his brother-in-law to wimp out and not support his wife when she needed him. Had it been him and Noreen he would have put his own feelings aside and been there if she wanted.

That wasn't ever going to happen now. Maybe he

should say it to Noreen straight away and not be letting her go around with false hope. It wasn't fair. She was going to have to deal with their situation one way or the other. He pushed away his half-eaten scone. He had no appetite. First thing in the morning he was going to tell Noreen about his test results. There was no point in putting it off.

'I'm scared. What if something's wrong?' Maura cried as Andy overtook a lorry at ninety miles an hour.

'Andy, slow down, we want to get to the hospital in one piece,' Noreen said calmly as she squeezed her sister's hand. 'Stop worrying, Maura, you'll be fine—'

'Oooohhhh!' squealed Maura as a contraction enveloped her. Andy nearly had a heart attack.

'What's wrong? What's wrong? Don't say she's having it?'

'She's *not* having it, Andrew, keep driving.' Noreen couldn't hide her exasperation. What a useless tool her brother-in-law was. 'Maura, breathe like they taught you in prenatal. Deep breath now, breathe slowly,' she instructed firmly.

'They're getting closer,' Maura whimpered.

'There's plenty of time between them. Stop fretting, Maura. You're not going to have it in the car. Trust me, I'm a nurse.' She smiled at her sister, from whose tear-rimmed eyes streaks of mascara ran down her red sweaty face. Noreen fished a clean tissue out of her bag and wiped Maura's face. 'You don't want to arrive at Holles Street looking like a wreck,' she soothed, glad to withdraw her hand momentarily from Maura's vice-like grip.

'The traffic is awful,' moaned Maura as they came to a halt in a tailback at a roundabout.

'It's not too bad, we made good time from Kilronan to Navan. Stop panicking, you'll be fine.'

'I hope there's nothing wrong with the baby, four weeks is very early.' Maura's eyes were bright with fear.

'Not at all, remember our cousin Aideen had twins ten weeks early and look at them now. Blooming. The baby will have to go into an incubator for a while, that's all. Don't be worrying, Maura, just concentrate on your breathing and getting through the labour and you'll be fine,' Noreen encouraged, in her calm, reassuring, professional voice. She hoped everything was all right; obviously there was always some cause for concern when a baby came prematurely.

'I'm so nervous I think I'm going to puke,' Maura groaned.

'Don't puke in the car, for crying out loud,' Andy blustered. 'Do you want me to pull in?'

'Take deep breaths, Maura,' Noreen encouraged. If she got her hands on Andy she'd flatten him. He was *less* than useless. She didn't envy her sister the rearing of her child. Somehow or another she didn't think her brother-in-law would be a hands-on father.

At least he'd be a father, she scowled. It was so unfair. Oliver would be a very conscientious father if he got the chance. He took his responsibilities seriously. She knew he'd take care of her and be with her at the birth if she was lucky enough to be pregnant. She banished the thought. Daydreams, that's all they were. She'd want to start facing reality that there might be more difficulties ahead. About two weeks after he'd had the test, she'd delicately mentioned the subject and asked if he'd had any word.

'I've to go for another one,' he'd muttered and she had known better than pursue the matter apart from asking if he'd like her to go with him.

'I'll be fine,' he'd retorted and walked out of the kitchen. If he was to go for another test it meant there could be problems and that was worrying to say the least. Maura groaned again and Noreen forgot her own situation as she turned to her sister and gave her her full attention.

As it happened it was a smooth, uncomplicated birth, and as she held her baby nephew for a quick minute before he was whisked off to the Special Care Unit, she looked into his scrunched-up little face with his little flat nose and felt a wave of longing that almost crucified her.

'He's a lovely little fella, Maura, congratulations,' she whispered smiling at her sister, who was totally overwhelmed.

'Oh my God! Oh my God! I can't believe I did it, Noreen. I thought I'd go to pieces. It was amazing. Andy is a fool to have missed this.' She held out her hands for the baby. Noreen placed the little bundle carefully into the curve of her elbow.

'You were terrific, you did very well, Maura,' she said warmly, all the years of resentment she'd felt for her sister evaporating as they looked at the baby that had brought them close for the first time in their lives.

'I want you to be the godmother.' Maura looked up at her.

'But what about Rita?' Noreen said in surprise. 'I think she's expecting to be godmother.'

'She won't mind. I'll explain to her that because you were with me, there's a special bond with the baby, and that's true isn't it?' she asked anxiously.

Noreen's eyes glazed with tears. She nodded. Maura would never know just how much of a bond she felt for that gorgeous little being that the nurse was taking to the Special Care Unit.

'God, Noreen, I never saw you crying before,' Maura said, shocked. 'And it's me whose hormones are awry,' she joked awkwardly.

Noreen wiped her eyes and took a deep breath. 'I'm just glad everything's all right. Do you want to ring Andy and let him know he's got a son?'

'I suppose so,' Maura muttered resentfully. 'He could have stayed around instead of going off into town. I'll get him to drive you home.'

'No, no, let him stay with you,' Noreen said hastily, the thought of being driven to Kilronan by Andy not an enticing prospect. 'I'll give Oliver a ring. He'll come and collect me. Now I'm going to go outside and let the nurses get on with it and I'll come to the ward with you when you're ready.'

'Thanks for everything, Noreen. There's just one thing I want to say to you.' Maura looked agitated.

'What's that? Do you want me to do something for you?'

'No, no, you've done enough. It's just . . . just

I'm sorry I wasn't more of a help to you with Mam. I feel very bad about it.' She burst into tears. Noreen looked at her dishevelled younger sister and thought of how much she'd despised and resented her when their mother was ill. She'd often wanted to slap Maura's smug face. She remembered Oliver's words about being able to look herself in the eye and actually felt sorry for her sister. She had to live with her regrets about how she'd behaved towards their mother. That was one burden she didn't have to carry, Noreen thought gratefully.

'Don't trouble yourself about it, Maura. You need to concentrate on your baby and getting your strength back,' she said evenly. 'Stop crying now.'

'I used to think you were so hard, and you're not, you're very kind, Noreen.' Maura wept. 'I'm really sorry.'

'Shussh, stop now, forget it,' Noreen soothed. 'You'll be fine after a cup of tea. I'll see you in a little while.' She handed her sister a tissue. 'Come on now, wipe your eyes or you'll set me off again. Twice in one day would be just *too* much!'

Maura gave a watery smile. 'Thanks, Noreen, for everything.'

So her sister had finally acknowledged that she had something to apologize for regarding their mother, Noreen thought dully as she walked out into the corridor. Somehow in the light of all that was going on in her life it didn't seem to matter any more, which was probably a good thing. There was no point in being eaten up with bitterness and anger.

She punched in Oliver's number.

'Hello,' she heard his familiar deep voice at the other end.

'Can you collect me?' she asked shakily. 'Maura had a baby boy, four and a half pounds. Everything's fine. I just don't feel like going for the bus.'

'That's OK. It's Holles Street, near Merrion Square, isn't it?'

'Yes, I'm in the Merrion Wing. I'll go down to the ward with Maura and wait with her until Andy gets here, and then I'll go and have a cup of tea.'

'It will take me a while,' Oliver warned.

'I know,' she said quietly.

'Are you OK?' Oliver asked gruffly.

'I'll be glad when you're here,' Noreen admitted. 'I just want to go home. See you when I see you.'

'OK, 'bye.'

Noreen heard him click off and felt an ache of loneliness. She longed for Oliver to put his arms around her like the old days. She wanted to pour out her sadness, and tell him what lay behind it, but she knew she would be reluctant to lay her burdens on his shoulders now. If he had asked her to marry him, rather than the other way around, she would have felt more comfortable baring her soul. She would have felt enabled to do it in the knowledge that he had wanted her to share her life with him. The nagging uncertainty that he might never have married her had grown far stronger since their row at Christmas and she knew their relationship had changed irrevocably because of it.

The door to the delivery suite opened and Maura was wheeled out. She looked flushed and tired against the pillows. 'Did you ring Andy?' Noreen asked as she fell into step beside her.

'I did. He was having something to eat in the Davenport. It's not far away. He's going to stay the night there. I think he's had a few drinks,' she confided.

'Wet the baby's head.' Noreen smiled, privately disgusted with Andy that he couldn't have waited until later to start celebrating. *Selfish bastard*, she thought. *Just like Pete.* Funny that she should think of him now. He rarely came into her consciousness. Difficult though her relationship was with Oliver, she completely respected her husband in contrast to the contempt she held her former partner in. She wouldn't mind a trip to London though. The last time she'd visited was just before her wedding and that seemed another lifetime ago. She kept in touch with her friends through email mostly and the telephone. Kay Thomas, her best friend and a nursing sister at St Mary's in Paddington, was always asking her to come for a visit.

Maybe after Maura's baby was christened she'd go for a couple of days. She knew Oliver wouldn't mind – he'd probably welcome the break from her, she thought wryly, as Maura was wheeled into a pretty, sunny, two-bed ward.

Her sister was sleeping when Andy arrived two hours later, full of the joys. The whiff of brandy was unmistakable. He had a bunch of straggly flowers and a blue teddy under his arm. *Full marks for originality*, Noreen thought nastily as she stood up to leave.

'Hasn't she the life, asleep at this hour of the evening?' Andy boomed, giving her a jovial puck in the arm. 'Well, what's my son like?'

Too good for the likes of you, she was tempted to retort, but she restrained herself. 'He's lovely,' she said shortly. 'I'm just going to go and give Oliver a call and have a cup of tea. See you later.'

'Grand.' Andy was ogling the young woman in the bed next to Maura, who was cuddling her baby. 'Howya doin'? Is he a good grubber?' he leered, and Noreen slipped out of the room before she clattered him.

Oliver was trying to find parking around Merrion Square when she phoned him and he sounded distinctly tetchy.

'I'll wait for you at the front door. You better pop in and see Maura for a minute,' she suggested.

'Right, see you – I see a space,' he informed her and then she heard an explosion of profanity and the sound of a car horn as someone else pipped him to the space. Noreen prudently hung up. She walked downstairs to the front hall and sat down to await his arrival. After a while she felt like a breath of air and stepped outside. It was good to feel the breeze cold against her face after the heat of the hospital. Darkness had fallen and the rush hour was in full swing. It reminded her of London. Now that she'd got the idea of going for a visit she was looking forward to it. Life in Kilronan was quiet and uneventful most of the time. There was a sameness about the days that got to her sometimes. If she and Oliver did more things together as a couple it might not be so bad, but he was immersed

369

in his work and for the most part she was left to her own devices. Some retail therapy, meals out, trips to the theatre and meeting up with old friends and catching up on hospital gossip were just the diversions she needed, Noreen decided as she watched her husband stride towards the hospital with a face like thunder.

'By God, there's some crazy hoors driving around this place,' he grumbled as he reached her. 'I bought this for Maura, until you get some baby stuff.' He held out a bottle of champagne.

'That was kind, Oliver, and thoughtful.' She reached up and gave him a peck on the cheek. The first kiss she'd given him since their row.

He looked surprised. 'Well, I didn't like to come empty-handed. A bottle of plonk seemed a bit mean in the circumstances.'

'That other yoke arrived with a wilted bunch of flowers and a teddy-bear and he'd been drinking.' Noreen led the way into the hospital and up the stairs towards the private rooms.

'How's the baby doing?' Oliver asked.

'Very well for a premmie. He's a lovely little chap. She asked me to be godmother.' She arched an eyebrow at him.

'How do you feel about that?' Oliver slanted a glance at her.

'I was surprised. I thought Rita was earmarked for that position. She said it was because I was with her, and to tell the truth I'm glad I was. She won't be getting much support from that bollox, I wouldn't say. She even apologized for not helping out more with Mam. She said she was really sorry.'

'And what did you say?' Oliver was more than surprised at this revelation.

'What could I say, Oliver? There's no point in holding on to old grudges. At least she had the grace to apologize. She was very upset about it. Hormones all over the place, I suppose. I told her to forget about it and concentrate on getting back to strength for the baby.'

'Good girl, Noreen. It's best to let bygones be bygones,' Oliver approved warmly and they smiled at each other, a touch of their old affection breaking through as they walked down the corridor to Maura's room.

'Oh . . . hello, Oliver. Thanks for coming up.' Maura was surprised to see him.

'It's just for a minute. I'm sure you're tired after all the hard work. This might refresh you.' Oliver smiled at his sister-in-law and handed her the bottle of champagne.

'Well, thank you, Oliver. Oh, it's Moët,' she said, delighted.

'I'll take charge of that,' Andy declared jocosely.

'No you won't,' Maura said sharply, putting it in her bedside locker.

'So, Maura, when will you be able to take the baby home?' Oliver asked.

'They said it shouldn't be too long. He's in an incubator and when his weight comes up to five pounds and they're happy with his progress they'll let me have him,' Maura said. 'Would you like to look in at him? I'm going down to feed him.'

Oliver looked at Noreen. 'We can have a look at him on the way out, we'll walk down to Special

Care with Maura,' she said as she handed her sister her dressing-gown.

'I'll wait outside,' Oliver said hastily as Maura made to get out of bed.

'Are you going to come and see your son?' she turned to Andy.

'I suppose I'd better see if he's a chip off the old block,' he agreed, and Noreen couldn't get over his casual attitude. They made their way to the unit and watched as Maura went in and lifted the baby out of the incubator. She brought him to the window and stood proudly with him in her arms.

'That's my boy!' Andy exclaimed. Oliver forced a smile. He was glad for his sister-in-law that all had gone well but today was possibly the worst day ever for him to have to oohh and aahh over a baby. Looking at Maura's proud expression brought it home forcibly to him just what Noreen was being denied. Seeing Maura's reaction to her child, he began to understand the strength of Noreen's desire to have a baby. And because of him she might never experience her greatest desire. He felt awful. A failure as a man and a husband.

'We should go and give them some privacy,' he said quietly to Noreen.

'Arrah, stay for another while and we'll go for a pint,' Andy urged.

'No thanks, Andy, I want to get going, I've a busy day ahead of me tomorrow,' Oliver replied politely. Noreen muttered a brusque goodbye. She was raging with his carry-on.

'Did you ever see the likes of him, he should

be ashamed of himself,' she complained as they walked towards Merrion Square.

'He's a cool customer all right.' Oliver marched along, forcing her to quicken her pace.

'Would you slow down a bit, Oliver, we're not in a race,' Noreen protested.

'Sorry. I'm tired. I just want to get home.'

'I'll drive if you want,' she offered.

'Ah, you're all right, you're probably tired too after being at the . . . being with Maura,' he amended.

'She was very good actually, she did what she had to do without any fuss.' Noreen felt herself begin to relax. It was the first time in weeks that they'd had a normal conversation. She was half tempted to ask him would he like to go somewhere for a meal but he looked really whacked.

'It's over there,' Oliver took her arm to cross the road. He was a real gentleman in that regard. She'd always liked his courteous ways. Maybe things might start improving between them. The new baby had brought healing to her and Maura's relationship, Oliver had been proud of her when he'd congratulated her on letting bygones be bygones. She should try and do the same with him. Try and put those wounding words out of her head, not give them any more space.

She got into the car feeling easier with him than she had for a long time.

30

Fourteen straight hours on a building site wouldn't
have left him as tired, Oliver felt as he sat in the
Haven with Noreen waiting for their meal to be
served. She had asked him on the way home if he'd
like to stop for a meal somewhere, but under the
circumstances he hadn't felt like going anywhere
posh, so he'd asked if she minded if he kept on
driving and having something to eat in Kilronan.

'Suits me fine, too,' she said tiredly, and his heart
sank once more at the prospect of telling her his
news. Noreen deserved better, he thought discon-
solately. She was a good woman, she'd be a loving
mother. All the unwanted children in the world,
and she, who wanted one so badly, was deprived. It
wasn't fair and it wasn't right. Should he say to her
that if she wanted to find someone else, she should
do so, he wondered? But, especially after his un-
kind words at Christmas, she'd surely think that he
didn't love her or was trying to get rid of her and
that was not what he wanted. He just wanted for
her to be happy. She looked weary as she sat
sipping her glass of wine. And she'd got thinner, he
noticed. Weight she could ill afford to lose. There

was no happiness in their marriage and it was taking its toll on her. He'd want to start making a bit more of an effort. The last couple of weeks had seen them drifting further apart. That was no way to live.

'Traffic was brutal, wasn't it?' he remarked, fiddling with a vinegar sachet.

'I'd hate to have to commute,' Noreen said. She made a face. 'When I was standing outside the hospital it reminded me of being in London. I drove in city traffic for years over there and never thought anything about it.'

'I'd go crazy being stuck in traffic like that day in, day out,' Oliver said truthfully. 'But you know me, no patience.'

'Ah, you're not that bad,' she said lightly.

'You know I'm sorry about what I said,' he said awkwardly.

'Let's forget it, Oliver, and start over,' Noreen said quietly. 'It's been horrible.'

'I know. I don't like not talking.' He was half tempted to tell her about his tests but a pub lounge was not the place to tell a woman she might never have a child, he thought ruefully as the waitress placed a plate of steak, onions and chips in front of him and a smoked salmon salad in front of Noreen. Let her eat her meal in peace, she'd be in turmoil soon enough.

They ate in silence. But it wasn't an uncomfortable one, and he was glad when Noreen ordered dessert for herself. The lounge was starting to fill up and the sound of talk and laughter was relaxing and brought a little balm to him after his day.

'Have another pint and I'll have another glass of wine,' Noreen suggested.

'OK so.' He smiled at her, glad that at least they were back on speaking terms. It would have been a nightmare to have to tell her the news when they were hostile with each other. He watched a couple walk over to a table in the corner with their arms around each other's waists. The girl was glowing, smiling at her boyfriend, engrossed in him with eyes for no one else. It was touching to see, but he wondered how long it would last when life's hard knocks began to take their toll.

Don't be such a cynical bastard, he reproved silently. Just because he and Noreen were having problems didn't mean everyone else would have them.

By ten thirty he was yawning his head off. Two return trips to Dublin after a sleepless night had been a killer and all he wanted to do was get into bed. 'Are you ready to go home?' he asked.

'Yeah, it's been a long day.' Noreen shrugged into her coat and linked her arm into his. Just like old times, he thought heavily, except that everything had changed only she didn't realize it yet. The nearer he got to home the more heavy-hearted he got. He wished he could tell her and get it over with. When was the right time? Was there a right time? He followed her into the house and hung up his coat.

'Will I come back from Siberia?' Noreen smiled up at him when he said goodnight.

'Will you get a flight at such short notice?' he teased as he put an affectionate arm around her and they walked up to their bedroom together.

'I need to have a quick shower, Oliver. It was awfully stuffy in the hospital. I used to be used to that too,' she said ruefully as she slipped out of her trousers and polo-neck and threw them in the linen basket. Oliver sat on the end of the bed and unbuckled his belt. His stomach was tied up in knots. He could hear the sound of the shower spray. Should he tell her now or let her have a good night's sleep? He kicked off his shoes and socks, pulled the rest of his clothes off and got into bed, remembering to stay on his own side. For the past few weeks he'd sprawled spread-eagled in the middle.

The sheets were cold. He was cold. He lay tense in the bed until she came out of the en suite. 'Feel better after that?'

'I certainly do.' She slipped out of her towel and slid in under the duvet. 'Oh God, it's freezing.' She snuggled in immediately and he put his arms around her. 'Put the light out,' she whispered.

'OK,' he whispered back as she raised her lips to his. They kissed tentatively and then with more passion as their bodies moulded together in old remembered positions, hands stroking and touching, caressing and teasing. She was stroking him, arousing him, when he suddenly remembered his test results. To his horror he felt himself grow soft and in the light of a stray beam of moonlight that drifted in through the window he saw the dismay in her eyes.

'Sorry, sorry,' he muttered, turning away.

'It's OK, Oliver, it's been a long day. You're tired. Go to sleep.' She leaned over, kissed him and put her arms around him. He closed his eyes and clenched his hands and felt more shattered than he'd ever felt in his life.

Noreen lay beside Oliver, wide-eyed. She tried to tell herself that Oliver was tired. He'd had a couple of pints. Pete was never able to perform after a few pints, she reassured herself, but she couldn't quell the bubbles of fear that were rising uncontrollably. Maybe he no longer wanted her. Maybe he'd only been doing a duty shag. Oliver was as healthy as an ox and had never had trouble doing the business.

Why did it have to happen tonight, just when things were getting back on an even keel? She'd been enjoying their intimacy. The feel of his arms around her had been comforting and reassuring and at the back of her mind she was heartily relieved that they were making love again. Conception had some chance of occurring at least. It had none when they were sleeping in separate rooms.

Poor Oliver. At least women could fake it, men couldn't. Knowing her husband as well as she did, she knew he'd be mortified by this insult to his manhood. But there was no point in saying anything, no point in even trying to reassure him. That would only make him feel worse. He couldn't bear to get into a discussion about it. He would hug that to himself now, the barriers would go up and she'd never hear another word about it.

Hopefully it was only tiredness – the last thing they needed was impotency to add to their problems. She closed her eyes and drew deep even breaths trying to relax enough to sleep. She remembered the tiny little hands of Maura's baby and his little scrunched-up face and envied her sister so badly she could almost taste it. The longing overwhelmed her and hot tears slid down her cheeks. How could the pain of wanting feel so physical, she wondered, feeling the ache so strong it almost smothered her. Did her sister know how truly blessed she was?

She remembered Andy. Well, every cloud had a silver lining, it had to be said. Who'd want the likes of him to be father to their child? Who'd want to be married to him? Maura certainly had her own problems, she acknowledged. Oliver was a stalwart husband, a man of integrity, and she had got the far better man. It was a comfort of sorts, she reminded herself, before she eventually drifted off to sleep.

The dawn chorus woke him and for a moment he lay comfortably in that relaxed place between sleeping and waking, until he remembered the events of the day and night before and the heavy burden of turmoil descended once more. Noreen lay beside him breathing evenly, her face relaxed in repose.

Maybe last night was a once-off, a fluke, he thought miserably. Bad enough that he couldn't father a child without being a bloody eunuch as well. Just say he was never able to perform again. A deep spasm of dread twisted his guts. He was only gone thirty and he enjoyed sex as much as the next man. The nightmare his life had turned into was getting worse.

Apprehensively he slipped his hand down between his legs and tried to get some response. Nothing was happening, not a quiver. Noreen stirred beside him and he put his hands behind his head, almost guiltily. *Go back to sleep, woman,* he willed her silently, but she rubbed her eyes and opened them.

'Morning,' he said quietly.

'Good morning, Oliver. Did you sleep well?' she murmured.

'Well enough,' he lied.

She raised herself up on one elbow and traced a finger along his stubbly jaw. 'It's nice to wake up in the same bed as you again,' she said softly.

'Is it? Even after last night?' he grimaced.

'Don't be silly, Oliver. It happens. So what?' She leaned down and kissed him. He wanted to turn his head away but he knew that would hurt her so he kissed her back, hoping a miracle would happen, but it didn't, and when she drew away he sat up against the pillows and looked her straight in the eye. There was no point in putting it off. In the light of what was happening, or rather not happening, it was only fair to tell her.

'Noreen, I need to talk to you.' He tried to keep his tone steady.

'What's wrong?' He saw the anxiety in her eyes.

'I got the test results. It's my fault. I can't father a child,' he said bluntly. He saw the colour drain from her face.

'Oh . . . Oh!' she stuttered in dismay.

'I'm sorry, Noreen—'

'How bad is it? Could we do IVF?'

380

'Oh, Noreen, I don't know. Doctor Lawson said something about harvesting—'

'Well, that's what we'll do. What hospital did you go to? We'll go to their fertility clinic. Who is this doctor you went to? Can we go and meet him together?' Noreen shot bold upright and looked at him.

Oliver groaned. 'Oh, Noreen, do you really want to go down that road? What happens if it doesn't work? Can you cope with the disappointment? God Almighty, I can't even get it up for God's sake.'

'ED can be treated, it's quite common,' she said firmly.

'What's ED?' he muttered.

'Erectile dysfunction. It's probably psychological after getting the results of the tests. The doctor will refer you—'

'Noreen, I'm not going near a bloody doctor to tell him I can't function. I've had enough of bloody doctors and their personal questions.' He threw back the bedclothes and leapt out of bed. He slammed the door of the en suite and stood with his head in his hands. Why wouldn't Noreen just let it go? Was that all he was to her? A sperm bank? Could she not live with the idea of it being just the two of them? It didn't look like it, he thought bitterly as he stood beneath the spray of the shower, angry and humiliated.

Noreen wrapped her dressing-gown around her and went down to the kitchen. She filled the kettle and stood looking out at the breaking dawn. A pearly mist rose over the lake and pink-tipped wisps of clouds drifted across the horizon.

She didn't know what to think. She was in shock. So there had been a reason that she hadn't conceived. And it wasn't her fault. At one level, there was a little comfort in the fact that the fault lay with Oliver and not her. Part of her felt pity for him. And it was bad enough that he was sterile, but being impotent on top of it was a disaster for him. His outburst about going to see more doctors was understandable. He'd never been to a doctor in all the time she'd known him. And to have to answer the intimate questions they'd be asking him must have been awful for him.

If she could get the name of his doctor she could ring him. Her mind raced, seeking solutions. Of course his doctor would be bound by his oath of confidentiality, so that wouldn't be a good idea. Oliver would just have to bring her to see him, she decided as she slid a couple of slices of bread into the toaster and began to whip up scrambled eggs.

She heard him moving around upstairs. Resentment began to bubble. Why hadn't he told her about his visits to the doctor and let her come with him? What was the point of being married if you weren't going to share the burdens as well as the good times? She was angry with him for excluding her. Didn't he realize how hurtful it was to her? Did he realize and just not care? She bit her lip as she salted the eggs and put a knob of butter on top.

She'd better let him calm down a bit and get used to their situation, but in the meantime she was going to read up on everything she could about male infertility. She was going to find out where he'd had his tests and contact the infertility clinic. It would be easy enough to pretend she was Douglas Kennedy's receptionist. Or she could always go through Oliver's cheque-book stubs. He would have had to pay. Finding out wouldn't be a problem, she assured herself as she made a pot of coffee. If Oliver could do things behind her back she could do things behind his. She was his wife, for crying out loud. Not some perfect stranger. If he couldn't talk to her and confide in her, who could he confide in? She wondered had he said anything to Cora, but dismissed the idea out of hand. If Cora knew anything was amiss she'd never be able to keep it to herself.

Well, Oliver was her husband whether he liked it or not and he'd better get used to the idea that this problem was going to be shared and talked about and thrashed out between them. She was going to explore every avenue of treatment, she promised herself grimly, as she heard Oliver coming downstairs for his breakfast.

31

Noreen held her baby nephew as cameras clicked and she and Oliver tried to look happy. It was his christening, and he was lying placidly in her arms gazing up at her. Maura had called him John. He was putting on weight and thriving.

'It suits you, Noreen,' Rita remarked. 'I suppose it will be your turn next.'

'Who knows?' Noreen said lightly. Did people ever stop to think when they made their silly, intrusive, thoughtless remarks to childless couples? she raged silently. Just that very morning she'd gone for an early swim. In the changing-room afterwards a group of mothers had been dressing their children. One of the youngsters was fractious and whinging. 'Be quiet or I'll give you away,' his mother reprimanded. The others laughed and the talk turned to pregnancy and motherhood.

'No one ever tells you it's a life sentence,' whined one.

'If I'd known what I was letting myself in for I'd have made him have the snip,' moaned another.

Smug, ungrateful bitches. Noreen's lips tightened as she pulled up her jeans. Did they not know how lucky they were? They might not be so smart with their comments if they were in her position. A pain in her lower back gave advance warning that her period was on its way. Not that that was a surprise. Oliver had not come near her since that disastrous night that John had been born. He wouldn't talk about the problem, he was working all the hours God sent. They were back to square one and she was at her wits' end. She was trying her best not to be hostile and resentful but it was extremely difficult when he was being so uncooperative.

She'd phoned a fertility clinic and asked what were her options, but rightly, they had pointed out that they needed to be able to assess both of them and they needed Oliver's test results and would probably have to do more tests to investigate his sterility thoroughly.

John gave a little sneeze, bringing her back to reality. 'God bless you, Baba.' She smiled down at him.

'Here, give Oliver a go,' Rita ordered from behind her camera. Noreen felt she was still smarting at not being godmother. She'd been quite snippy with her since the birth. It was obvious a little bit of jealousy had crept in because of Maura's and Noreen's new bond.

Oliver glowered at his sister-in-law. 'I'm sure the poor baby has had enough of being passed from Billy to Jack. Why don't you put him in his cot and let him have a snooze?'

'Don't be ridiculous, Oliver, he'll have to get used to it,' Rita said snootily, not impressed with his tone.

'Oliver's right,' Noreen interjected swiftly. The

last thing she needed was a row at her godson's christening and in the humour Oliver was in he'd take no prisoners. Rita might have a sharp tongue, but if Oliver let fly he'd make mincemeat of her with a few choice words.

'Maura, would you tell these pair it's *normal* to have photos taken at a christening,' Rita drawled sarcastically. 'Honestly, you'd think he was a piece of china the way they're going on. Easy to see they're not used to children. Oliver, take that child and let me take a photo of him with his uncle!' she ordered imperiously. Someone had claimed Maura's attention so she was quite unaware of the tension that was building.

Noreen took one look at Oliver's face and froze. She had only seen that look once or twice in their relationship, but Rita had clearly overstepped the mark in his eyes and he was having none of it.

'Rita, don't order me around, save it for Jimmy,' he said coldly, his eyes like flints. 'I've had enough photos taken. I'm going to get a beer.' He turned to Noreen. 'Would you like a drink, Noreen?'

'I'll have a G and T,' she said.

'See you at the bar then.' He turned and strode away.

'Touchy bastard, isn't he?' Rita said angrily. Two bright spots of pink staining her cheeks.

'He doesn't like getting his photo taken,' Noreen said evenly. She wasn't going to let her sister rile her.

'Oh, for God's sake! It's a christening,' Rita retorted.

'Rita, we stood there for the last fifteen minutes, posing. Oliver was right to go and get a pint and

I'm going to put the baby in his Moses basket, he's ready for his nap.'

'Noreen's right.' Maura joined them again. 'Give him to me, and I'll put his Moses basket down at the far end of the room. It's getting a bit smoky here. I'm not staying here all day. As soon as the buffet's over I'm taking him home. Andy can say goodbye to everyone. He looks like he's here for the day anyway.' She glowered at her husband, who was propping up the bar surrounded by a gang of his golfing cronies.

'We'll bring you home if you want,' Noreen offered.

'Thanks, Noreen. I'm trying to keep the baby in a routine. They said that was important, but trying to explain that to his father is like talking to the wall,' Maura said wearily.

'Oh, for God's sake! Don't start letting a baby dominate and dictate. I never did it with my pair. You'll have no life if you go down that road,' Rita sneered.

'Rita, the baby's only two months old, it's not a question of dictating. Maura's right to keep him in a routine. It's the best possible thing for a baby.' Noreen was annoyed at her sister's attitude.

'What would you know about it?' Rita said rudely. 'You nurses are all the same.'

'*Rita!*' Maura exclaimed. 'That's uncalled for. Apologize to Noreen.'

'Oh you're so pally-wally with her all of a sudden, aren't you, Maura?' Rita was hopping mad at her turncoat sister. 'You've certainly changed your tune. You were always giving out about her and now it's Noreen this . . . and Noreen that—'

'*Rita!*' Maura was mortified, her face flaming. 'Don't mind her,' she said to Noreen.

'I'm going to have a drink with Oliver. If you want a lift home after the buffet, let me know,' Noreen said mildly. She wasn't getting involved in a row with Rita, whose jealousy had clearly got the better of her. She had enough on her plate without letting Rita get to her.

'That was *really* bitchy,' she heard Maura say furiously as she walked away.

Let them at it, she was now going to have to pacify Oliver. Noreen sighed deeply. She was sick of the whole bloody lot of them. London seemed like a more enticing prospect day by day.

'The minute this meal is over I'm out of here,' Oliver growled as she joined him at the bar.

'Fine,' she shrugged. 'Just give me a lift home to collect my car. I told Maura I'd give her a lift home.'

'Have you forgotten we told Mam we'd take her to tidy up the grave for Dad's anniversary?' Oliver reminded her.

'Well, I told Maura we'd give her a lift. It looks like Andy's here for the day,' Noreen retorted.

'Right. We'll give her a lift, go home and change and then go to Mam's. Just let Maura know we've something else on,' he said testily.

Noreen remained silent and took a sip of her G and T. Now she felt under more pressure. Family occasions were always fraught but it wasn't fair, she thought resentfully; she had to put up with Cora, and that was no easy task. He could put up with her family for a couple of hours, even if Rita had overstepped the mark.

By the time they got to her mother-in-law's she had a thumping headache.

'How did the christening go? I thought you'd be here an hour ago,' Cora said snippily.

'It went fine,' Noreen said shortly.

Cora gave her a studied look. 'If you and Oliver are having problems conceiving you'd want to get it seen to. I'd like to be alive to see a child of Oliver's being born and that's all that I'll say to the pair of you,' she declared as she settled her hat on her head.

The nerve in Oliver's jaw jerked in anger at her temerity but she'd gone out of the door before he could respond.

'I have a good mind to tell your mother in no uncertain terms that I'm perfectly willing to get "our" problem sorted but you're not, Mister. She'd better never say anything like that to me again, Oliver, or I really will let her have it.' Noreen was incandescent at her mother-in-law's unwarranted interference.

'I didn't know she was going to say that,' he snapped.

'I don't care. You let her know it's your fault, not mine, that we can't have a baby.' Noreen didn't care if she hurt him. He was hurting her by not dealing with the problem and she was damned if she was going to have Mrs Flynn blaming her for their childlessness.

'Thanks for putting the boot in, Noreen,' Oliver snarled as he followed his mother out the front door.

'You're welcome,' she muttered to his retreating back.

That night as they lay in bed, having not spoken a word to each other for the rest of the evening, she turned to him and said curtly, 'I need a break. I need to get away and have some time to myself. I'm going to go to London for a week or so as soon as I've arranged it with Kay.'

'Suit yourself,' Oliver said coldly.

I bloody well will, Noreen thought as she pulled the duvet up over her shoulders. *I've a good mind to go and never come back.*

Two weeks later she stood at the check-in at Dublin Airport. Oliver had dropped her to the airport but when he'd indicated to go into the car park she'd said coolly, 'There's no need for you to come in, just drop me off at the departures and you won't be delayed.'

'Fine,' he said tightly and swung the wheel sharply to the left to drive up to the departures ramp, causing her handbag to fall off her lap. Her lips tightened. She was *delighted* to be getting away, she thought, still angry with him.

'I'll get your case out.' He made an abrupt stop in the set-down area.

She felt like telling him not to bother but she restrained herself. What a way to be going on holiday. And imagine having to go off on holiday on her own, she thought bitterly. If he was any sort of a decent husband he'd come with her. She was so annoyed and irrational she didn't stop to think that she'd never even asked him to come with her.

'Goodbye, Oliver,' she muttered when he'd placed her case on a trolley for her.

'Have a good time,' he said, his face carved out

of granite. He didn't lean towards her for a kiss and stubbornly she decided if he wasn't going to make the first move, neither was she. She turned away and pushed the trolley towards the automatic doors, and didn't look back.

Oliver drove out of Dublin Airport and felt a vague sense of relief that Noreen was on her way to London. There was no living with her these days. He knew she was angry that he wouldn't go to the doctor and get himself seen to. He knew she was anxious to investigate further the causes of his sterility. She wanted to see if they were suitable for IVF. But the more she pushed the more harassed he felt.

When she'd turned on him at his mother's it had been the last straw. He was sick of it, he was sick of her, and there seemed no way out of the nightmare. London would be a respite for him and for her. It would give them some breathing space. He needed it.

Noreen peered eagerly out the window as the plane made its descent into Heathrow. It was a clear, sunny day and the snake-like winding curve of the Thames was clearly visible. As the plane flew lower she could clearly see the Millennium Dome and the majestic Houses of Parliament. She felt a flicker of excitement and anticipation. It was good to be back. She was looking forward to seeing Kay and her other friends.

The relief of getting away from her marriage and Kilronan for a while was almost intoxicating. The further she'd got from Ireland the more the tension eased out of her body. It was as if she'd been holding her breath for a long time and now she was exhaling slowly, with great relief.

Kay was waiting for her at arrivals and they hugged warmly.

'You've lost weight!' Her friend looked at her with concern.

'Ah, I'll put it back on here with a few nosh-ups,' Noreen grinned. She was delighted to be here. To hell with Oliver, she was going to enjoy herself. 'Well, tell me all the gossip,' she ordered her friend as they made their way to the car park.

'Well, Mia and Will have separated, he went off with Kira Reid—'

'Kira Reid!' Noreen was agog! 'Tell me more . . .'

The gossip lasted all the way to Westbourne Park Road, where Kay had a first-floor flat in an elegant, cream-painted three-storey house.

'Come on, let's have lunch on the balcony, it's a gorgeous day,' she urged after she'd shown Noreen to the guest room at the front of the house. The French doors in the kitchen led to a small balcony overlooking the back garden. Spring had come early and a glorious pink cherry blossom waved gently in the balmy breeze. Noreen had always liked London in the spring. Sitting on the balcony, eating creamy smoked salmon and pasta and a Caesar salad, and sipping chilled white wine with Kay, Kilronan and all her problems seemed very far away.

'I've got tickets for *Stones in his Pockets*, the Marie Jones play, for us and there's an exhibition of

Chinese art that you might like and tonight we're going to meet the gang for a meal in Rajiv's.'

Noreen's eyes lit up. 'Oh, Kay! You've gone to so much trouble. It will be like old times won't it. I always liked going to Rajiv's. How is he?'

Rajiv Bashra was the owner of Rajiv's Star of India Restaurant, and Noreen had always got on very well with him after she had taken care of his mother, who had taken a bad turn when she'd been having lunch in the restaurant one day. A widower with a grown-up son, he was a gregarious, chatty man with a kind heart. He'd held a party for her when he heard she was leaving to go home to nurse her mother, and told her that he would miss her.

'Rajiv's good. Delighted that you're coming to visit. He told me to tell you he'll have his best tablecloths out for you.'

Noreen laughed and thought suddenly with a little shock, *that's the first time I've laughed for months*. She frowned. She hadn't even thought to let Oliver know that she arrived.

'What's wrong? Maybe you'd prefer to go somewhere else?' Kay mistook the reason for her frown.

'No, no, I'm chuffed to be going to Rajiv's. I couldn't think of anything nicer. I was just thinking that I forgot to call Oliver to tell him I was here.'

'Is everything OK with you two?' Kay probed delicately.

'Why do you say that?' Noreen hedged.

'You haven't mentioned him once since you arrived, and to be honest you don't look great,' her friend said bluntly.

Noreen looked down at her hands. Kay had

always been very perceptive. She was a very dear friend.

'Things couldn't be worse,' she said quietly.

'Oh dear . . . I'd better put the kettle on,' Kay said sagely. She stood up and went into the kitchen. Two minutes later she reappeared with another bottle of wine. 'While we're waiting for the kettle to boil,' she suggested. Noreen made no objections.

It was a relief to unburden herself, having kept her unhappiness bottled up for so long, and Kay listened quietly, interjecting a comment here or there.

'So that's where we are now,' Noreen said sadly after telling her sorry saga.

'Why don't you tell him?' Kay asked.

Noreen shook her head. 'It's too late now. It would only make things worse. I pushed him too far and he resents me. I don't blame him.'

'I'm sorry, Noreen.' Kay stood up and gave her a hug. 'I don't know what advice to give to you.'

'I think the only way to save our marriage is to give up the idea of having a baby of my own,' Noreen admitted.

'Maybe you're right. Look, you're here for ten days. Relax, don't beat yourself up about it. A little distance is a very good thing. Now why don't you go and unpack while I tidy up here and then we'll stroll down the Portobello Road,' Kay suggested.

'I'll give you a hand.' Noreen jumped up.

'No you won't, you're on your holliers. Go and give Oliver a ring and tell him you've arrived,' Kay ordered.

'Yes, Sister.' Noreen grinned. She went into her

room and sat on the side of the bed and called up Oliver's mobile number. She got the out-of-range message and wasn't sure if she was glad or sorry. She left a brief message, and rang home just in case he was there, but the phone rang out so there was nothing more she could do. If he wanted, he could call her back.

By ten thirty that night she was in flying form. Just like her old self, Kay whispered approvingly as she sat at a big round table in Rajiv's restaurant chatting and laughing to colleagues, as if she'd never been away. Rajiv had been delighted to see her and hugged her warmly.

'Hello, my friend. You left it a long time to pay us a visit,' he said in his lovely Indian accent.

'Yes, Rajiv, much too long,' Noreen concurred, returning his hug.

'You see, my best linen tablecloths.' He laughed as he led her to a beautifully dressed table in an alcove in the pale yellow and terracotta restaurant.

'Oh Rajiv . . . freesias, my favourites,' Noreen exclaimed in delight as she saw vases of yellow and purple freesias on the table. 'You remembered.'

'Of course I did.' Rajiv smiled at her. 'And I've a dish of aloo saag made just the way you like it.'

It was a great evening, the best she'd had in a long, long time, and as she eased herself into bed, rather the worse for wear, it was with the realization that some of the friends she had here in London were closer to her and knew more about her than her own family, and even her own husband. Before she fell asleep she checked her mobile. There were no messages. Oliver had not phoned back.

32

'Better go, Noreen, enjoy the rest of the day and I'll see you tonight.' Kay stood up, waved at Rajiv and left the restaurant to go to work the late shift. It was the second last day of Noreen's holidays and it was lashing rain. She wasn't sure what she'd do. She didn't fancy trudging around the shops in the rain. She sipped the remainder of her wine and considered ordering another coffee.

'So what are you doing for the rest of the afternoon?' Rajiv slid into Kay's empty chair.

'The weather's miserable. I'm all shopped out. I might just go back to Kay's and have a read.' Noreen leaned back in her chair and smiled at her companion.

'That's far too boring and lonely,' Rajiv said firmly. 'Let's go to the pictures. I love playing hooky on a wet afternoon.'

'Will we?' Noreen perked up. Going back to Kay's *was* a bit dull. She could spend her time reading when she got home. 'What's on?'

'Hold on, I'll get the paper.' Rajiv said with alacrity. Five minutes later he was back with another bottle of wine and a paper. They perused the films on offer and narrowed it down to *A Beautiful Mind* or *The Shipping News*.

'Don't really like Russell Crowe—'

'Then *The Shipping News* it is,' Rajiv declared gallantly. 'I'll order a taxi.'

'I'm drinking like a fish,' Noreen remarked as he topped up her glass after ordering the taxi.

'You're on your holidays, Noreen. Relax. Enjoy.'

'I'm having a lovely time and I *am* relaxed.' She smiled.

'Much more relaxed than the first night. You looked very tired.'

'God, I must have looked a bit of a wreck,' Noreen retorted lightly. 'Kay said the same thing.'

'So tell me all about life in Ireland. Is it everything you wished for? Peaceful and balming after London?' Rajiv smiled his lopsided smile, his brown eyes warm and kind behind his glasses.

'It's different,' Noreen said slowly. 'Now that I'm back here for the few days, I've realized that I actually liked living in London very much.'

A waiter politely interrupted. 'Your taxi is waiting, sir.'

Rajiv thanked him and ushered Noreen to the entrance. 'They'll all be talking now,' he whispered conspiratorially. 'Rajiv's gone off for the afternoon with the woman from Ireland.' He laughed heartily.

Noreen tucked her arm in his. 'You know, Rajiv, you should be with someone. Isn't there anyone nice on the scene? Do you still miss your wife so much?' she asked gently.

'If I tell you something you will be shocked,' he murmured as he held the taxi door open for her.

'You have someone?' Noreen was delighted for him.

'No, no,' he shook his head. 'But I don't miss my wife at all. Isn't that a terrible admission to make? And I've never said it to anyone.' He lowered his voice, 'Noreen, she was so bossy. "Rajiv, do this," "Rajiv, do that." "Not like that, Rajiv,"' he said in a sing-song voice. 'Now I do exactly what I like with no one to give me orders. She is not the boss of me any more. And neither is my mother.'

'You don't really like women, do you?' Noreen twinkled.

'Not true at all. I like Kay and I like you. When you went off to Ireland I missed you very much.'

'Did you really?' Noreen was amazed. 'I thought you were just saying it out of politeness.'

'But, Noreen, the talks we had. It is so unusual to have really good talks with a woman,' Rajiv declared endearingly. 'We got on very well.'

'Yes, I suppose we did,' she agreed.

'Your husband is a very lucky man. I'm sure you have the most wonderful talks. My wife used to talk at me, not to me,' Rajiv observed with a sigh.

'But you meet so many people in your restaurant, Rajiv, surely you've met someone you like?'

'I suppose when my son was still living with me, until January just gone, I wasn't lonely, but he's been promoted in his job and gone to live in Paris and I do find life lonely now. You're right, Noreen, I should get out and about and start meeting people. I'm fifty now, more than half-way there.'

'Fifty's not old,' Noreen scoffed as the taxi pulled up outside the cinema.

'Wait until you get there,' Rajiv said drily as he paid the taxi driver.

Noreen thoroughly enjoyed the film, having read Annie Proulx's book when it was first published. The last film she and Oliver had gone to, he'd slept through most of it. Rajiv was a witty companion and his amusing asides made her laugh. The afternoon flew by. It was still raining when they left the cinema, and Rajiv hailed a taxi for them and gave Kay's address.

'Are you rushing back to work?' Noreen asked when the taxi eventually reached Westbourne Park Road. 'Have you time for a cup of coffee, or a drink?'

'Why not? I'm not a slave to my restaurant. I deserve an afternoon off now and again,' Rajiv declared.

'Indeed you do,' Noreen grinned. 'You've got to learn to be impulsive.'

'Is your husband impulsive?' Rajiv asked as she inserted the key in the front door.

'Not in the slightest,' Noreen said drily. 'If I suggested going to the pictures on a weekday afternoon, he'd think I'd lost my marbles.'

'Aren't you happy, Noreen?' Rajiv asked forthrightly as he followed her up the stairs.

She gave a deep sigh, 'I'd be lying if I said I was, Rajiv,' she answered candidly. 'We're going through a bit of a rocky patch at the moment.'

'So soon into the marriage. That's a shame. Is it something that can be sorted?'

'Well, you're a man, Rajiv, maybe you could give me an idea of what's going on in Oliver's head, because I'm at my wits' end,' she confessed. 'Go and sit down and I'll get us a drink. How about a brandy? I brought Kay a bottle, she won't mind,' Noreen said recklessly. It was such a treat to have a good conversation with a man again. Oliver and she hardly talked any more and until she'd come on holiday she hadn't realized how lonely she was.

'We are being impulsive aren't we?' Rajiv chuckled. 'If my staff could see me they wouldn't believe it. And my wife would tell me I was being lazy and intemperate.'

'Ah, we only live once.' Noreen took two brandy goblets out of a cabinet and poured two generous measures. Life was for sharing. If she was at home in Kilronan she'd be coming home from afternoon surgery to an empty house. The thought of going home to her lonely existence made her feel unhappy.

Three brandies later, she was feeling no pain and she'd opened her heart to Rajiv. He was a good listener; he was like Oliver in that way, she thought sadly, as her friend stood up to go. 'I had a lovely, lovely time, Rajiv.' She hugged him warmly. 'You're a dear, dear friend.' He smiled down at her.

'Now I'll really miss you. It was so nice spending time with you. You made me feel young again.'

'Oh Rajiv, you *are* young. I told you, fifty's nothing.' Noreen cupped his face in her hands, her expression earnest. 'You should believe me.' They looked at each other.

'I want to kiss you, Noreen,' Rajiv whispered. It seemed so long since any affection had come her way, and the tenderness in his eyes was such a balm to her she raised her lips to his and felt his arms tighten around her. The whole taste and texture of him was so different from Oliver, she thought fleetingly, his desire for her a welcome affirmation that she was still an attractive, desirable woman. The loneliness and worry of the past few months seemed like a bad dream as she returned Rajiv's kisses with brandy-induced abandon. Casting inhibitions and guilt to the wind, she took him by the hand and led him to her bedroom.

I deserve this, she thought woozily. *Because Oliver abandoned me*.

Rajiv was a kind and considerate lover, and afterwards as she lay in his arms, drowsy and sated, she refused to entertain any thoughts of guilt. Thoughts of this interlude with Rajiv would keep her going through the difficult times.

'I think we were a little drunk.' Rajiv stroked her cheek.

'I don't care, Rajiv. I'll always remember this day.' Noreen smiled at him. 'It was special and lovely and I'm glad we had it. I'm going home in two days' time, I'll have a precious memory to bring with me.'

'I'd better go, Noreen. Kay would get an awful shock if she arrived home and saw us like this.'

Noreen groaned. 'How am I going to explain all the brandy that's gone? I better run out and get a bottle somewhere.'

Rajiv jumped out of bed. 'I know an offie not far from here. I'll go. I won't be long. It's only eight thirty. Kay won't be home for a little while yet,' he offered.

'Are you sure?'

'Of course I'm sure, Noreen. I'd do anything for you. You made me feel alive again.' He smiled, his teeth very white against his smooth olive skin. She watched him dress. It had helped that he was so different to Oliver. Shorter, stockier, his chest smooth and satiny compared to Oliver's hairy chest. His silky black hair, sprinkled with grey, not at all like Oliver's tight-cut brown hair. Rajiv was a soft, kind man, with none of Oliver's hard strength. They couldn't be more unlike.

'I'd better get dressed and make the bed,' she said drowsily. She would have liked to stay in bed for the rest of the night, but Kay would worry that there was something wrong with her. By the time Rajiv got back with the brandy she'd showered and was dressed in a tracksuit.

'I won't stay, dear friend.' He kissed her hand. 'Thank you for everything.'

'No, Rajiv, thank *you*.' Noreen kissed him tenderly. 'You'll never know what comfort you gave my spirit.'

'And a beautiful spirit it is, too. Try to be happy,' he said kindly, before closing the door behind him.

Noreen replaced the bottle of brandy in Kay's drinks cabinet and wrapped the well-depleted bottle they'd been drinking from in a towel in her case. Her behaviour this afternoon had been totally out of character, she acknowledged with a bashful grin as she caught sight of herself in the mirror, her eyes betraying the amount she'd had to drink. After she'd remade her bed, she made herself a strong cup of coffee to help counteract the effects of the brandy.

'I'm bushed,' Kay announced when she got home. 'We never stopped all day. Would you mind if we rang for a takeaway tonight, Noreen? I don't think my feet are up to going out.'

'I don't mind at all, Kay, as long as it's not an Indian,' she laughed.

'We'll have Chinese, the one that delivers to me does chow mein to die for,' Kay informed her as she kicked off her shoes and sank on to the sofa. 'Well, what was the rest of your day like? What did you do with yourself?'

'I had a perfectly lovely time,' Noreen said truthfully, and began to give an edited version of her doings.

That night as she lay in bed, woozy again after another bottle of wine with Kay, she hugged her precious memories to her, replaying them in her mind. Oliver had not phoned once while she was away and she hadn't phoned him, angry with him that he couldn't be bothered to contact her. Her infidelity was his fault, she rationalized sleepily. If he had looked after her properly, emotionally, she would never have ended up in bed with Rajiv. And she wasn't sorry she had either, she thought crossly. Rajiv had made her feel like a *wanted* woman. Not someone to be endured. She fell asleep and slept like a log.

Forty-eight hours later she sat on the plane winging its way to Dublin and wished she could have stayed in London longer. She'd enjoyed herself. She hadn't felt under pressure, or tense and agitated like she was feeling now. What had she to look forward to? Only hostility from her husband. She wondered if he would kiss her at the airport. That was if he *was* at the airport, she thought wryly, as the plane began a slow bank to the right and the coast of Wexford appeared far below them.

Oliver looked up at the monitor and saw that Noreen's plane had landed. He put his empty coffee cup in a bin, folded his paper and made his way to the arrivals area. She hadn't even phoned him once, just left a message on his mobile to say that she'd got there ten days ago. He felt very hard done by, especially as he'd had the exterior of the house painted in her absence, washed and vacuumed her car, had the gardens tended to by a gardener so that they were in tip-top shape, and even done the shopping. She probably wouldn't even say thanks, he thought crossly, as he stood glowering with his hands shoved into his hip pockets waiting for her to emerge into the arrivals hall.

He saw her before she saw him. She looked relaxed, rested. He was glad of that. He walked forward to take her trolley.

'Oh . . . Oh! Hello,' she said coolly. 'I wasn't sure if you'd be here.'

'Here, let me take that.' He took the trolley from her. 'Why wouldn't I be here?' he demanded.

'Well, you could be busy,' she said huffily. 'You never rang to say you'd be here. You never rang me at all.'

'You mean *you* never rang *me*,' growled Oliver. 'You were gone ten days and not a peep.'

'*Excuse me*, I left a message to say I got there,' Noreen retorted.

Oliver manoeuvred the trolley through the crowds. 'You might have phoned back. It was quite obvious you weren't the slightest bit interested—'

'Oh Oliver, *please* let's not bicker,' she burst out agitatedly. 'Don't ruin my holiday with a row.'

'Sorry,' he muttered.

They walked in silence to the pay booth. And when he'd paid the parking fee he turned and took the trolley again. 'We're in C,' he said. 'I couldn't get any closer.'

'That's OK,' Noreen murmured and he felt a bit of a heel.

'Did you have a nice time?' He made an effort.

'Yeah, I did. Kay was really kind to me.'

'Good. I'm glad,' he said gruffly and touched her arm briefly. To his dismay, she burst into tears. 'What's wrong?' He gave her a look of dismay.

'Oliver, please let's not fight,' Noreen wept. 'I don't want to go home to fighting and not talking.'

Oliver swallowed hard. He took a step forward and put his arms around her. 'We won't fight, Noreen,' he said firmly. 'Stop crying and let's go home.'

Noreen tried to eat the fillet steak Oliver had cooked for them but her throat felt closed and tight. The minute she'd seen Oliver lope towards her in arrivals she'd been swamped by guilt. He looked tired and careworn. It wasn't easy for him either, she acknowledged. He was a good man and she'd slept with someone else behind his back. If he ever found out he'd feel a bigger failure than he felt now, and she'd hate that. He was hurting enough with all that was going on, she didn't want to plunge the knife in even deeper.

I'm sorry, Oliver, she apologized silently to him as he poured her a glass of water. She wasn't drinking for at least a week, she vowed. She hadn't drunk as much in years as she had when she'd been on holiday and look where drink had got her, she thought guiltily.

'The house looks great, Oliver. The paint really freshens it up, doesn't it?'

'I thought it would be good to get it done when you were away so you wouldn't have to smell the fumes,' he said, sprinkling more salt than was good for him on his potatoes.

'Go easy on the salt,' she said out of habit, feeling worse than she'd ever felt in her life as his thoughtfulness heaped even more guilt on to the load she was already carrying.

'Is your dinner OK? The steak's a bit tough. I battered it around a bit to tenderize it.'

'It's lovely, Oliver. Thanks very much.' She thought she was going to cry again as she saw him smile at her, his clear blue eyes even bluer against his tanned skin.

'We need to put a few pounds on you, woman, so eat up. There's more gravy and veg if you want them. Would you like some more?'

'No I'm fine, honest. They served a snack on the plane; it took the edge off my appetite.' Making a superhuman effort, Noreen ate some fried onions and wished with all her being that she had never invited Rajiv back to Kay's flat. As long as she lived she would never drink brandy again, she vowed miserably, as Oliver updated her on the goings on in Kilronan while she'd been away.

Later, she unpacked. The sight of the half-empty bottle of brandy wrapped in her bathtowel jolted her and guilt came flooding back. Hurriedly she stuffed the bottle to the back of her wardrobe. She'd put it in the drinks cabinet when Oliver was at work. She sighed deeply. She felt awkward and unbalanced. All the relaxation she'd felt in London had ebbed away. Although Oliver was being kind and making an effort, the tension was there between them and she dreaded going to bed that night.

She pretended to be asleep when he came to bed an hour after her. She'd pleaded tiredness but as she lay with her back to her husband with her eyes closed she was wide awake and utterly on edge. She couldn't bear it if he tried to make love to her. Guilt boiled and bubbled inside her, burning her soul, and she wanted to tell him about Rajiv and get it over with. If he ranted and roared and called her names it would have to be better than what she was enduring now.

The bedsprings creaked as Oliver got into bed. Noreen tensed. She heard him sigh and roll on to his side away from her. She prayed that he would fall asleep soon so that she could open her eyes and stop pretending to breathe deeply, and just endure her misery.

33

'He never gets up to him at night, he carries on as if there's no baby in the house. He's off playing golf whenever he wants and I'm not getting a wink of sleep,' Maura moaned.

'Well, if you like I'll take the baby for a walk around the lake for an hour and you could nip up to bed for forty winks,' Noreen offered, feeling more than a little sorry for her sister. Gone was the smartly dressed, immaculately coiffed Lady-Who-Lunched. Maura had bags under her eyes, her roots needed touching up and her jumper had creamy puke stains on it.

'Would you, Noreen? Are you sure? I'll take the phone off the hook and just have a quick snooze. He's had a bottle so he might even sleep for you.' Maura's eyes lit up at the prospect of sleep.

'Get me his coat. It's a bit cool, so stick an extra blanket on the buggy,' Noreen instructed. 'I'll go and put his seat into my car. Where are your car keys?'

'On the table in the hall.' Maura couldn't believe her luck. Noreen laughed and went out to struggle with the intricacies of baby seats. Twenty minutes later she was pushing her nephew through the gates that led to the pathway that circled the lake. It was a grey, gloomy day. The sky and lake seemed to merge and even the vibrant yellow gorse seemed dull today.

Noreen sighed. She was restless. Since she'd come back from London she was finding it hard to settle down. Even her job in the surgery was losing its lustre. Was this what it was going to be like for the rest of her life? she wondered moodily as she negotiated a hole in the footpath. Oliver was doing his best. He'd offered to go to the Rotunda Fertility Clinic with her, but she knew his heart wasn't in it. Their easy companionship was gone. A jagged edge of tension underlined their relationship now. She knew he felt he was walking on eggshells. She could feel the tension in him at night when he put his arms around her, and she would pretend to sleep until he fell asleep himself and then lie awake thinking of her time in London, wishing she could turn the clock back.

Oliver had tried to make love to her shortly after she'd come back from London. It had been a disaster. She'd tensed up, he'd got tense too, nothing happened and he'd just turned away from her and not said a word.

It had to be because he didn't fancy her any more, she tormented herself, even though the rational, medically trained part of her knew that Oliver's problem was psychological, induced by the discovery of his sterility. *But if he really wanted me, he'd be able to get it up*, was the thought that rampaged around her head in spite of herself. The notion plagued her so much she wanted to shake him and shout, 'Look, just say you don't want me any more. Tell me to my face that I don't turn you on. Stop punishing me for asking you to marry me.'

She pulled the buggy in beside a seat and lifted her nephew out on to her knee. He smiled happily at her and she kissed his rosy little cheek and held him tenderly against her, loving the feel of his tiny little legs kicking away.

'You are a beautiful little fellow, and when you grow up, I hope you meet a woman you love enough to propose to. I hope you meet a woman you can talk to, and I hope you'll never have an unhappy day in your life, my little precious,' she crooned. John gooed away animatedly, head bobbing from side to side as if he understood everything she'd said, so that she had to laugh. She sat and held him for about ten minutes, and felt calmer and soothed when she put him back in his buggy to resume their walk. She felt quite sure that Maura would welcome any involvement she cared to have in the baby's life. Maybe John would be her lifeline, she mused as she tucked the blankets around him tenderly. She could do up a room for him so that he could come and stay the odd night when he was older, although no doubt Rita would get in a snit that her pair had never been invited.

You couldn't win in this place, she frowned, her humour dipping again.

The baby was asleep when she got him home and she lifted him gently from his car seat and rang the doorbell. 'One sleeping child,' she said smugly when Maura answered the door.

'Great, I'll put him in his cot and we'll have a cuppa. If you've time, that is?' her sister invited.

Noreen glanced at her watch. 'I have another three-quarters of an hour before surgery. I wouldn't mind a cup of tea, thanks. I'll just put the car seat back in your car.' When she got in Maura had the kettle on. Her eyes were puffy from sleep and she yawned widely.

'Sorry,' she apologized. 'I think if I was to sleep around the clock it still wouldn't be enough. Nothing's prepared me for motherhood, Noreen. I never thought it would be so all-consuming.'

'The first couple of months are the hardest, all the feeding, changing, washing . . . it will get easier,' Noreen consoled.

'Do you think so?' Maura said doubtfully, placing a generous chunk of coffee cake and a mug of tea in front of Noreen.

'I know so,' Noreen fibbed. She had taken her third sip of tea and a mouthful of cake when a heat suffused her and a wave of nausea swamped her. She swallowed hard. Don't say she was starting a tummy bug. She usually had a cast-iron stomach. 'Need to use your loo,' she murmured.

'Use the one in the hall,' Maura said, too busy shovelling coffee cake into her to notice anything untoward. Noreen made her way to the loo and threw up as discreetly as possible. She felt most peculiar, she thought as she splashed her face with cold water and took deep breaths, casting her mind back to what she'd eaten in the last twenty-four hours that had sickened her. Nothing came to mind and she took several deep breaths before rejoining Maura.

'Finish your cake,' her sister ordered. Fortunately John began to whimper and Noreen said hastily, 'I'll head off, Maura, I need to get to the surgery a little early today, I'll see you later in the week.'

'Thanks very much for taking him, Noreen, I'd a lovely sleep.' Maura hastened to the baby's cot, and Noreen left her to it.

She sat in the car, beads of sweat on her upper lip and forehead. She felt grotty, but she couldn't very well let Douglas down at such short notice by not turning in for work. But if it was a bug she could spread it, she argued silently as she drove towards town. She found a packet of chewing-gum in the window pocket and chewed on one. It helped her nausea subside and she decided she'd go to work.

The surgery was half full already and she had a busy afternoon. The queasiness ebbed and flowed, but nothing as dramatic as she'd endured in Maura's. Still, she was glad to say goodbye to her colleagues and drive home.

The thought of cooking dinner was less than enticing so she phoned Oliver on his mobile and told him to get a takeaway for himself on his way home. 'I don't feel the best, I'm going to lie down,' she informed him.

'Will I get anything for you?' he asked.

'No, I'll have something later, a few crackers or something,' she told him, as she drove into the driveway.

She went into the kitchen, drank a glass of water

and went to lie down on the sofa. It was so unusual for her to be sick, she thought, perplexed. She had the constitution of an ox and was immune to most bugs after all her years of nursing. It was hardly her period, she thought vaguely as she lay down. She often felt sick at the onset but she'd never barfed before. She shot bolt upright as the blood drained from her face.

'Mother of God! It couldn't be,' she muttered as she raced upstairs, galvanized. It just couldn't be after all that had happened. She scrabbled in her bedside locker until she found what she was looking for. Thank God she had one. Five minutes later she was looking at two blue lines on her pregnancy test kit.

'Pregnant! I'm *pregnant!*' she said in disbelief, unable to absorb the enormity of what had happened. For one brief moment a wave of joy flooded her being. *She* was going to have a baby. God had not deserted her. She was exhilarated. 'Thank you, thank you, thank you.' She fell to her knees, burying her head in her hands, and cried at the knowledge that she had not been forsaken.

'I'm having a baby.' Noreen spoke aloud the words she had longed for an eternity to say. Then the stark realization of her situation hit her.

She was pregnant and Rajiv was the father. Now, not only Oliver but the whole world would know that she had betrayed her husband. No child of Rajiv's would ever be mistaken for a child of Oliver's. Well, God had granted her her dearest wish, she thought bitterly. Now she was pregnant, but look at the circumstances. Oliver would be gutted. It would be such a kick in the teeth for him. What the hell was she going to do? she thought in panic.

She couldn't tell Oliver. It was as simple as that. She'd have to leave Kilronan. She lay down on the bed, her heart racing, her thoughts a blizzard inside her head. She had money of her own from her mother's estate. She'd need a roof over her head.

London. She'd go back to London. What other choice had she got? Kay would help her sort herself out. And Rajiv deserved to know he'd fathered a child. If he wanted to be involved, fine. If not she'd cope, she thought distractedly. The thing to do was move fast. There was no point in dragging things out. She needed to be sorted before the baby was born. And besides, she couldn't live with Oliver knowing that she was pregnant by another man and knowing that she was going to leave him. The fairest thing on both of them was to get it over and done with quickly.

Maybe he'd be relieved, she thought frantically as she heard his key in the door. She sat up and shoved the test into her drawer and took a deep breath as she heard him run upstairs.

'Are you OK?' he asked anxiously.

'No, Oliver, I'm not.' She felt sick with tension. 'Oliver, I have to talk to you.' She took a deep breath, twisting her hands in her lap. 'I want to go back to London. I can't stay here any more. It's doing my head in. You're not happy. I'm not happy. It's the best thing for both of us.'

Oliver looked at her, stunned. And then he

414

turned away and walked to the window so she couldn't see the expression on his face.

'If that's what you want, Noreen,' he said flatly.

'I'm sorry, Oliver,' she whispered, her throat constricting.

'When are you going to go?' he asked, his back still turned to her.

'I . . . I . . . probably the day after tomorrow,' she hesitated. 'It's the best thing for us, Oliver.'

'If you say so,' he said tonelessly. 'I'm going to have a pint. See you later.'

''Bye,' she whispered as he left the room. That was it, he was going to the pub, he hadn't even tried to argue with her or persuade her to stay. He probably couldn't be more relieved, she thought bitterly as she heard the door close behind him. She walked into her closet and pulled her big, battered black case down off a shelf. Briskly, methodically, she began to pack her clothes and uniforms. It was best to go quickly. If she could she'd go before he came back from the pub, but she needed to tell Douglas she was leaving. Maura and Rita, well, they'd know soon enough. She'd phone them from London, she couldn't do it face to face. And Cora. Noreen gave a twisted smile as she folded a pair of jeans. Her mother-in-law would be the happiest woman in the world.

Oliver sat in a dark corner in the pub nursing his fifth beer. So Noreen was leaving him. He couldn't say he was surprised. As a husband he was a total failure. Couldn't give her a child, couldn't make love to her, no wonder she was going. Why would she stay with a dud like him? He didn't know whether he was glad or sad. He didn't know what he was feeling except this huge, ferocious anger and despair that was eating at him, making him want to pound his fists into a brick wall or something.

Why had this happened to him? What had he done to deserve it? One thing he knew for sure, he was finished with women. They only led to misery and he was never going to get hurt the way Noreen had hurt him again. 'Goodbye and good riddance,' he muttered drunkenly, a salty tear sliding down his cheek.

34

'I'm not going to a fortune-teller, Ruth,' Heather snapped sulkily.

'She's *not* a fortune-teller, she's a psychic,' her sister said indignantly, 'and I've made the appointment and you're coming.'

'Oh Ruth,' groaned Heather. 'What's the point?'

'It might cheer you up.'

'What? To be told I'm going to be on the shelf for the rest of my life?' Heather scowled.

'You're not going to be on the shelf for the rest of your life. Don't be ridiculous.' Ruth couldn't help the edge in her tone. She was at her wits' end with Heather. Since she'd found out about Neil and Lorna she'd sunk into a depression that was completely out of character. 'Come on,' she urged, 'just to please me. I've been to her before and she told me about meeting Peter. She told me he was the one, and he is.'

'Yeah, but maybe there's no one for me,' Heather said glumly, munching on a piece of toast dripping with butter.

'Well, just come for the day out anyway. It's a nice trip to Kilcoole, we can have lunch and a poke around the Avoca Handweavers on the way home.'

'OK, whatever you say,' Heather said dispiritedly as she buttered another piece of toast.

Ruth threw her eyes up to heaven. This was hard going, and if she could get her hands on Lorna Morgan she'd wrap them around her skinny little neck and throttle her.

Heather sat in the passenger seat beside her sister as the traffic crawled along at a snail's pace towards the Merrion Gates. The sun shone in a clear blue sky. People strode briskly along the seashore walk, the sea a sparkling azure in the curve of Dublin Bay. She stared unseeingly through the window, seeing none of it, too focused on the heavy, dull ache that had been her constant companion since she'd found out about Lorna and Neil.

It was six soul-destroying weeks since her life had been turned upside-down. This day six weeks ago she'd had a good job, her own place and a man she thought she loved. Now she was living at home with her parents, working in Fred's Fast Food Emporium, and there were times she wished she was dead.

Tears smarted her eyes and she turned her head so that Ruth wouldn't see. Her sister had been her rock. She'd come to her aid the minute she was needed. It seemed like only yesterday, the memories were still so raw.

As soon as Neil had left the flat after she'd cursed him to high heaven, she'd sat on the bed, shaking, and phoned Ruth. She could hardly talk for crying.

'What's wrong with you? Is it Mam? Is it Dad? For God's sake, Heather, tell me what's wrong?' Ruth started panicking.

'Neil . . . Neil slept with Lorna,' she managed before breaking into shoulder-shaking sobs.

'*What!*' The shock in her twin's voice made her worse and she cried with abandon. 'I'm coming right now,' Ruth said hastily. 'Where are you?'

'The flat,' Heather gulped, relieved beyond measure that Ruth was coming.

'I'm on my way,' Ruth said and hung up.

Lorna and Neil, Neil and Lorna. She kept repeating it over and over, still unable to take it in. She would have been shocked to hear that Neil had slept with another woman, but for him to have slept with Lorna beggared belief. That he could hurt her so deeply and obviously not care was the most painful thing she had ever experienced. Had he no loyalty in him at all? She knew that Lorna was capable of a lot of things, but Heather had never dreamed that she would stoop so low. It was almost as if Lorna's contempt for her was so great, it hadn't cost her a thought to inflict the hurt she'd inflicted on her.

She lay huddled on the bed until Ruth arrived an hour later, and fell crying into her arms as they embraced at the door.

'Come on. Get packed. You can tell that bollox he can stuff his flat. Here, I brought a roll of black sacks.' Ruth was nothing if not practical. 'You can tell me all about it while we're packing.'

Heather told her sorry story as Ruth began to stuff the duvet into a black sack.

'Whatever about *her*,' Ruth's voice dripped scorn

419

as she referred to their cousin, 'I never thought he would do such a scummy thing.'

'Yeah, well, he did,' Heather said bitterly.

'Well, it's happened and there's nothing you can do about it right now so let's get the hell out of here. That little bastard will be the sorry man when he comes into work on Monday and you're gone, lock, stock and barrel.' Ruth whipped the pillows off the bed, followed by the sheets, and stuffed them into another sack. 'Come on, stop standing there. Get your clothes out of the wardrobe.'

Ruth's brisk no-nonsense attitude focused Heather's mind and the two of them worked like Trojans, not speaking much until all of Heather's possessions were packed into eight large black plastic sacks. Heather looked around her. How bare the place looked, how lonely.

'Take down those curtains, Mam made them,' Ruth ordered.

'The *curtains*?'

'The curtains,' insisted Ruth. 'Why should he have them?'

Heather obeyed with a weak smile. Ruth never did things by half.

'Now can you go downstairs to the office and delete any files or mix them up and make his life a misery? I take it you're not doing another second's work for him.'

Heather's eyes widened. 'God, I never thought of doing that.'

'How could you think straight?' Ruth retorted, her eyes full of sympathy. Heather started to cry again.

'How could he do it to me, Ruth? Did he think I was such a doormat that he could wipe his feet all over me? They never even liked each other, until she came back all Flashy Glam, saying she was going to New York. She flirted with him to get the best price she could for that car. He wouldn't tell me what he paid for it. And he fell for it and went running when she clicked her fingers and I didn't count with either of them.'

'Ssshhh, don't waste your tears on that little slapper and him. They deserve each other, Heather. They're users. Come on. We'll teach him to mess with the Williams. Let's see what we can do with the computers. He'll be *such* a bloody sorry little toad by the time I'm finished with him.' Ruth's eyes glittered dangerously. Heather sniffed and wiped her eyes.

'You were always my champion, even when we were small.' Heather laughed, suddenly buoyed up at the idea of taking revenge. 'Come on.' She led the way downstairs to her own office. No one could ever accuse her of being the spiteful type, but right this very minute she wanted to get her own back on Neil and Ruth had hit the nail on the head. Mucking up the files would cause him a lot of grief.

Half an hour later she had files renamed, hidden, and disguised to her satisfaction. She'd drawn the line at deleting them, not quite willing to go that far. He'd have a hell of a search looking for the wages, tax and VAT files, she thought with satisfaction as she reformatted all the floppy disks that had held copies. Ruth in the meantime was flicking through the filing cabinet, taking sheafs of papers

421

out of files and inserting them, willy nilly, into others.

'Deal with that, you slithery bastard!' she declared, as Heather shut down the computer. In spite of herself, Heather laughed again. She felt almost on a high. Neil might have thought that she didn't count. He'd think twice in the morning and know exactly how much he needed her. He might think he'd got where he was on his own, but in the couple of months that she'd worked for him she'd reorganized his business completely and left him to do what he was best at, selling cars. Office management was definitely not her ex-lover's strong point.

'Now I think we're finished. Let's go pack the car.' Ruth yawned.

'I can collect the stuff tomorrow.' Heather took a look around the little office she'd made her own and felt a deep sense of sadness.

'No, Heather. We'll bring them with us now. You're not setting foot in this place again. Mam's expecting us.'

'What did you tell her?' Heather asked in alarm.

'Stay calm,' Ruth soothed. 'I said that you and Neil had had a falling out and you were leaving. I never mentioned that other little fucking cow. You can tell Mam and Dad yourself if you want to.'

'Thanks, Ruth. Ma would have a fit. She'd probably go haring off around to Jane's and there'd be a fine family row,' Heather said faintly. 'I suppose I'll have to tell her some time. It's going to be all around the town anyway.'

'Well, not tonight. Come on. Let's go home,' Ruth said kindly, giving her a shove out of the door. For the next ten minutes they lugged the black sacks down the stairs and into Ruth's Mazda. 'Here, you sit in the car and give me the keys. I'll lock up,' her sister ordered.

Heather swallowed. She'd been really happy in her flat with Neil, challenged and interested by her work, and now it had all evaporated. She sat tiredly in the car, her high dissipated. She was almost numb. She watched her sister turning the key in the lock. Ruth was the salt of the earth, she thought gratefully. She'd taken control and given direction just when it was needed.

She glanced up at the windows of the flat. How cold and bare they looked without the curtains. She was right to leave, though. She had some pride. If it had been anyone else, she might eventually have forgiven Neil. But he'd betrayed her with Lorna. There could be no going back.

Her mother and father greeted her kindly, lovingly. 'Come in, pet,' said her dad. 'You can tell us all about it another time if you want, but for now, you're home where you belong and that's all that matters.'

Her mother took one look at her daughter's pale, strained face and said firmly, 'Up to bed with you. The blanket's on. I'll bring you up a cup of hot chocolate.'

Heather didn't argue. She was too exhausted. Her mother had the bed turned down, the big plump white pillows utterly inviting. She stepped out of her clothes, pulled on a nightie and slid into the warm comfort of her bed. She lay looking at the faded Laura Ashley wallpaper with its little cornflower sprigs, and the matching curtains that her mother had made. It was a homely bedroom that held many happy memories. Heather couldn't help but think that even though it had been the worst day of her life, she had a lot of loving support to cushion the blow. Some people had to deal with betrayals and broken hearts on their own.

Her mother knocked gently and came in with a cup of steaming hot chocolate. 'I put a drop of brandy in it to help you sleep. Everything will work itself out, love,' she said comfortingly.

'Thanks, Mam. We had a row. I'll tell you about it in a little while.'

'Whenever you want to, don't be worrying.' Her mother patted her as if she were a child. Heather sipped the hot chocolate and lay back against the pillows. She felt as though she were in a dream. That none of it was real. It was a very weird feeling. Anne slipped out of the room, and when she'd finished the hot chocolate Heather switched off the light and lay watching a sliver of moonbeam through the curtains. The old familiar shapes and shadows of the room weaved around her and she closed her eyes, too tired to think any more, and fell asleep.

Surprisingly, she slept until noon the following morning and when she woke up she lay in the half-awake state wondering why on earth she was sleeping at home in her old room. Remembrance hit and she buried her head under the pillows and cried, trying to smother her grief, afraid her parents would hear. How could she get up and face them and pretend to be normal? She just wanted to die rather than face that stabbing, aching pain, grief and shock that assailed her. *Lorna and Neil, Neil and Lorna*, round and round it went in her head until she felt like screaming.

A little while later Ruth rapped smartly on the door.

'Why aren't you at work?' Heather asked tearfully as Ruth came and stood beside the bed. Her sister carried a mug of tea and a bacon sandwich.

'It's Sunday, silly, and I felt you might need some sisterly affection.' She surveyed her twin's tear-stained face. 'Come on, eat this and get up and we'll go for a walk around the lake before dinner. It will give you an appetite. You know if you want to come back to Dublin you can move in with me for a while. Peter and I are buying a place soon. You can move in with us if you want,' she offered.

Heather shook her head and took a bite of the sandwich. She was actually hungry, she thought in surprise. Typical. Lots of her friends had lost their appetites and shed pounds when they'd been dumped, but not her. Her appetite was large as life, she thought crossly as she took another mouthful of hot, sweet tea.

'I don't know what I'm going to do,' she confessed to Ruth as they walked around the lake an hour later. It was a fine, bright day, the scent of spring unmistakable. Cotton puffs of clouds drifted on a cerulean sky, the birds sang lustily, but there was no balm for her spirit.

'Don't make any decisions yet. I just want you to know there's a place for you if you need it. It can be hard living at home with the parents when you're used to your own space, especially when you're upset.'

'I'll need to get a job. I can't sponge off Ma and Da.' Heather sighed. The thought of looking for employment was daunting, the thought of going back to Dublin even more stomach-lurching.

A magpie flew right in front of her and she cursed. 'Where's your blasted mate, the last thing I need is to see one magpie,' she grumbled, craning her neck to see if she could see the second one. 'Come on, you don't believe that malarkey,' Ruth chided as they began to move on.

'I hate seeing one magpie and I just don't need to see a single one today,' Heather snapped. She knew it was superstition but nevertheless she was always happy when she saw the pair. She scanned the treetops. It wasn't to be, there wasn't another magpie to be seen, and Heather walked on and felt the whole universe was against her. They passed Oliver Flynn, striding along with his head down.

'Hello,' he said politely but kept moving. He looked as miserable as she felt, Heather thought glumly as she panted after her fitter sister.

'I always thought he was a fine thing,' Ruth confided. 'I wondered why did he marry Noreen Lynch? I would never have thought of her as his type. And she's older than him.'

'I would never have thought of Lorna as Neil's type and definitely not of Neil as Lorna's,' Heather reflected grimly.

'I suppose,' Ruth murmured, not quite knowing

how to respond. Which was unusual for her to say the least. They walked for half a mile or so in silence.

'We'd better go back. Mam will have the dinner ready. Do you want to come to Dublin with me for a day or two? It might be easier,' Ruth suggested.

'I suppose I could. I know it's running away. I don't want to have to see Neil for a while.'

'Fine. We'll go to Dublin after dinner and you can stay as long as you like.'

Heather didn't particularly want to go to the city, but it would give her a chance to try to come to terms with what had happened and she wouldn't be under the concerned gaze of her parents, which was a little trying.

'It's a good idea. A break at Ruth's will do you all the good in the world,' Anne declared as she served up the dinner.

'Does that fellow owe you any money or anything?' Her father lowered his paper and glanced out at her over the top of his glasses.

'No, I got paid on Friday and I'm not giving him any notice so we're quits,' Heather said defiantly.

'Hmm,' said her father.

'Look, the thing is, he spent the night with someone else,' Heather muttered. 'That's why I'm leaving.'

'The *pup*!' Anne exclaimed indignantly. 'Well, I thought more of him than that.' Ruth caught Heather's gaze. A little smile flashed between them. If their mother only knew who Neil had spent the night with, there'd be real ructions. Her father frowned but remained silent. This type of thing embarrassed him. Still, Heather was glad that the awkward bit was out in the open; at least her parents wouldn't be conjecturing about the reasons for the row. Nor would they be dying of curiosity, she thought fondly as she caught sight of her mother's grim expression. If Anne bumped into Neil she'd let him have it good and proper, so Heather took the precaution of asking her to say nothing if she met her erstwhile boyfriend.

'Well, I'd like to tell him what I think of him,' Anne retorted as she ladled gravy on to Heather's grilled chops.

'Mother, I'm a big girl now. I fight my own battles,' she said evenly. 'Just stay out of it.'

'But—'

'Heather's right, Ma,' Ruth interjected.

'Very well,' her mother said tightly as she sat down to say grace.

The twins remained silent. It was the best policy when their mother was annoyed.

'That's Neil Brennan in Ma's bad books, she'll have a go at him one way or another,' Ruth observed as they drove towards Dublin a couple of hours later.

'I know. She's really mad, maybe I should have said nothing.' Heather groaned.

'Forget it,' Ruth advised.

Easier said than done, Heather thought rue-fully. Idly, she rooted in her bag for a tissue and switched on her mobile phone. The message icon flashed and she keyed in 171. Neil's indignant tones assaulted her ears.

'That was a bitchy thing to do, taking the

curtains. You're really childish, Heather,' he ranted before hanging up.

Heather turned to her sister. 'Neil left me a message to say I'm bitchy and childish because I took the curtains. Wait until he gets to grips with the office and the computer.'

'I wish him the joy of it.' Ruth grinned.

After three days sleeping on the floor at Ruth's, Heather decided to go home. She had to face it some time. And she had to make decisions about her life. She needed a job, any job to keep her going until she decided what she was going to do.

'Come and visit at weekends,' Ruth urged as she deposited her sister at the bus stop on the quays, where Neil had picked her up that fateful night before Christmas.

'I will,' Heather promised. 'And thanks for being there for me.'

'Don't be silly,' Ruth snorted. 'You'd do the same for me.'

As the bus pulled away from the bus stop, Heather felt tension curl around her insides. What was she going to do now? If she stayed in Kilronan she ran the risk of bumping into Neil at any time. Could she deal with that? She'd have to if she wanted to stay living at home. A car horn beeped loudly beside her and she looked out through the grimy bus window and saw a driver shaking his fist at a motorcyclist. A car was being clamped further along. If she came back to the city, she'd have to get a flat on her own. She wouldn't impose herself on Ruth and Peter. People living together for the first time needed to be on their own to get used to each other. She didn't want to come back to Dublin, she thought unhappily as the bus lurched forward, coming to a stop half a minute later as the traffic lights ahead turned red.

As the week passed by she got more agitated. It was horrible getting up in the morning with nothing to do and no job to go to. She hadn't left the house, reluctant to walk through the town, apprehensive of seeing Neil, and hating the idea of people talking about her. Her mother's cake box was a constant source of temptation and one evening when dusk had fallen she decided she had to go for a walk. All her trousers and skirts were getting tight at the waist and because she hadn't gone to basketball training or played any matches she was rapidly losing tone.

Head bent, muffled up in a scarf, she walked along the main street. Further ahead she could see the bright halogen lights illuminating Neil's forecourt. She paused, reluctant to go that far. Neil would have the showrooms open. She didn't want to see him. Since that one bitter message there'd been no contact, but she kept her mobile switched off most of the time, just in case. She wondered if he'd gone to New York for his weekend with Lorna. It tormented her to think of them in bed together. Couldn't he see that she was only using him and that when someone better came along she would drop him like a hot potato? It wasn't Lorna Neil should have been going to New York with, it should have been her, she thought bitterly, hating her cousin with a viciousness she didn't know she possessed. She blinked the tears from her eyes, raging with herself for being such a weeping willow.

Fred's Fast Food Emporium looked bright and cheerful and she suddenly got a longing for a comforting, piping hot single of crispy chips, drenched in vinegar and smothered in salt. She pushed open the door and felt a welcome wave of warmth. 'A single, please, Tom,' she said to the gangly youth behind the counter.

'I just put in a fresh batch, it will take a while,' he informed her grumpily.

'I'll have a coffee while I'm waiting,' she said.

She took her coffee to a small alcove. A notice-board hung on the wall, filled untidily with a variety of leaflets and posters. Babysitters wanted. Reflexology and aromatherapy available. Typist wanted to type thesis. She could do that, she supposed. It would be a bit of income. She noted down the number and then saw a notice saying: STAFF WANTED. APPLY WITHIN. Impulsively, she marched over to Tom. 'See the notice, staff wanted? Are you still looking for staff?'

'Yep.'

'Who do I talk to?'

'You!' He looked surprised. 'Don't you work for Neil Brennan?'

'Not any more,' she snapped.

'Oh. Well, Fred's in the back if you want to go in.' He pointed to the door that said Staff Only. Heather took a deep breath, walked behind the counter, knocked on the door and went in. Fred Kelly, the owner, sat watching a gardening programme, a pint of beer in one hand, a cigarette in the other.

'Hello, Heather,' he said in surprise. 'What brings you here?'

'Staff wanted, apply within,' she said drily. Fred looked at her in surprise.

'What about the job in—' he looked at her shrewdly. 'Aahh, I heard a rumour all right.'

Heather blushed.

'He's a bloody idiot,' Fred said kindly. 'Get a white coat out of the press there and go on out to Tom. He'll show you the ropes. The salary won't be what you're used to. But it's the going rate and I fancy you won't be staying with us that long,' he said astutely. 'You better stick a hat on your head. They're real sticklers for the health regulations.'

'Now!' Heather exclaimed.

'Might as well. I'll be out to help at the rush when the pubs close. You're in charge of seating areas. Keep the tables clean and set. Serve the meals promptly. And if you're helping behind the counter don't be mean with the chips. Fill the bag and a few over. Punters don't like to be short-changed on their chips. And Fred's are proper chips, not like those thin stringy yokes they serve over in that burger place,' Fred said proudly.

'Thanks, Fred.' Heather smiled at him. She knew him from her time working in the accountant's. He was well liked in the town for his decency.

'Make me proud,' Fred chuckled wheezily.

What in the name of God am I doing? Am I mad? Heather was heartily regretting her impulse as she

432

pulled on a white coat and a little white cap with a red braid. A small cracked mirror showed her face to be as red as the braid and she closed the door hastily.

'Go on and don't forget . . . Clean tables and plenty of chips.'

Tom surveyed her warily. 'Staff can't eat on the premises,' he said bossily.

'Just give me my single, Tom, and then you can show me the ropes,' Heather retorted. Tom Foley was at least five years younger than she was and she was taking no nonsense from him.

'Well, it's not allowed,' he said sulkily as he handed her a single.

She'd lost her appetite and didn't finish them, feeling a right prat in her hat.

'What do I do?' she asked the expert as politely as she could.

'If all the tables are clean you can make up some boxes, I'll show you how and I'll show you what to do with the bags. Always make sure there are bags and boxes ready,' Tom instructed her, bristling with importance as he demonstrated the art of making snack boxes and puffing out chip bags.

Two of her team-mates from basketball pushed open the door.

Oh no! she groaned silently.

'Heather!' Imelda Cooney exclaimed. 'What on earth are you doing here?'

'Well, I could hardly stay working at Neil's,' she retorted defensively.

'I suppose not,' Imelda agreed. 'Err . . . Could we have two snack boxes please?'

'I'll deal with it,' Tom interjected bossily. 'To eat here or take away?'

'Err . . . er . . . take away, please,' Imelda said hurriedly.

'Are you going to come back to the basketball? We lost our last match,' Caitriona Walsh said kindly.

'I will, yeah.' Heather puffed open some bags the way Tom had shown her. He was bustling around shaking the chips out of the oil, all business.

'Is everyone talking?' she asked hesitantly.

'Ah, you know, today's gossip is yesterday's news. It will be something else next week. I wouldn't take any notice,' Caitriona assured her.

'Lorna, though! That must have been an awful shock,' Imelda butted in. Heather didn't like her much. She was the type who would enjoy another's misfortune.

'That's men for you. Remember when Terence Nolan did the dirt on you?' she riposted spiritedly. Caitriona grinned and gave her a supportive wink.

Imelda went puce. 'At least he didn't sleep with my own cousin,' she retorted swiftly.

Heather kept silent.

'This job won't be great for basketball practice,' Caitriona tried to lighten the atmosphere.

'It's just until I get something more suitable,' Heather said quietly.

'Wrap the boxes in paper after you've asked if they want salt and vinegar,' Tom ordered. Heather cringed. This was *so* embarrassing. She must have been off her rocker to set herself up for such humiliation.

'Salt and vinegar?' she asked crisply, trying to appear normal.

'No thanks,' both of them echoed, and she foostered with the paper until Tom showed her how to fold it just so.

She couldn't get any more humiliated, she decided, as she watched Imelda and Caitriona walk out the door. She might as well stay. It couldn't get any worse.

Over the following weeks there were plenty of dropped jaws as people she knew did a double-take when they saw her behind the counter.

'Don't ask,' she'd say firmly, not engaging any of them in discussion. Fred was kind to her and Tom thawed when he saw that she was more than prepared to pull her weight. It meant less work for him.

One day Neil walked in. 'I heard you were working here. You made a right mess of my office – you're a spiteful bitch,' he blustered.

'You shut up and get out of here. Go get your chips somewhere else,' Tom said belligerently, much to Heather's amazement.

'Yeah, well, look at you, serving in a chipper, good enough for you,' Neil taunted.

'At least I'm working with decent people who have some code of honour,' Heather retorted, stung. How dare he take the offensive after what he'd done to her? 'And don't you dare even speak to me, Neil Brennan. You're the lowest of the low.'

'Out!' ordered Tom, pointing an imperious finger.

'Shut up, ya little nerd,' Neil exploded.

Tom raced out from behind the counter. Heather nearly fainted. It all happened in the space of a few seconds. One minute Neil was standing in front of her, the next he was manhandled out of the door. 'I'd stay out if I were you. I'm a black belt in karate,' Tom warned.

Neil paled, and trying his best to reclaim his dignity walked back towards the garage.

'Nobody calls me a nerd and gets away with it and I didn't like the way he was talking to you,' Tom said gruffly.

'Thanks very much, Tom.' Heather's heartbeat started to return to normal. It had been horrible when Neil had marched in. Her stomach had flip-flopped with dismay and then when he'd started calling her names it had made her feel sick. A sadness that they had come to such a pass had swept over her as she watched Neil walk away, shaken. Tom had astonished her with his reaction. Behind the surly gruffness he wasn't a bad old stick, she thought fondly.

'Are you a black belt?' she asked, adjusting her cap which was always falling down over one ear.

'Naw!' Tom smiled sheepishly. 'I'm only a yellow, but he wasn't to know that.'

Heather smiled at the memory as she sat driving to Wicklow with Ruth. Tom had stood up for her and she was very grateful to him. He was a decent sort, something Neil could never claim to be, she thought angrily as Ruth took a sharp right at a signpost that said Kilcoole. 'I don't want to go to this fortune-teller,' she moaned.

'I told you, she's not a fortune-teller. She's a

436

psychic and you need to get off your ass and go to *someone*. How long are you going to work in Fred's for heaven's sake? That's a cop out. Are you not mortified knowing that little shit is only down the road looking down his nose at you?' Ruth burst out, unable to contain herself a moment longer.

'Ah, don't be giving out to me,' Heather snapped as the car bounced up and down over the hilly road. 'Are we nearly there? What's this one's name?'

'Her name is Anne Jensen and you're lucky to be getting an appointment, so stop whinging.' Ruth indicated left and then drove right into an attractive tree-lined estate. She pulled up outside a neat semi-detached house and looked at her sister. 'Go in, she'll give you a sense of direction at the very least. You need it, Heather.'

Heather swallowed. She felt fluttery and nervous. In her heart of hearts she wanted to go back to Neil, although she'd never admit that to Ruth in a million years. Her loneliness and misery were greater than her pride. She missed her life with Neil. She was tormenting herself imagining him emailing and talking to Lorna. Surely he couldn't see a future for them? Couldn't he see that Heather was the one he should be with? They were a great team. He couldn't love Lorna the way he loved her. Maybe when all the bitterness had eased, they'd get back together. Maybe this Anne woman would give her good news.

She knocked at the door. A little dog started to bark. A tall, slender woman with soft ash-blonde hair opened the door and smiled. 'Hi,' she said. 'I'm

Anne, don't mind Precious barking, she's very friendly. Come in and sit yourself down in the kitchen.' She waved out at Ruth. 'You're not peas in a pod, that's for sure,' she remarked as she led Heather into a large, bright, airy kitchen.

'I've never been to a fortu— a psychic,' she amended, 'before.'

'Nothing to worry about,' the woman said matter-of-factly. 'Sit down and relax and let me do the work.'

Heather sat down, palms sweaty. The little dog licked her hand. It was comforting somehow. Her heart was racing. *Please let her tell me that Neil loves me and wants me back*, she prayed as Anne handed her a pack of well-used tarot cards and told her to shuffle them.

35

Neil pulled off his overall and ran a comb through his hair. One of his mechanics was out sick and there was a backlog of cars waiting to be serviced. Having to do ramp work at this stage of his career wasn't on, he thought crabbily as he got a whiff of BO. He had a client coming at nine on the dot, he wouldn't have time for a shower. He yanked his T-shirt over his head, applied some deodorant, rooted out a clean shirt and buttoned it up. He splashed some aftershave on to his hands and rubbed it over his face.

Heather couldn't have left at a worse time. He'd been working his butt off to get a franchise, he was practically ready for the sign-up, but everything was getting on top of him. The office was a shambles, Larry was out sick, there were three cars still to be serviced. Vince, the other mechanic, was working flat out, and Neil was thoroughly browned off.

He saw a dusty, maroon Vauxhall Vento drive on to the forecourt. The driver, a crusty middle-aged bachelor farmer, eased his lanky frame out of the car. Neil had persuaded him to trade in for a brand new BMW. It had been hard work and it was only when Neil assured him that women went mad for new Beemers that Morris Mullen had taken the bait.

It was another hour before Morris finally drove off, proud as punch in his new car. Neil bent his head to finish the paperwork. The new girl he'd taken on to look after the office had flatly refused to work Saturdays and she was a stickler for leaving at five on the dot too. Neil chewed the top of his pen and gazed unseeingly out of the big plate-glass windows. The last six weeks had been a nightmare, from the moment Heather had come up the stairs with that damn email. He hadn't covered his tracks very well, he had to admit. He should have deleted the damn thing. He'd thought he had.

Heather would have found out about him spending the night with her cousin one way or another. Sleeping with Lorna in the Lake View was a really daft thing to do, no doubt about it. But then, how many men got to pull a classy bird like Lorna Morgan? It had been an intensely satisfying encounter. She was a challenge and he wanted more, but Lorna hadn't got in touch since that unexpected email inviting him to spend a weekend in New York. To issue an invite like that and then ignore him was downright rude and that pissed him off big time. He hated the idea that he was only a one-night stand for her.

They could go places together, climb up the social ladder, be a powerful team. The more he got involved in the business the more he realized how important business and social contacts were. Lorna could be a huge asset to him if she were willing to be in a relationship with him. And if that happened it would be worth the break-up with Heather.

Heather was a great girl. She was a tremendous organizer, great for giving encouragement, great for listening to his plans, but she was a small-town girl. Provincial, parochial. There'd been no challenge in getting Heather into his bed. She was a soft touch with few ambitions.

Lorna was a sophisticate who could carry herself anywhere and she looked the part. Her dress sense far outshone Heather's and she had a figure to really carry it off. He wanted her. He wanted to show her just how far he could climb. He knew she looked down her nose at him and he wanted that to change. One day Lorna Morgan would look at him with respect, even awe, in her eyes, he daydreamed, gazing around at his chrome and glass showrooms with pride. He missed Heather at work, he couldn't deny it, but at night in the dark it was Lorna he lusted after and Lorna he fantasized about.

Neil felt a stirring of desire, remembering their night together. Resolutely he bent his head and finished his paperwork. He could do with a bit of breakfast and a cup of coffee, he was hungry. He wondered could he risk Fred's. If that idiot Tom was working he wouldn't bother. Shoving him out the door like that. That had been embarrassing. He scowled at the memory.

What a comedown for Heather to end up working in a fast-food joint. Surely she could have found a better job for herself, she was so capable and qualified? He shouldn't have gone into Fred's shouting the odds, he supposed, but he was as mad as hell and under pressure. He'd had to get some-one in to sort out the desktop and it had cost him a pretty penny.

He felt a dart of guilt. He'd treated her extremely badly, he knew that. He'd been shocked at her vindictiveness, mucking up the files in the com-puter and even taking the curtains off the windows, but he understood it, respected it even. If she'd said and done nothing, he would have respected her less. His sleeping with Lorna would have cut her to the quick. He'd betrayed her, there was no denying it, but at the end of the day a man had to look out for himself, and a woman like Lorna would be a far better asset on his arm climbing up the social ladder. Heather had no ambitions, Lorna had. He recognized a kindred spirit in her. If only she'd bloody well get in touch. He didn't like the feeling of being used – it brought back bitter memories. Been there, done that, worn the T-shirt. Women were horrible creatures sometimes. And yet, the one woman who had treated him with love, respect and consideration was the one he had treated most shabbily. In spite of himself, he felt ashamed.

'Oh, for God's sake,' he muttered irritably, not enjoying his moment of introspection. He flung his pen on the desk and grabbed his jacket. He was going to have a fry-up and to hell with whoever was in Fred's. Heather didn't work on Saturdays as far as he could see. That only left Sir Galahad to deal with.

Fortunately the Karate Kid wasn't on duty, and Neil ordered the full Monty. Now that Heather was no longer cooking for him, his diet had gone to the dogs, he thought ruefully. He glanced at his watch. Almost eleven. New York was five hours behind; Lorna no doubt was catching up on her beauty sleep in some posh uptown pad. She'd probably already met some wealthy yuppie guy and she'd never again look down her pert little nose at him.

'Get in touch, Lorna, get in touch,' he muttered as the smell of sizzling bacon wafted through Fred's Fast Food Emporium.

Lorna groaned as the shrill penetrating ring of the alarm clock brought her reluctantly to consciousness. She couldn't face going into work this morning. She'd spent the previous night at a club in TriBeCa, drinking cocktails, and she was in flitters. Her feet still ached from standing in her pointy, backbreakingly high Manolos. They had cost a week's salary.

She sat up in bed and ran her fingers through her hair. It was dark and the rest of the house was quiet. Carina and her friends were going skiing in the Catskills for the day, but Lorna really needed to work. Saturday was the best day for getting tips in the Times Square diner that she worked in. Unfortunately, she was rostered on the early shift and it was a bummer. If she didn't go in, Zack Pedroski, the owner, would kick her out. She'd missed a shift once and he'd told her in no uncertain terms that two strikes and she was out. 'Ya don't get more than one chance in my diner,' he warned.

'Ah, stick your diner,' she muttered aloud, tempted beyond measure to snuggle back down and go asleep, and then wake up and ride into Manhattan and eat brunch in a posh uptown restaurant before spending the day shopping on Fifth Avenue. But she was smashed, totally smashed. She had to make enough money for her rent this week. She shouldn't have bought the damn sandals. They were her first Manolos, and she'd been on such a high buying them, even Carina had been impressed.

Being broke was the pits. New York was heaven and hell, she decided as she got out of bed and gingerly made her way down the hall to the bathroom. Her head throbbed. She'd really hit the sauce last night. The loose group she socialized with played hard. Those cocktails were knockout strong. For an hour or two she'd felt like Samantha, her heroine in *Sex and the City*, but the reality was so different.

Being a waitress was the worst thing. She was going to get an office job come hell or high water. It was difficult though. She'd tried a few places. Everybody was tightening up after 9/11 and she had no visa. Once she had a green card she could come back and try again, she was told. Zack Pedroski didn't worry about the niceties like green cards and visas. As long as people covered their shifts efficiently, he didn't care if they came from the moon.

It was hard to believe she'd been in New York six weeks. It was the most wonderful, vibrant, magnificent, noisy, brash, dirty city. It was everything she'd dreamed of and more. If only she was loaded, she'd adore it. If she were as rich as

Charlotte in *Sex and the City*, she would be perfectly happy. She'd live in a duplex on Madison or Park, and spend her days in Saks and Armani's and Bergdorf's and Tiffany's. She'd never forget the first time she'd seen Tiffany's. She'd walked past it, so understated and elegant and not at all what she was expecting. The small, perfectly dressed window so at odds with the larger, brasher stores. She thought she'd faint with excitement and frustration as she entered its hallowed portals, which oozed class. To be in the place of her dreams and have no money to spend was the pits. She'd wandered around looking longingly at the glorious jewellery and the silver giftware that made the most perfect presents and felt totally inadequate. Tiffany's was out of her league and that disturbed her greatly.

In her heart and soul, Lorna admitted that in New York you had to work hard to get places, and working hard was not her. She'd hoped at this stage to have met a rich eligible, but even though she was looking her best and wearing classy clothes, she was one of thousands with the same ideal, and there were far more women than men in the cocktail bars and at the parties she'd so far attended. Her confidence was wavering bigtime.

Lorna brushed her teeth. She felt like crying. She had a hangover, her period was killing her and she had to go and spend the next eight hours toing and froing carrying heavy trays, clearing tables, and having to listen to whinging kids change their minds a dozen times while she waited to take their order. This had not been the plan at all. She

445

wouldn't be seen dead waitressing at home, but she was broke and she needed the money.

The first week in the city had been the most exciting, exhilarating week of her life. She'd flashed her father's money around with abandon. If her life was like it had been those first few mind-blowing days she'd be in Paradise, she reflected, shivering as she hurried back to her small bedroom.

Coming in to land at JFK and seeing the unmistakable skyline in the distance as they made their approach had been a truly memorable moment. Carina's friend Fiona had met them in arrivals and the drive from the airport had been the most nerve-racking experience. New York drivers were crazy, the honking of car horns a nerve-jangling cacophony. The famous yellow cabs dominated the streets and she couldn't wait to stand on Fifth Avenue and yell 'Taxi!' just like her heroines. Preferably carrying large carrier bags with prestigious names emblazoned on them.

The nearer they got to Manhattan the more excited Carina and herself became, pointing at this and that, gazing at the skyscrapers in the distance. As they drove across town towards Grand Central Station, Lorna felt she had died and gone to heaven. They were taking the train to Yonkers but Lorna wanted to dump her luggage and begin exploring immediately. Carina and Fiona were deep in conversation, catching up on news and gossip, and Lorna felt impatient with them that they were perfectly content to carry on to the suburbs when the city of cities waited to be experienced.

Dragging their luggage through Grand Central

and down to the subway was not a pleasant experience, and Lorna was crotchety as they sat on the swaying train, leaving Manhattan behind. As they rode north, Lorna was surprised at how green the countryside was. Yonkers was only a short distance from the Catskill Mountains. She and her friends spent a lot of time skiing and walking the trails, Fiona told them. Walking in mountains was not what she had come to America for, Lorna thought sulkily. She might try skiing, but it was so bitingly cold, she didn't think it would really be her scene. The journey to Yonkers took less than half an hour and that cheered her up. At least she wouldn't be spending hours commuting.

The house they were to share was in the suburb of Woodlawns. A two-storey over basement. It had a surprisingly large back garden with a patio area. People lived on their patios in summer, Fiona assured them. The front was open-plan. So middle-class, Lorna relected, not New York hip, and not for her. As soon as she could she was going to get a place in Manhattan.

Lorna smiled at her naïvety as she sat on the train waiting to go to work. She'd gone into Manhattan the next day with Carina and they had spent a fortune. That whole week they'd eaten out, hailed taxis with abandon, bought clothes that cost an arm and a leg, and had a ball. The next week they'd gone waitressing in an attempt to repair the damage to their finances.

Lorna, fed on a diet of glossy novels where heroines arrived in New York and plum opportunities, not to mention sexy men, dropped in their laps, soon had a good dollop of reality. Fiona and her friends were perfectly content to work double shifts waitressing and to party hard with their boyfriends, mostly builders and electricians. All Irish. Lorna didn't want Irish. That was why she had come to New York. She wanted glitz and glamour and she certainly wasn't going to get it hanging around Rory Dolan's Irish bar, or in the little delis and bars on McClean Avenue. She might as well be living in Rathmines or Ranelagh for all the good it was doing her.

And she was permanently cold, she thought dolefully as the train rattled into Ludlow. She knew the names of all the stations now. Riverdale was next, she might as well have been on the Dart. A drunk got on at Morris Heights and swayed down towards her. She froze. The carriage was only a third full, and she hoped he'd leave her alone and not start to annoy her. He fell into a seat and Lorna breathed a sigh of relief as they rolled through Harlem towards 126th Street. It was bad enough having drunks on the train at night, but not at the crack of dawn.

It was a bitterly cold morning as she emerged from Grand Central, and as she always did, she looked up at the Chrysler building. It was still hard to believe she was in Manhattan. Dawn was streaking across the eastern sky. Skiing in the Catskills suddenly seemed inviting as she trudged across town to Times Square and another day's drudgery.

Late afternoon found her marching wearily along West 57th, an Internet printout clutched in her hand. 'Uptown but not Uptight' was the motto of Le Parker Meridian, and they had the only glass enclosed rooftop pool in Manhattan. Two blocks south of Central Park, she could see Fifth Avenue from where she was standing. She lifted her chin and squared her shoulders as she walked into the classy foyer. Minimalist chic, a little like the Clarence, she noted, impressed. She wouldn't mind working here. Her mother would love it. She marched over to the concierge service and waited for someone to deal with her. After a moment or two a young man smiled politely and asked if he could help. Lorna explained that she was inviting her mother to stay in New York for a week and was looking for a suitable hotel. She was particularly interested in the pool area, could she view it? The young man called one of the bellhops over and asked him to escort Lorna to the 42nd floor. A small TV in the elevator showed Laurel and Hardy and a couple, arms entwined, giggled as it moved smoothly upwards.

'This way, madam,' the bellhop indicated as they exited on the 42nd and he led her to the pool area. Lorna sighed with pleasure as she saw the sparkling pool, and the bare-branched trees of Central Park in the distance. Luxurious loungers lay poolside and potted ferns gave an exotic air. The sky was deepening to pink and mauve as dusk stole westwards, and a man sliced powerfully through the blue water, his broad shoulders deeply tanned. Probably a millionaire, she thought wistfully, wishing she was draped in her turquoise bikini on one of the plump-cushioned loungers.

'Thank you.' She smiled at the bellhop and reluctantly tipped him one of her precious dollars. This was definitely the hotel for her mother, only she wasn't going to come until May at the earliest. And that seemed ages away. She'd love to spend a weekend in this fabulous place, she thought as the elevator descended to the foyer. Another couple entered as she exited and she observed them enviously. Why couldn't she find a man who would bring her to this Nirvana? Neil Brennan would, she had no doubt about that, but she'd been hoping that she would have met a far richer, successful man by now.

Still, Neil would do for a weekend, she thought excitedly as she peered in at Norma's, one of *the* places to go for brunch in NYC. She was tempted to have coffee and a muffin but it would probably cost an arm and a leg. Let Neil treat her to brunch when he came. It was the least he could do.

Heartened at the idea of a luxurious weekend in a classy hotel, minutes away from Tiffany's and Saks, Lorna smiled charmingly at the doorman as he held the heavy doors open for her. The next time she came to Le Parker Meridian, it would be as a guest.

36

'You've been through the mill.' Anne Jensen frowned as she studied Heather's palm and then glanced at the cards that were laid out on the table. 'You suffered a double betrayal. Your partner's been with a woman who's related to you in some way. She's blonde.'

Heather nearly fell off the chair. 'My boyfriend slept with my cousin,' she said faintly.

'Hmm. He's not the one for you anyway. You're far better off without *him*.' Anne said briskly. Heather's heart sank.

'Isn't he?' she asked forlornly, her heart plummeting at the words she'd dreaded.

The psychic looked at her in surprise. 'Why would you want him? After what he's done to you? He's shallow and selfish and only interested in what's best for him. There's a far better man waiting for you, Heather.'

'I don't think I'll ever fall in love and trust anyone again,' Heather retorted, angry that she wasn't hearing what she wanted to hear. Who was this man waiting for her? Any fortune-teller would tell you that there was a man for you. That's why women went to them. What a swizz, she scowled, raging with Ruth for bringing her.

'Stop that nonsense,' Anne instructed sternly. 'Of course you will! And sooner than you think, you listen to your Auntie Anne. That man you were with only wanted you because you were of use to him. And your cousin is so jealous of you—'

'Jealous of *me*?' Heather was astonished.

'Yes, *you*!' Anne smiled as she threw out another card. She had beautiful hands, and a lovely slender figure. Heather would give anything to be able to wear a polo tucked into her jeans the way the other woman did.

'Your cousin is a very unhappy, confused young woman. She thinks material things will make her happy; she'll never have what you have. She never has. She's jealous of your relationship with your family, especially with your sister. She was jealous of you when you got together with that Neil and she wasn't happy until she broke you up, but she'll never get the chance to do that again. The man that's coming into your life will see through her right away. You are going to have a relationship that will sustain you all your life. It will be a friendship first. Then it will become deeper and sustaining. That gift will never be hers.'

'Is she going to see Neil again?' Heather willed the psychic to say no.

'Heather, I know you would love me to tell you that Neil is the man for you and that he'll realize that he's made a mistake. But I don't give people false hope. I don't say things that they want to hear just to suit them. I tell them the truth. I don't abuse

452

my gift. When you see what's waiting for you, you'll realize that there is no comparison with what you had. Neil and your cousin will use each other as it suits them but their relationship will never be from the heart . . . Yours will. Pick out another few cards there.'

Heather reluctantly did as she was told.

'I see a key of a door, a new job and a new man.' Anne flicked the cards on to the table in front of her.

Heather looked sceptical. 'What's this man like? Where will I meet him?'

'You already know him. He's someone on the periphery of your life at the moment. Soon he'll be ready for you to come into his life. It will be a great friendship first. You'll be the first woman he's ever fallen "in" love with. I'm not saying that he hasn't loved, we all love, but you'll be the first he's fallen "in" love with,' she emphasized again. 'And the relationship will be for life. Look,' she pointed to a card. 'It's Divinely ordained.'

'And what's the new job?' Heather felt she might as well go along with the charade.

'It's like a job you did before. The skills that you learned in that job will help you.'

'Will I leave Kilronan?'

Anne gazed down at the array of cards in front of her. 'I don't see a move from your area, just a key of a door. It's all going to work out, you know, and I know you don't believe a word of it but you'll see. And you're going to be very happy. That Neil fella was very shocked but impressed by what you did to get your own back,' she added slyly.

Heather blushed to the roots of her hair. 'How did you know that? Were you talking to Ruth?'

'No I wasn't. I can see it. Just as I can see that he will be going over water to see that woman and you are not to give it one second of energy. Don't waste time on them, they're not worth it. Close the door on it and let it go and open yourself to the new energy that's coming in to your life. You're a very lucky woman. Not many women will know the love that you'll know. It will be a deep and lifelong bond.'

She smiled at Heather. 'Keep in touch and let me know what's happening.'

'OK,' Heather agreed, privately feeling that it had been a complete waste of time. A man on the periphery of her life indeed. Ruth had no sense, dragging her to a psychic. Mind, the woman had known about Heather's revenge and according to her Neil was going to go to see Lorna over water. Heather hadn't even mentioned that Lorna was in New York.

'Trust your Auntie Anne,' Anne exhorted as she opened the front door for Heather. 'Tell your sister I was asking for her.'

'Well?' demanded Ruth as Heather got into the car.

'There's a man on the periphery of my life, and it's going to be a deep and lifelong bond,' Heather said sarcastically.

'Great, and what did she say about Neil and that other wagon?'

Ruth ignored her sister's obvious scepticism.

'Well, she did say he was going to visit her over water and she did seem to know I'd done

454

something to get my own back on him,' Heather admitted. 'Did you tell her about the files?'

'No I didn't,' Ruth retorted indignantly. 'I'm telling you, she sees things.'

'Yeah, well, we'll see,' Heather said glumly. She was sorry she'd come. According to Anne Jensen, Neil was going to visit Lorna and that was a dagger to the heart no matter how shallow he was.

The few hours they spent in Avoca Handweavers took her mind off her troubles but the heartache was never far away and the journey home to Kilronan left her as troubled as when she'd left. It didn't help that she saw Neil driving past, laughing as he spoke to someone on his mobile. How dare he laugh, she thought irrationally. How dare he be happy when she was as miserable as hell. So much for psychics.

Tom did his best to cheer her up the following evening at work, but she was glad when he went on his tea break so she could be miserable in comfort. She was puffing up bags when Oliver Flynn pushed open the door. He looked grey and tired. 'A cod and chips, please,' he said and then gave her a look of surprised recognition.

'Doing a nixer, Heather?' he asked.

'Em . . . not really, Oliver. Neil and I split up. I left the garage . . . and the flat,' she added wryly, remembering how he'd wished her the best in her new home.

'Oh, oh, sorry to hear that,' he said awkwardly.

'That's OK,' she murmured unhappily.

'You wouldn't go back to live in Dublin?' he ventured.

'Not really. I don't want to go back there. I like Kilronan.'

'Me too,' Oliver sighed.

Two young lads came in and ordered burgers and chips so she applied herself to her tasks, thinking that she really should start looking for a job that paid more and challenged her more. It was time to get on with things again. She remembered Anne Jensen's words that the skills that she'd learned in her previous job would help her. She could always drop in to the local auctioneer's and see if they had any vacancies, she supposed. Or maybe she should try the accountant's, maybe she was referring to that. It could be anything, she thought crossly as she wrapped Oliver's cod and chips for him and gave him his change.

Oliver took his fish and chips and drove out to the lake. He didn't want to go home. It was strange how empty the house was without Noreen. It was lonely. He missed her. He'd told Cora that she was in London looking after a friend who was sick, but he was going to have to tell her the truth, sooner rather than later.

The birds sang all around him as he sat on a bench and unwrapped his meal. The days were getting longer. He'd be able to put in a couple of extra hours on the new site he was developing. Twenty-two apartments with lake views would give him plenty to do and plenty to think about. The first phase was well under way. He wouldn't have time to be lonely. One thing he was good at was his job, even if he was a failure at everything else. He'd spoken to Noreen a couple of times on the phone, stilted, awkward conversations that he was glad to end. She was going to go back to nursing, she'd told him. That sounded pretty final. She'd left him, and why wouldn't she? he brooded. He couldn't give her a child, he couldn't even make love to her properly. Why would she stay with a failure like him? Why would any woman ever want to be with him? He'd be on his own for the rest of his life, he'd better start getting used to it.

Neil's heart leapt in his chest when he saw Lorna's email address in his inbox. It was about time. Eagerly he clicked on the icon.

Hi Neil,

Can I possibly be missing you?????!!!!!! When are you going to spend a sexy weekend with me? I found us a fabulous hotel, see attachment. Just let me know when you're booking the room so that I can make sure to take the weekend off? New York is a dream. You'll love it. They have a chain of lingerie stores called Victoria's Secret, should I splash out?????

Lorna xxxxxxx

'Yes! Yes! Yes!' he punched his fist in the air. A weekend in bed with Lorna Morgan wearing a see-through creation was just what he needed. He couldn't wait. He opened the attachment and read the details she had sent about the hotel. It sounded fine. He couldn't care less where he stayed. She probably wanted to stay in a hotel so that they could have some privacy. She hadn't given him a telephone number, which was frustrating. He'd far prefer to talk to her, it was much more intimate than sitting at a computer. He flicked through his diary. He could organize a few days off without too much difficulty. So what if he had to pay Vince a bit extra to keep an eye on the showrooms on the Saturday. He deserved a holiday, he'd worked bloody hard for it. Lorna could have booked the hotel instead of leaving it to him, she was living in the damn city. He'd book it over the phone. Fiddling on the Internet drove him nutty. Heather was far superior at doing things like that. She'd probably be very hurt if she found out that he'd gone to see Lorna for the weekend. But it was time for him to move on, and her too, he thought irritably, annoyed at his feelings of guilt.

She was really letting herself go to the dogs, working in a chipper, putting on weight. She must have been crazy about him. It was reassuring to know he had that effect on women. Neil hoped that he'd have the same effect on Lorna, eventually. That would be something to aspire to. He smiled to himself as he rooted in his pocket for his credit card and dialled the hotel number she had emailed him.

Ten minutes later the hotel was booked. He sat down at his keyboard and logged on.

Hi Lorna,

Hotel booked from Thurs to Sun the weekend after next. Black suspenders would be something

else on a sexy woman like you. Can't wait. Will book the flight tomorrow and let you know the details. Just thinking about you makes me as horny as hell, wish I was with you now,

See you soon beautiful woman,

Love Neil

He pressed send and heard the musical ping as his email went winging its way to Lorna. It was great that she was making all the moves. It meant she wanted to be involved. He was so used to Heather's giving nature, it was like being on a rollercoaster with Lorna, but it sure as hell wasn't boring. Whistling, he shut down the computer and went up to the flat to get his gym gear. He had less than two weeks to tone up and look his best. With Heather it hadn't mattered, he'd never felt worried about his body, but Lorna was a different kettle of fish. She was so perfect herself, he didn't want to feel flabby and unfit in front of her. And he must buy himself some new boxers, the ones he had really didn't enhance his image. Image was everything, he assured himself, wishing his stomach wasn't rumbling and that he didn't feel so hungry.

37

'Noreen, you really should tell him, it's not fair on the chap, and you have to tell Rajiv as well,' Kay said firmly.

Noreen groaned. 'I know, Kay, I know. I just can't bring myself to.'

'Get it over and done with. Invite Oliver over if you want to. If it would be easier for you.'

'No, I'm not imposing on you any more, Kay. I'm going to get a place of my own very soon. I know I've been putting it off. I just seem to be in a fog.' Noreen nibbled on a slice of toast.

'That's because you need to act decisively. You need to sort out your relationship with Oliver.' Kay poured them another cup of tea.

'What relationship?' Noreen said wryly.

'Ah, don't be like that,' Kay admonished. 'He's a good man.'

'But even before all this blew up he was never at home. He kills himself working. He'd rather work than spend time with me,' Noreen said mournfully.

'Don't look at it like that, Noreen,' her friend said patiently. 'Some men work like that because it's how they define themselves. It's where they get affirmation of who and what they are. It makes them feel good about themselves and when wives and partners nag and moan about it, that drives them to work even harder. It's nothing to do with a lack of love for you. That's the way he is, Noreen, and you have to accept it because you won't change him.'

'But I'm lonely, Kay, really, really, lonely,' Noreen said quietly.

'Well, maybe he's not the man for you. But at least tell him the truth and don't have him beating himself up over all that's happened. It's not fair on him.' Kay looked her squarely in the eye.

Noreen smiled. 'You know you're the straightest person I know and the best friend I've got. I'll book a flight home and tell Oliver face to face. It's the least he deserves.'

'Do you want me to come with you?'

'No thanks, Kay. This is something I have to do myself. I got myself into this mess, I have to get myself out of it.'

'At least you're pregnant,' Kay said gently.

'I know. It's hard to believe. And I feel so well after only a couple of weeks of morning sickness.' Noreen stretched lazily. 'I'll see if I can get a flight today. The sooner I get it over with the better.' She glanced at her watch. Nine thirty – she could be back in Kilronan before teatime.

Sitting on the bus as it drove along the quays, five hours later, Noreen yawned tiredly. It had been a day of trains, planes and buses. It had been all go since breakfast. She'd got a flight from Stansted no problem, and had hailed a taxi at Dublin Airport to take her into town. Now, sitting on the Kilronan

461

bus as it made its way out of the city, she started to feel nervous.

How on earth was she going to tell Oliver she was pregnant? It was six weeks since she'd run away to London in a panic and nothing in her life was sorted. She'd talked to him on the phone a few times, but they had been stiff, uncomfortable conversations and she'd felt his resentment and anger at the other end of the line.

Kay was right. She had to tell Oliver everything. It wasn't fair to let him think that their break-up was all his fault. Kay had been such a brick, she reflected as she stared unseeingly out the window. When Noreen had told her that she was pregnant and that Rajiv was the father she'd been stunned. Noreen grinned, remembering the absolute shock on her friend's face. If it wasn't so serious, it would be comical.

'Right!' she'd said. 'Right. Now you have to stay here until you decide what you're going to do. Are you going to tell Rajiv you're here?'

'Not yet,' Noreen groaned. 'I need to get used to the idea of being pregnant for a while.'

'Fine, take all the time you need,' Kay ordered and had looked after her like a baby for the past few weeks. They were closer than sisters; she was lucky to have her, Noreen thought drowsily as her head lolled on to her shoulder. She'd heard women talking about the tiredness that could envelop women in early pregnancy, they hadn't been exaggerating, she thought, as she fell asleep.

She slept for the duration of the journey, and woke to find Mrs Larkin, one of her ex-patients, shaking her by the shoulder. 'Nurse Flynn, Nurse Flynn, wake up, we're just coming into Kilronan,' she urged kindly.

Noreen came to with a start. 'Where . . . what . . . Oh, Mrs Larkin, I must have fallen asleep.'

'Indeed you did, dear. I got on in Navan and you were sleeping like a baby.'

Noreen blushed. Surely Mrs Larkin couldn't tell she was pregnant! *Don't be ridiculous*, she chided as she sat up straight and ran her fingers through her hair.

'Were you away? We've missed you in the surgery,' Mrs Larkin enquired chattily.

'I was,' Noreen smiled.

'And will Oliver be waiting at the bus for you with that heavy bag?'

'Aaahhh, I got home earlier than I expected.'

'I hope he has the house tidy,' chuckled Mrs Larkin. 'Did you hear young Neil Brennan and Heather Williams broke up? I think she caught him with someone else, her cousin if you don't mind. A right little madam, thought she was too good for the town. She's gone to New York and poor Heather's working in Fred's chipper. Terrible,' she tutted, delighted to be first with the gossip. 'And Aileen Kelly broke her arm in two places and had to go into a nursing home. And poor Maddy Hill only has a few weeks to live, they took her into hospital and opened her up and she was riddled with cancer, *riddled* with it,' she emphasized, with great relish. 'Nothing they can do,' she added triumphantly. She delighted in her role as the bearer of bad tidings. In fact the worse they were the more satisfaction she got. She was a sad woman, Noreen

463

thought irritably, imagining the older woman's shock if she suddenly announced that she was pregnant and Oliver was not the father.

The bus pulled into the bus stop and Noreen grabbed her bag and walked purposefully towards the exit, followed closely by Mrs Larkin. 'Can you manage ther—'

'I'm fine, Mrs Larkin, take care,' Noreen said crisply and took to her heels as soon as she stepped off the bus. She had no intention of listening to that old gossip for the length of North Road.

Now that she was home, she felt agitated again. And she was hungry. She wondered if Oliver would have anything in the fridge. Maybe she should have phoned him to tell him she was coming home. She took out her mobile and keyed in his number, but got the out-of-range message. 'Damn,' she muttered. She didn't particularly want to go shopping for groceries. She wanted to get out of sight as quick as possible. She was not in the mood for social chit-chat with neighbours and ex-patients.

It was strange putting the key in the lock when she got home. She felt she had no right and that she was invading Oliver's privacy. She felt most uncomfortable, but she shrugged off the notion and went into the kitchen and put the kettle on. The kitchen was neat and tidy; typical Oliver, she thought fondly, as she rooted in the fridge and found a hunk of cheese and a jar of chutney. She found brown bread in the bread bin and buttered a slice, smeared on some chutney and added a piece of cheese. It would do to tide her over.

She pulled out the freezer drawers and found a

couple of salmon steaks. They'd do fine for dinner, if only she could locate Oliver and find out what time he'd be home. She was peeling potatoes when she heard his key in the door. Her heart leapt and she turned and saw the look of astonishment on Oliver's face as he walked into the kitchen.

'Hello, Oliver,' she said nervously.

'Hello, Noreen,' he responded warily. He looked wretched, she thought as guilt overwhelmed her. She'd planned to wait until after they'd eaten to tell him but she couldn't keep it to herself a minute longer.

'Oliver . . . I . . . I've something to tell you. And I want you to know I never meant to hurt you in any way. I'm sorry . . . I'm really sorry.' Her face crumpled and she started to cry.

'Oh, Noreen,' he groaned. 'Don't be crying.'

'Oliver . . . Oliver, I'm pregnant. I slept with a man when I was in London and I'm pregnant.'

Shock, pain, hurt flitted across his face as he stared at her. The silence stretched taut between them. *Say something*, she willed.

'Well, you got what you always wanted,' he said eventually. 'I'm glad that you found a real man,' he added bitterly.

'Don't say that, Oliver! You *are* a real man. You're the most decent, manly man I've ever met.'

'So decent that you go behind my back and sleep with someone else, is that it?' he raged.

'It wasn't like that, Oliver, I swear,' Noreen said heatedly. 'I was drunk. I was upset about us.'

'Well, you've a funny way of showing it,' he snarled.

'Oliver, will you listen to me for a minute. I need to tell you something. I need you to understand why I was so driven to get pregnant. Please, Oliver. This is the hardest thing I've ever done. Please don't judge me,' she pleaded, walking to where he stood and looking up into his eyes.

'Oliver, before I met you, when I lived in London with that man I told you about, Pete, I had an abortion. I've regretted it every second since. I was tormented with guilt. I kept thinking about the baby, especially around the time it would have been born and at Christmas and when I'd see children playing. I'd try and imagine . . . imagine . . .' She broke down sobbing as though her heart would break and Oliver held her, stroking her back, saying nothing, his eyes shadowed with pain.

She managed to compose herself, wiping the tears from her cheeks with the back of her hand. 'He told me he'd leave me if I didn't have it. I loved him and I was afraid I'd lose him. But I couldn't stay with him after I'd had the termination. I began to hate him for giving me an ultimatum like that. You were so different, Oliver. So kind, so responsible. I knew you'd never treat me badly. I wanted a child so much. I felt if I got pregnant that God would forgive me for what I'd done and give me the chance to be a good mother to another child. When I wasn't getting pregnant I felt it was God's punishment. Oh Oliver, I've been to hell and back these last few years.' She rested her head on his chest and wept again. His arms tightened around her. She looked up at him. There was no anger in his eyes any more or judgement, just pity and sadness, and she rested against him.

'Why didn't you tell me?' he asked after a while. 'At least I would have understood.'

'I couldn't. I was ashamed,' she said simply. 'Oliver, I'm so sorry I put you under pressure to have a baby. I know I did your head in.'

'I didn't know what you were going through. I wish I had.'

'I'm sorry,' she whispered.

'Did you know the man that you slept with?' he asked hesitantly.

'He's an old friend.' She buried her face against him.

'That's good. At least he wasn't a stranger. Have you told him about the baby?'

'Not yet. I wanted to tell you first.'

'You don't have to tell him. You don't have to go back to London, you know. Nobody need know that it wasn't mine.'

Noreen wiped her eyes and shook her head. 'Oliver, love, the whole world will know it's not yours. Rajiv is Indian,' she explained.

'Oh! Oh!' He couldn't hide his surprise. 'Well, fuck everybody, it's none of their business,' he said gruffly, and Noreen knew why she loved him.

'I think it's better for me to stay in London. I think too much has happened for us to be . . . to be . . . easy with each other,' Noreen said honestly. 'You're not a saint, Oliver. You're human, and my child would always be a reminder of what's happened between us.'

'I'd try,' he said indignantly.

'I know you would, but Oliver, I don't want you

to be miserable. I want you to be really happy in your life. Find someone—'

'Noreen, I won't be inflicting myself on another woman again, you can rest assured about that,' Oliver retorted.

'Ah, stop that, Oliver, any woman would be lucky to have you.' Noreen frowned. 'Don't be like that now.'

'Just don't hold your breath, Noreen. I'm probably better off on my own.'

'No, you're not. You need someone in your life and when they come into it, cut down on the work, and share your feelings with them. Don't shut them out.'

'Did I shut you out?' He was taken aback.

'Yes, love, you did and it hurt,' Noreen said quietly.

'I'm sorry, I didn't mean to. I'm just not good at all this emotional stuff,' Oliver scowled.

'Well, you've had plenty of practice with me,' Noreen said lightly, relieved beyond measure that she had unburdened herself to him.

'Where will you live?' he asked tiredly.

'There's plenty of accommodation in London at the moment. Loads of people are buying to let, so rents aren't too high—'

'Rents! That's money down the drain. You need to buy a place. I'll sell this place and give you half. You're entitled.'

'You can't do that.' Noreen was shocked.

'Noreen, I'm not rattling around this place on my own and besides, you have as much of a stake in it as I have. You did all the decorat—'

'No, Oliver. I couldn't.'

'Well, you'll just have to take the money, Noreen, it's not all about you any more, you have the child to consider,' Oliver said firmly, and threw his eyes up to heaven when she burst into tears again.

'For God's sake will you stop bawling, that baby will be dehydrated,' he urged.

'Sorry, Oliver. I don't deserve such kindness.' Noreen could hardly talk, the lump in her throat was so big.

'Yes you do,' he said firmly. 'And you should never think that God punishes – it's an insult to Him to even consider it, Noreen. God is love and love does not punish and you are worthy of every good thing that comes into your life. So stop tormenting yourself with thoughts of punishment and unworthiness. You are a good person.' His blue eyes were bright and intense as he stared down at her, and she felt the strength and goodness of her husband that were unique to him.

As she lay in bed in one of the spare rooms that night, she wondered if she were making a mistake not staying with Oliver. Maybe they could leave the bad times behind them and make a new start. He'd been so kind when she'd told him about the abortion. It was such a relief to tell him. It had been a terribly heavy burden to carry all this time. Only Kay knew. Oliver's words had been a balm to her soul. God *was* love. And she loved Oliver. She wasn't in love with him but she loved him. How could she not? In her heart of hearts, she knew it wouldn't work. She'd feel too guilty every time she looked at her baby and there was no equality in guilt. She had to make a fresh start and so did he. Her child would fulfil her. And no matter what Oliver felt, some woman would fall in love with him and give him the life he deserved.

She rested her hand on her tummy. She'd been given a second chance; Oliver would be given one too.

Oliver tossed and turned, unable to sleep. Noreen's unexpected arrival and her subsequent bombshells had left him drained and shattered. It was hard to believe that Noreen had slept with another man and was pregnant by him. He felt gutted and totally rejected. He wouldn't, couldn't let Noreen see it of course, she had enough to contend with. Why couldn't she have told him about the abortion? At least he would have understood why she was so hung up on getting pregnant. And the irony was he could never have given her that baby. Maybe it was a sign that they weren't meant to be together. At least he knew the score now, knew why she'd left so suddenly. He didn't have to be torturing himself.

He'd wanted to rant and rave and ask what about him, but she looked so woebegone and was so distraught he didn't have the heart. But part of him was angry, damn angry. She'd asked him to marry her and now she'd left him in the lurch and no matter what nonsense she said about some women falling for him, he was never getting involved with one of the species again. They only brought misery, he told himself, as he pummelled his pillow into a more comfortable shape and lay staring wide-eyed at the ceiling.

38

'I'm sorry, Heather, we have no vacancies at the moment, but if one does occur and you're still interested, I'll certainly give you a shout,' Eddie Mangan assured her kindly.

'Thanks, Eddie, I appreciate it.' Heather hid her disappointment and shook her ex-employer's hand.

'You could try the hotel, it's coming into the summer season,' he suggested, tapping his long, bony fingers on his desk.

'I might do that. It's an option anyway. See you.' She hurried out of the office, not stopping to chat. Maybe it wasn't going to be as easy as she thought getting a job in Kilronan. She bit her lip and walked along briskly, then on impulse crossed the street. Carleton Auctioneers and Estate Agents had had a revamp, she noted in surprise, approving the smart new navy blue façade. After her experiences at Brooke, Byrne & O'Connell she didn't really feel like working in the property market, nor did she particularly want to work for Clarence Carleton, a crotchety old buzzard if ever there was one.

She stood peering at the notices in the window, wishing she could afford to buy a place of her own.

She missed having her own space. She wanted to wallow in her unhappiness but she couldn't really do that in front of her parents. It wasn't fair. Nor did she enjoy the experience of feeling like a child again, which inevitably surfaced when she lived at home and felt no longer in control of her own destiny. Living at home at her age was not a grown-up thing to do, especially after she'd been used to living on her own and standing on her own two feet. Not only that, her mother was intent on feeding her up, which was playing havoc with her figure.

'Hi, Heather, thinking of buying?' She heard a friendly voice in the region of her left ear. She turned and saw Ray Carleton, Clarence's eldest son, smiling at her.

'I wish,' she grimaced. 'I like the new façade. Very posh.'

'Do you think so? I've taken over the business and between you and me it needs a revamp badly.'

'Have you? Has Clarence retired? I never thought he'd go.' Heather was surprised. Clarence was an institution in Kilronan.

'Ticker's giving him trouble,' Ray confided. 'And so's Ma.'

Heather laughed. 'So you've come back home to take over. Do you miss Dublin?'

'Not in the slightest,' Ray declared emphatically.

'I used to work with Brooke, Byrne and O'Connell in their lettings department.'

'Did you? They've an awful reputation.' Ray looked at her in surprise.

'Tell me about it,' Heather said wryly.

'I used to work for BWH in Dublin after I finished studying for my B.Sc. in Property Studies. What a shower of chancers. Their ethics were non-existent, especially selling property abroad. People thought they were a reputable company with their fancy name and logo and glossy brochures. They just took the money and left clients to their own devices, and lots of them had terrible problems out in Spain and Portugal. I was glad to get out of it, I can tell you. Some of those big estate agents and auctioneers are the lowest of the low.' Ray clearly was unimpressed with the big boys in the business. BWH were supposedly the biggest and the best. Brooke, Byrne & O'Connell were only in the halfpenny place in comparison, and had looked upon them with envy.

'Will you come in and have a cup of coffee?' he invited.

'OK,' she agreed, following him into the bright, airy office and display area, where a young woman sat typing busily at her computer.

'This is Lia, my secretary, and I'd be lost without her.' He flashed her a grin.

'He always says that when he wants me to make him a cup of coffee,' Lia retorted, but she smiled at Heather and asked did she want milk and sugar as Ray led her into an extremely tidy inner office, which housed a big antique table where his computer sat. Two easy chairs and a small coffee table made the office less formal for client discussions. He motioned her to sit down opposite him. 'I keep my desk absolutely clear except for my in-tray otherwise I wouldn't be able to find my way around the debris. I take after my dad in that respect. His filing system was a shambles. So I have to be ruthless with myself.'

'I'd say Lia could be fairly ruthless,' Heather remarked.

'As tough as they come, thank God,' Ray agreed with a smile.

An hour and a half later they were still chatting. Ray had plans for his father's firm. He wanted to set up his own website, and he wanted to start up a makeover service for houses that needed it before they went on the market.

'You see, some of these old cottages need a lick of paint, a few tubs of flowers in the yard, new lamps or throws just to brighten the place up and give a better impression. It's a service I want to develop, there's an opening for it. What do you think?'

'I think you're spot on, Ray. It was always much easier to let a place that looked smart and present-able.' Heather felt a *frisson* of interest. This sounded good and she liked his enthusiasm. Her heart lifted, maybe he might offer a job.

'There's just one fly in the ointment, unfortunately,' the auctioneer was saying. 'You know Joan Nolan who worked for my dad?' he raised an eyebrow and made a face.

Heather nodded.

'She's driving me around the twist. Everything I do that's different, she says, "Your father never did it like that. Your father did it this way." She won't work on the computer and she gives Lia a dog's life. I'd love to let her go but she'd probably sue me for unfair dismissal or something. Dad would have a fit anyway, but it's a hell of a problem and unfortunately I can't afford to take anyone else on at the moment. She's really holding me back.'

Heather's heart sank. Ray obviously wouldn't be making her a job offer. She felt a dart of disappointment. It had been interesting talking to Ray. She wouldn't have minded at all, working for him.

A sharp rap on the door made Ray throw his eyes up to heaven. 'Talk of the devil,' he grimaced, heaving a great sigh. 'Come in.'

Joan Nolan marched in, gave a brusque nod in Heather's direction and plonked a file on Ray's desk. 'We need to discuss the Marshall property,' she announced gravely.

'I better go, Ray. Thanks for the coffee.' Heather stood up and gave him a little wink. 'Good luck with the business. See you round.'

'Thanks for dropping in, Heather.' Ray politely walked her to the door. Joan stood, arms folded, a wisp of grey hair escaping from her bun, with a face on her that would turn milk sour. Heather felt sorry for the auctioneer. What a battleaxe. And what a difficult position to be in. She dawdled along, wondering where else she could look for a position. It looked as if she was going to be staying at Fred's whether she liked it or not.

'Oliver, are you sure you want to sell the house? Would you not wait a while before making a decision? You might change your mind after a while,' Noreen asked as she drank a cup of coffee in the bright, sunny kitchen that had been her pride and joy.

'What do I want to be rattling around it on my own for? I don't need four bedrooms and three bathrooms,' he said and his tone had an edge of bitterness.

'You might meet someone,' she persisted.

'I told you, Noreen, I'm not going down that road again.' His face was grim as he stared out the window.

'Where will you live?' Noreen demanded.

'I might move into one of the apartments I'm building, the first block is nearly finished. I can bunk in there for a while until I decide what to do.'

'You'd hardly go back to living with Cora?'

'Nope.'

'What about all the furniture and everything?'

Oliver turned to look at her. 'Take what you want, Noreen. When you get a place to live, tell me what you want and I'll get it shipped over.'

'That's not very fair. I don't expect anything from you. I know it's all my fault and I'm really sorry,' she said miserably.

'Don't be. That's life, Noreen, and you're welcome to the stuff, what would I be doing with the half of it?' He drained his coffee and rinsed the cup under the tap. 'Are you sure about going to live in London? You don't have to, you know.' He turned to look at her again, his blue eyes unwavering in their gaze.

Noreen stared back at him. She knew if she said she wanted to stay, that would be that and he would row in behind her and support her. But

476

it would be a duty call. She'd seen the way he shouldered the burden of his mother. She would not add another burden to the ones he already carried.

'I think it's for the best all round,' she said quietly.

'Right. Let me know when you want to go to the airport, I'll take you. You're not taking the bus,' he said firmly, and then he strode out of the kitchen and she heard the front door close behind him.

Noreen sat at the kitchen table. She felt numb. She should tell her sisters, she supposed. Once she would have dreaded telling Maura, but motherhood had taken the smug pomposity out of her younger sister's sails and as for Rita, nothing would change her, so Noreen resolved to get the ordeals over and done with as soon as possible.

She rang Maura, who responded with an uncharacteristic warmth at hearing her sister's voice. 'You're back from London, great. You won't recognize your nephew,' she declared. 'Are you coming over?'

'Just for a quick visit, Maura. I'm going back to London,' Noreen said calmly.

'What! So soon? Does Oliver mind?' Maura was astonished.

'I'll tell you all when I see you. Stick the kettle on,' Noreen said crisply, although her heart was in her boots. What on earth was she going to say to her sister? She'd have to tell her she was pregnant. She didn't want to keep her child a secret. She wanted her child to know its family, roots, and background. Confessing that the baby wasn't

Oliver's was daunting. Once it was born it would be clear for all to see. Better for her to look like the baddie anyway. Oliver had to live in Kilronan, and she didn't want him being blamed for their break-up.

'My God, Noreen, no one ever told me it would be like this,' Maura groaned half an hour later when Noreen arrived to the sound of John bawling at the top of his voice. 'He's like a little bull today, listen to that racket,' her sister grumbled as she led the way into the kitchen, which was not in its usual pristine condition. Maura had been making up feeds and a container of dried milk lay open on the counter, little creamy flecks of powder all over the place. The breakfast dishes were still on the table and Maura was in her dressing-gown.

'Will I pick him up?' Noreen asked, peering into the pram where her red-cheeked nephew lay howling.

'You might as well or we'll get no peace,' Maura said wearily. She looked tired, the bags under her eyes puffy and dark.

'How's it going?' Noreen asked sympathetically as she lifted her nephew and rocked him gently. His cries turned to a whimper and he nestled into her neck. She sniffed his lovely baby smell, longing for the moment when she would hold her own child.

'God, you're good with him,' Maura said in surprise as she poured boiling water into the tea-pot.

'Just as well,' Noreen remarked evenly. 'I'm going to have one of my own.'

'Noreen!' Maura exclaimed in delight. 'That's

marvellous. Is Oliver thrilled? They'll be great company for each other, the two little cousins. When are you due?'

'Early December, but er . . . well, Maura, Oliver and I are splitting up. The baby's not his,' Noreen said baldly.

Her sister's mouth formed a perfect O. If it hadn't all been so heartbreakingly sad, Noreen might have laughed at the expression of pure shock on her sister's face.

'Whose is it?' she asked faintly.

'Someone I've known for a long time when I lived in London. That's why I'm going back to live there. He's Indian, owns his own restaurant. He's a widower in his early fifties.'

'I'm . . . I . . . I don't know what to say. I'm really sorry that you and Oliver are breaking up. He's a very good man, Noreen. I always thought you were lucky with him.'

'I was,' Noreen said sadly, 'but things weren't working out between us.'

'That's a pity. He wouldn't have left you looking after a baby on your own,' Maura said bitterly and burst into tears.

Noreen let her cry. 'Get it out of your system,' she encouraged.

'He's such a bastard, Noreen, he won't even feed the baby, he says that's woman's work. And he never gets up in the middle of the night and he plays golf three nights a week and every weekend and I'm finding it so hard to cope and I'm starting to hate him. I don't even want to have sex with him and I don't even care if he goes and finds himself

479

another woman. He's the most selfish, lazy, untidy bastard going. He was bad enough when we got married but he's twice as bad now.' She sobbed brokenly, her fists clenched in anger.

Noreen wasn't the slightest bit surprised at Maura's outburst. Men's true colours often came to light when a baby was born and many marriages suffered under the strain. Andy had never been the type to put himself out, and it was clear he wasn't going to change.

'Oh, Noreen I wish you weren't going away, you've been such a help to me.' Maura raised her head from her elbows and sniffled.

'You and John can always come and visit me in London, I'm sure I could do with a bit of help myself when the baby's due,' Noreen suggested.

'Of course I will. I like London, that would be something to look forward to. Are you going to live with the baby's father?' she asked, wiping her eyes on her dressing-gown sleeve.

'To be honest, Maura, I don't know. The truth is, I think I don't really like men. After Dad and all that stuff at home I got involved with a man in London who was an alcoholic too and he treated me like shit. I'll tell you about it some time. I like Oliver and I respect him very much, but he's a workaholic and he can't give me the emotional security I need. I don't think I'll go looking to another man for it. I think I might be better off on my own.'

'I might as well be on my own,' Maura observed bitterly. 'And Andy's got a drink problem, I've been denying it for ages but it's obvious. They say the children of alcoholics often marry alcoholics, I wonder why?'

'It's patterns that are ingrained in us since childhood,' Noreen sighed. 'I'm sorry you're unhappy, Maura.'

'Oh, I'll get over it, I suppose. I really thought Andy would change when I had a baby, more fool I.'

'Well, try to enjoy John,' Noreen urged. 'I'm really looking forward to having mine.'

'Strange, isn't it? We weren't close until now. I'm glad we are.' Maura smiled at her sister.

'It's about time.' Noreen kissed her nephew's soft downy head. 'I suppose I'd better go and tell Rita.'

'Don't tell her anything I said to you, sure you won't?' Maura said hurriedly.

'I won't say a word,' Noreen assured her.

'It's just I couldn't say the things I said to you about Andy to Rita, she's a bit . . . you know the way she goes on?'

'I know, don't worry, Maura. I'm not looking forward to telling her my news.'

'Do you want me to tell her?' Maura offered.

For a moment, Noreen was tempted, but she shook her head. That would be the cowardly way out. 'Thanks. I'd better do it myself or it would give her something to moan about. Take care, Maura. When I get my phone I'll give you the number, you have my mobile one. Keep in touch.'

To her surprise her sister stood up and kissed her on the cheek. It was the first time they had kissed in years. 'Thanks for everything. I'll definitely be over when the baby's due. Mind yourself,' she said awkwardly as she took the baby from Noreen.

'If you see Oliver around, say hello to him won't you? It wasn't his fault,' Noreen urged, anxious that no blame be attached to her husband.

'Of course I will,' Maura reassured her. They smiled at each other again, and as Noreen walked to her car she felt at least that her new, improved relationship with her sister was one positive thing to emerge over the past few months.

She didn't know whether to be relieved or not when she got no answer at Rita's door. She scribbled a note to say that she had called – it would be easier to tell her sister her news over the phone. Rita was a far different kettle of fish from Maura. She'd always been hostile towards Noreen, especially when she'd married 'Mister Moneybags' as she had sarcastically christened Oliver. Noreen wouldn't put it past her to be pleased about the marriage break-up, she thought unkindly as she hastily got into the car, half afraid her sister would arrive home before she left.

She drove back into town and stopped at Brennan Motors. She might as well sell the car and use the money to go towards buying a new one in London.

Neil Brennan was talking to a man on the forecourt, so she sat on the bonnet of her car waiting until he came over. He'd done a good job on the place. She remembered Oliver telling her that he'd turned the rooms upstairs into a flat for Heather Williams. That relationship hadn't lasted long, she reflected, as she remembered Mrs Larkin saying something about Heather catching him with her cousin.

Bloody idiot! Heather Williams was a nice girl, not like that snooty consequence of a cousin of hers. Noreen had seen her prancing around the gym in her skimpy leotard, showing off in front of the men, before she'd gone away to work. Neil Brennan's wallet was probably the attraction there, Noreen thought nastily, as she saw him gesticulating expansively to the man he was talking to. Obviously doing his car salesman act, she thought, unimpressed, fed up at having to hang around. Car salesmen never took women seriously. She remembered buying her car from the most disinterested, patronizing, fat lump of a bloke with egg stains on his tie, and swore she'd never go to him again. If Neil Brennan didn't come over to her in the next five minutes she was driving out of here, she told herself crossly. She gave him five minutes exactly, and got into her car. She saw him move across the forecourt. In her direction.

'Too late, you ignoramus,' she muttered as she drove on to the main street. Oliver would sell it for her and probably get a better price too; no doubt Master Brennan would have time to do business with him. She saw a woman on a bike on the other side of the road and recognized her mother-in-law. Cora pretended not to see her as she cycled slowly along. She was a great woman for her age, Noreen had to admit. She pulled in in front of the church grounds and phoned Oliver on her mobile.

'Yes, Noreen?' he said flatly.

'Oliver, I've just seen your mother. I . . . er . . .

well, would you like me to tell her about us? I'll tell her it's all down to me, of course,' she added hastily. There was silence at the other end of the phone.

'I don't think that would be a good idea, Noreen. Leave it to me.'

'Are you sure?'

'Yeah, God knows what she might say to you. I think you're better off leaving me to handle Mam.'

'Well, I would do it if you wanted, you know that. I told Maura. Rita wasn't in. I'll call her.'

'I see,' Oliver said heavily.

'Would you sell the car for me? I called into Neil Brennan's but he was too busy to deal with me.'

'I'll take care of that for you,' Oliver said, and she felt even more of a heel, if that was possible. Why didn't he tell her to fuck off out of his life and leave him alone? Why did he have to be so decent? She'd never experienced the kindness of men until she'd met Oliver, she thought unhappily, as she thanked her husband and hung up. There was nothing else to keep her here now; she might as well go home and book a flight for herself. The longer she stayed here, the worse she'd feel about herself, if it was possible to feel any worse, she thought dispiritedly as she eased out into the traffic and headed for home.

'Ah, Oliver, how's it going? I saw Noreen here the other day, but I was dealing with a fella and she must have been in a hurry, she didn't wait.' Neil put on his best hail-fellow-well-met voice as he advanced on the builder, hand outstretched. Oliver

484

Flynn was a good customer – he wouldn't like to lose him.

'Don't worry about it,' Oliver said drily.

'So what can I do for you?' Neil rubbed his hands. 'Is there something wrong with Noreen's car?'

'Not a thing. She wants to sell it, will you have a look at it there and make me an offer?'

'Is it a trade-in?' Neil couldn't help the note of anticipation in his voice.

'Nope.'

'Oh.' He couldn't hide his surprise or disappointment. What was she selling her car for if she wasn't getting a new one? Or was she getting a new one elsewhere? He couldn't help but wonder.

'Have you had any offers from anyone else?' he pretended to be casual as he walked around the car and gave the tyres a little kick.

'No.' Oliver was a man of few words sometimes, Neil thought irritably.

'Oh! OK so.' Neil sat in the car and turned on the ignition. It was in good nick, and well cared for. He'd have no trouble making a few bob profit on it.

'Nine thousand Euro.' He eyeballed Oliver.

'Is that your best offer, Neil? Because if it is, I'll try Jenkins in Navan where she bought it.'

'Nine fifty.' Neil grimaced.

'Ten,' Oliver said firmly. Neil knew there was no arguing with him. Best to keep him on-side for future sales.

'Done.' Neil held out his hand and Oliver gave him a firm shake.

'Come into the office and I'll get Carol to do the paperwork.'

'Carol?' Oliver looked surprised.

Neil reddened. 'Heather doesn't work here any more.'

'Oh, right, I forgot. I saw her in Fred's a while back,' Oliver said awkwardly.

'Easy come, easy go,' Neil said jocularly. Oliver didn't look too impressed, in fact he looked downright dour.

'Are you thinking of changing your own car, yet?' Neil changed tack.

'Naw.' Oliver folded his arms across his chest and waited for the young girl at the desk to fill out the forms while Neil wrote the cheque.

'That's my spending money for New York gone,' he joked as he handed the cheque to Oliver.

'Off to New York, are you? Enjoy it,' Oliver said politely. Neil gave up. Oliver was not in the mood for idle chit-chat, and there was no point in pushing it. He was sorry he hadn't hung out for nine fifty.

'Tell Noreen if she's looking for anything special I'll see her right,' he said to Oliver after the paperwork was finished.

'Will do,' Oliver said and marched on.

'Moody bugger,' Neil muttered as he went back into his own office. He was restless. He wanted to be in New York right this minute. He'd emailed Lorna to tell her of his impending arrival and that the hotel was booked and she'd just sent back a one word email saying 'great'. Talk about keeping a fella on his toes. It should be the other way around. With his mind only half on the job, Neil sat down to attend to the paperwork for Noreen Flynn's car.

39

'Would you like me to come over and find a place with you?' Oliver lifted Noreen's bags out of the car and hoisted them on to a trolley. 'I can take a week off next week if you want,' he offered.

Noreen took a deep breath. His offer was tempting. There was something so solid and reliable about Oliver. It was easy to repose in his strength and be minded. But it wasn't fair on him, she admitted. As long as he felt linked to and responsible for her he couldn't get on with his own life.

'I *really* appreciate your offer, Oliver, you're very kind to me, but you're not responsible for me and you never were. I have to stand on my own two feet and accept my responsibilities. I'll be fine in London. I've got some very good friends there and I know when I tell Rajiv about the baby he will be very concerned to do the right thing for the child. Don't feel in any way that you have to do things for me. You've done more than enough,' she said earnestly.

'As long as you're sure,' he said gruffly as he strode off pushing the trolley, with her trying to keep up with his long strides. He lifted her cases on to the check-in desk, where, fortunately, there was no queue, and when she had her boarding card they stepped away and he slanted a glance at her as if unsure what to do next.

'Would you like a coffee or anything?' he asked politely. Noreen shook her head. 'Oliver,' she blurted, 'if you don't go now, I'm going to start crying.'

'Don't do that, woman,' he said hastily. She managed a laugh at the look of horror on his face.

'Oh Oliver, Oliver, I'll never meet a man like you again.' She took his hand and held it to her cheek, then brought it to her lips and kissed his callused palm. 'I wish it had been different,' she said. 'Will you just answer me one thing?'

He looked at her warily. 'If I can.'

Noreen took a deep breath. 'Did you ever love me, Oliver?'

He blushed a dull red, mortified at her question, and looked away.

'Did you, Oliver?' she persisted.

'I suppose I did,' he said.

Noreen sighed. *Suppose*! That had always been the problem. There should be no supposing about it. Even now he couldn't say emphatically, 'Yes, I loved you.'

'Oliver, we should sort out a divorce eventually to leave us both free, but just let me give you one word of advice for the future. When you do fall in love, and you will, don't wait for the woman to ask you to marry her. *You* do the asking, and that way she'll never be wondering if she's loved,' Noreen said with a hint of acerbity in her voice. 'And try and spend a bit of time with her; time is the most precious gift you can give to someone.'

'Don't be wasting your breath, woman, it's not going to happen,' he growled, irritated by her remarks. 'By the way, I lodged twenty-five thousand Euro into your account. When I sell the house I'll send you the rest of your share.'

'God Almighty, Oliver, there was no need for that! I certainly wasn't expecting it.' Noreen stared at him, horrified. 'I'm not a moneygrabber, Oliver. I don't feel you owe me anything. I'm the one who behaved badly.'

'Don't talk like that,' he frowned. 'Whatever you think, I *do* have feelings for you and I'm not going to turn my back on you.'

'Oh Oliver, you make me feel like a heel,' she said forlornly as they walked towards the security check.

'That's enough of that now, Noreen,' he said in his best no-nonsense tone and she smiled in spite of herself.

'Yes, Oliver,' she said meekly. They stopped at the barrier and he turned to her and put his arms around her. She nestled into his strong, hard chest and felt the steady beat of his heart under his shirt. They hugged tightly, unable to speak, then parted and walked away in different directions. Crying, Noreen showed the security guard her boarding card and walked into the security area without a backward glance. She was on her own now, but that was her own choice. She could have stayed under the mantle of her husband's protection but that would have been cowardly and unfair. To have found a man of his strength and integrity was a rare blessing. If only it hadn't gone so disastrously wrong.

So that was the end of it. Oliver clenched his jaws tight as a deep, painful sadness smote him. He felt a complete and utter failure. The prospect of a long lonely life ahead of him was daunting. He missed Noreen around the house. It was horrible going home to an empty house after a day's work. He had taken her a bit for granted, he supposed. If he was honest with himself, he'd deserved her crack at him about spending time with whatever new woman he fell in love with. Where did Noreen get her notions from? He glowered as he passed through the automatic doors at the exit. How could he even consider going with another woman with all his flaws? Sterility, impotence, who'd want him? And besides, he wasn't setting himself up for another fall. He never wanted to experience what he'd experienced with Noreen again.

It hurt that she was so determined to start afresh in London. He'd offered to just get on with things and he thought that was pretty fair of him, but she wasn't having it. She really did want to leave. She wasn't prepared to fight for their marriage. She'd given up so easily, it hurt. For better or worse had meant nothing to her, he thought bitterly as he dropped his coins into the parking machine. Well, he'd just have to get on with things. And putting the house on the market was first on his priorities. It was too lonely living there on his own. It held too many memories.

He'd better tell Cora too. She was giving out yards about Noreen being away 'minding her sick friend'. He might as well get that ordeal over and done with. Cora would want him to go and live with her, but he'd have to stick to his guns there. He didn't mind looking after her, doing her shopping and running her here and there, but he was not going to live at home again, no matter what pressure she put on him. With a heart as heavy as a lead brick, Oliver drove out of Dublin Airport wishing he was going anywhere but home.

'You're splitting up! She's going to live in London! Why?' Cora Flynn couldn't believe her ears. Although she'd never liked her daughter-in-law, she'd never foreseen her and Oliver ending their marriage. Shock was her main emotion.

Oliver thrust his hands into the pockets at the back of his jeans. 'Ma, it was my fault we couldn't have a baby and we weren't getting on so well. It's the best thing,' he said resignedly.

'Well, I don't think so. Couldn't you have adopted? You just don't up and leave your husband like that. Has she no consideration for your feelings?' Cora exclaimed indignantly. 'What kind of a wife is she at all?'

'That's enough, Ma. Whatever differences Noreen and I have are between us,' Oliver said sharply and Cora frowned. Even though that one had upped and left him he was still ready to defend her.

'You'd better come to me for your dinner every day. I want to make sure you're eating properly,' she ordered.

'Now we'll see, Ma. I'm up to my eyes at the minute—'

'All the more reason to have a good dinner inside you,' Cora retorted.

'Look, how about if you cook me the odd dinner now and again and I can heat it in the microwave,' he suggested. Cora's lips tightened. She had no time for these modern conveniences. Food didn't taste the same as fresh out of the oven or saucepan – still, if it meant she'd see more of him, it was better to agree, she argued silently with herself.

'Right. You'd better take me shopping so I can get in a few extra stores.' She hopped up in a sprightly manner from her chair. She was in fine fettle these days, thank God, only the odd twinge of arthritis. 'I'm just going to get my hat and put on a bit of powder. It won't take a minute.'

'No rush,' he said, but it was clear that his mind was miles away. Cora pursed her lips and her nostrils flared. The cheek, the absolute cheek of that Noreen rip to dump her son. How dare she! Who did she think she was, treating the Flynns like that?

She was very vexed over the whole affair. If Oliver had thrown Noreen out, Cora would have been as happy as Larry about it. She'd be glad to see the back of her, but how could she be glad when Oliver looked as miserable as could be? What kind of a fool was he to have fallen for a biddy like her? He should have listened to his mother. Cora had always told him that Noreen wasn't the right one for him and now she'd been proved right. And the annoying thing was, it didn't make her feel one bit better to have been proved right. All she could see was her poor, fed-up son, looking like he carried the weight of the world on his shoulders. It wasn't good enough, and she was going to have serious words with the Sacred Heart tonight when she got into bed to say her prayers.

Oliver deserved to be treated much better and if she had that Noreen one on her own for a few minutes she'd let her have the sharp edge of her tongue and not mince her words either. Cora was hopping mad as she dusted her cheeks with powder and dabbed some Lily of the Valley on her wrists.

40

Heather was absent-mindedly cleaning table tops one wet and windy morning when Ray Carleton popped his head around the door of Fred's.

'Good, you're on your own. Something brilliant has happened,' he exclaimed exuberantly, clenching his fists.

Heather laughed at him. 'What?' she asked, tickled by his behaviour.

'Joan Nolan tripped going into an old cottage half-way up White Heather Hill and she broke her leg and her arm and she's not coming back to work . . . ever. Oh happy, happy day! Oh there is a God, Heather.'

'Stop that, the poor woman,' Heather giggled.

'So?' Ray challenged.

'So what?' Heather said, dimly.

'So when can you start? You'll be doing a bit of everything but I would like to get you involved in the makeover side of the business. I'd like to get it up and running as soon as possible. I've made an arrangement with one of the big furniture shops in Navan to start up a fitting-out service for new apartments, houses and show houses. Oliver

Flynn's developing a big site near the lake and I'm pushing him to let me do the show house. Are you on?'

'Are you offering me a job?' Heather stared at him.

'Well, of course I am, if you're interested. How can I let you go to waste? Can you drive?'

She nodded, flabbergasted.

'You'll need a car – we have farms and houses for sale up to fifty miles away. Dad had customers far and wide. I'll sort one out for you. It won't be top of the range but it will get you from A to B. Can you start next Monday? Same salary you were getting in Crooks & Co?'

'You bet,' Heather agreed excitedly. Ray's enthusiasm was infectious, and from talking to him he had high business standards, unlike her previous employers in the property world. The makeover scheme was up and coming in the bigger agencies, and she'd enjoy getting involved. Developing a website with him would be a challenge, something new to get her teeth into.

What had made her cross over the road that day to look in Ray's window at that particular time? Was this the serendipity people talked about, she wondered. Or was it one of her friend Margaret's growth opportunities? All she knew was, she'd gone into Mangan's looking for a job in accounts and had ended up back in the property business. This time it would be better. Ray Carleton seemed to have integrity and good business ethics; it should be totally different from the offhand carelessness that had pervaded Brooke, Byrne & O'Connell.

'Well, you landed on your feet there,' her mother said with satisfaction when she imparted her news. 'You deserve a bit of luck, Heather. I'm delighted for you.' There was a note of relief in her voice. Heather knew that she wasn't too happy with her working in Fred's. There was no future in it. It had been a respite from the real world, Heather acknowledged, but it had kept her going in those first, shock-filled days when her world had crumbled around her ears.

She gave Fred her notice that evening and he wished her well. 'Told you you wouldn't stay too long. You go and make a success of that new job for yourself, Missy. You're a great worker and a very nice girl,' he wheezed, and beamed broadly when she gave him a hug. 'Oh, and by the way, the chips will always be on the house,' he told her kindly, and Heather was touched by his generosity of spirit. He'd been good to her in her hour of need; she'd buy him a nice gardening book and a crate of beer, she decided.

That night as she undressed for bed, a thought struck her. Anne Jensen, the psychic, had told her that the man she was going to get involved with was on the periphery of her life and she'd also told her that she'd be using skills that she'd learned previously in her new job. Was Ray the new man? He was a nice chap, Heather acknowledged. They got on well. She liked him, and the psychic had said it would be a great friendship first. Maybe Anne *could* see things. Ruth swore by her. The job had come true, that was a start. And she was going to have a car. She hoped Ray wouldn't buy it at Neil's.

A dart of sadness stung her: he hadn't even tried to woo her back. Had she meant so little to him? It looked like it. It looked as if he'd just been using her until something better came along. Forget him, she ordered. He was history.

For the first time in weeks she felt a bit like her old self. Felt in control of things. It would be nice to be out and about in her new job. Ray was interested in the job and ambitious for his company, and that was enough to motivate staff. The clients were there, and there was no reason why there shouldn't be a lot more on his books. She'd work her butt off and help him expand, she decided, and every time Neil Brennan drove past Carleton Auctioneers and Estate Agents he'd see what he was missing.

Neil was edgy. He was flying to America this very week and the days were dragging. He needed to buy some new underwear. It was quiet enough in the garage – he'd take a stroll up the town and see what was on offer.

'Carol, just going up the town for an hour. Call me on the mobile if anything comes up,' he instructed his secretary.

'OK.' She didn't lift her head from her computer. She wasn't half as interested as Heather had been. Neil knew she was just putting in the time until something better came her way.

He was walking past the church when a pale green Ford Focus drove into a parking space outside Carleton's and he saw a woman dressed in a navy suit get out. He stared in surprise as he recognized Heather. She was carrying a briefcase and walking purposefully into the estate agent's.

What was that all about? Was she looking for a place to rent? And where did she get the car? And what was with the briefcase? He couldn't help feeling a bit miffed. She didn't look too heart-broken any more, not like she'd looked when he'd had a go at her in Fred's. He nearly got a crick in his neck looking in the window but it was tinted glass and he couldn't see anything. Was she still working in Fred's, he wondered. He couldn't very well waltz in and ask. It was none of his business now, he knew, but he was just curious. She certainly hadn't bought the car from him. It was two years old and had a Dublin reg plate. Was she working in Dublin? But why would she be going into Carleton's if that was the case? He was quite preoccupied as he ambled into McMahon's Quality Man Shop in search of some designer boxers.

When he came back three-quarters of an hour later the car was gone. For some odd reason seeing Heather unexpectedly, all dressed up and business-like, driving a new car, put him in a bad humour.

To cheer himself up, he rang the leisure centre in the hotel and booked a session on the sunbeds. He didn't want to be all pale and pasty going to see Lorna. He wanted to look his absolute best. He'd get his hair cut and perhaps have a manicure. He was a successful businessman, he assured himself. He wanted to look the part.

Lorna stood on the pedals of her bike, spinning furiously. All around her, lithe, toned, tanned

498

bodies worked hard to stay with the pace. A guy on the bike beside her took a draught from his water without breaking his rhythm. She hadn't reached that level of competence yet. It was seven a.m. and her shift started at eight. She had joined a gym near Times Square and took spinning classes three mornings a week. Lorna felt it was a very NY thing to do. Her gym wasn't upmarket enough to meet an Upper East or West Side millionaire, unfortunately. There were a lot of resting 'actors' among the clientele, due to the gym's proximity to Broadway. They were a dead loss: they spent their sessions admiring themselves in the big wall-to-wall mirrors that lined the gym. Totally narcissistic, she thought disdainfully as she started to pant.

She was relieved when the class ended. Her butt was aching as much as her calves and thighs. But what toned calves and thighs they were, she thought with satisfaction as she lathered herself with Carolina Herrera shower gel. She'd gone mad and treated herself to a host of goodies in Sephora, in the Rockefeller Center. How she loved that shop, with its exotic scents and magical arrays of glass jars and bottles all stylishly displayed, teasing and tempting her. Dollars just disappeared out of her purse when she gave in to temptation after a hard day lugging trays around. She adored wandering around inhaling this perfume, sampling the other, testing this cream, or that jelly.

She'd bought herself a gorgeous Tod handbag yesterday and she was skint again. She was sick of it. She couldn't afford New York and it was getting her down. She was so looking forward to her luxury weekend with Neil. It was a pity he was only starting out in the motor trade; if he had a few garages under his belt he'd be loaded. He was probably in hock up to his ears, unfortunately. And if he wasn't he would be by the time she was finished with him. Her eyes sparkled at the thought of money being showered on her. Neil would want to impress her and she'd certainly let him.

She should ring him, she supposed. He would think it odd that she hadn't given him her phone number. It was just that everyone knew New York's code was 212/718. Unfortunately Yonkers was 914 and she didn't want him knowing that she didn't live in Manhattan. She might give him a call nearer the time he was coming over. She had no intention of trotting out to JFK, he could get a taxi to the hotel. She'd tell him that she couldn't get off work. She was going to tell him that she worked in publishing. It seemed to be a totally cool career in NYC. She could say she worked for *Vogue* or *Vanity Fair*, as a staffer. She was damned if she was telling him that she worked as a waitress in a diner off Times Square. She could hardly believe it herself, she thought despondently as she dried her hair. One of the girls in the house had got an office job but she'd gone back waitressing because the money was better. It all came down to money, the harder you worked the more you made, but she didn't want to work at all!

What a failure she was. Carina thought she was mad to feel like that. Her colleague was thrilled with the amount she was making in tips. She was spending all her spare time doing sporty things in the Catskills and having a ball, according to herself. She spent her night-time socializing in Irish bars. Lorna was much more interested in clubbing in the Bubble Lounge in TriBeCa, or Lansky's. She'd strutted her stuff but got nowhere in Cibar and had tried not to be in awe of the totally gorgeous model types that floated around sipping cocktails as if they were born to it. Cheetah cost a minimum of $100 a go and was full of Europeans, but it was clubby and different and she'd enjoyed it. Not so Carina, who claimed a night in Tir na Nog, the Irish pub in Penn Plaza, was far more fun and you never had to put your hand in your pocket. She was a grave disappointment to Lorna. She didn't seem to mind her long waitressing stints. She was always chatting and laughing with the customers. Lorna couldn't be bothered.

The realization that she did not want to work for the rest of her life had hit Lorna like a hammer blow. She didn't want to go back home with her tail between her legs and work godawful shifts as a receptionist in a hotel. Nor did she want to get married and live in a boring three-bed semi-detached. And she'd seen enough of life in NYC to realize that most single women worked to pay their rents if they lived in Manhattan, with not a lot left for retail therapy. *Sex and the City* was not about the likes of her, unfortunately, no matter how much she aspired to the lifestyle. It cost an arm and a leg to socialize. She wanted to be wealthy enough never to have to worry about money again but she just couldn't figure out how she was going to achieve that particular goal. She certainly couldn't do it on her own, she admitted.

Lorna sighed deeply. Under no circumstances could she say that she had taken New York by storm. That had simply not happened, nor was it likely to. She hadn't the drive or the nerve to crack it. The sophisticated façade that had worked for her in Dublin did not cut it here, because there was nothing to support it. She was on the make like everyone else and she couldn't hack it, and that was a bitter pill to have to swallow.

Perhaps she should start going to the theatre and art galleries to try and meet some eligibles, but it all seemed like such hard work after a ten-hour stint on her feet. If she could even find a sugar daddy she might consider that option, she thought ruefully as she crossed Eighth Avenue and hurried along West 43rd to work.

Heather twisted the key into the lock of the badly warped wooden door and let herself into the small two-bedroom cottage that Carleton had recently added to their 'For Sale' lists. The owner had died suddenly and the executors wanted a quick sale. They had told Ray that they would be prepared to spend some money on smartening the place up. Heather took out her pen and notepad and began to take notes. A thorough cleaning job was called for, windows in particular. A coat of paint throughout – perhaps a warm buttermilk colour would be nice, she pencilled in, in brackets. Throw out existing sofa and threadbare chairs. Better off not having them there at all. A few lampshades to cover naked bulbs. Some blinds on the windows to replace tatty curtains, she scribbled happily, in her element.

Only her second day on the job and she was given a nice meaty challenge. And the joy of having a car. Neil had been promising and promising that he was going to organize a car for her and he never had. She didn't need him or his cars now, she thought with satisfaction. She had a great job and her own set of wheels and all on her own merit. It made her feel good about herself. Better than she'd felt in weeks.

Today was a good day – she didn't feel lonely, forlorn and in the depths of despair. She hadn't thought of Neil for at least two hours. That was progress, she thought ruefully. 'Up yours, you bastard,' she muttered as she inspected the bedroom and wrinkled her nose at the stale smell that permeated the room. By the time she was finished with this place no one would recognize it.

When she was finished work tonight she might go for basketball practice. She'd put on ten pounds since her split with Neil; the waistband of her suit was digging into her uncomfortably and she had the beginnings of jowls where once she'd had cheekbones. Time to get a grip, Heather decided as she locked the door after her and sat into her gleaming pride and joy. She'd show Neil Brennan that life was just as good without him. She didn't need a man in her life, she was perfectly capable of managing without one. She was going to buy a place of her own and be completely independent. She drove down the narrow winding lane, ablaze with brilliant yellow gorse. The sky was cloudless and the heat of the sun warmed her. She was so glad she hadn't left Kilronan, she thought gratefully as a field of young corn came into view, a rich emerald carpet of green ringed by dark green hedgerows. She was about ten miles from the town, in the depths of the countryside. It was a peaceful place to be. She smiled remembering how she'd sat cursing in traffic, waiting to get to an apartment or town house in Dublin. There really was no contest, she thought happily as she pulled in and rolled down her window, content to sit for a little while and enjoy the vista.

41

Heather was busy typing out an inventory when she vaguely noticed that someone had come into the office.

'Hello, Heather,' a familiar voice said, and she looked up to see Oliver Flynn looking at her in some surprise. 'You do get around.' He smiled.

'Well, let's hope I get on better in this job than I did down the road,' she said wryly.

'I'm sure you'll be fine. Er, is Ray around?'

'He's not, I'm afraid, he's showing two properties and he won't be back until this afternoon.'

'Oh!' Oliver looked disgruntled.

'Can I help?'

'Well, I'm putting the house up for sale, I was hoping he'd look after it for me.'

'Oh, I'm sure he will. Are you moving?' Heather asked innocently, wondering why Oliver and his wife would want to move from that beautiful house overlooking the lake.

Oliver flushed. 'I'm in the same boat as yourself, Heather. On my own again. Noreen and I are separating,' he said gruffly.

'Oh! I'm sorry, Oliver. That's rough,' Heather

505

sympathized, trying to hide her surprise. What had gone wrong there?

'That's life. You never know what's going to happen next.' Oliver smiled ruefully and her heart went out to him. What a horrible thing to happen. He seemed such a nice bloke.

'Well, I'll get Ray to make an appointment with you to have a look around and give you a price guideline. And I can organize for a photographer to take a few photos. We'll get the signs up in the next few days, get the ads in the property pages and organize the viewings. If you'll just give me a number we can contact you at, that's all I need for the moment,' Heather said matter-of-factly.

'I'll give you my mobile number.' He called out the digits and she took it down, feeling sorry for the harassed-looking man in front of her.

'As soon as Ray comes back I'll get him to give you a call. If I can get my hands on our photographer, would tomorrow morning be all right for him to take a few photos? Exterior shots are fine, if that's what you prefer, but a few interior shots always help that little bit extra,' she said tactfully.

'That's no problem, Heather. I'll take a couple of hours off.'

'If you like, I can come and let him in so that you don't have to hang around,' she offered.

'Would you? I did have a meeting with architects that I'd prefer not to postpone. I'd appreciate that, Heather.'

'OK, I'll be at your house for nine and I can set the alarm when we're finished,' Heather assured him.

She watched him leave. At least she and Neil hadn't been married or even engaged when they'd parted. Break-ups must be even worse when you were married. All that legal stuff that had to be dealt with. She chewed the top of her pen, glad that she hadn't had those complications in her break-up. Sighing, she flicked through her Rolodex for the photographer's number.

'Call for you, Neil, I'll transfer it.' Carol stood at the door of her office and yelled at her boss. 'You better hurry, it's transatlantic.'

Neil's heart did a somersault. 'Catch you again, Tony,' he said to the man he was talking to and took off at a trot to his office. He took a couple of deep breaths before he picked up the receiver.

'Hello, Neil Brennan,' he said coolly.

'Well, hello there, big boy,' Lorna drawled down the phone. 'Are you getting in training for me?'

'Do I need to? I'm fairly fit,' he riposted.

'You could never be fit enough for New York and a demanding woman.' Lorna giggled. 'Listen, we're putting the latest edition of the magazine to bed so I'm not going to be able to meet you at the airport. Just take a cab to the hotel and I'll meet you in Jack's bar. You should get there around four, NY time.'

'Oh, I was looking forward to a big kiss in arrivals.' Neil was crestfallen.

'Sorry about that,' Lorna said airily. 'It's not like home here. I'm lucky to be getting time off. You know, the mighty dollar and all that. Make sure your credit card is clear. I'm going to take you

507

shopping. Saks men's department is waiting for you. No one in Kilronan will be able to keep up with you.'

'Sounds good. We might go shopping to that Victoria's place too,' he suggested.

'We'll see. I have my eye on a few things that I might allow you to buy me. And we're only a stone's throw from Tiffany's.'

'Steady on, Lorna,' Neil said in alarm.

'I'm high maintenance, Neil, don't ever forget that,' Lorna warned. 'Have to go now, I've to go to a meeting with the editor-in-chief. 'Byeeee.'

Neil heard the click of the receiver being put down. She was something else. And the thing was, she was perfectly serious about Tiffany's. He was paying a fortune for a top-notch hotel, now she was looking for jewellery from Tiffany's. Lorna hadn't been exaggerating when she announced that she was 'high maintenance'. Was she worth it though? That was the big question. At least she'd phoned him. He'd better get down to the bank and see if he could increase his credit limit on his Visa card. His accountant would have a fit, but it was a once-off, he comforted himself. He couldn't go to New York on a shoestring.

Whistling, he shrugged into his jacket and headed for the bank.

'Noreen, you're back in London.' Rajiv couldn't hide his delight at the other end of the phone.

'Yes, I am. I wondered could we meet. Somewhere private?' she asked, feeling butterflies doing tangos in her tummy.

'But of course, Noreen. Is something wrong?'

'I just need to talk to you,' Noreen repeated.

'There's a very nice hotel in Knightsbridge, just behind Harrods, called the Franklin, they have discreet drawing-rooms that we could talk in, and a rather good restaurant downstairs if you'd like dinner,' he suggested.

'That sounds perfect, Rajiv. Could we meet tomorrow?' she asked hesitantly.

'This evening if you wish. I can be free,' he said in his melodic lilting voice.

'OK,' she agreed, wanting to get it over with.

'Shall I pick you up? Where are you staying?'

'No, no,' she demurred hastily, preferring to make her own way there. 'I might indulge in a little bit of shopping first,' she fibbed.

'OK, Noreen, whatever you wish. The Franklin for five thirty? Six?'

'Five thirty's fine. I'll see you there,' Noreen said lightly. ''Bye.' She put down the receiver and exhaled deeply. Telling a man that you've slept with once, and only then because you were pissed, that you were pregnant was not what she had ever planned for herself, and at her age it was ridiculous. Once she'd told Rajiv and got that out of the way she was going to rent a flat of her own until she found a place where she wanted to live.

She took a deep breath and keyed in Rita's number. She hadn't phoned her since she'd missed her when she called at the house. Rita was another ordeal to get through.

'Halloo,' her sister's lawdy-daw tones floated down the line.

'Rita, hi, it's me—'

'Very poor line,' Rita remarked. 'Where are you ringing from?'

'Sorry about that. I'm phoning from my mobile. I'm in London,' Noreen said briskly.

'You've gone back! How long—'

'Rita, I won't be back. Oliver and I have separated. And I'm having a baby in December and it's not his,' Noreen declared bluntly.

'Good *God*!' Merciful hour!' Rita was flabbergasted. Noreen felt like laughing hysterically. It was rare for Rita to be completely floored.

'So that's the way it is, Rita. I don't know when I'll be back in Kilronan again.'

'But . . . but . . . Noreen, are you mad? Getting pregnant by someone else. Mind, I always felt that Oliver was a surly ignoramus. His behaviour at the chris—'

'Rita, Oliver is the most steadfast man a woman could wish for and I won't hear a word against him. Now I have to go. I'll be in touch,' Noreen said coldly.

'Oh! Well! Suit yourself,' Rita said huffily.

''Bye, Rita,' Noreen retorted and hung up. She was certainly not going to allow her sister to call Oliver names under any circumstances. Still, at least she'd got Rita out of the way, now she only had to break the news to Rajiv and she could get on with things.

The afternoon dragged by and she was like a cat on a griddle by the time she hailed a taxi to take her to Knightsbridge. Her stomach was queasy and tight with tension. What would Rajiv say? Would he want her to have a termination like Pete had all those years ago?

It doesn't matter what he says.

This is not about him.

It's about you and your baby.

You don't need him if he's not prepared to support you, she argued silently in the back of the taxi. Noreen suddenly sat up straight. She wasn't a pathetic, lovestruck doormat any more. She was a strong, determined woman. And Rajiv was no Pete. This time it would be totally different.

The traffic wasn't too bad, and she felt better when she got out at the elegant redbrick building with the discreet gold nameplate gleaming in the late afternoon sun. A small reception area led on to two reception rooms with comfy chairs and sofas. Both were empty. She choose the smaller one and went back out to reception to order a pot of tea. 'English breakfast, please,' she said briskly as the receptionist recited her litany of teas.

It was a peaceful room and she picked one of the daily papers off a side table and flicked through it as she waited for her tea to arrive. It and Rajiv arrived at the same time, so she ordered another cup for him.

'Hello.' He smiled at her with a hint of embarrassment. Noreen felt herself blush and laughed.

'Let's not be embarrassed, Rajiv,' she said warmly, giving him a hug.

'I never did anything like that before,' he confessed as he sat beside her on the sofa.

'Me neither,' Noreen admitted. 'Oh, Rajiv, I've something to tell you and I just want you to know that I'm happy about it in one way. I'm going to have a baby. It's yours. And Oliver and I have split up.' It all came out rather breathlessly and not in the calm measured way that she had been practising earlier in the afternoon.

Rajiv could only stare, his brown eyes getting bigger and rounder as he assimilated the news. 'A . . . a baby . . .' he stuttered. 'Mine? Does Oliver know?'

Noreen nodded. 'I told him a few days ago. He was very kind, Rajiv, he wanted us to stay together and just get on with things. But I didn't think it was fair. Everyone would know it wasn't his. He'd know every time he looked at it and I think I've caused him enough hurt and damage in his life,' she said sadly.

'No . . . no . . . don't say that. It wasn't intentional.' Rajiv gave her a comforting pat on the shoulder.

'How do you feel about it?' She looked him in the eye, not sure of what she'd find.

He smiled his warm lopsided smile. 'I feel joyous, Noreen. Here I was living an empty sort of life and now you are back. And having a baby that I fathered. Children are joy. So indeed I feel great joy. I hope I can be part of the child's life. And if I am, I hope it will be a little girl. I always wanted a little girl, but my wife felt one child was enough.'

Noreen burst into tears. 'Oh Rajiv, I'm happy to be having this baby. You'll never know how happy. But I feel so bad about Oliver and I miss him. I'll need your help.'

'You'll have it. I promise. I promise. We must

find you somewhere nice to live. But are you sure leaving your husband is the right thing?' He looked perturbed as he handed her a fresh hanky, completely unabashed by her tears – so unlike poor Oliver, she thought fleetingly.

'It is, I know it is, for him and for me. We weren't really suited, Rajiv. He couldn't give me what I needed. And I only caused him grief. And I didn't mean that I needed financial help or anything like that,' she added quickly, anxious that he wouldn't think she was looking for money from him. 'I just want to know that I can share the good times and the difficult times of our child's life with you.'

'With pleasure, Noreen, with pleasure. Just tell me what you want from me and I will try my best to give it,' Rajiv said earnestly. 'But you must let me help look for somewhere to live. That I insist.' He spoke quite firmly.

'Well, if you insist then, Rajiv, that's fine,' Noreen agreed.

'Excellent! Now, are you well? Do you have sickness? Have you had a scan yet? When is the baby due?' The questions came pouring out, and relieved that she no longer had to shoulder her pregnancy alone and that everyone she needed to tell had been told, she sipped her tea and brought him up to date.

Oliver vacuumed the bedroom, dusted, and used a couple of Flash wipes to clean the en suite. What a pain this was going to be, keeping the house tidy so that strangers could wander at will through the rooms. Half the town would probably come to poke their noses in, he thought grumpily as he jiggled the toilet brush up and down the loo and sprayed it with bleach. Heather Williams and that photographer were coming first thing. Noreen would go mad if she thought that the house was like a pigsty. Pity she wasn't here to do the cleaning, he thought resentfully, angry with her that things had come to this.

Maybe he was making a mistake putting the house on the market, but he'd told Noreen he was selling and he'd better do it now, he frowned, as he flushed the toilet.

His mother had phoned him on his mobile to say that there was a dinner ready for him, so he supposed he'd better drive over and have it. Then he was going to go to the pub and lower a few pints for himself. He couldn't get mouldy drunk. He had a meeting in the morning and he needed his wits about him, but one of these days he was going to go on a batter and blot everything out for a few hours. It was the least he deserved.

42

What a city! What a city! Neil didn't know which side of the cab to look out of. He was wide-eyed with excitement. All around him skyscrapers soared into the clear blue sky. Horns honked. 'Walk Don't Walk' signs flashed overhead, just like he'd seen in numerous films and TV series. Even if he hadn't been going to spend a weekend with Lorna he'd have a ball here. He could feel the buzz. Whatever the weekend cost, it would be well worth the money. He was on an absolute high.

He thoroughly enjoyed the attentions of the doorman and bellboys when the taxi drew to a halt outside the hotel. He signed his registration form with a flourish. *This is the way to live*, he thought proudly as he was taken to his room and respectfully ushered in. The bed was huge. It was the first thing he noticed. As wide as it was long, with big fluffy pillows, he'd have a great time in it with Lorna. Neil was surprised at the size of the room. He'd stayed in London a few times and had found hotel rooms small and cramped. He'd expected the same if not worse in New York. This was a very pleasant surprise.

There was a state of the art entertainment deck with a VCP and DVD, a safe, desk, fax machine, data port and voicemail, call waiting and modem. He could work from here if he wanted. Lorna had chosen well. Terrific room-service menu as well, he noted as he flicked through the hotel information folder. Pity he was only staying for three nights. He felt hot and sticky after his flight so he headed into the bathroom and had a quick shower. He wanted to appear cool, casual and in control when Lorna walked into the bar. He was sipping a cold, refreshing Bud when she sashayed into the bar, dressed in a short suede skirt and a body-hugging white shirt, with her suede fringed bag slung casually over her shoulder. She looked a million dollars and he felt a flicker of nervous anticipation when he saw her.

'Hi, babe, I'll have a Margarita,' she said insouciantly, as though she'd only seen him hours ago. She leaned across and kissed him lightly on the cheek. He inhaled the scent of her. *What a woman!*

'So you made it,' she said coolly, when he'd ordered.

'Wild horses wouldn't keep me away,' he said huskily. 'Let's go up to the room.'

Lorna laughed. 'Neil, you're like, so unsubtle. Totally uncool. Really! There'll be plenty of time for that.' He flushed at her rebuke, feeling crass and unsophisticated. What a daft thing to say. She eyed him curiously. 'How did you manage to get here? What did you tell Heather? Are you supposed to be at a conference?'

'Heather found out about us a week after you flew out. She flipped, needless to say.' Neil grimaced. 'Left my computer and the files in a right mess before she left. It took me ages to get it sorted. I never thought she could be so bitchy. I was shocked,' he said plaintively, playing the sympathy card.

'Oh dear, are we the talk of the parish? Mum can't have heard anything or she would have said it to me. Just as well she doesn't hob-nob with the plebs.' Lorna gave a little giggle. Kilronan was thousands of miles away and she didn't give a hoot. Heather would get over it and find someone else.

'It's not funny. Heather hates my guts,' Neil reproached.

'Mine too, I'm sure.' Lorna sipped her Margarita. 'Let's face it, Neil, we weren't exactly discreet. We didn't care if we were found out.'

'I suppose you're right,' he agreed. 'What does that say about us?'

'Not a lot,' Lorna said cheekily. 'Now drink up and come on, you're in New York and you're only here until Sunday. Where do you want to go first?'

'Bed,' he said hopefully, not caring if he sounded gauche or un-PC. Lorna was right, he only had until Sunday afternoon to have his wicked way with her.

'Later! I told you. We're going to do the tourist thing now and tomorrow, interspersed with serious shopping. Bed is for night-time. I've booked us a table at the Russian Tea Rooms for dinner. It's just a few blocks down the street. That means we've time to walk across to Fifth Avenue and Madison, to do a little shopping, come back here, change, have dinner, fall into bed, get up at the crack of dawn to go for a swim, do some sightseeing, more

517

shopping, go to dinner and a club, fall into bed, make mad passionate love, get up, go for a—'

'Whoa!' Neil laughed. 'I'm exhausted already.'

'Welcome to New York.' Lorna smirked.

The jelly was cold and slithery against her tummy and her heart raced with excitement. Noreen studied the monitor carefully. Was she seeing things? It couldn't be right. She looked again and looked at the doctor. She was smiling at her. 'You're not seeing things, Noreen. Congratulations, you're having twins.'

'Oh my God.' Noreen was stunned. *God, You really have forgiven me*, she thought with a great burst of happiness as she turned to Rajiv. His eyes were aglow with delight, a melon-sliced smile creasing his face.

'We've been doubly blessed, Noreen. This is a *very* good day,' he said tenderly, bending down to gently kiss her on the forehead.

Two little babies, two little souls entrusted to her care; she would be the best mother she could possibly be, she vowed. She couldn't believe it, but there they were, on the monitor, with two fine strong heartbeats. Tears of happiness brimmed in her eyes. This was much more than she deserved.

Oliver would be happy for her. He'd understand what a joy it was for her to be having *two* babies. Part of her wished with all her heart that it was him that was holding her hand and kissing her on the forehead and sharing her happiness. But that was a path she couldn't go down, she *had* to look forward. She owed that to her babies. They would be attuned to every emotion, tucked snugly in her womb. She couldn't wallow in regrets and sadness. She had to be as positive as she could possibly be. It wasn't all about her any more. Noreen resolutely banished all thoughts of Oliver from her head. The past was the past, she had to move on.

'I hear *Mister* Brennan's gone off to New York. I wonder will he bump into Lorna?' Anne Williams said disdainfully as she poured Heather a cup of tea and handed her a plate of buttered toast.

Heather's stomach lurched and the old familiar heartache returned with a vengeance. He was going to *her*! They must be keeping in touch. Maybe it was serious between them. She just couldn't bear it if Neil and Lorna ended up together. He could go and see anyone else, she'd get over that, but she so much wanted for things to end badly between her ex-boyfriend and her cousin. Her favourite fantasy was of Neil seeing Lorna in her true colours and coming back to her, broken and penitent, begging her to take him back. And how she would enjoy his grovelling before telling him she wanted nothing to do with him.

Anne took a closer look at her, noting her pallor. 'Maybe I shouldn't have said anything. Sorry, Heather, it was a bit tactless of me,' she said contritely.

'Ah, why should it bother me any more. They're welcome to each other,' Heather said despondently.

'*What!* What do you mean, welcome to each other?' Anne said sharply.

Oh no! Heather could have kicked herself. It had slipped out in an unguarded moment. Now her mother was going to do handstands.

'Are you telling me that that . . . that two-faced slug slept with Lorna? Are you telling me that that little bitch did that to you, Heather?'

'Forget it, Mother, I'm doing my best to,' Heather said tightly.

'Indeed I won't. I've a good mind to go over to Jane and Gerard and tell them what that little tart of a daughter of theirs has done. How mean and underhand. Who does she think she is?'

'Oh, Mam, *don't*! Just stay out of it. I mean that now,' Heather exclaimed angrily.

'I'm only standing up for you, Heather,' her mother declared indignantly.

'Mam, I don't need you to stand up for me. I'm not a child. I can stand on my own two feet, but thank you anyway.'

'Well, it's a disgrace! An absolute disgrace, and if I ever get my hands on that pair they'll be the sorry ones.' Anne was fit to be tied.

'I'm off to work, Ma. I'll see you, and for God's sake please don't say it to Dad,' Heather warned.

'Don't worry, he's the last one I'd tell,' her mother said grimly.

'You idiot!' Ruth declared later, as Heather gave her the low-down on her mobile.

'I know. I wasn't thinking. I just got such a shock when I heard he'd gone to New York. It hurt,' she said defensively.

'What do you care what that bastard does any more? Didn't Anne Jensen tell you there was a much nicer man for you? She was right about the job, wasn't she? Forget that pair and don't be wasting your energy on them.'

'Ah, it's easier said than done,' Heather said mournfully, feeling very sorry for herself. Ruth had no idea what she was going through. She'd never been dumped. And certainly not in favour of her own cousin. 'I'll talk to you later,' she said crossly. ''Bye.'

She drove directly to Oliver's house. She had a couple coming to view at nine thirty. She now had a set of keys. She knew the house would be shipshape. Oliver was very good like that, she approved, as she turned left off the main street and headed towards the lake. She liked showing Oliver's house and she enjoyed her conversations with him. He had an extremely dry sense of humour and often made her laugh with his wry observations. To her surprise his car was parked outside. She knocked on the front door. Moments later he opened it.

'Hi, Heather,' he said politely. 'I had to come back to get my chequebook. I forgot it this morning. Who's coming today? Any nosy parkers?'

Heather shook her head. 'No, this couple are from Dublin. They want to move to the country and still be within commuting range to visit their family.' Unconsciously she gave a deep, deep sigh as she followed him into the kitchen.

'That came from the toes,' he observed.

'Sorry,' Heather apologized. 'Bad day.'

'Tell me about them,' he said wryly. 'What's up?'

'Ah, I just heard that Neil's gone out to New York to see Lorna. I feel like stabbing them,' she said viciously.

Oliver laughed. 'Woman, don't let bitterness eat you up, it's not worth it.' He looked at her in some surprise. 'Is that Lorna Morgan, your cousin?'

'Yep. That's who I got ditched for. My own cousin.' She made a face.

'He's a bit of a moron, isn't he?' Oliver remarked. 'Anyone can see she's only interested in herself.'

'I know. But he can't see that. He mustn't have had any feelings for me at all.' Heather started feeling sorry for herself again.

'Do you think that he's thinking about you or your feelings, right now?' he asked bluntly.

She shook her head.

'Well then, don't give him free lodgings in your head any more. Just get on with it.'

'It's hard, though,' she protested, taking the cup of tea he poured for her.

'I know. No one knows better than me. I don't say it lightly,' he said kindly.

'Are you bitter about Noreen?' Heather was curious. He was surprisingly easy to talk to. It helped that they were in the same boat.

'I'm trying not to be,' he said gruffly.

'How do you keep her out of your head?'

'Work! Work! Work! And then you're so tired when you fall into bed you conk out. Walking's good too.'

'Yeah, but your work is very physical,' she pointed out. 'It wears you out. Mine doesn't.'

'Go to the gym, walk, swim,' Oliver advised, matter-of-factly.

'I need to. I put on ten pounds comfort eating, and I couldn't afford that anyway.'

'Better to be looking at it than looking for it,' Oliver said diplomatically with a twinkle in his eye, and she started to laugh.

'There's a lovely view from this window. This house won't take long to sell.' She changed the subject. 'No, no, wait, don't look out now,' she said hastily, spying a single magpie on the lawn as he turned his head to look out.

'Why not?' He looked startled at her vehemence.

'There's one magpie out there,' she informed him, scanning the skies for his mate. 'I hate that,' she muttered.

'Do you believe in that old nonsense?' Oliver jeered.

'Well, I know it's silly, I'd just prefer to see two,' she said defensively. 'Two for joy, you know!'

'I suppose you read your stars too,' he teased. 'You women, always looking for signs and portents.'

'Oliver, I went to a fortune-teller a while ago and she told me I'd change my job and use skills that I'd learned in a previous job. And she was right. Don't dismiss it all out of hand.'

'What else did she tell you, that you'd win the lottery?' he scoffed.

Heather laughed. 'No, smarty-pants, but she told me there was a new man on the periphery of my life.'

'And is there?'

'I don't know, he's staying rooted to the periphery

so far, but I live in hopes.' She smiled, feeling much more cheerful after her little chat with him.

'I wonder what she'd say to me?' Oliver raised an eyebrow.

'You should go to her, she's good,' Heather said earnestly.

'Ah, I'll leave that to you, Heather. The next time you go you can ask her if she sees anything nice for me.'

'I will,' she promised as he rinsed his cup and left her to await her clients.

Lorna was pleasantly tipsy as she pointed out Carnegie Hall to Neil on their way back to the hotel. It was a balmy evening, a lovely end to one of the best days she'd had since she'd come to New York. They'd gone shopping with gusto and Neil was the proud owner of two new suits, one an Armani, a Calvin Klein sweater, and some classic Ralph Lauren casuals, from the snazzy Madison Avenue store. A leather belt in Saks had cost him $200. He'd been reluctant to buy it but she'd persuaded him; the spirit of New York had overtaken him and he'd thrown caution to the wind and treated her to a DKNY little black number to die for and a beautiful Nicole Farhi top and trousers that made her look a million dollars.

Exhilarated, she had taken him to the Rockefeller Center for coffee when he'd started to flag, the five-hour difference beginning to kick in.

'That's Saint Patrick's Cathedral across the street. I haven't actually visited. Churches aren't my thing.'

'Me neither.' Neil grinned. 'Will we go to the Empire State?'

'No, not with all these parcels, it will be packed now anyway and you have a lot of queuing to do. We'll go first thing in the morning. I think we should go back to the hotel, drop our stuff and go for a swim and then change for dinner. We shouldn't waste the hotel; after all, it's one of the best in New York and has one of the top ten health clubs.'

'I couldn't agree more.' Neil stared lustfully at her. Lorna felt her heart sink. What would the sex be like this time? She'd been as drunk as a skunk the last time. She felt nervous.

She needn't have worried. Neil was so horny it made her horny too, and it was all over in less than five minutes. And she'd felt quite tingly. Definitely getting better, she thought happily as she swam in the rooftop pool, with the lights of New York's skyscrapers twinkling above her like a multitude of diamonds. She floated along lazily, utterly relaxed. Their room was perfect. She was very pleased with her choice of hotel. Minimalist chic, muted greys and blues.

Tasteful. So unlike the boring creams and yellows of the hotels she'd worked in. This was the life she was cut out for! How was she going to endure going back to work in Zack's crummy diner, when Neil went home?

He was extremely impressed by the fact that she knew her way around so well. He didn't realize yet that it was practically impossible to get lost in New York with the grid system. Still, it was nice that he believed her façade and saw her as a chic, sophisticated, uptown babe. It helped her believe that she was one for a little while. Lorna sighed. Why couldn't she be like Carina and simply enjoy the buzz and the different lifestyle? Why was she always grasping for something that seemed so out of reach? It was a pity Neil wasn't rich enough for her. She'd really enjoyed shopping with him. He too liked the good things in life. He too had social aspirations.

She climbed elegantly out of the pool, conscious that his eyes were on her, and wrapped herself in the luxurious terry-towelling robe that had been waiting for her in the room. She was tired now, and Neil was exhausted. Just as well they were dining close by.

The Russian Tearooms had impressed Neil no end. Lorna thought the bright golds and reds more than a tad garish but the food was luscious, the caviar with buckwheat blinis and melted butter a culinary delight. Neil had wolfed down his beef Stroganoff in mustard cream sauce. Lorna had gone for the flame-grilled skewered lamb.

Neil had brought her up to date on the home gossip as they lingered over brandies.

'I think Oliver Flynn and his wife have split. I heard she's in London. He sold me her car just before I came over. And the house is up for sale. It all happened out of the blue in the last few days.'

'They didn't last long. That's a fabulous house, I had a look at it when it was being built. I wouldn't mind a house like that,' Lorna said wistfully.

'I'll buy it for you,' joked Neil. 'I wouldn't mind

living in it myself. What else? Heather has a new, well, second-hand, two-year-old Ford Focus. I saw her getting out of it the other day. She was working in Fred's—'

'The chipper!' squawked Lorna, agog at this titbit. 'Is she mad? How common.' She turned up her pert little nose.

'Yeah, well, it was only temporary. I saw her going into Carleton's the other day all dressed up in a suit and carrying a briefcase. I don't know if she's buying some place or working there. I've seen her driving around in the car, so she must be still living in Kilronan.'

'She'll never speak to me again.' Lorna made a little moue.

'Or me,' sighed Neil.

'Anyway, there's nothing we can do about it, let's forget it and not ruin our evening. I wonder why the Flynns split up. He's a fine thing, very sexy bod. And he's loaded. He won't stay on his own for long. I wonder would I have a chance?' Lorna stretched sensuously, thrusting out her boobs.

'Hey, less of that. You'll be giving me a complex,' Neil exclaimed, unable to take his eyes off her.

'Well, he *is* sexy. I saw him once with his shirt off. What a chest. What shoulders. He's not my type though, unfortunately. He *really* is a clod-hopper.'

'You used to think I was a clodhopper,' Neil accused.

'You're coming on. That gear we bought today will really help the image. Looking smart is so key in business.'

'Image is everything,' Neil agreed, quoting his favourite axiom. 'I'll just have to come to New York every season to update my wardrobe.' He smiled at her and Lorna found to her surprise that she felt quite fond of him.

They strolled back to the hotel arm in arm and she was quite looking forward to some passionate lovemaking, now that she was getting the hang of it. Definitely the best day she'd had since she came to America, she decided as they entered the hotel.

They kissed in the lift and when they got to their room Lorna huskily told him to give her a moment to change into the sexy outfit she'd bought in Victoria's Secret. Tingly with anticipation, she changed into the see-through black wispy chiffon creation and emerged seductively into the bedroom. Only to find that Neil was flakers, snoring like a train. Technically because of the five-hour time difference he'd been up all night, she realized, and they'd had a few drinks. Nevertheless she was still miffed. Lorna slid out of her lingerie and got in beside him. So much for a night of passion. She pummelled her pillow into shape and snuggled down in her side of the bed, pleased that the bed was so big and that she could lie comfortably without touching him. She liked her own space in bed, hated men's legs and arms flung over her as they slept. She yawned. It had been a long, busy, but very enjoyable day; they could have sex in the morning. Minutes later, she was asleep herself.

Heather tossed and turned restlessly. She could hear the birds chirruping, signalling the dawn. What were Neil and Lorna doing now? They were probably entwined together, making love and laughing at her. Did he whisper endearments into Lorna's ear the way he used to with her? Was he feeding her croissants, dripping with butter and jam, for breakfast? Were they walking hand in hand through Central Park, or skimming stones across the lake? She'd never been away with Neil. They'd been meant to be going to the Slieve Russell, which was supposed to be pretty luxurious, until she'd found out about Lorna.

She'd have been waiting a long time before he took her to New York, she thought bitterly. Lorna no doubt had clicked her fingers and he'd gone running. He was probably spending a fortune on her. Lorna would wheedle money out of Scrooge. Her cousin was such a manipulating little cow. It had taken her years to see it, despite Ruth's constant nagging about it. Neil, the fool, probably couldn't see beyond his dick. Well, one day he'd know the truth, and that day couldn't come soon enough for Heather.

It was all right for Oliver Flynn to tell her not to waste her time being bitter. She had invested a lot of time and effort into Neil Brennan and it hurt desperately having it all thrown back in her face. Heather lay tormenting herself, knowing she'd have to get up for work in a few hours' time. She'd hardly slept a wink all night and she was bog-eyed.

If only she could get them out of her head. Where was this man on the periphery of her life? Was it Ray? She liked her new boss very much. He was a couple of years older than her and he was hugely interested in his work, but she wasn't sure if she fancied him. And so far he had made no move to let her know if he fancied her. Her grandmother always said the only way to get over one man was to find another. Heather's mystery man couldn't make an appearance in her life quick enough as far as she was concerned, she thought tiredly, yawning so hard her jaw ached as the birds outside her window twittered and chirruped exuberantly as the sun rose high in the sky.

The shrill ring of the phone startled Oliver. It was only ten to eight, who on earth would be ringing him this early? Maybe there was something wrong with Cora.

'Hello?' he said anxiously.

'Oliver, hi, it's me.' He heard Noreen's voice down the line.

'Is anything wrong?' he demanded.

'No, no, not at all. I just wanted to catch you before you went to work. You know the way your mobile can be out of range sometimes?' Noreen said hastily.

'How are you?' he asked, surprised to hear his wife's voice at this hour of the morning.

'I'm fine, Oliver, feeling much better actually.'

'That's good,' he said briskly.

'I had my scan, Oliver. You'll never guess. I'm going to have twins!'

'Twins!' exclaimed Oliver. 'How do you feel about that?'

'Oh, Oliver. How do you think after what I've

told you? I'm chuffed! Two little babies. I really do feel forgiven,' she bubbled.

'Noreen, you weren't ever being punished. You were the one that was punishing yourself.'

'And you,' Noreen said quietly.

'Forget it. I'm delighted for you. Is everything OK with the bloke? Have you told him?'

'Yes, Rajiv's fine about it. He was with me for the scan.'

'Good,' Oliver said succinctly. 'It's running late, Noreen. I'd better head off.'

'Keep in touch, won't you,' Noreen urged.

'Yes, I will. There's been plenty of people looking at the house. There's a few more coming over the weekend. Heather Williams is looking after things, she's working for Carleton's now.'

'She's nice,' Noreen remarked. 'Make sure to wash the dishcloths so they don't get smelly and—'

'Everything's taken care of in that department,' Oliver said curtly, annoyed at her remark.

'I know, it's just little things like that can tend to get overlooked,' Noreen explained.

Well, if you were here where you should be, I wouldn't have any of these problems, Oliver thought angrily. 'Yeah, well, don't worry about it. Just make sure to do what the doctors tell you. And I'm glad about your good news. I'll talk to you again.'

'OK, Oliver, take care,' Noreen said, and hung up.

Oliver scowled. He was glad for Noreen that she was having twins, but he almost felt as if his nose was being well and truly rubbed in it. He couldn't even father one child and mister super-duper in

531

London could give her two. And she had the nerve to tell him to wash the dishcloths, he thought irritably as he sniffed the one he'd been using. It probably could do with a wash, he sighed, and shoved it into the washing machine. He threw in a few tea towels and a hand towel and set the controls, before adding the powder. He was well capable of looking after himself without a woman interfering, no matter what Noreen might think. Oliver headed off to work feeling extremely hard done by.

43

'I can't believe the weekend's gone so quickly. I had a great time.' Neil leaned over and kissed Lorna.

'Good,' she purred, sliding her hand down between his legs.

'Lorna, Lorna,' he whispered huskily as he became instantly hard.

'Just so you won't forget me,' she murmured into his ear as he rolled on to her.

'As if I would,' Neil groaned, wanting to make the most of this last lovemaking session with Lorna but wanting to explode into her at the same time.

Lorna wriggled beneath him and then wrapped her long legs around him, holding him tight. Those legs so taut and toned and silky to touch. It had never been like this with Heather, and never would have been, he thought fleetingly as he enjoyed every second of this last lusty joining.

'You'll just have to come over again soon,' Lorna murmured when they were finished.

'It'll be a while, my accountant will probably cut up my credit card when I get home,' Neil confessed. He'd spent a small fortune this weekend so far, and he still had to settle his hotel bill.

'Tsk! Don't think about it.' She looked annoyed. 'Come on, let's go up to the pool and have a swim, take a quick walk in Central Park and then we'll have brunch in Norma's downstairs. It's one of *the* places to have brunch in New York and I'm dying to try it out.'

'Well, if you're dying to try it out, try it out we will,' Neil said gallantly. He wouldn't mind a strong cup of coffee to wake him up. It had been the early hours when they'd got to bed. Lorna had walked the legs off him the previous day and then she'd taken him to a very loud, crowded, hip club that had cost $100 each to get in, not to mention the rip-off prices they'd charged for drinks. Lorna had told him it used to be one of Madonna's favourite haunts. Madonna might have the money to spend in such a place, he hadn't, but he couldn't let on to Lorna that it was way out of his range. She was obviously used to socializing in these sort of places.

The swim woke him up, and he enjoyed his laps underneath the glass roof that allowed a hot, bright sun to shine through. Hard to believe that this time tomorrow he'd be back home in Ireland. He'd work his butt off to try to get another trip before the end of the year. Not only was he hooked on Lorna, he was well and truly hooked on New York.

By the time the waiter put a big juicy doorstep of a steak in front of him some hours later, he was ravenous. He'd enjoyed his walk in Central Park among all the NYC residents out strolling, cycling and rollerblading with panache, with Lorna pointing out areas of interest as knowledgeably as if she were a native, he thought admiringly. She'd really settled in here, practically a native New Yorker.

It had been a rush to get packed and checked out and he'd paid his hotel bill without flinching. It wasn't bad value considering all the luxurious extras and its prime site. Even though the prices in Norma's reflected its status as *the* place to have brunch, it was his last meal in the city, he might as well enjoy it.

Lorna was having a popover chicken and vegetable pie, pushing it around her plate, toying with it. He noticed that whenever she ate, she left at least half of her meal on her plate. Obviously she was watching her fantastic figure, but it grieved him that the food that had cost him half a day's pay was being wasted. She should order child's portions and be done with it. At least Heather ate what was in front of her.

Stop that!!! he ordered himself, silently. There was no comparison between Lorna and Heather. Lorna was a sophisticated woman of the world, Heather a nice but parochial homebody. He knew who he wanted to be with, whether she picked at her food or not.

'Isn't it a fabulous place? The buzz is terrific. Oh Neil, I wish I could do brunch here every Sunday,' Lorna said wistfully, gazing around at the smart, crowded, airy restaurant.

'Why don't you?' he asked, puzzled.

'Er . . . there's so many places to try out, Neil, you can't keep going to the same place,' Lorna drawled. 'I should have brought you to the

Carnegie Deli as well. It's famous and it's only a few blocks away, they have queues out the door.'

'When I come back, next time.' Neil smiled as the waiters arrived to top up their coffee and juice.

'When do you think you'll come back?' Lorna slid a tiny sliver of chicken into her mouth.

'As soon as I can! Maybe I could stay in your place next time. It wouldn't be so expensive either. If I'm going to keep coming over it makes sense to stay with you,' he suggested. 'Is it big? I'd love to have seen it.'

'Just your average brownstone apartment in Chelsea near the piers,' she said airily. 'Le Parker Meridian is much more romantic, *much* more us.'

'And OK if you're loaded,' he retorted. Lorna frowned and he quickly changed the subject. She was touchy about money. 'Are you sure you won't come to the airport? The concierge told me I shouldn't leave it too late.'

'No, don't,' Lorna agreed. 'Everyone will be coming back from Westchester and the Hamptons, traffic's always crap on Sunday afternoon and evening. I really don't want to spend hours in cabs each way.'

'Oh, OK,' he sighed. 'Just let me settle the bill.' He half hoped that she would offer to treat him. She hadn't put her hand in her purse since Thursday, but then it was obvious she was used to men wining, dining and looking after her. She expected the same from him. He supposed he'd got off lightly by not having to buy any jewellery at Tiffany's, although she'd dropped enough hints when she'd taken him in to 'browse'. He didn't feel one bit guilty. He'd spent a king's ransom on clothes for her, time enough for the jewellery as they got to know each other better. He'd been stung before by girlfriends dumping him after he'd bought expensive jewellery for them. Sometimes, he couldn't quite put his finger on it, but he felt Lorna was toying with him. He'd noticed especially the night they were in the club that she kept looking around and over his shoulder, trying to make eye contact with other men. Not a very nice trait.

Stop! You're being paranoid, he chastised himself, annoyed that his old lack of confidence should suddenly resurface.

'I suppose I'd better go.' He made a face as he pocketed his credit card, having paid yet another small fortune for their meal.

'I guess you'd better. The doorman will call you a cab. I might just stay and have another coffee. I don't really want to watch you leaving, Neil.' Her lower lip trembled.

'Ah, Lorna!' He patted her hand awkwardly, touched at her emotion and disgusted with his earlier lack of charity. She did care about him, it was obvious. She seemed upset.

'Just go, now,' she said forlornly. 'I'll call you.'

'OK.' He leaned across the table and kissed her gently. 'I had a wonderful, wonderful time. Give me your number so I can keep in touch. Let's call each other a couple of times a week as well as emailing,' he suggested.

'I'll email you my number. You'd really want to get a move on, Neil.'

Was it his imagination or was she a trifle testy? It was just that she was upset, he assured himself, looking at her downcast face. He shrugged into his new black leather jacket and walked down the steps of Norma's. When he looked back she was sitting with her face cupped in her hands, looking so sad he felt like running back and taking her in his arms. Taking a deep breath, Neil kept going and ten minutes later was sitting in the back of a yellow cab on his way to JFK, and a future reckoning with his accountant.

Lorna tried to keep the tears at bay. She couldn't believe that her weekend of pampering and luxury was over. If she didn't get a move on she was going to be late for her shift at Zack's. Not that she gave a damn. How could she go back to waitressing after spending a weekend eating in upmarket restaurants in the hottest spots in town? How could she slum it back in that tacky, noisy diner?

She'd thought Neil would never get a move on. Time was getting tight and she had to change her clothes, she certainly wasn't working for the next eight hours in her Nicole Farhi outfit. She finished her coffee and reluctantly left the restaurant, collected her weekend bag, and got a swipe card for the loo. Like Cinderella, after midnight, she divested herself of her finery and emerged into the foyer in her jeans and Gap T-shirt.

She was damned if she was taking public transport to Times Square, she decided, having spent the last four days being whisked around in taxis.

The doorman smiled at her and whistled for a cab. Sick at heart, Lorna climbed in.

She wouldn't have a weekend like this again until her mother came. Neil was a dead loss. *Imagine* suggesting he stay at her place the next time. As if. He'd really blown it big-time. If that was his attitude, he could forget her, she decided. Neil was OK but definitely not what she required. He kept going on about his accountant. How cheap was that? Even this morning while they were having brunch she'd considered keeping him on a long leash, prepared to keep in touch until he came out again, but when he'd suggested doing it on the cheap and staying in her place, that had put the kibosh on that. He wasn't worth it.

She shouldn't have bothered flirting with him, just so she could knock the smug smile off Heather's face. Heather was such an idiot anyway, she thought crossly. Imagine falling head over heels in love with Neil. In spite of all his best efforts, he'd never be able to shake off his country-boy leanings. Looking for a cheap place to stay indeed. Lorna was raging with him for that. She felt really let down; even the fact that he was the only man who'd given her pleasure in bed wasn't enough. She'd invested a lot of time and effort in him and he'd proved to be a loser.

He'd even wanted to visit Ground Zero, how uncool was that? How ghoulish and voyeuristic. Lorna didn't even like to acknowledge that such a place existed. It made New York seem vulnerable, and she didn't like that feeling, she felt vulnerable enough herself as it was.

Lorna sighed. Her place was uptown, and if she wanted to be there she'd better find someone to keep her, and fast. As the flashing billboards of Times Square hove into view, Lorna felt sick with disappointment as reality hit home hard.

It had not been the best weekend ever, Heather thought glumly as she squeezed some lemon juice into a glass of warm water and sipped it slowly. All her hard-won equilibrium seemed to have disappeared in an instant when she'd heard about Neil going to New York. The hurt and grief had hit her again, twice as hard, and that shocked her. When did the pain stop? When did the heartache disappear? Was she going to feel like this for the rest of her life? she wondered in despair. She'd thought she was over him. She'd tormented herself for the entire weekend, thinking about what they were doing, and hated herself for being such a wimp.

It still hurt that Neil had dropped her like such a hot potato. Apart from that horrible episode in Fred's he hadn't spoken to her at all. He'd cut her out of his life as if she'd meant nothing at all to him. Didn't he miss her even a little bit? Didn't he miss their talks about the business? Looking back, he'd only ever talked about himself. It had been all about him and his plans. He could talk about himself for hours. Surely he didn't get away with that with Lorna. All she ever talked about was herself. That they'd ever got together at all was a miracle. They were two horrible people, Heather thought bitterly.

She chewed the side of her lip. Was it Lorna she was more mad at than Neil? It was the humiliation of it all that got to her. Her pride had been well and truly dented. Sometimes she wondered if it was her pride that hurt the most or her heart. Looking back, she felt she'd been more in love with the idea of living with Neil and being a couple, than actually in *love*. Was she just as shallow as Neil and Lorna at the end of the day? She wished these horrible questions would stop buzzing around her head.

She slipped a slice of bread into the toaster and sipped more of her warm lemon-flavoured water. Today was the start of her diet, she vowed. She'd disgraced herself over the weekend, stuffing herself with chocolate-covered Kimberleys, crisps, slices of fruity Maltana slathered in butter. She'd gone on such a binge she hated herself. It had to stop, *now*!

She was driving towards Carleton's just a few hundred metres from the garage when she saw Neil's car parked on the forecourt under the flat, with the boot open. Slowing down, she saw him lifting suitcases out of the boot. He must have flown in this morning. She glowered, feeling a fierce stab of jealousy. He looked extremely well in a pair of black trousers, black shirt and black leather jacket. She could see Lorna's influence and it galled her. If he'd looked hunted and miserable it would have given her some consolation. She put her foot on the accelerator and decided to comfort herself with a chocolate éclair for her tea break.

'Oh, I like this!' Noreen exclaimed as she walked into the light-filled, airy fitted kitchen and dining-room that led out to a sunny, shrub-filled garden. 'I'll need a good garden, Rajiv, for two of them. It's the nicest one I've seen. And the flat's decorated in the colours I like. I had a beautiful house in Kilronan, you know.' Sadness flickered across her face. She'd been so proud of that house. So chuffed to show it off to Rita and Maura, but in the end it had become a place of great unhappiness for both her and Oliver.

She'd spent the weekend looking at houses, apartments and flats, none of them appealing to her until she'd seen this high-ceilinged, immaculate ground-floor flat with garden, in a large Victorian house on a quiet, leafy, tree-lined road not far from Kay, Rajiv and St Mary's, where she was back working part-time.

A garden had been high on her list of priorities and this one, walled, mature and private, was perfect. The flat itself had three bedrooms and a good-sized lounge, with a beautiful bay window, and it was in her price range.

'If you like it, go for it, Noreen, house prices are starting to rise. Don't delay buying,' Rajiv warned. He was being extremely kind, supportive and helpful to her. It was the first time in her life that she'd ever had such a *relaxed* relationship with a man but she was finding it difficult to come out of her I'm-An-Independent-Can-Stand-On-My-Own-Two-Feet-Woman mode. She and Rajiv had an easy friendship but she had not had sex with him again. She wasn't sure if she would in the future, but for now she was holding back. It was as though being pregnant had satisfied every need and want for the moment and she was content to savour that particular joy for the time being.

'You know, Rajiv, I feel that Oliver shouldn't be selling the house and giving half the proceeds to me. Why should he? He worked hard to build that house. I feel terribly guilty about it,' she added despondently as she walked out into the flower-filled garden. Great drifts of clematis tumbled down over trellises. Bluebells and irises waved softly in the breeze under two damson trees that formed a natural archway as their foliage intertwined. It was a peaceful place. Soothing and restful. A bird sang exuberantly. It was an oasis in the midst of the city. She could do far worse for herself and her children than buy here, she reflected as she waited for her friend's answer.

Rajiv took a deep breath and studied her with his kind, trusting eyes. 'I understand how you feel, but from a man's point of view, if I may, I think if you don't let him sell up and give you half the cash, you'll make him feel worse than he feels already. It can't be easy for him to know that you are expecting twins. I'd say the poor man feels he's let you down and this is a way of trying to make up for it. Giving you the money will be an honourable ending of it for him. What do the Americans call it? Closure, isn't it? An interesting concept if you don't believe in karma,' Rajiv said honestly as he bent down to smell a tuft of lavender.

'But I'm the one that feels I've let *him* down. Oh Rajiv, I kept at him and at him to have a baby. I can't take his money. It's not fair. I've walked out on him, he has no obligation towards me,' Noreen fretted.

'You can't stay with Kay for ever. And if you don't take his money you won't be able to afford a place half as nice as this unless you let me—'

'No, Rajiv,' she said sharply. 'You can help with the babies but that's it. I'm not going to sponge off you too.'

Rajiv held up his palms. 'Fine, Noreen. I respect your wishes,' he said calmly, 'but I think you should let Oliver keep some sense of pride and dignity, if you want my honest opinion.'

Noreen bit her lip at the gentle, implied rebuke. 'I don't mean to be ungracious, Rajiv. Until I got married I was used to fending for myself.'

'Time to learn how to receive as well as to give,' Rajiv said mildly. 'Much harder sometimes. You must honour people's divinity, my dear, and accept their kindness so that they can be infinitely rewarded for their generosity. Kindness from another can sometimes be reparation for a wrong done in a past life.'

'Oh!' murmured Noreen. 'I hadn't thought of it like that. I'm not sure about past lives and all of that. OK then, I'll use the money I have for a deposit. My salary will pay the mortgage and when I get the proceeds from the house I can pay it off. That should keep you *and* Oliver happy.' She smiled at him. 'You see life so differently to the way I do. I value independence and you tell me to learn to receive . . . we're going to have some interesting discussions, I can see.'

'Be open, Noreen. Our children will learn a lot of

wisdom from both our cultures,' Rajiv said easily.

'They'll be very lucky to have a lovely daddy, which was much more than I had.'

'Let the past go, Noreen. Your father made karma for himself that no one would want; bless him and send forgiveness and it will come back to you a thousandfold.'

'I'm not that much of a saint, Rajiv, but I'll try, some time,' she said drily. 'Come on, I'll go and make an offer to the estate agent. The sooner I have a place of my own, the sooner I can decorate a nursery.'

Oliver could hear the doorbell shrilling, making his head throb. 'Piss off, whoever you are,' he muttered. 'Leave me alone and get away from my door.' After a while the bell stopped ringing and he fell asleep again.

He woke again to feel someone shaking him vigorously. 'What the fuck,' he muttered, opening red-rimmed eyes and closing them quickly as shards of bright sunlight caused immense pain.

'Oliver, Oliver, wake up. I've two couples coming to see the house,' he heard a woman say agitatedly. 'Oh, for God's sake, Oliver, you're as drunk as a skunk! And the room smells like a brewery. Will you get up and let me get the place sorted,' Heather Williams exclaimed in exasperation as he opened his eyes again and she swam into focus, staring down at him in dismay.

44

Heather stared down into Oliver Flynn's bleary eyes and her heart sank. He was mouldy drunk. There were beer cans strewn on the floor and an empty brandy bottle on its side and the room smelt stale and skanky. She went over to the windows and opened them wide.

'Come on, Oliver, get up. The Reillys from Mount Kilronan are coming and I'm not going to have them see you like this,' she exclaimed, pulling him up out of the chair. He swayed, but steadied himself.

'You can't stay here. Come out to my car and sit in it until the viewing is over. I'll drive it up the lane a bit, then afterwards you can go up to bed and sleep it off,' she ordered. She took him by the upper arm and pushed him towards the door.

'OK, Heather,' he slurred, the alcohol fumes emanating from him, pungent to say the least. She managed to get him into the car and he slumped down in the seat as she got in beside him and reversed rapidly out of the drive.

'You know shomething, it was my birthday yeshterday and I thought I'd have a few beers, thatsh all,' he mumbled. 'Had to drown my sorrows, ya know. I mean, I couldn't give her a baby, I can't even get it up and she rings me and tells me she's having twins with this Indian bloke. What do you think of that, Heather? It'sh enough to turn a man to drink isn't it?' he demanded aggressively.

'Yes it is, Oliver,' Heather soothed, stunned at his drunken revelations. Noreen was having twins and Oliver wasn't the father. No wonder the poor chap had hit the bottle.

'Not that I'm much of a man,' Oliver continued dolefully. 'Had all the tests. Embarrashing, Heather. Can't have kids, can't do the business, what woman is ever going to want to be with me?'

Heather didn't know what to say. 'Don't worry about it now, Oliver, you just go for a little snooze until the viewings are over,' she murmured as she pulled in between two bright, yellow gorse bushes that hid the car from view of the house. 'Stay there now,' she said urgently, afraid that the people would arrive early and she wouldn't have the lounge sorted.

'Don't leave me,' he slurred. 'I like talking to you.'

'We'll talk in a little while, Oliver, I promise. Now have a rest there for a few minutes and I'll be back.' She patted him on the arm. 'Close your eyes, like a good fella,' she ordered and felt a wave of relief when his head drooped and his eyes closed.

She grabbed a bag out of the back seat that contained a duster, polish and a room spray. She always carried it with her to freshen up empty houses that she was showing. Oliver was still half asleep, so she opened the window on her side, closed the door gently and legged it back up the lane as fast as she could in her tight skirt. She rooted around the kitchen presses until she found a bin liner and filled it with the empty beer cans and brandy bottle. A plate held the remains of a cheese sandwich so she tidied that up, ran a brush over the floor and liberally sprayed air freshener around the room. She hurried upstairs to see what the main bedroom was like but the bed was made. Oliver clearly hadn't slept in it. She plumped up the pillows and tweaked the duvet so that it was uncreased. It was a beautiful room with magnificent views; she felt sorry for Oliver that he had to sell the house. She sprayed some polish in the air to give a nice 'just polished' smell.

She had just finished wiping the crumbs off the kitchen table when the doorbell rang signalling the arrival of the Reillys. Mr and Mrs Reilly were a wealthy couple who owned several businesses in the town. They lived in a luxurious bungalow about a mile out of Kilronan and Heather was sure there was more than a hint of nosiness in their desire to see the Flynns' house. She hated people who came to view with no intention of buying. Already they had a firm offer in, giving the asking price, but both Ray and herself felt that it could go higher if they persevered for a while longer. Oliver had given them another week. He was anxious to get the sale complete.

The Reillys proved to be exremely thorough in their prying, opening every single press and wardrobe. Oliver would be mortified if he realized. He was such a reserved, private man.

'And why exactly are they selling up? They haven't lived here all that long.' Joan Reilly couldn't contain her curiosity.

'I just show the houses, Mrs Reilly,' Heather said politely.

'Oh, the reason I'm asking is that I was wondering was there some fault or flaw?' the older woman riposted frostily, a faint hint of pink in her cheeks at Heather's implication.

'Well, of course, if you are interested in buying the property, you will be able to have it surveyed. It's always advisable.' Heather smiled sweetly.

'We'll be in touch with Ray if we decide to put in an offer,' Mrs Reilly said snootily, putting Heather firmly in her place. The doorbell rang. It was the next couple, a freelance tax consultant and his wife who were interested in relocating from Dublin. He was in his mid-thirties, intense and bumptious, his wife a quiet, self-effacing young woman who didn't have much to say for herself. Mrs O'Reilly looked them up and down and swept out the door without so much as a thank you. Her husband grunted something in her direction and followed his wife down the steps.

'It's got possibilities!' the tax consultant told her twenty minutes later, 'but I wouldn't be prepared to pay what they're looking for.' Heather knew he was chancing his arm.

'We have an offer in for the asking price already,' Heather assured him.

'Well, they're paying far too much,' Shay

Lincoln blustered. 'It's too far from Dublin for that price.'

'Well, the couple who've put in the offer are from Dublin and they don't seem to think so. It's all a matter of perception, isn't it?' Heather remarked.

'Come on, Chloe, let's view that house outside Navan,' Shay said peremptorily, giving a curt nod in Heather's direction.

Up yours too, she thought, but she smiled politely, thinking that the whole morning had been wasted. She filled the kettle and switched it on, waiting until their Merc had disappeared before she headed off to rescue Oliver. He was snoring loudly, oblivious to everything. Heather drove the car back to the front of the house and gave him a poke in the ribs. 'Come on, Oliver, wakey, wakey.' He opened one eye and looked at her bleary-eyed.

'Don't ask,' she said kindly. 'I have the kettle boiling. What you need is a good strong cup of coffee.'

Oliver groaned and ran his hand over a dark, stubbly jaw. 'I think I went on a bender,' he muttered, but this time he seemed more with it, his voice less slurred than earlier.

'I think that about describes it,' Heather said cheerfully as she led the way into the house. 'Sorry about leaving you in the car. I thought it was the best thing to do, especially as the Reillys from Mount Kilronan were the first viewers.'

'That pair!' Oliver exclaimed in disgust as he sank on to a chair at the kitchen table and put his head in his hands. 'I don't care if they offer more than the asking price, I'm not selling to that pair of snobby hoors!'

Heather laughed.

'Sorry about the language,' he apologized.

'Ah, don't be silly, Oliver. You should see me in full flow, especially when I'm describing Neil and Lorna,' Heather scoffed as she placed a mug of coffee in front of him. 'Would you like anything to eat?'

Oliver winced. 'No thanks. Look, Heather, I'm very sorry that . . . em . . . er . . . sorry about this,' he muttered, embarrassed.

'Forget it, Oliver, you're going through a rough time, it's allowed. Look, when you've finished that why don't you go up and have a shower and go to bed and I'll come back later on this afternoon and drive you to wherever you left the car,' she offered.

'I think I left it in the car park behind the Haven. I was on the way home from Ma's when I dropped in for a drink . . . or two. I walked home. I wasn't too bad at that stage. Then I went on the brandy,' he confessed.

'Well look, you go and sleep it off and I'll call back in the afternoon. All part of the service.' She smiled.

'OK so,' he said wearily, too under the weather to argue with her.

Impulsively she stood up from the table and gave him a hug. He looked so miserable and unhappy her heart went out to him. It must be horrible for him to know that Noreen was expecting twins and he couldn't father a child. She'd thought she was unhappy, but his misery far outdid hers, she decided magnanimously.

'What was that for?' he looked astonished.

'Thought you might need one,' she said good-naturedly.

'Thanks, Heather,' he said awkwardly. 'You're a nice person.'

'Arrah, you're not bad yourself,' she said lightly, not wanting him to be embarrassed. 'See you later.'

Well, you never knew what you were going to encounter when you went showing houses, that was for sure, she reflected as she drove back into town. She had another house to show at lunchtime, she'd want to get a move on.

It was after four before she got back to Oliver's. There was no sign of his car, so he obviously hadn't collected it. She wondered if he was at home. She rang the doorbell and waited patiently for him to answer. She heard him run down the stairs and smiled. That sounded more like the Oliver she knew. He was shaved and dressed in fresh clothes when he opened the door and she knew by him that he was mortified.

'You want a lift into town?' she asked lightly.

'You shouldn't have bothered, Heather. I could make my own way in, the walk wouldn't kill me,' he said awkwardly.

'It might with that hangover.' She grinned.

Oliver managed a wry smile. 'It's pretty impressive all right,' he agreed.

'Come on, hop in and I'll drive as carefully as I can over the potholes,' she promised.

They drove in silence, but it wasn't a strained one

and when she pulled up outside the Haven he turned and smiled sheepishly at her. 'Thanks, Heather, if ever I can do you a favour let me know,' he said.

'The next time you're going on a bender let me know and I'll go with you,' she laughed. 'We can drown our sorrows together.'

'And how are your sorrows? Any better?' he enquired.

Heather threw her eyes up to heaven. 'Bad weekend. You might have gone on the beer, I went on a food binge, and then I went on a diet this morning and I saw him arriving home from America so I had an éclair at break time.' She looked at him. 'Speaking of food, my mam's off on a Ladies Club day out and my dad's playing golf so I'm fending for myself. Do you feel like coming into the Haven for something to eat before you pick up the car? I'll treat you for your birthday.'

Oliver laughed. 'Did I tell you it was my birthday? I *must* have been pissed. Come on then, but I'll treat you for what you did for me.'

Heather shook her head. 'No. My treat. I suggested it, and besides, then you'll have one good thing to remember this birthday for,' she said firmly.

'You're a real old softie, aren't you?' Oliver declared, but he looked pleased.

'Me, I'm as hard as nails,' Heather assured him as she reversed into a parking space.

'Yeah, I believe that all right. You're the toughest nut in Kilronan.' They walked into the smoky darkness of the Haven, Oliver holding the door open for her to precede him.

Nice manners, she thought. Neil had been very hit and miss on the manners. They sat in a quiet alcove and studied the menus in silence. 'Scampi and side salad for me I think,' Heather decided. 'Oliver?'

'Aah, I think I'll go for the plaice and chips. That can't do too much damage.'

'A drink?' she suggested.

'I think I'll stick to Seven-Up,' Oliver said ruefully as a waitress came to take their order. 'Er . . . Heather, I was just wondering, when I told you it was my birthday, did I reveal any more dark secrets?' he asked warily when the waitress had moved away.

Heather dropped her gaze. She could lie and say he'd said nothing, but what happened if he vaguely remembered saying something? He'd know she was lying.

'It was drink talking,' she said offhandedly.

'And *exactly* what did drink say?' he probed.

'Does it matter, Oliver?' she shifted in her chair. How did she answer him, for God's sake?

'Just tell me, Heather, I can take it on the chin,' he said firmly.

Heather cleared her throat. 'Well, you told me that Noreen was expecting twins and that you weren't the father. And er . . . you said that you couldn't give her a child,' she said quietly. That was as far as she was going, she was damned if she was going to embarrass himself and herself any further by his confession that he couldn't get it up.

Oliver looked her squarely in the eye and she admired him for it.

'Heather, for Noreen's sake I'd ask you not to

554

mention this to anybody. I'd be very grateful for your discretion.'

'Oliver, I assure you, I promise you, you have it. It's nobody's business but yours and Noreen's. I'll never say a word to a sinner, honestly,' she said earnestly.

'I know you won't. You're a real pal.' Oliver gave her hand a quick squeeze and she felt very honoured to hear him call her a pal. Instinct told her that when Oliver Flynn paid a compliment he meant it.

'Now tell me how are you getting on with Ray Carleton? He seems to be a decent bloke. Do you think he's the one on the periphery that your woman told you about?' Oliver teased, relaxing after clearing the air.

'No, I found out he's seeing someone. A teacher up in Dublin. Strike him off the list.' Heather shrugged.

'Maybe it's someone you'll sell a house to? Don't give up.' Oliver stretched his long legs out in front of him.

'And what about you, have you seen anyone?' Heather asked.

'I'm not looking.' His face darkened.

'Well, they say that it's when you're not looking that *lurve* strikes! So watch out.'

'I'm not going down that road again, Heather,' Oliver declared.

'Tell you what,' she suggested. 'Whichever of us gets fixed up first the other one has to buy a bottle of champers.'

'Well, you'd better decide what you like, Moët, Dom P, because you'll be the one drinking it.'

555

'Go to Anne Jensen, the psychic. I *dare* you.' Heather's eyes sparkled with mischief.

'Are you mad, woman?' Oliver growled. 'Thank God, here's our food. That will keep you quiet for a while.'

'Coward,' she taunted.

'That's me,' he agreed as he sprinkled salt and vinegar on his chips, but Heather was glad to see that at least he was smiling.

45

Oliver sighed and turned over on to his back. something was different, he thought vaguely, and then realization dawned as the full, tingling sensation that he hadn't had for months reminded him that he was normal again. No need for Viagra after all. A huge wave of relief enveloped him. He'd seriously begun to wonder if he'd ever enjoy the pleasures of sex again. This was a step in the right direction. He felt a weight lift off his shoulders and for the first time since the beginning of the year he began to feel optimistic about life again.

Life wasn't too bad at the moment, as it happened. He yawned. The first six apartments were finished, so he could move in any time he wanted, once he had the place painted. Heather had told him she'd give him a hand decorating and arranging furniture and curtains, and stuff like that.

Heather Williams was one really nice girl, he thought sleepily. And very easy to talk to. He felt as if he'd always known her. She had a relaxed way about her that made him feel comfortable in her company. He liked her very much. They'd had a few good laughs since he'd put the house on the market. It was a pity he was the way he was, he wouldn't mind getting to know her better. Still, at least he wasn't moping around the place like he had been. And now this. He was half-way normal again. It was a very pleasant start to the day.

Neil Brennan felt like thumping his computer. He had connected to his emails and surprise, surprise, there wasn't one to be had from Lorna. It was weeks since he'd been to New York and he hadn't heard a peep from her. What a bitch! She'd really used him, let him spend a fortune on her and dumped him. He'd sent email after email but to no avail. She might as well not be on the planet.

If he'd known she was so shallow, insincere and manipulating he'd never have gone near her. It would take him months to pay off his credit card expenses. He'd had a stinker of a letter from the credit card company for exceeding his credit limit, and he still had to endure a talking to from his accountant later in the afternoon.

He was totally browned off. That new girl, Carol, wasn't at all interested in her job and he'd had to speak to her about her use of the phone for personal calls. He had a feeling that she wouldn't be staying for long and then he'd have the hassle of looking for someone else. He wondered if he offered Heather more money would she give up her job in the estate agency and come back to work for him? They didn't have to be personally involved. They could keep the relationship strictly business.

Surely she couldn't turn up her nose at more

money, not if she had any sense, and she had to be over her huffs with him by now. 'Ah, come on, Lorna, get in touch,' he muttered, tapping his pen impatiently against the desk, staring at his empty 'in' box. He knew in his heart of hearts that there was no chance she was going to contact him after all this time. She had his email, his office number, the flat number and his mobile number. Lorna had done the dirty on him and he might as well forget her. But if he ever saw her again he'd let her have it. By God he would!

'Are you going home next month?' Carina plonked herself down beside Lorna on a banquette during a break on their shift.

'If I don't get out of this dump soon, I am.'

'Aw, come on, it pays much better than office work and it's a bit of a laugh. I'm staying another year at least. I might even have the deposit on an apartment saved when I get home.' Carina yawned.

'You wouldn't be seen dead waitressing at home,' Lorna snapped resentfully. She hadn't saved a penny but she had a terrific new wardrobe, a dozen bags and eight pairs of shoes, her latest being a divine pair from Prada with their distinctive silver buckle that oozed uptown chic.

'I know,' Carina admitted cheerfully. 'But you'd never make at home what you make here. Come on, we'd better get our butts in gear. Oh look, there's Suzie. What's she doing here on her lunch break?' She waved at one of their house-mates.

'Hi, girls.' Suzie sank on to the banquette wearily

and wriggled her feet out of her shoes. 'Any chance of a latte?'

'Coming up.' Carina went to oblige.

'Actually it was you I wanted to see, Lorna. You can type can't you? And you did reception work?' Suzie asked, flicking her blonde hair back over her shoulders. She worked as a PA to a wedding planner.

'Yeah, why?' Lorna felt a flicker of excitement.

'Well, a friend of mine who works in my building on the floor below me wants to go to Europe for six months, and she wants someone to take over her job and take a sublet on her apartment. She works for an agent.'

'Where's the apartment?' Lorna demanded.

'The East Village—'

'I'll do it. I'll take it. When? Where?'

'Hold on, you have to go and be interviewed first,' Suzie interjected.

'Fine. When?'

'I'll sort it. Get me a muffin to go with my latte,' her housemate ordered.

'Yes, ma'am,' Lorna deadpanned and Suzie grinned.

'Now!'

Two days later, dressed in a businesslike taupe suit with navy accessories, Lorna presented herself at Sandra Winston & Associates. Alanna, the girl she was hoping to replace, was sitting at the cherry-wood reception desk facing the elevator.

'Hi, Alanna isn't it? I'm Lorna Morgan. I'm hoping to stand in for you. Suzie told me you wanted to go to Europe.'

Alanna eyed her up and down. 'Waal, hi yourself. I guess Suzie's filled you in on what I'm doing. Six months off to do Europe. I just can't wait to get to Paris, France, and meet some sexy Frenchmen.' She grinned. 'Sandra's fine to work for as long as you do your work and don't look for time off Friday or Monday. She goes out of town Thursday lunchtime and doesn't come back until Monday lunchtime. She has a farm in Westchester. She breeds horses.'

'Wow! She must be rich.' Lorna was impressed.

'Stinking. She has an apartment on Park!'

'That says it all.' Lorna sighed.

'Anyways like, mostly you're answering the phone, making appointments with editors and authors, typing letters, that kind of stuff. I use Word, are you familiar with that?'

'Sure,' Lorna nodded.

'Cool. If you want, you can come and spend a half day here once Sandra OKs you, and I can like, train you in. If you want to come around and see the apartment later this evening that's fine. It's a studio, kitchenette, and toilet and shower on the first floor. No AC unfortunately, but I've got plenty of fans. It's just off First and Eight.'

Lorna's heart sank. A studio! No AC. Already the humidity levels were very high. She'd heard that New York in August was a stinker. No AC was a bit of a bummer. Some parts of the East Village were a bit on the seedy side, and she hoped Alanna's pad was in the more bohemian, trendy neighbourhood. Still, it was too good an opportunity to miss. And it would give her a breathing space for six months, doing a job she was much more suited to. The relief of knowing that she might never have to work in Zack's goddammed diner again was indescribable.

'When are you thinking of going?' Lorna asked.

'Mid May.' Alanna broke off to answer a call.

That would be perfect, Lorna thought happily. Her mother was coming out the week after next. That would bring her up to the end of April. She'd do double shifts in the diner next week so that she'd never need to set foot in the crappy joint again.

'Let me introduce you to Sandra.' Alanna stood up from behind her desk. She was tall and thin and dressed impeccably in a grey pinstripe suit.

'Great,' agreed Lorna, although she felt a tad nervous as Alanna led her into a beige and off-white office where Sandra Winston reclined in a cream leather chair, dictating a letter. She was the epitome of Park Avenue chic in her black Chanel suit, with a single strand of pearls and a discreet gold bangle her only jewellery. Her ash-blonde hair was impeccably cut in a short asymmetrical style that sharpened her fine features and emphasized the smoky grey of her eyes. Her sculpted nails were state of the art, Lorna thought enviously as she stared at the perfectly groomed woman in front of her. She could be any age from thirty-five to fifty. It was hard to tell.

'This is Lorna Morgan, the girl I was telling you about, Sandra,' Alanna said breezily.

'Good to meet you.' Sandra held out her hand and gave Lorna a firm handshake. She had a soft, beautifully modulated voice. She was everything Lorna aspired to be, if just a little too old.

'I've read your CV, it's fine. You've done front-line reception, which is what you'll be doing here for the six months Alanna is away. I expect you to keep on top of your in-tray. Be polite at all times to callers and clients. You will after all be the first interface callers will have with Sandra Winston & Associates. First impressions are lasting impressions. But I'm sure I don't have to tell you that, having worked in the hotel trade. I may have to call on you to run errands occasionally. And I like my coffee black, first thing. You know your way around Midtown and Uptown?' Sandra arched a perfectly shaped eyebrow that caused not a wrinkle on her smooth, botoxed forehead.

'Oh yes, I spend a lot of my free time shopping,' Lorna assured her.

'Perfect! I think we'll work extremely well together. Please come in for at least half a day so that Alanna can familiarize you with the office.' Sandra stood up, indicating that the interview was over.

'Whew,' Lorna exhaled when Alanna had closed the door behind them.

'She's totally hot.' Alanna grinned. 'But it's a good position and you meet lots of people. I enjoy it. Why don't you call around to my building after work? I'll be there from seven on. I can tell you more about the job and you can see if you like where I live,' the other girl suggested.

'Sounds good to me.' Lorna took the address that Alanna had written and left the office walking on air. Standing in the elevator as it sped silently from the fiftieth floor, Lorna looked in the mirror and smiled. At last it was starting to happen. Who knew who she'd meet during her sojourn at Sandra Winston & Associates? Now she really had something to boast about.

She wasn't too sure if she'd be boasting about the apartment, she thought with a sinking heart when, several hours later, she knocked on the door of Apt 1C and felt the oven blast of heat as Alanna unfastened what sounded like a multitude of locks before opening the door to the small, cramped studio apartment that looked out on to a fire escape and the wall of an adjoining apartment block.

'Vista's not to die for,' Alanna admitted as she offered Lorna a beer, 'but there's plenty of restaurants and shops around. Little India is just a few blocks away between First and Second. Great little restaurants, very cheap to eat out. There's lots of clubs and cafés, I'll leave you a list of must-sees!'

Lorna gazed around at the studio, which was about as big as the bedroom she'd shared with Heather so long ago in Dublin. The house in Yonkers was a palace in comparison.

A sofa-bed took up the wall opposite the two sash windows. A built-in shelf space contained a TV and stereo unit. An armchair with a multi-patterned throw stood in front of an unsightly radiator. A small table and two chairs completed the furniture. The room was painted in a soothing pale green and white, its only saving grace.

A closet filled the wall at the end of the room,

off which two doors led to a tiny kitchenette with a cooker, sink, small fridge-freezer and microwave. The other door led to the toilet and shower.

'The john's a bit noisy when you flush, so if I have to go at night I don't bother flushing. You'd be awake for an hour listening to the cistern filling up,' Alanna advised.

Lorna tried to quell her sense of disappointment. She'd been expecting a roomy loft, or an elegant brownstone. This poky little kip was from a different era, and the rent was not insubstantial, but this was Manhattan, she admitted. Living space did not come cheap. Unfortunately. If she was ever going to get the apartment on Park, she had to make a start somewhere. If Neil saw this, her image would be totally blown, she thought wryly as Alanna offered her another beer and began to tell her what would be expected of her as PA to the perfect Sandra Winston.

Jane Morgan kissed her elderly mother goodbye and hurried out of the nursing-home. She hated visiting. When her mother's health had started to deteriorate two years ago, Anne had offered to take her to live in her home and Jane had been mightily relieved. She was not good with sick people. They upset her, made her feel fearful about what might happen to her in the future. Her sister was much better at dealing with things like that. Their mother, however, had a streak of independence that was unquenchable, even in her eighties.

'I'll be a burden to no one. I'm going to sell the house and move into that Tranquillity House

565

nursing-home,' she declared. Jane thought it was a marvellous idea. Anne had been horrified.

'We're not putting Mum into a home,' she fumed.

'It's what she wants and that's what's important,' Jane said firmly, and her sister couldn't argue the point. The care in the nursing-home was excellent and their mother settled in well; nevertheless Jane disliked visiting, especially as her mother had become frailer and a little senile. It was distressing when she didn't know her, and whereas Anne had great patience with her, Jane found herself becoming irritable.

She hurried down the steps of the nursing-home to where her husband was waiting to drive her to the airport. She couldn't wait to get to New York. Lorna had been bubbling with excitement during her last phone call. Telling her mother about a new job and a new apartment that were on the cards. It did Jane good to hear her. She wanted her daughter to be happy. At least if she was happy it would help Jane smother the guilt she carried around with her after her daughter's traumatic outburst at Christmas. If only Lorna could find the right man and settle down it would be almost perfect.

'How was Mother?' Gerard asked as they set off towards the capital.

'Dozing. I don't know if she even knew I was there.' Jane sighed.

'Well, she's not in any pain. She's warm and comfortable and well looked after, so try not to be upset,' her husband advised.

'Thank you, Gerard,' she said more warmly than

usual, appreciating yet again that while her husband might not be the most ambitious, successful man in the world, he had a good heart.

They didn't talk much, as was their wont, but as he stood with her at the check-in he smiled at her and said kindly, 'Don't be afraid to use the credit card. I've upped the limit to ten thousand Euro so don't be stuck.'

'Don't encourage me,' Jane warned as she raised her face to his and kissed him lightly on the cheek. 'Thank you for the chance of this holiday with Lorna, Gerard. I appreciate it.'

'A bit of daughter/mother bonding is always a good thing, but try to get her to think about coming home in May. She needs to set herself up in a career here, buy a house, establish roots.'

'She's young yet, Gerard. Let her get it out of her system,' Jane argued.

'She'll be an illegal, I worry about that. If anything happens to her she won't be able to pay for healthcare.'

'I'll talk to her,' his wife promised as she took her boarding card from the clerk and with huge relief waved her husband goodbye before setting out, alone, on her much longed-for holiday.

'And that's Jackie's apartment block, Mum,' Lorna pointed out the green canopied entrance to 1040 Fifth Avenue. 'Isn't it magnificent? Look at the length of the canopy, it's longer than a limo.'

'It's so elegant,' Jane murmured, staring with unashamed curiosity at the place where one of the greatest icons of the twentieth century had lived.

'Look at the views she had over Central Park, and how near she was to all the shops that matter.' Lorna was in her element in her spiritual home of the Upper East Side. It was the third day of her mother's visit and they were about to have lunch in the Metropolitan Museum and then do a tour of it. Museums weren't normally Lorna's bag, but the Met was different and she knew her mother would enjoy its bright, airy, impossibly stylish ambience.

Jane had taken to New York like a duck to water and already her hotel room was filled with designer bags full of joyfully purchased goodies. It was the first time Lorna had ever spent time with her mother and to her surprise she was enjoying the experience. She'd gone out to JFK to meet her and her heart had lifted when she saw her elegant mother emerge into arrivals, her face lighting up with pleasure when she'd seen Lorna. They'd even hugged briefly.

It helped of course that they both enjoyed and shared a taste for the fine things in life. Jane thought Le Parker Meridian lived up perfectly to its 'Uptown But Not Uptight' motto. She was like a child in Aladdin's cave as they plundered the stores on Fifth Avenue, and Lorna began to realize that her mother had never done the kind of things she took so much for granted. She'd never gone on holidays with girlfriends, never shared a flat, never gone clubbing and most probably never had sex before marriage. She'd gone from her parents' house to marriage and motherhood, and while she had travelled with Gerard, she'd never done the girly things she was now doing with Lorna. They'd even got tipsy on champagne in Jack's the previous evening after enjoying a delicious room-service dinner, so exhausted were they after a day of serious shopping that their swollen feet would take them no further.

When they got back to their hotel room later that evening, after their cultural afternoon, the flashing light on the phone caught Lorna's eye. 'There's a message, Mum, you'd better check it out,' she said as she rooted around in the mini bar for some still water.

She heard her mother lift the phone, and then give a little gasp. 'Oh no,' she muttered. 'Oh no.'

'What is it?' Lorna jumped to her feet and hurried over to where her mother was standing. 'Mum, what is it?' she repeated. Jane raised a trembling hand to her mouth.

'It's Mummy, she died an hour ago. We've got to go home!'

46

Heather knelt beside her grandmother's bed, along with the rest of her family, and looked at her face, which held a peaceful smile as though some secret knowledge had been granted to her and all life's cares and worries had been wiped away.

She'd miss her gran, who had always had time to listen and advise, up until the last year when she'd grown frail and forgetful. Heather knew she'd been her gran's favourite. When she'd made her will she'd told Heather she'd left her the cottage by the lake. Ruth had been left a site, and Lorna and the boys a sum of money from the sale of land. But Martha had wanted Heather to keep the cottage and live in it. She knew her granddaughter loved the lake.

If Gran had known about Neil she'd have been urging her to get out there and get another man. 'Best way to get over a man is to find another,' she'd say.

'You help me find my new man, Gran,' Heather whispered.

'*You've found him!*' Heather looked up, startled. Had someone spoken? No! no, she was imagining things, but for one second as clear as anything she was sure a voice had told her she'd found a man.

Pondering on men who might be, or not be, in her life, she wondered if Neil would come to the funeral. He didn't know her grandmother so it was hardly likely. An unwelcome thought struck her. Perhaps he'd come to offer support to Lorna.

Oh no! That would be very, very difficult. Seeing them together would be the pits. Hell, seeing Lorna on her own would be the pits. It was bad enough that they were burying her beloved grandmother without having to deal with all the Lorna and Neil stuff. Would Lorna swan around trying to rub her nose in it? Bet she would. Would Heather have the longed-for dismissive conversation where she told her man-stealing cousin exactly what she thought of her? She'd practised that speech so many times in her head, did she want to get the chance to use it? Her heart sank at the prospect. It seemed so horrible and petty to be thinking of spite and revenge in front of her grandmother's corpse. Heather suddenly felt ashamed and very much alone.

Ruth drove herself and Heather home from the hospital. As sad as her twin was at this moment, she was looking so much better than the last time she'd stayed with her in Dublin, Ruth thought approvingly. It was a real stroke of luck that she'd got that job in Carleton's. It suited her perfectly, having gained such experience in Dublin. She was talking about buying a place of her own. That was great! Positive stuff. She wasn't looking for a man to provide for her and that was good, Ruth reflected. Although it would be nice for her sister to have a decent man in her life. It was so enriching. She smiled thinking of Peter. He would be coming for the removal later; it would be a solace of sorts to have the comfort of him.

Their Aunt Jane was trying to get a flight home from New York. It was unfortunate that her holiday had had to be cut short. Ruth wasn't sure if Lorna was accompanying her. She sincerely hoped that she wasn't. She was the last person Heather needed to see. But if she did appear, Ruth knew one thing: Lorna Morgan was going to be a very, very sorry young lady, once she'd dealt with her.

'What removal do you want to go to?' Oliver tried to keep the irritation out of his voice. It seemed as though half the parish was dying lately. Cora was always ringing him to bring her to this funeral or that.

'Martha Jackson's. She lived in that little cottage just beyond Rooks Point on the lake.'

'Oh, right.' Oliver pretended to know who she was talking about. He couldn't remember a Martha Jackson, but then his mother had so many friends and acquaintances. He had a vague recollection of the cottage though. A little stone one with a wild, overgrown garden.

'What time is it at?' He glanced at his watch and saw that he was running late.

'Six sharp, pick me up at twenty to. I don't want to be late for the hearse like we were for poor Annie Clarke's. I was mortified,' Cora ordered.

'Yes, Ma, twenty to six it is. Have to run, 'bye.' He put his phone into his shirt pocket, mentally trying to rearrange the rest of his day to suit his mother's desire to attend yet another funeral in the county.

The Aer Lingus airbus roared down the runway at JFK, lifted its immense bulk into the sky and headed for home. *Oh, Gran. Why did you have to die right now?* Lorna whinged silently, horrified to find herself sitting in a plane flying home to Ireland. Only that she knew her mother would be extremely hurt if she didn't attend, she would have stayed put. She'd been very fond of her gran, of course, but she was gone now and she wouldn't know who was at her funeral or not.

She was literally going to have two days to attend her grandmother's funeral and then it was straight back to New York to move out of the house in Yonkers and start her new life in Sandra Winston's and the East Village. It was just as well it had happened now, if her grandmother had died the following week her new job would be up the Swannee.

A thought struck her and her heart sank to her toes. She was going to have to face Heather at the funeral, and even *worse*, that virago, Ruth. Ruth would never let her get away with what she'd done to Heather. She was always interfering, fighting her twin's battles. Would she be crass enough to have a go at her at their gran's funeral? Knowing Ruth, the answer was yes. Lorna felt tension twist around her intestines like a snake.

'Er . . . Mum have you been talking to Anne or Heather lately?' She turned to her mother, who was gazing regretfully at the faint, hazy, unmistakable outline of Manhattan in the distance as JFK faded away beneath them as they gained altitude.

'No, funnily enough, I haven't. I saw her at Mass a couple of weeks ago but she was in an awful hurry and didn't stop to talk. I left a message on her answering machine to say I was going to New York. I thought she'd phone me back but she didn't. She's always so busy with parish activities. I'd hate her life,' Jane admitted.

'And Heather?' Lorna tried to keep her tone casual.

'Don't you keep in touch? I thought you and she were all sorted?' Jane looked at her in surprise.

'Em . . . we don't, no. Mum, I should tell you something.' She took a deep breath. 'Heather won't be speaking to me because I had a bit of a fling with her boyfriend and she found out about it.' There, it was said. She waited for her mother's censure.

'Ah, *Lorna!* What on earth did you do that for?' Jane frowned. Had her daughter no cop on? There were some things you just did not do. Jane sometimes feared for Lorna. She had no loyalty to anyone but herself.

'Don't ask me,' Lorna said sulkily. 'It happened. It was one of those things.'

'But not with your cousin's boyfriend. Heather's always been very good to you. There *are* boundaries, Lorna. You can't be totally selfish for the rest of your life.'

'I was only looking for the same thing as you were when you slept with that man,' Lorna retorted, and immediately felt regret for her horrible barb when she saw the flush rise to her mother's cheeks.

'Lorna! That was uncalled for,' Jane said quietly.

'Oh, Mum, I'm *sorry*. I was only trying to explain,' Lorna apologized hastily. 'I don't know what comes over me. I think I've found what I'm looking for and then it just crumbles away. Don't be cross,' she wheedled.

'I'm not. I just worry about you,' Jane sighed.

'Well, don't. I'm going back to a job that's going to be a real stepping-stone for me and I'm very happy about it. And Mum, please don't ever tell anyone that I was waitressing, sure you won't?'

'Of course I won't,' Jane exclaimed, understanding her daughter perfectly on that score. 'That's why Anne was avoiding me? As if it were my fault,' she added indignantly. 'Is Heather still working for him?'

'I don't think so. Will they have to have a post-mortem for Gran?' Her daughter changed the subject.

Jane shook her head. 'No, not at her age and with her history of heart trouble. I was talking to your dad. He's arranged the funeral with Anne. Solicitors are good at things like that. Gerard is always very good in a crisis.' She shook her head at her daughter. 'Try to stay out of Anne and Heather's way,' she suggested, as the air hostess came down the aisle with the drinks trolley.

That injunction proved to be easier said than

done. When they went to the funeral parlour later in the morning after arriving home, the first people they saw coming out were Anne and Ruth. Lorna nearly puked. Her cousin's lips tightened and her eyes flashed contempt, but she said nothing and turned away from Lorna as though she had the plague.

Anne ignored her niece completely as she went to kiss her sister.

'Are you all right, Jane?' she asked. 'It must have been awful to get that news so far away from home.'

'I'm a bit shocked and jet-lagged. I wasn't expecting Mummy to go,' Jane murmured, subdued.

'No. It was sudden, she went in her sleep. I'm glad she didn't suffer.' Anne started to cry and Jane put an awkward arm around her. 'She looks very peaceful, Jane, would you like me to go in with you?'

'Please, Anne, would you?' she said gratefully. 'I'm a bit apprehensive. I'm not great at things like this.' She looked troubled and very tired.

'Mummy looks like she's asleep, she's very peaceful,' Anne comforted, putting her arm around her sister's shoulders. They walked back into the funeral parlour and Lorna, who had no desire to see her grandmother's dead body, but was anxious to get away from her cousin, made to follow. But not fast enough.

'Just a minute, you little slag,' Ruth hissed.

'Fuck off, Ruth,' Lorna hissed back. 'Show a bit of respect.'

'Do you hear who's talking about respect, you

little hypocrite. What kind of a bitch goes off with another girl's bloke, especially when that girl is the cousin you've grown up with and shared a flat with? You are the pits, Lorna Morgan. You're scum.' Ruth then turned and deliberately spat at her. Lorna was faint with horror.

'You spat at me?' She couldn't believe it. 'You dirty wagon. You *spat* at me!'

'If we weren't outside a funeral parlour and *I* wasn't mourning my grandmother,' the emphasis on the 'I' was unmistakable, 'believe me, Lorna, I'd *thump* you because you need a good thumping, you spiteful, two-faced little cow.' Ruth was puce with fury and Lorna felt a twinge of apprehension as she hastily stepped backwards. She wouldn't put it past her cousin to sock her one on the jaw.

'One good thing,' Ruth threw over her shoulder. 'At least Heather has finally seen you in your true colours. I've been trying to tell her what a cow you were for years. At last the penny's dropped and she'll never have anything to do with you again. You'll have to find someone else to use!'

She disappeared through the doors of the funeral parlour, leaving Lorna feeling extremely shaken. The verbal attack, the spitting, the names were appalling. She had never felt such naked aggression directed towards her in her life, and it rattled her. But for one brief, fleeting moment she envied Heather for having such a champion. There was no one in her life who cared as much about her. Her brothers were a dead loss in that regard. Feeling very forlorn and weary, Lorna sat on the steps of the funeral parlour, rested her head on her knees and cried.

When her mother came out, red-eyed and weepy, she was sitting in the car. They drove home in silence and went to bed exhausted. Lorna was asleep as soon as her head hit the pillow.

Neil read the funeral notice in the paper and his mouth tightened into a very thin line. Lorna Morgan would surely be at her grandmother's funeral. Not even she would be self-centred enough to miss it. He flung the paper on to his desk and stared out at the forecourt.

This might be his only chance ever to get to talk to her again. To tell her what he thought of her. His face darkened with fury. The longer it lasted that she hadn't contacted him, the more outraged and indignant he'd become. What made a woman treat a man with such disrespect? Did she really think him of so little consequence? She'd always looked down her pert little nose at him, now she was just rubbing *his* nose in it. What made her feel she could use him like that and get away with it? The more he thought about it the angrier he got. He was eaten up by his anger. It was all-consuming. He was going to have it out with her come hell or high water, and if the only way to do that was at her grandmother's funeral, so be it.

Lorna woke up around three thirty, woolly-headed and jet-lagged. She had a shower and spent half an hour trying on various combinations of clothes to see which would make the biggest I'm-a-New-

York-Success statement. There were usually more people at the removal ceremony than at the funeral, she figured. This evening was the evening for the biggest impact! After many changes and discarding this and that, Lorna finally decided on her DKNY little black number with a short black cardigan and a single string of pearls à la Sandra Winston. She pulled her hair back off her face and applied her make-up with extra care. Even if she said it herself, she had never looked better, she thought with satisfaction. Let Kilronan look on and be impressed as hell. To add to her look, she slipped on a pair of dark glasses. Very Princess Di, Jackie O, Catherine Zeta Jones, she approved, studying her reflection in the mirror.

It was a shock to see Heather at the funeral parlour, weeping, red-eyed and red-nosed, as they knelt to pray for their late grandmother. Her cousin was wearing a dark navy suit and her hair was cut in a shorter, sharper style. It quite suited her, she thought with a little jolt. For one brief moment Heather looked in Lorna's direction, a dismissive, disinterested look that bugged Lorna by its apparent indifference, then she picked up a prayer sheet and resolutely began to answer the prayers.

Lorna felt a flicker of shame.

All's fair in Love and War.

But you didn't love him and she did.

More idiot she.

I did her a favour.

Oh, stop it. Can't do anything about it now.

The internal dialogue went on and on, until with

relief they began to file out after the coffin to begin their journey to the church.

Lorna quite enjoyed the drive to the church in the funeral limo. It added to her sense of importance and she was definitely dressed for a limo ride, she reflected, as the car drove into the church grounds thronged with friends and neighbours. She climbed elegantly out of the limo making sure to show a discreet flash of toned, tanned thigh. She'd had a tanning spray job done the evening she'd found out that she had to come home – it had cost a fortune but it looked so real and so golden it was worth every cent. She looked as if she'd just come back from the Caribbean.

She saw Oliver Flynn's tall form in the middle of the crowd and remembered her conversation with Neil about his eligibility, now that he and his wife had separated. He was an extremely good-looking man, she decided. A real man, who didn't give a hoot what people thought of him. Not like Neil, to whom image was everything.

She wondered would he be here. She'd just play it very cool and ice-queeny, she decided. After all, she was flying back to NY the day after next and as she was in mourning she couldn't be going out socializing. That's what she'd tell him anyway, she determined as she followed her grandmother's coffin up the aisle, her impossibly high heels making a very satisfying click-clack as she went.

It was a little awkward at the top of the church. The front pew held her parents, her aunt and uncle, her grandmother's two younger sisters and their husbands. Grandchildren had to sit in the row behind. Lorna grabbed her two brothers and whispered, 'Let me sit between you,' so that she didn't have to sit near her twin cousins who were also in the same row.

Strangely, when the choir sang 'Be Not Afraid', she remembered how as a child her grandmother would take her to tea in the Lake View, before it had been refurbished, when waitresses in black dresses and little white aprons and caps would serve them beautiful scones with jam and cream. She'd always felt very important sitting beside her grandmother, sipping tea out of fine china cups. A lump rose in her throat and to her horror she started to cry. If she wasn't careful her make-up would be ruined. She could see her mother silently crying in front of her and that made her feel worse. Poor Jane had been having such a carefree time in New York and it had been cut short so abruptly. Once Lorna started working for SW, as she had started privately calling her new boss, she'd never have any time off for the next six months. Even if Jane did come back out, she would only be able to spend evenings and a weekend with her. Life was mean sometimes, she thought glumly as she slanted a glance through her glasses and saw both Ruth and Heather in tears. Once again a wave of loneliness enveloped her and she cursed herself for her weakness.

It took a good thirty minutes for everyone to come up and offer their condolences, and Lorna was rigid with tension wondering would Neil appear. She breathed a sigh of relief when it was done. Why would Neil come anyway? He didn't know her grandmother after all.

She emerged into the bright sunlight, glad to be out of the church. It was eerie to think that her grandmother was in the coffin at the foot of the altar. Little knots of people stood chatting in the warmth of the evening sun, and she saw Oliver Flynn lope over towards Heather. Why he should go to her first to offer condolences she had no idea, she thought sniffily. After all, she had been a full guest at his wedding. Heather had only made the afters. She watched them talking and smiling at each other. They seemed very comfortable in each other's company, she thought enviously, wishing she had someone to share the sadness of her grandmother's funeral with.

'Well, Lorna! Dropped any *hot* potatoes lately?' Neil suddenly appeared in front of her and she nearly jumped out of her skin.

'Don't be tacky,' she whispered. 'This isn't the time or the place.'

'Really,' Neil derided. 'And when is there a time and a place? You made a fool out of me, Lorna Morgan.' His voice was rising, his face red with suppressed fury.

'Shut up, Neil,' she hissed, aware that people, and especially Heather and Oliver, were looking in their direction, surprise written all over their faces.

'You let me spend a fortune on yo—'

'Oh, get over yourself, Neil,' she snapped, annoyed that he would doorstep her at her grandmother's funeral. No class. 'If you want to play with the big boys act like one of them and stop whingeing and moaning every time you use your credit card. Grow up and cop on.'

'You *bitch!!*' he roared. 'You selfish little user, you had no feelings for me and yet you slept with me and let me spend a fortune on you. You know what that makes *YOU*?'

'How *dare* you!' Lorna, incensed, raised her hand and slapped Neil hard across the cheek, leaving a stark red imprint.

Neil's eyes glittered and the veins in his neck bulged, but the next moment Anne Williams, outraged at the carry-on at her mother's funeral, marched over and said icily, 'How *dare* you, the pair of you. If you want to behave like alley-cats don't do it at my mother's funeral. Get out of my sight, you,' she said to Lorna. 'And as for you, Neil Brennan! You and she are well matched. Sly, slithery worms the pair of you. Get out of here and show some respect for the dead.'

Furious, mortified, Neil walked out of the church grounds knowing that he'd be the talk of the town tomorrow and, even worse, knowing that his image as a sophisticated, successful businessman had just been shot to hell.

Scarlet-cheeked that so many neighbours had witnessed her public humiliation, Lorna slipped into the black limo and scowled at the two smirking faces of her brothers. She could see Heather and Oliver laughing, looking towards the limo. They were laughing at *her*. The cheek of them! How dare they. She, who had come back home intent on making a dazzling impression, was the laughing stock of the town. It was too much to bear, especially when her father got into the car and gave her an uncharacteristically cold, unfriendly look and said icily, 'I think you have some explaining to do, Lorna.'

Her sophisticated façade dissolved in an instant. She couldn't call it back. Sitting in front of her flint-eyed father, she felt about seven years old. She hated Kilronan and everyone in it, but most of all right now she hated Heather and Oliver Flynn.

'Well, all doesn't look well in Love's Happy Garden,' Oliver whispered to Heather from where they'd been observing the fracas that had just taken place. 'I know this isn't the place for it, but I bet that gave you some amount of satisfaction.' His eyes twinkled down at her.

Heather giggled, half with shock, half with amusement. Oliver was right. To see Lorna engage in a slanging match, and then to see Neil get his face slapped, had been deeply, deeply satisfying. And she didn't mind admitting it to Oliver – after all, he would understand it more than most.

It was obvious they were finished. She didn't care who Neil saw now. And then for Anne to interfere and send Lorna off to her limo with her tail between her legs had been almost too good. Both Ruth and her mother had had a go at Lorna. They must think she was an awful wimp not to be able to stand up for herself. But when she'd seen Lorna in the funeral parlour earlier, all dolled up like a dog's dinner, looking like someone out of a cheap TV soap, she'd thought how pathetic her cousin was and remembered Anne Jensen saying that she was jealous of all Heather had in her life.

All Lorna had were her posh frocks and silly notions. Heather couldn't even be bothered engaging with her. What was the point? She was back on track again, she had a great new job with a bright future ahead of her and the right man on the periphery of her life, or so she'd been told.

'Will you take him back if he comes running?' Oliver was curious. His mother was standing among a group of pensioners, in her element, so he had time to stop and chat for a while.

'Will I take him back? Are you mad, Oliver? What would I want him for?'

'But didn't you love him?' he probed.

Heather frowned. 'Oh, Oliver. I've been asking myself that question over and over. I thought I did. But I mustn't have loved him enough. Maybe I was in love with the idea of being in love. I don't know. If I'd really loved him I'm sure I'd want him back but I don't. I think my pride was hurt, more than my heart. That's a sad admission to make, isn't it?'

'No, not at all. It's an honest one. So is this the end of the moping?' he teased.

'Oliver Flynn, stop teasing me at my grand-mother's funeral.' She couldn't help smiling.

'Sorry, I thought you might have been a bit upset by the drama.'

'Childish and mean-spirited though it is, as you can see I enjoyed it,' she said drily. 'But then again I'm only human. It was great to see them at each other's throats. When you've been the one who's been dumped for someone else, you never want the dumper to be happy with that someone else. It's a woman thing,' she explained with heartfelt honesty.

'God preserve me from "the woman thing"! I don't understand you creatures at all.'

'Oh, I think you understand us more than you let on,' Heather said astutely. 'Will I make a date with you for the psychic?'

'You will in your hat, Heather Williams. You're the one who's teasing me now. I'd better get this mother of mine home. I'm sorry about your grandmother, but I'm glad that you gained some satisfaction at least, on the broken heart front.' Oliver smiled down at her.

'I'm glad *you* gained some amusement from it all. It was better than a TV soap,' she admitted ruefully. 'Don't forget that couple from Dublin want to have one last look on Friday, before putting in a final offer. Told you we'd get a better offer than the asking price.'

'Yes, little Miss-Know-All. I haven't forgotten. And I'll be on my best behaviour, not a beer can or brandy bottle in sight.'

'Friday should see the end of it. I'll bring you for a drink to celebrate,' Heather declared. 'I suppose I should go and thank people for coming.'

'You should, you're being very remiss,' Oliver said gravely. 'I'll look forward to the drink. See you.'

'See you, Oliver.' She smiled as he strode off, noting that he had gone to the trouble to put on a smart grey suit and tie out of respect for the dead. It looked good on him too, she thought admiringly, before turning to go and comfort her grandmother's best friend who was standing quietly crying at the church door.

It so happened that by chance both she and

Lorna arrived at the church together the following morning.

'Let's hope you can remember this is a funeral and not a two-bit soap opera,' Heather drawled sarcastically, feeling immensely superior to her cousin for once in her life. After yesterday's episode, Lorna had lost all credibility.

'You can have Neil Brennan back, I'm finished with him,' Lorna retaliated contemptuously.

'Thanks, Lorna. I don't want your leavings. Being with Neil showed me exactly what I don't need in a man. In fact, I don't need a man at all.' Heather smiled sweetly.

'It didn't look like that when you were giggling like a schoolgirl with Oliver Flynn,' Lorna retorted, eyes flashing with temper.

'You know, Lorna, there's something you don't realize, and I feel sorry for you because of it. Men and women can actually be friends. It's not *always* a drama. Oliver and I have become good mates, really good mates. We do after all have something in common. Both of us have endured a parting of the ways, which wasn't of our choosing. But we're doing fine. We talk about anything and everything. And you know something? I *value* his friendship. And you know something else? There is no man or even woman in your life that you can truly say that you're a friend to, and I feel sorry for you for that. Grow up and get a life, Lorna, or you'll end up a sad, sorry, lonely old woman.'

Heather swept into the church on an absolute high. Never again would she feel inferior to her cousin. It was one of the best moments of her life and she couldn't wait to tell Oliver. She'd meant it when she'd told Lorna that she really liked him. It was always a pleasure to see him. She hadn't fibbed when she'd said that she could talk to Oliver about anything. It was true. And he clearly felt just as relaxed with her, which was nice. Her jaw dropped.

Good God! The man on the periphery.

Oliver Flynn.

It couldn't be. Or could it?

Why not? He was one of the nicest men she'd ever met. They got on like a house on fire. He was dead easy to talk to. He seemed to like her. Anne Jensen had said there'd be a great friendship first before the relationship turned intimate. And then she remembered. He couldn't father children.

If she fell in love with Oliver and he with her they'd be childless. Would she mind?

Calm down, she ordered as she walked slowly up the aisle. Was she being totally ridiculous and over-imaginative thinking that any man that came into her sphere could be the one? Was she just looking for someone on the rebound? Feeling more confused than she'd ever been in her life, she touched the gleaming wood on her grandmother's coffin as she slipped into her seat.

'My God, Gran,' she whispered. 'Is it Oliver?'

A shaft of sunlight burst through the stained-glass window, illuminating the altar and the coffin, the choir began to sing 'I Will Raise You Up on Eagle's Wings' and the soughing of the wind through the conifers outside seemed to whisper: '*Yeessss*.'

47

Noreen woke from her sleep with a start. It was almost dawn. A strange unfamiliar sensation enveloped her and then as clear as anything she felt the little fluttery movements in her tummy. Joy leapt in her as her hand slid down to the smooth curve of her lightly rippling belly. Her children were kicking in her womb. How magical.

How good that sounded. Her children.

'Hello, my darlings,' she murmured. 'How are you today? I wish it was time for you to come out so I could see you. Are you two little girls or two little boys or a girl and a boy? I'm doing up a lovely nursery for you. Uncle Oliver told me that the house is being sold today so I'm bringing over some of the furniture I had at home and our new home will be very comfortable.'

She lay serenely against her pillows. Oliver had phoned to say that the house was almost sold and she should make a list of what she wanted from it so that he could ship it over to her. He sounded much more like his old self, brisk, businesslike, organized. That was good, she thought gratefully. The quiet, subdued, depressed Oliver was so unlike his true nature. *God, please send a good and loving woman into Oliver's life*, she prayed. She didn't like to think of him being alone. She had Kay and Rajiv and she'd have her twins to devote herself to. Oliver was the only thing she had left to feel guilty about. If Oliver was sorted, everything would be fine.

Neil Brennan lay tossing and turning in bed. He hated Lorna Morgan. She'd ruined his life, the she-witch. The whole of Kilronan would be laughing at him. Heather and Oliver Flynn had been sniggering at him when Heather's mother had ordered him out of the church grounds. His accountant had had a Mickey fit when he'd studied the New York Visa bill. Neil was seriously up to his ears in debt. He was going to have to knuckle down and get the show on the road again. But somehow he didn't feel like getting up for work and getting out there and competing. He'd lost his edge. All he could think about was that sly, freeloading cow and how she'd ripped him off.

Well, he *would* get off his ass and get out to work, he decided grimly. He was going to become so fucking rich, she'd cry every time she heard his name mentioned. Because she could have had it all and she'd blown her chance. He'd show her. By God, he'd show Lorna Morgan just what she'd turned her back on, Neil vowed.

But as soon as he got to the office he was going to make one very important phone call. One person could get him back on track workwise. That would be the start of it.

Lorna didn't know what she felt as flight EI 105 took off from Dublin and headed west towards Shannon. Her mother had brought her to the airport and hugged her tightly. The only good thing to come out of all this was that she'd grown a lot closer to Jane, she thought despondently as she unbuckled her seatbelt. Her father was hardly talking to her, so disgusted was he at her taking Neil away from Heather, and Heather . . . Lorna cringed. Her cousin really despised her and pitied her. That was skanky. How dare she talk to her the way she had at the funeral? She *did* have friends, she assured herself. Carina was a friend. Suzie, her housemate in Yonkers, was a friend. Weren't they? Lorna's heart sank to rock-bottom. Heather was right. She had no one. Carina and Suzie weren't bosom pals that you could share anything with, the way she'd shared with Heather.

Oliver and Heather had looked so . . . so *comfortable* together. There was no one now that she was comfortable with. No one she could truly be herself with. No one who knew what was behind the façade. Once she got back to New York the mask would have to go on again, and this time it all seemed like a bit of an effort. Would she have the energy to sustain it? she wondered dully, accepting a small bottle of red wine from the air hostess. Imagine arriving in New York with no one to meet her and then having to move by herself. Carina and Suzie would probably be off hill-walking in the Catskills if they weren't working. They had a great social life with lots of friends. Lorna's policy of not mixing with the Irish, while she was on the hunt for Mr Upper East Side, had ensured that she had no male friends to lug black sacks of possessions from Yonkers to the East Village. She'd probably have to do it all by herself.

Feeling lonelier than she'd ever felt in her life, Lorna sipped her red wine and wondered how she could have got it all so terribly wrong.

Heather took extra pains to look her best for the final viewing at Oliver's today. She applied a light frosting of pink lipstick and then sprayed herself lightly with White Linen. She felt a little nervous. After her realization at her grandmother's funeral the previous day that Oliver could be the one, she'd lain awake imagining scenarios of how they would fall into each other's arms and confess their love to each other. It felt very right, somehow. These past few weeks getting to know him had lifted her out of her depression. But then she'd wonder if Oliver viewed her in the same light as she was starting to view him. He'd never flirted with her or made any attempt to go beyond the teasing, friendly, easygoing relationship that had developed between them. Maybe he just didn't fancy her either, she fretted. His wife had been very slim and tall, not on the short, curvy side like Heather. Up and down her emotions seesawed as she pondered the unknowable.

And just say she was the one, what about the children thing? She was young enough now, but might she feel desperately unfulfilled in her midthirties when she hadn't become a mother? It wasn't that she was particularly maternal, she decided. She didn't have much to do with children and what you didn't have you didn't miss. At least she could make a decision based on knowledge. Noreen hadn't had that option, the poor thing.

Was she mad or what? Oliver probably never gave her a thought when she wasn't with him.

Heather stared at her reflection in the mirror, noting how her new shorter layered look highlighted the copper glints in her chestnut hair and made her hazel eyes seem wider. She'd lost a few pounds too, she noted, pleased with the reappearance of cheekbones, on to which she brushed some blusher to add emphasis. She wanted him to fancy her. Somehow it seemed terribly important now.

'That hairstyle really suits you,' Lia complimented when she walked back into the office to get her briefcase.

'Thanks, Lia. I'd had the bob for yonks. It's nice to try something different.' Heather smiled at her colleague. Lia was always chatty and good-humoured. The atmosphere in the office was so different from that awful place she'd worked in in Dublin. She looked forward to coming to work every morning. The phone rang. Lia answered it.

'It's for you. I just want to pop into the chemist for a packet of Feminax, I'm in bits,' she grimaced.

'Fine,' Heather said as she picked up the phone. 'Hello?'

'Heather, hi,' a familiar voice said. Heather's eyes widened in recognition.

'Neil, can I help you?' she said coolly.

'Well, I hope so, Heather. I've a proposition to

put to you. Whatever you're getting in Carleton's I'll pay you fifty Euro a week more if you'll come back and run the office for me. All business and above board – you probably wouldn't want to get back with me again,' he said in a 'poor me' sort of voice.

'You can say that again, Neil. You're the last person I'd want to get back with if I was to be on my own until the day I die—'

'OK, OK, I appreciate that, but I'm offering you a good job. I'll throw in a car as well.' He sounded desperate.

'No thanks. Not interested. 'Bye,' Heather said crisply and hung up. What an idiot, she thought, smiling. He hadn't got a clue. But his phone call made her feel good all the same. It gave her a nice, satisfying sense of closure, just like she'd had with Lorna yesterday.

Lia arrived back, munching on a bar of chocolate. 'PMT,' she explained, offering Heather a couple of squares.

'No thanks. I'm on a diet,' Heather said cheerily. Things were really going good so far today – it was unusual for her not to be tempted to eat chocolate. 'I'm off to Oliver Flynn's for that last viewing, see you later for the Fennelly auction.' Taking a deep breath, Heather set off with a tingle of anticipation, which was completely dashed when she arrived at Oliver's to find that he wasn't there. She let herself in feeling utterly disappointed. There was no need for him to be at the viewing, but from the way he'd been talking at the funeral she'd felt he was going to be there.

'See! He doesn't fancy you!' she muttered as she plumped up the cushions on the sofa and tweaked the curtains to hang perfectly from their tiebacks.

Oliver stood in a florist's in Navan while the assistant put the finishing touches to the bouquet he'd just purchased. He'd gone to Navan because if he'd bought flowers in Butler's in Kilronan, the whole town would have known about it. He felt nervous. He'd never done such an impulsive thing before where women were concerned but he wanted to thank Heather for all the effort she'd put into selling the house and also because she'd been so completely understanding about the time he'd gone on the batter. He smiled thinking of her. Heather was great fun, he thought warmly. He liked talking to her, she had an unusual slant on life that was refreshing. He'd been really impressed by how honest she'd been with him the day Neil Brennan and Lorna Morgan had had their bust-up outside the church. She'd openly admitted that she'd enjoyed it and was glad they were going their separate ways. She'd been honest enough to admit also that it might have been her pride more than her heart that was affected. If he was honest with himself there was a touch of that in how he felt about what had happened between him and Noreen. It was only when he'd heard Heather admitting the truth to herself that he'd allowed himself to think about his own situation.

His pride *had* been hurt. And his ego and his vision of himself as a fit, healthy, virile male. That had been dented badly but it wasn't fair to blame it on Noreen. Her insistence on trying for a baby hadn't helped but that was all water under the bridge now and there was no point in revisiting it. Since the day he'd been on the batter and blurted it all out to Heather he hadn't felt so badly about himself. She'd been very understanding and sensitive, and surprisingly, he wasn't at all embarrassed with her. That in itself was a miracle for him. He was looking forward to their drink tonight. It was nice to have female companionship, apart from his mother's. What would she think of Heather? Oliver had a feeling Cora might like her.

Stop thinking like that, he told himself. It wasn't as if Heather would give him a second look, especially knowing that he couldn't have children. Suddenly he wondered if the flowers were such a good idea. Too late now, they were paid for. Was he going over the top, he wondered. Would Heather be embarrassed? But he wanted her to know that he was grateful to her for her friendship when it mattered. What was wrong with letting her know that he was grateful? Oliver marched out of the shop with his bouquet, looking grimly determined.

Heather was just locking Oliver's front door when he drove up looking harassed. She felt her heart lift and beamed at him like an eejit. 'Hiya,' she said shyly when he got out of the car. 'They went up another five thou! They want it badly. Told you.'

Oliver grinned. 'They're afraid of you. That psychic has probably put a spell on them.'

'Stop it, Oliver. She has a gift, you know.'

Heather laughed, starting to feel relaxed again. It was so nice to see him, to be in his company. She wanted to hug him.

'Have you to go rushing off?' he said diffidently.

'Well, I haven't had my lunch yet and we have an auction this afternoon.'

'Have you time for a cup of tea?'

'Yeah, why not,' Heather agreed happily.

'Go in and put the kettle on, I've to get something out of the car,' he instructed.

'Yes, sir!' Heather inserted the key in the lock once more.

She had her back to him at the sink when he walked into the kitchen.

'I thought you might like these. I know women set store by them. I hope you like the colour. Thanks for everything,' Oliver said awkwardly, thrusting a huge bouquet of baby pink roses laced with frothy white gypsophila at her.

'Oh, Oliver!' Her eyes widened with delight. 'Oh, Oliver, they're *beautiful*. Oh, Oliver,' she repeated inanely.

'That was my name when I got up this morning all right.' He grinned, delighted with her reaction.

'Oh, Oliver,' she said again and started laughing. 'Thank you. I've never had such beautiful flowers before. Neil always got his from the newsagent's,' she added drily. 'Pink roses are my favourites.'

They smiled at each other and she was struck by how blue his eyes were.

'You're lovely, Oliver.' It burst out of her.

He flushed shyly. 'You're fairly lovely yourself, Heather,' he managed, dropping his gaze.

'Don't be shy with me.' She put the roses down on the table and went over and put her arms around him in a hug.

His arms came up and tightened around her. 'What are we doing?' he whispered.

'Being dear friends,' she whispered back.

'That's all we can be,' he said slowly, drawing away from her.

'Why?' she looked at him, puzzled.

'You know why. You know what I told you about having children.'

'Oh that,' she murmured, hugging him again, enjoying the hardness of his chest against the side of her face and the manly clean scent of him.

'Yes, that,' Oliver said firmly.

'OK, Oliver,' she said meekly. 'Whatever you say.'

'Are you teasing me?' he demanded, looking down into her laughing eyes.

'Me?' she said innocently. 'Sure aren't I committed to finding the man on the periphery of my life? You'll just have to keep me going until he comes along.'

'OK then,' Oliver agreed, caressing her cheek.

'Great. Have you any food in the fridge, I'm starving!'

'Bacon sandwich?' He disentangled himself from her hug and went to the fridge. Heather stood grinning from ear to ear. She felt ridiculously happy.

'Sounds perfect to me,' she declared.

Oliver turned to look at her and before he knew it she was in his arms again and they were kissing hungrily, tenderly, hungrily again.

Breathless, he drew away from her.

'Are you sure about this, Heather?' he demanded. 'Are you very sure?'

'As sure as I've ever been about anything, Oliver. I think I love you,' she whispered.

'Oh, Heather, you foolish woman,' he groaned. 'I'm not the man for you. You need a husband who'll give you children, a family.'

'Says who?' Heather said crossly. 'Will you stop your nonsense and take me up to bed. I've only got an hour.'

Oliver stared at her and then he started to laugh. 'I don't know if I can do it, I've been having a few problems in that area.' His eyes never left her face.

'Well, we'll never find out standing here.' Heather took him by the hand. 'Come on, we deserve it.' She smiled at him, happier than she had ever been in her life. He *was* the one for her, she just knew it. Anne Jensen had been right about everything.

'Did you say you'd been having problems or something?' she enquired innocently an hour later, after she and Oliver had made glorious, lusty, abandoned love, twice.

'You must have cured me.' He smiled down at her where she was nestled in the curve of his arm, her cheeks bright and flushed, her eyes wide and happy.

'I was wondering how I would feel making love to someone else, after Neil. Oliver, there was no comparison, I feel completely at home with you. I feel peace, and joy, and I'm bursting with happiness,' she bubbled.

'I feel the same, love. I feel as if I've known you all my life. It's unbelievable. I never thought I'd be happy again and I am. I'm just worrie—'

She pressed a finger to his lips. 'Please stop, Oliver. It will be different with me because I know what's what and it's my decision. I love being with you. I love talking to you. Isn't that all that counts at the end of the day?'

'I suppose you're right, Heather. I'm just afraid you might become unhappy further down the line.'

'Oliver, what you don't have you don't miss. As long as we can be like we are and have a bit of fun out of life and tease each other until the day we die, I'll be happy.'

'Will you?' he looked down at her, stroking her cheek with his fingertip.

'Look what we have! A great bond, a great friendship and a huge affection for each other, even before we had this. Lots of people never experience even one of those things. Look at poor Lorna,' Heather remarked. 'We're lucky, Oliver.'

'You're beautiful, Heather. Neil Brennan was a fool. You accept me after what I've told you. You make me feel loved,' he said huskily, his eyes darkening.

'You *are* loved, Oliver. You're loved very, very much, my darling,' she whispered, hugging him to her with all her strength.

How her grandmother would be pleased for her, she thought joyfully as she stroked her fingers through Oliver's dark hair and sent a prayer of thanks heavenward for sending her the greatest gift of her life.

Oliver watched Heather's car disappear from sight and took a long deep breath. He was overwhelmed. The speed of this beautiful thing that had happened between them had taken him by surprise. He'd made love to her *twice*. And it had been fantastic. There was no pressure, just joy and love and lust. Afterwards they had talked so openly about their feelings. The first time he'd ever done that with a woman. His natural reserve had melted away. He felt free to be himself with her and that was immensely liberating. She knew his deep, sad secret. The thing that had caused him to question his whole essence as a man. It was out in the open between them and it didn't seem to bother her. It was unbelievable. Maybe there was a future for him. Maybe, at last, it was his turn to have some happiness.

His face creased into a smile as he looked up at the sky. Him and Heather Williams. Who would ever have thought it? She'd told him that she loved him and he knew that what he felt for her was completely different to any feelings he'd ever had for any other woman. He felt he'd come home.

He walked into the hall and picked up the phone. He needed to tell Noreen. He wanted to have everything out in the open. It was important that she heard it from him. She answered and he felt a little pang. He wouldn't hurt Noreen for the world. He hoped she wouldn't mind too much.

'Hi, it's me,' he said with a hint of uncertainty.

'Hi, Oliver. How's things? Is everything OK?'

She sounded cheerful enough. He took a deep breath.

'Fine . . . er . . . Noreen, I . . . I . . . think we have a buyer.' He chickened out.

'Oliver, are you sure about this?' she asked for the umpteenth time.

'Yes, I'm sure. It's good to sell the house and let the past go. Er . . . I . . . I've something else to tell you . . .'

'What's that, Oliver?' Noreen asked lightly.

'I think I've met someone I'd like to have a relationship with,' he said steadily.

There was a long pause. *Speak to me. Say something,* he willed her.

'Oh . . . Oh, I see.' He could hear the hurt in her voice and he knew she was thinking the same thing he'd thought. *It didn't take him long to get over me.*

'Do I know her?' she asked.

Oliver cleared his throat. 'Yes, actually. It's Heather Williams. She was dealing with the sale of the house and we got to know each other. I've told her about . . . well, you know. She knows the score.'

'Oh!' He could hear the surprise in her tone. 'I . . . I . . . She's a very nice girl.'

'Yes, she is, Noreen. I hope eventually you can be happy for me. And I just want you to know that I'll always be here for you. Whatever happens with Heather and me will never change our friendship.'

'Thanks, Oliver. I am happy for you. It's just a bit of a shock.' He could hear the quiver in her voice.

'I know. But I wanted to tell you. I didn't want you to hear it from anyone else. And I think with this and selling the house and you having the babies it's a chance to move on and get on with things.'

Noreen gave a little laugh. 'Oliver, that is so you. Don't hang around wallowing. Get moving, get going, even with the emotions.'

'That's me, Noreen. I don't think I'll ever change.'

'No, don't ever change. You're you and I'll always try and remember our happy times. Because we did have happy times, didn't we?' There was a note of pleading in her voice.

'Yes, Noreen, we did,' he said gently. 'And we'll have a lot more, just different.'

'Thanks for phoning, I know it wasn't easy. We'll talk soon,' she paused for a moment and added quickly, 'And I'm glad it's Heather, I don't think she'll ever hurt you. 'Bye, Oliver.'

''Bye,' he said and heard the click of her phone. Oliver gently laid the receiver back in the cradle. That was it. He'd told Noreen. That was the hardest part. It made their split very final. Maybe he needed that, he thought ruefully.

Cora could like it or lump it. He'd been given a second chance and he was going to grab it with both hands. If his mother had problems with it, she'd just have to get over it.

He walked into the kitchen to tidy away their lunch dishes and felt as if a burden had lifted from his shoulders. For the first time that he could remember, Oliver felt carefree and exhilarated.

*   *   *

Noreen looked at the wedding ring on the third finger of her left hand. She still wore it. Her heart twisted with pain. Oliver had found someone else. It hadn't taken long. It hurt.

Was it on the rebound, she wondered. Was Heather someone he could make a go of things with or just someone to tide him over his hard times? Maybe she was on the rebound too after Neil Brennan. They'd been ripe for each other, she thought sadly. It didn't really matter what the reasons were. She and Oliver were finished as a couple. She had to face that.

She slid her ring off her finger. It felt naked. Part of her had subconsciously seen Oliver as her safety net but now he'd pulled that net from under her and was moving on.

Noreen squared her shoulders. He was right. They had to get on with things and it would have been most unfair of her to expect him to live a solitary life. She felt terribly lonely all of a sudden. Hot tears slid down her cheeks.

'Oh, stop it,' she muttered irritably, annoyed at herself. She was the one who had left the marriage, she was the one who was pregnant with another man's babies. Of course Oliver was entitled to be with someone else. Why was she being so begrudging? Why did she feel so alone?

Her hand slid down to her tummy. Soon enough she'd have two little lives to share her own with and she wouldn't have time to be lonely. Poor Oliver would never have that joy. Heather Williams was a nice girl, not a walking wagon like her cousin. Oliver deserved some happiness in his life; she'd have to try hard not to let feelings of bitterness and hurt eat away at her. She had to take responsibility for her own part in all of this and she was not going to act like a victim, Noreen lectured herself silently.

She slipped her wedding ring into an envelope and put it at the back of a drawer. It was time to let go of the past and look to the future. And a good future it was going to be, Noreen assured herself firmly as she pulled out the ironing board and began to iron her uniform for work.

'You had sex with Oliver *Flynn*!!!' Ruth's voice rose several octaves and Heather had to hold the phone away from her ear.

'It wasn't sex, it was *much* more than that,' she emphasized. 'Oh Ruth, I'm *so* happy.'

'But when did all this happen? What about the other yoke, do you still have feelings for him?' Ruth was clearly hardly able to believe her ears.

Heather laughed. 'I wouldn't care if I never saw him again. Remember Gran used to say the only way to get over a man is to find another? She was right. To think Oliver was under my nose and I never realized. He's lovely, Ruth. We have the greatest fun. I'm dying for you to meet him properly.'

'Are you sure about this?' her twin demanded. 'How do you know it's not a rebound thing?'

'I know I never felt like this about Neil, that's for sure,' Heather retorted. 'You know when you just *know* he's the one? You know when you feel completely comfortable with someone? Isn't that how you feel with Pete?'

'It sure is,' Ruth agreed.

'Well, that's how I feel about Oliver. We've got to know each other well the last few weeks when he was selling the house. I love being with him. I love talking to him. I can say anything to him, tell him anything and today we made love and that was the icing on the cake.'

'So Oliver Flynn was the one on the periphery of your life. Anne Jensen was right! I'm delighted for you, Heather. I'm dying to hear all the ins and outs. I just hope it all works out,' Ruth declared.

'Me too,' Heather agreed fervently. 'Better go. I'll see you on Sunday. 'Bye.'

She hung up, smiling, and started the car ignition. She'd just come from an auction and it was the first chance she'd got to give Ruth her momentous news. She and Oliver were going for a walk around the lake later, and she couldn't wait. Who could believe it? Finding someone like Oliver was a miracle. She wanted to make him happier than he'd ever been in his life, because he had made her the happiest woman in the world. Of that there was no doubt.

48

December

Lorna gazed around the customer service
mezzanine at Tiffany's, marvelling at its elegance.
The flowers were always fresh, the lighting subdued. She never tired of it, and loved it when SW
sent her off on errands such as the one she was on
today, getting a solid silver photo frame engraved.
Tiffany's was jam-packed with early Christmas
shoppers and she'd already been here at least half
an hour. Sandra had told her to be prepared to wait.
Even though it was Friday, her boss had stayed in
the office to conduct a particularly thrilling auction
between one of her authors and a half a dozen
frantic publishers. 'We're going to hit the million, I
just know it,' she'd confided to Lorna as she sat in
her cream chair, sipping hot water and lemon, and
having a manicure.

It took another twenty minutes before Lorna
followed a petite young woman down the dark blue
hall and around the corner to the long row of
mahogany desks. 'Desk seven,' the young woman

indicated politely. Lorna took her place, half sorry that her errand was nearly complete. She'd had a wonderful morning people-watching.

She dawdled along Fifth Avenue swinging her distinctive duck-egg blue Tiffany bag, in no rush to get back to work. It was one of those perfect, cold, crisp, blue-skied New York days and she was tempted to nip into Sephora and then have coffee and watch the ice skaters in the Rockefeller Center, but reluctantly she nixed the idea. She'd been delayed too long in Tiffany's to skive.

Sandra was radiant when she got back to the office. 'I've done it, Lorna. I've got Trenton Hawks one million big ones. Now I need you to organize press releases to the trade and media. I want interviews, TV slots. Ring my contacts. Pity about Oprah not doing the Book Club any more, still, we'll never say die. I need you to organize a bottle of Krug for Trenton, ASAP, ditto his editor who stayed the course and paid the bucks. I also need you to send press releases to the UK trade, the *Bookseller* and *Publishing News*.' Sandra's list of instructions went on and on and Lorna's hands flew over her pad trying to keep up. Her heart sank, she'd be working fine and late tonight.

Sandra was a hard taskmaster. Lorna had worked her ass off from the first day she'd taken over from Alanna, and although she had weekends off, she badly needed them to recover from her gruelling week in the office. Working in Zack's had left her physically exhausted, working for Sandra left her mentally wrecked, stressed and tired. She returned to her own desk with two pages full of instructions and a thumping headache.

'Honey, you made that reservation for me for lunch in the Waldorf with Kendal McDonnell, didn't you?' Sandra buzzed her on the intercom.

'Yes I did, Sandra.' Lorna stopped mid type.

'Fine. Oh and honey, Alanna called me from Europe. She'll be back in three weeks, so I guess you might need to start looking for another job and a new pad. And honey, can I get you to make an appointment for me for a pedicure, body exfoliant and facial in Bliss as early as possible next week? Thank you.' The intercom went dead and Lorna stared at it. In shock. Was she imagining things or had she just been given the boot?

Had the last six months of slave labour meant absolutely nothing? What a hard-hearted bitch. Alanna had earlier in November extended her leave and was not due back until the end of January. Now, just because she had changed her mind, Lorna was going to be left high and dry.

She sat, staring into space. What on earth was she going to do now? She was way, way beyond her ninety-day visa, her papers weren't in order. Ten Irish illegals had recently been deported, her father had told her during their last phone call. She so did not need to hear that, she'd assured him.

Who was going to give her a job and where was she going to live? She didn't want to go back to commuting from Yonkers, besides, her room had been let to another girl. She didn't want to move into another ancient, poky little studio. Sahara in summer, Siberia in winter. She certainly didn't fancy spending the rest of the bitterly cold NY winter shivering and listening to creaky radiators that made so much noise she had to wear earplugs to sleep.

True, she had gained invaluable work experience, but she was going to have to start from scratch again and she just didn't have the heart for it.

Her mother had promised that she would fly out the day after St Stephen's Day. Nevertheless, the thought of spending Christmas Day on her own was daunting. Carina was going skiing with friends. Suzie had family commitments.

Heather's words came back to haunt her. *There is no man or even woman in your life that you can truly say that you're a friend to, and I feel sorry for you for that.*

Jane had told her that Heather and Oliver Flynn were an item and having seen them together at her grandmother's funeral, she wasn't totally surprised. Heather would be happy with Oliver, she thought enviously. He wouldn't let her down. Not the way Lorna had been let down by men. Heather and Oliver suited one another. They were the same sort of people, country people, happy to vegetate in their little cocoons.

Maybe they were right, she sighed. Lorna might always have felt the superior one in her and Heather's relationship, but right now, with a lonely Christmas and an uncertain future staring her in the face, it didn't seem like that. Heather was the lucky one. What a difference a year made. Who would ever have thought that she would envy her stick-in-the-mud-cousin.

Sandra swept out of her office. Today she was wearing a black Jil Sander trouser suit with the sharpest creases Lorna had ever seen. Her mink was thrown casually over her shoulder. She dropped an envelope on Lorna's desk. Lorna knew it was her pay cheque.

'Honey, will you please call Kelly Dunlop and tell her she's number eight on the UK Booktrack 100 and rising,' Sandra instructed. 'And honey, will you call my personal trainer and reschedule for eight a.m. tomorrow and will you call my caterers and ask them to do a sushi lunch for ten, for Sunday, at noon, and don't forget to type up our contract for Karl Neiderman, we've renegotiated and it's not standard, so make sure to check it thoroughly.' She waved a hand in languid farewell and disappeared into the elevator.

Lorna stared after her and felt resentment and hatred. No wonder Sandra was a millionairess living on Park and Lorna was a wee slavey living in a hencoop. She had more or less told Lorna she wouldn't be requiring her services and still she issued orders like bullets from a machine-gun and expected Lorna to execute them. It just wasn't on.

Lorna picked up her pay cheque, dropped it in her bag, shrugged into her coat, and took a last look around the office. She had no photos or personal effects to collect. The phone rang. Lorna ignored it. She'd had enough of hard-nosed Sandra Winston and her complete lack of appreciation and gratitude for a job well done, enough of hard work and nothing to show for it except a wardrobe to die for, enough of living in a dingy, seedy street in Manhattan, enough of being manless and friendless. She was going home. Going home to regroup and start over.

She picked up the phone and dialled home. She might as well get a freebie in before she went. Her mother answered. It was good to hear her voice.

'Mum . . . Mum . . . it's me. I'm coming home. I've had enough,' she confessed, her lip trembling.

'You come home, Lorna, if that's what you want to do. Just let me know when you're arriving and I'll be there to collect you. What's wrong?' Jane's sympathetic tone was balm to her spirit. Lorna told her sorry tale.

'Never mind, just come home,' her mother urged after listening to her daughter's tale of woe. 'Let me know your arrangements when you've made them.'

'I will, Mum, and thanks,' Lorna assured her before hanging up. One person did love her, warts and all, no matter what her stick-in-the-mud cousin said. She felt some of her old fighting spirit infuse her.

The day *would* come when Heather Williams would eat her words and envy *her*.

'You can't give me a week's notice just before Christmas. It's the busiest time of the bloody year,' Neil exploded at his secretary as she stood in front of his desk, chewing gum, unfazed by his outburst.

'Sorry, Neil, I'm going to do a beauty therapist's course in Dublin in January and I want to take a couple of weeks off before I start,' Carol said jauntily, sauntering back to her own office.

'Selfish bitch,' Neil muttered, running his hands through his hair. Now he was going to have to advertise, do interviews, the whole palaver. It was a disastrous end to a disastrous year. The sooner the new one started the better. He looked out his window and saw a familiar green Ford Focus whiz by. Neil scowled. Heather certainly hadn't taken long to get over him. Now she was living with Oliver Flynn and they were the talk of the town, not that they seemed to care. He'd seen them in the Haven the other night, laughing and joking and looking so happy he'd wanted to slap their faces. How dare she forget him so easily? What was it with women?

Some Christmas he was going to have. Himself and his father sitting over a dried-up turkey they'd be cooking themselves. So different from last year, when he and Heather had been getting the flat sorted and the world seemed like their oyster. He'd mucked it up. He should never have let himself be taken in by Lorna Morgan. He only had himself to blame. And that was what made it all the worse.

Cora bustled around her parlour polishing and tidying. Oliver was bringing his young woman to dinner on Sunday and she wanted everything to be just so.

When he had sat her down all those months ago and told her that he had met someone else and that he loved her she'd been very taken aback. But she'd stayed quiet. This was different from that Noreen one. She knew by him. It was the first time she'd ever seen real happiness in her son's eyes and she wasn't going to be selfish enough to take it away from him. There'd been times after Noreen had left him that she had felt like ringing the other woman up and pleading with her to come back, just to take away the lonely despondency that had afflicted him.

She'd worried about him night and day, grieving for him, and cursing Noreen for inflicting such sadness on her son. Now Martha Jackson's granddaughter had changed Oliver into a different man, and even though the church might frown, Cora didn't care. They weren't ones to judge any more with all their scandals. The Lord was the one she went to in times of need. She'd discussed the matter with the Sacred Heart in the quiet of her bedroom and saw in His smiling gaze mercy and compassion. He would not deny Oliver love in his life, and neither would she. Besides, it was a comfort to know that when she was gone Oliver would have someone to care for him.

Cora felt a lump in her throat. He was a great blessing in her life. She had made him miserable about Noreen with her criticism, she admitted that with a dart of shame, remembering how she hadn't even gone to his wedding. Well, this time it would be different. Not one bad word would she utter. In fact – she went out to her linen chest in the hall and took out the pristine linen and lace tablecloth that was only used on the rarest of occasions – she would set the table with her precious cloth and then Oliver would know how she felt. Happy at the thought of pleasing him, Cora hummed 'The First Noel' to herself as she hurried into the kitchen to make a dozen mince pies.

*   *   *

Heather raced up and down the supermarket aisles, anxious to get home and have the fire lit and the dinner cooking before Oliver got home. It was a wild, windy night and she looked forward to cuddling up with him later, to chat and laugh and relax at the end of a busy week. Friday night was her favourite night of all. She chucked a packet of chocolate Kimberleys into the trolley; he liked them as much as she did, and he liked Maltana too, fortunately. But his favourites were Tunnock's Teacakes, so she got two packets of those. She felt a warm little glow as she shoved her trolley up and down, shopping for their groceries. It was going to be lovely this year buying a Christmas tree together and decorating it. She'd never been as happy, she thought gratefully. Sometimes she felt ready to burst, she was so full of happiness. Being with Oliver filled every need, every want. The more she got to know him, the more she loved him and the wonderful thing was that she was greatly loved in return. She was perfectly content.

When he'd moved out of the house into one of the apartments he'd built, she'd helped him organize the move. She'd spent the first night with him there, to 'help him settle in' as she'd laughingly put it, and she'd never moved out. It was as easy and simple as that. They'd spent a glorious summer tramping around the lake, rowing on it, swimming in it, happy as could be with their own company. When Heather had told him that her grandmother had left her the cottage, Oliver had offered to refurbish it for her. 'Only if you'll come and live in it with me,' she cajoled. 'I know you're only interested in me because I'm a woman of property.'

'I'll show you why I'm interested in you.' He grabbed her and made love to her there and then on the sofa and then they'd sat grinning at each other like idiots.

They'd decided to make the cottage their home and they'd had an architect draw up plans to extend and enlarge it. Oliver was going to start work on it in the new year.

She was busy putting away the groceries when the phone rang. She answered, hoping it wasn't Oliver to tell her that he was delayed.

'Hello?' a woman's voice said. 'Would that be Heather?'

'It is,' Heather answered.

'Hello, Heather. It's Noreen. I was trying to catch Oliver on his mobile but there's no signal.'

'Oh. Oh, hello,' Heather said warily. It was strange to be talking to Oliver's wife. 'Sometimes on Fridays the network gets so busy it crashes. Can I give him a message and get him to call you?' she said politely.

'Well, thank you. I just wanted him to know that I'm going into hospital tomorrow. If I haven't gone into labour by myself, they're going to induce me on Monday.'

'Oh, right, Noreen. The best of luck.'

'Heather, I just wanted to say that I'm so glad Oliver's with you. You must know how wonderful he is or you wouldn't be with him. He deserves every happiness and I really mean that,' the other woman said quietly.

Heather felt a lump come into her throat. 'He is wonderful, isn't he? He's the most special man I've ever met.' She gave a little laugh. 'But then I'm biased.'

'Me too,' Noreen said, and Heather could tell she was smiling. 'It's been very nice to talk to you, Heather. I hope we can meet again some time.'

'I hope so too, Noreen,' Heather said warmly. 'I'll light a candle for you tomorrow. And I'll get Oliver to phone you tonight. Goodnight.'

She put down the phone and sat at the kitchen table. Noreen obviously had feelings for Oliver, but at least she wasn't alone in London and her dearest wish had been granted to her. And it was good that she and Oliver had remained friends. The babies' father was very supportive and Oliver had told her that Noreen was far happier living there than she ever had been at home. So perhaps it was a case of 'All's well that end's well', she reflected as she put away the remainder of the shopping and began to slice a pork steak into medallions, ready to cook in cream and wine.

When Oliver's key turned in the lock, she rushed out to the hall and planted a big kiss on his lips, making him laugh at her enthusiasm. 'Dinner smells nice,' he said as he strolled into the kitchen with his arm around her.

'You have ten minutes to shower, and by the way Noreen rang, she couldn't get you on the mobile.'

'Is she OK?' Heather noticed the flicker of alarm in his eyes.

'She's fine. She's going into hospital tomorrow

and if she doesn't go into labour herself she's going to be induced.'

Oliver made a face. 'I don't want any gory details,' he warned.

'Don't be such a wussy. Go and have your shower and give her a call.' Heather kissed him again and gave him a little shove out of the door.

'Will do.' Oliver pinched her ass, making her squeal.

Heather smiled to herself as she boiled the water for the basmati rice. Now that he was home, she felt perfectly content.

'Hello, Noreen,' Oliver said as he sat, wrapped in a towel, on the side of the bed. 'Heather told me you called.'

'She sounds lovely, Oliver. I'm really glad for you,' Noreen said warmly.

'Are you, Noreen?' Oliver said gravely.

'Honestly I am. I guess I don't feel so guilty about us, knowing you're happy with someone else.'

'And are *you* happy, Noreen?' he asked quietly.

'I'm very contented, Oliver. I'm so looking forward to bringing the babies home. Can't say I'm actually looking forward to the birth itself.'

'That's understandable. And Rajiv will definitely be with you? You know I would have come if you'd been stuck.'

'I know that, Oliver. He's here with me right now. And thank you. I'm fine. I'll ring you as soon as I can once they're born. Say a prayer for me, won't you?'

'You know I will, Noreen. Be assured of that,' he said firmly.

There was a silence at the end of the phone and he knew she was crying. 'For heaven's sake, woman. Not the waterworks again. We should send you to Africa to cure the drought,' he teased.

'Oh, Oliver,' Noreen gulped, half laughing, half crying. 'You're very special.'

'You're pretty special yourself.' He smiled down the phone. 'Go and get him to cook you a curry – I heard that's supposed to bring on labour.'

'Yes, Doctor Flynn,' Noreen managed a laugh. 'I'll call you as soon as I have two little babies.'

'You do that, and take care of yourself. 'Bye now.' He hung up the phone gently and sat towelling his hair dry. It was good that they could keep in touch and be concerned for each other. It meant that their relationship wasn't a total failure. He wished for her sake that the birth was over, then she'd be truly in her element with the children she'd always wanted.

Would that beautiful, warm, loving woman down the hall in the kitchen ever want babies, he wondered. She kept saying no, that she was happy as they were, and she certainly looked very happy. Maybe it was different for her from how it had been for Noreen, because she had made the choice herself. She knew what the score was with him and she'd still wanted to get involved. They could always adopt if she wanted. He only wanted what she wanted.

Smiling, Oliver dressed in the clean clothes Heather had laid out for him on the bed and went down to the kitchen. He stood beside her at the cooker and wrapped his arms around her.

'Are you sure you're happy?' he asked against her hair.

'Oliver, dearest, I'm the happiest woman in the universe.' She turned sideways in his arms to look up at him. 'Why wouldn't I be? I'm with the most wonderful man in the world.' She kissed him soundly, winding her arms around his neck until all he could do was believe her.

'Push, Noreen, one last push, that's all,' the midwife encouraged as Noreen, red in the face, hair plastered against her head, pushed as hard as she could and was rewarded moments later with a lusty roar.

'One fine healthy boy, to join his fine healthy sister,' the gynaecologist said cheerfully. Noreen burst into tears. It was all over. Finally all over and she had two healthy babies, born normally, and Rajiv standing beside her in his mask and gown looking as though he would burst with pride. The nurse put her son in her arms.

He was beautiful, with melting brown eyes, a little snub nose and a shock of black hair that made her laugh. His sister, born five hours earlier, was asleep in her cot, awaiting the arrival of her brother.

Noreen's heart swelled with love and joy as she held her son's tiny hand and felt his fingers curl tightly around her little finger. What perfection. What blessings God had bestowed on her, she thought gratefully, as all the years of pain and grief she had endured wafted away and vanished into nothingness. It was five thirty on a frosty December Sunday morning in London and she felt she was the luckiest woman in the world.

'Here, Rajiv, you hold him,' she whispered.

'We will hold him together, Noreen,' Rajiv murmured tenderly as he put his arms around them both and kissed her lovingly on the top of her head.

'Will you ring Maura for me later if I'm still asleep and tell her she can book her flight whenever she wants to? And will you ring Kay?' Noreen asked.

'Of course I will, my dear. And what about Oliver?'

'I'll ring him myself as soon as I wake up. He's the one person I want to tell myself.'

'And rightly so.' Rajiv smiled. 'He's the most important one of all.'

'When I dropped Ma home after early Mass, I had a cup of tea with her. I can tell you one thing, Heather Williams, you're getting an honour bestowed on very few,' Oliver informed Heather as they tramped around the lake, crunching frost-curled leaves underfoot, their breath freezing on the icy morning air.

'And what's that?' Heather asked with a smile, delighted to see Oliver so carefree. He'd been a bit tense, to say the least, about his mother's invite to Sunday lunch. He'd warned her to take no notice if she made snippy remarks about their situation. Now it looked as if he had no worries on that score.

'You're getting her very best linen and lace

tablecloth, reserved only for visiting clergymen and royalty. I couldn't believe it. When I commented, she said she wanted the table to look nice for Martha Jackson's granddaughter.'

'Ah, Oliver. Isn't that nice?' Heather snuggled in to him, chuffed. 'I hope she likes the book of quilting I bought for her, and the shortbread.'

'She will, Heather, stop worrying. If you're getting the linen and lace tablecloth you're away on a hack. Now come on, we have another twenty minutes to go to get our hour's walk in. You'll be hungry for your roast beef and Yorkshire pudding by the time I'm finished with you,' Oliver announced.

'Wait a minute,' she demanded, reaching up and wrapping her arms around him before kissing him passionately. He kissed her back until they drew away breathless and red-cheeked, grinning from ear to ear.

'You're a brazen hussy,' he told her, 'and I know exactly what you're up to with these delaying tactics. It's still twenty minutes, you'll just have to walk faster. Stop dawdling, woman, you'll never lose weight meandering along like this,' Oliver instructed, setting off at a brisk pace.

'Slow down, you meany,' Heather protested, but he was gone, loping along, urging her to keep up with his long-legged stride as she panted behind him, protesting loudly all the while. His phone rang and he stopped to answer it, giving her a chance to catch up.

'That's wonderful, Noreen,' she heard him say. 'I'm very happy for you. Was it hard going?

You don't have to tell me everything,' he added hastily.

Heather saw his face, intent and serious, as he listened to his wife at the other end of the phone. 'That's good. Of course we will. Noreen, say hello to Heather and let her congratulate you.' He handed her the phone.

'Hi, Noreen. Are you all right? Did it all go OK? Were you induced?' Heather asked excitedly.

'No, I went by myself and I've got a little boy and a little girl, five and a half pounds each. We're calling them Meera and Michael. Will you and Oliver come over for the christening in the spring?'

'Oh, thank you, Noreen, we'd be honoured,' Heather said delightedly.

'Would you mind if I asked Oliver to be one of the godfathers? Rajiv's son is going to be the other and Kay and Maura are going to be the godmothers. I haven't asked him yet – I wanted to ask you first if you'd mind?' Noreen said hesitantly.

'Of course I wouldn't mind, Noreen. When they're older they can come and spend holidays,' Heather said warm-heartedly. 'Ask him now.'

She handed Oliver back the phone and watched his face crease into a smile. 'Of course I will, Noreen. Thank you for asking. Get some rest now and we'll talk later in the week. Take care, and congratulations to Rajiv.' He clicked off, put the phone in his pocket and smiled at Heather. 'Thank God that's over for Noreen. She's on a high. I'm really glad for her,' he said, tucking his arm into hers as by unspoken agreement they turned and began to walk back towards the hotel.

'Don't you even feel a little pang that it's not you?' Heather asked, uncertain of his answer, wondering if he would prefer to be with Noreen.

He stopped and looked at her in surprise. Seeing the look in her eyes, he cupped her face in his hands. 'But Heather,' he said. 'If I was with Noreen, I wouldn't be with you and would never have known it could be like this. How could I have any pangs or regrets now? I do love you, you know that. You bring joy to my life.' His eyes were warm and loving as he stared down at her.

'Oliver, that's the nicest thing you've ever said to me,' she murmured tearfully.

'Oh woman, don't go all weepy and mushy on me,' he groaned, hugging her tightly. 'Quick, quick, look! There's two magpies for you.' He turned her in the direction of the lake and she saw two beautiful black and white magpies gracefully soaring and dipping in flight. She nestled in against him and his arms tightened around her as they watched the birds glide over the treetops in consummate symmetry.

'How perfect, Oliver.' Heather squeezed his hand tightly. 'For Noreen, and for us. Two for Joy.'

THE END